LATENCY

CHRIS COPPEL

CRANTHORPE
—MILLNER—
PUBLISHERS

First published by Cranthorpe Millner Publishers (2024)

ISBN 978-1-80378-191-4 (Paperback)

www.cranthorpemillner.com

Cranthorpe Millner Publishers

Printed and bound by CPI Group (UK) Ltd
Croydon, CR0 4YY

CHAPTER 1
2007

Cynthia Harter was delighted at how well her party had gone. It was no longer enough to simply own a mountaintop home with views across Los Angeles, stretching all the way to Catalina Island. No. Every party now had to have a twist. Something chic, trendy, and when possible, unique.

The problem was that each year it became harder and harder to find something original enough to entertain the overly pampered guests. Magicians were way too passee. Dancers went out a decade earlier. If you had the money, having Cirque de Soleil perform in your backyard had been hot for a few years, but even that became tedious to the Los Angeles A-list crowd.

Thankfully, Cynthia had heard about a very unique act from one of her close friends and had decided to give it a try. The results had been spectacular. She'd never seen party guests more enthralled in all her sixty-three years.

As she started to wipe away the work of a five-hundred-dollar-an-hour mobile make-up artist, she could hear the last of the catering and wait staff finishing the clean-up, one

1

floor above. By the time she had returned her face to its unmade-up, surgically-improved state, the house had gone quiet.

Despite being obscenely rich, Cynthia refused to have any live-in staff within her seven thousand square foot home. Her maid, cook and general handyman arrived each morning at eight o'clock, and on nights when there wasn't a party, they left at seven, sharp.

Cynthia had made her fortune from real estate and divorce. The former, while running her own property investment company in Beverly Hills; the latter, after leaving three husbands with only half of their original wealth.

The divorces had all been messy. Cynthia had learned that where money was concerned you couldn't trust anyone, especially not the live-in help.

Cynthia had decided that there was no reason to have staff live in the house where they could overhear and see every dirty little secret of her life, and there quite were a few of those.

Cynthia had two major addictions beyond the usual alcohol, benzodiazepine and pot. Not a day went by when she didn't soften the edges of her world with a low-dose tab of ecstasy, taken at seven in the evening. The second little habit was screwing young men. Very young men. Her preferred age bracket was between eighteen and twenty-five.

None were romantic encounters, yet Cynthia never, ever wanted to be considered a cougar. Instead, whenever the

2

itch became too much and fresh talent was not already lined up, she would text a certain escort agency that knew exactly what she wanted and what she was willing to pay.

A knock on her bedroom door brought a smile to her carefully stretched features.

"Come in," she said in a raspy voice.

Pietro was one of Mansion Magic Catering's waitstaff, and the moment she'd seen him loading in the crates of glasses and china earlier in the day, she knew that she wanted to feel those rippling, muscled arms wrapped tightly around her.

When she approached him after most of the guests had left, she asked if he would care to stay behind for a private party.

Pietro smiled knowingly and whispered, "Five hundred."

Cynthia should have been surprised by his openness, but knew that a young, athletic, swarthy Hispanic would be a hot commodity among the single ladies of means within Beverly Hills and that she was unlikely to have been the first one to proposition him.

What did surprise her was his price. With his hard body, long hair, and deep blue eyes, he could easily have commanded four times that amount. Then again, he probably wasn't used to the level of stamina that Cynthia could muster when being serviced with the appropriate level of enthusiasm.

She stepped out of the bathroom and was pleased to see that Pietro was holding a chilled bottle of Cristal and

3

two champagne flutes. He took a long look at Cynthia and clearly liked what he saw. She might have been sixty-three, but thanks to the surgeon, her personal trainer and her obsessively strict diet, she could easily be mistaken for forty.

Pietro placed the glasses on a marble side-table and poured the champagne.

As he handed her a glass, Cynthia reached down with her other hand and felt between his legs. She had been caught out in the past by horny young men who had supplemented their visible manhood with socks, and on one occasion, a hot dog wrapped in cling film.

What she could feel at that moment was undoubtably real. She caressed him through his jeans until he let out an involuntary moan.

Cynthia smiled. She was in control and both of them knew it.

Pietro reached out to caress her right breast, but she stopped him and took a step back.

"I want to watch you undress," she said in little more than a whisper.

It was clear that he didn't object to her predilection at all.

Pietro drained his glass and placed it on the side table. He then kicked off his leather slip-ons and began undoing his belt, all the while keeping his eyes directed at Cynthia's. As he slipped his black jeans down his muscled calves, Cynthia could see that she had sorely underestimated his value.

Once his red Calvin Klein briefs were lowered, and Cynthia finally saw exactly what Pietro was bringing to the party, she couldn't wait to see what the young man could do with it.

Pietro kicked away his jeans and briefs and began slowly unbuttoning his white Oxford button-down shirt. He was about to say something when he suddenly began to choke. As he gasped for air, his face turned red, then purple, and his eyes began to bulge out of their sockets.

Cynthia was about to step over to him when she felt her own airway constrict. She couldn't seem to breathe. As she clawed at her magnificently restored throat, she felt her legs give way and she dropped to the floor. She tried to crawl towards Pietro, but without oxygen to feed her muscles, she couldn't seem to move at all.

The last thing she saw, even while her vision began to fog, was that Pietro's neck appeared to be elongating to an almost cartoonish length. His face had turned a greyish-green and his eyes had rolled back within his head.

Even as Cynthia lay immobile and nearing unconsciousness, she thought she heard something.

Something impossible.

Her last conscious thought was that something in her room was growling.

CHAPTER 2
PRESENT DAY

Mason Darby walked into the Robbery Homicide Division squad room with a sense of dread. He'd been away for just over a year, which was bad enough, but what really got his gut rumbling was how his co-workers were going to react to his return.

Mason wasn't concerned about the standard ribbing and pranking that went on as a way to maintain some sense of sanity as they dealt in death and extreme violence. He was specifically worried about how the other detectives were going to treat a fellow officer after what he had done.

Even more troubling was who the lieutenant was going to assign to be his partner, considering that he was relatively sure that nobody wanted such a toxic posting.

Mason couldn't even imagine all the shit that must have played out when it became known that he was coming back to work. He could almost hear the angry exchanges that must have gone on in the department.

The thing was, Mason understood their angst. If what had happened to him had happened to one of the other

6

detectives, he was pretty sure he'd have jumped up on the very same bandwagon. He would have made sure that those in leadership roles knew that he didn't want anything to do with the returning officer, let alone want to team up with him or her.

Even after Mason's version of events were proven to be accurate and all charges were dropped, his fellow officers still wouldn't forgive him. In their heads, there were a lot of lines you can cross so long as it was legal and justified, but killing your partner while on duty was not one of them.

The fact that they'd been on their way to interview a promising witness in what had been the ongoing investigation into the Runyon Canyon Strangler, seemed to only make things worse. Apparently, if you were going to kill your partner, you should do it off duty and if possible, in the heat of passion.

Mason hadn't had a choice. His partner, Detective Jesse Franks, had reached the witness first while Mason stepped away to find a cell signal and call for backup, after hearing from a neighbor that the guy they were visiting had enough weapons to start a war.

When Jesse saw that Mason had returned after hearing a gunshot, he explained that he'd been waiting next to the front door as planned, but the guy had made a break for it and had drawn down on him.

The problem was that Mason had finished his call in time to not just hear the gunshot, but to see what had really gone down. Jesse had knocked quietly on the side door, and the

7

second it started to open, he'd grabbed the guy and dragged him out into the open.

Mason had been in a perfect position to see his partner shoot the man, then place a throw-down .32 into the guy's right hand.

It was then that all the pieces had fallen into place for Mason. The reason that the Runyon Canyon Strangler always seemed to know who and what the police were going to investigate next was that the Strangler was himself a policeman. Not just any policeman. He was a homicide detective who just happened to be Mason's partner. Jesse had obviously decided that, by killing a guy suspected of being the Strangler, the task force would be disbanded, and with the investigation closed, the chances of Jesse being connected to the serial killings would be nixed once and for all.

When Jesse had sensed his partner's approach, he had thought that maybe Mason hadn't seen everything and that he still had some wiggle room.

One look at Mason's expression told him otherwise. For a moment, he considered trying to talk his way out of it, then decided that plan B would be cleaner and leave less of a trail. While pretending to stumble getting up off his knees, Jesse grabbed the throw-down and brought it to bear on his friend, classmate and best man at his wedding.

Their careers had been a mirror image of each other in every way except on the gun range. Mason could outshoot

8

anyone in the LAPD and had done so at numerous exhibition events.

Jesse got the first shot off, but despite it hitting Mason in the left lung, he was able to fire off three rounds before he himself collapsed.

Mason only found out later that all three headshots had found their target and that Jesse had been dead before his body hit the ground.

The next thing Mason knew, he was in hospital at Cedars with his right hand handcuffed to the bed frame and a uniformed officer was in the room with him.

When Mason came to, he tried to ask what had happened, but the officer guarding him had simply glared as he shook his head in disgust.

And thus began the worst year of Mason's life. Even before the evidence was evaluated, the story had leaked to the media that a rogue cop had gone berzerk and shot his partner, a decent family man with a wife and two kids.

A team of detectives from San Francisco were brought down to head up the investigation (the mayor decided that the local cops, even those in internal affairs, were way too biased to see beyond the smoke and mirrors), and were able to piece together enough evidence to show that Jesse had in fact been the Strangler.

Even that wasn't enough to initially clear Mason's name. His innocence wasn't fully accepted until a punk kid was dragged into the Hollywood police station by his father so he could hand over a 1TB memory card from the boy's Walmart drone.

The boy had been illegally videoing the entire Hollywood neighborhood, hoping to find something cool he could upload to his TikTok page. Instead, he had accidentally captured Jesse murdering the witness and then trying to kill Mason. He had been sitting on the footage for six months, terrified that his own life was in danger.

If his father hadn't needed to download a bunch of pictures from his laptop and had gone searching for a spare memory card, the video would never have come to light.

When it was viewed, then months later, fully authenticated, the LAPD realized that they had a big problem. Mason was a hero, and instead of having believed his version of events, they had tried every way imaginable to break him into confessing to murdering his partner.

Mason was immediately released from the county lockup as truckloads of Harvard-educated lawyers in expensive suits spent almost two weeks in the chief of police's conference room at the 1st Street headquarters in Downtown Los Angeles.

Their task was to find a way to mollify Mason before he sued the city and the police department out of existence.

The hardest part of the entire process, at least for Mason, was that his friends and co-workers at the LAPD had severed all contact with him long before he was found innocent. What shocked Mason the most was that, even once he had been cleared of all charges, he was still being ostracized by his peers, thereby leaving him with no network for finding out what was happening within the walls of police headquarters and City Hall.

On top of that, his fiancée had left him soon after he was charged with Jesse's murder, and even his parents chose to move back east so that, in their words, 'we can stop hiding in the shadows in case anyone recognizes us as the parents of a cop killer'. What made the situation even more otherworldly was that Mason had been beset with invitations from countless young women all wanting to hook-up. Apparently, someone as damaged and newly infamous as Mason was a prime target for the serial sickos that thrived on the fantasy of having a relationship with a violent murderer.

Considering the public backlash against him, as well as the open hatred from just about every officer within the LAPD, Mason had spent most of his post-incarceration banishment locked in his two-bedroom apartment on Havenhurst Drive in West Hollywood, waiting for any word from his lawyers.

One year to the day after shooting Jesse, Mason was looking out of his living room window at the low grey clouds that were hovering above the city when his landline rang. He'd had to give up his private cell phone when initially charged and had never got around to getting another one, especially as it would only have been another means the media could use to hound him into an interview.

Considering how rare it was for his landline to actually ring, Mason was reluctant to pick it up. Call it pessimism, but he doubted that anyone who wanted to talk to him would be someone that he would want to talk to.

After almost twenty rings the caller gave up, at least that was Mason's assumption. When it started again only a few seconds later, Mason sighed and reached for the phone.

He was surprised when a cheerful-sounding woman asked him to hold for Chief Balisek. The only time he'd ever talked to the chief of police since his arrest had been when she'd visited him in the holding cell in the headquarters building immediately after being charged.

At six foot one, Rose Balisek was intimidating enough. When, unannounced, she had appeared in his cell one morning and stood glaring down at him, she had been downright terrifying. Even through her chocolate-brown complexion, Mason had been able to see her face reddening.

The chief had basically read him the riot act. She'd informed him in no uncertain terms that he was a disgrace to the department, the city and even the planet. She had also made it clear that she would use the entire weight of the LAPD to ensure that he ended up serving the longest prison term possible in the state of California. Before leaving, she had even hinted that they might just find a way to get him tried in Texas where the death penalty was still an option.

Understandably, hearing that the same person who had basically threatened him with death now wanted to speak with him was mildly unnerving. Sure, he knew that the city found itself in a moral and legal quandary after the way

12

they'd treated him, but he was surprised that Balisek herself wanted to talk. That took some balls.

"Darby." The chief's voice filled his ear. "Let me start off by telling you that our lawyers told me that, no matter what, I was not to call or contact you directly."

"Yet here you are," Mason replied coldly.

"Yes. Here I am, ignoring the experts and in theory putting the LAPD at extreme legal and financial risk."

"As far as that's concerned," Mason said, "that boat sailed a year ago when you basically told me that you were considering sending me to Texas to die."

"I was upset. Losing Detective Franks was quite a blow."

"I know. Imagine how I felt. Actually, that brings up a good point. Did you at any time consider what I was going through?"

"No," she replied bluntly. "Everyone thought you'd murdered Detective Franks, and at that moment in time, there was even talk that you could have been the Runyon Canyon Strangler."

"What happened to innocent until proven guilty?" Mason asked.

"You were found unconscious, still holding the gun that killed Jesse, plus you had gunpowder residue on your hand. That sort of evidence spoke for itself."

"I tried speaking up for myself and I'm sure you remember how that went."

"Let me ask you a similar question to the one you just asked me. If you were me and one of your detectives shot his partner while investigating a tip about the Strangler, how would you have reacted?"

"That, Chief, may be your one saving grace," Mason replied. "I have asked myself that question a thousand times."

"And?"

"And I probably would have treated him or her exactly the same way."

There was a prolonged silence from the chief.

"What does that mean for the department?" she finally asked.

"I means that I don't intend to destroy something that, for the most part, does a lot of good."

"I'm glad to hear that," the chief replied.

"That said, you and the LAPD owe me big time. I basically solved one of the biggest modern-day murder sprees in the city's history, and instead of basking in the warmth of a little gratitude... well, you know what happened."

"And I hope you know that I wish I could undo what's already been done, but I can't."

"I know that," Mason said.

"So, what do you plan to do?"

"Just like you and the department, I've been surrounded by lawyers ever since that video came to light. If I was to agree to their strategy, you would be looking down the barrel of, at minimum, a twenty-five-million-dollar action, and that's if we deal. If I go civil, you could easily have to double that figure."

"Your contract forbids you suing the city or the LAPD," the chief interjected.

"That's the wonderful thing about the law. It always depends how you look at the facts. My legal team feels there is no question that my employment was terminated the second you arrested me and held a news conference at which you stated that I had been summarily fired. The contract was nullified by your own actions. If you like, I can have one of my legal team give you a call and explain it in more detail, but—"

"I don't think that will be necessary. I only called because I'd hoped that you were not going to try and harm the department. I guess I was wrong."

"Don't you even want to hear what I've decided?" Balisek asked.

"I assume that you will follow your legal team's advice."

"You know better than to assume, Rose," Mason replied, intentionally using her first name just to see if he could get a rise out of her.

The chief remained silent, realizing that she should have listened to her lawyers. It was clear that Mason still held a weighty grudge against the LAPD, and more specifically, her. She'd planned to try sweet-talking the ex-detective, but now realized that any chance of that being successful had already flown away long before she made the call.

The twenty-five million that Mason had mentioned hadn't shocked her in the least. The city's legal team had estimated anywhere from ten to fifty.

"Go on," she said almost begrudgingly. "What have you decided?"

"It's very simple. I want four things. I want two million dollars for myself after legal costs."

Mason thought he heard Balisek suck in her breath.

"Number two: I want an additional nine million, that's one million for the family of each girl murdered by the Runyon Canyon Strangler."

Mason waited for some sort of response. None came.

"Number three: The LAPD, the city and you personally will publicly apologize to me and to the families of the victims for having prolonged their pain while you tried to blame me."

Mason paused to let his terms sink in.

"What's number four?" the chief asked.

"I want my old job back."

CHAPTER 3

Mason felt all eyes glaring at him as he made his way to what had been his old desk that had been part of a cubicle farm put in place at the behest of an overpriced consulting firm. He felt his insides roil with an icy chill when he saw what his co-workers had done. Whether the new décor had been in place ever since his being charged, or if it had been created especially for his return, he didn't know.

What he did know was that it had to have taken some real dedication to turn the space into what he now saw before him. They'd plastered the grey, material walls with photos of Jesse, as well as other memorabilia. In the center of the workspace was his ex-partner's badge, which had been mounted in a picture frame, and a black silk band was draped lengthways across the gold-colored shield.

What concerned Mason most about the creepy display was that the detectives couldn't have accomplished the task without the tacit approval of at least the department lieutenant and captain.

Chief Balisek had warned him, after finally agreeing to Mason's terms, that he was not going to be welcomed back with open arms. Even though the external task force, the department, internal affairs and the city had cleared him of all wrongdoing, he had still put three bullets into the head of a respected and well-liked co-worker.

It wasn't that anyone still doubted that Franks had turned out to be the Strangler. It was the way he was dispatched. Even after the video showed that Jesse had already shot him, it was felt that Mason could have wounded him in any of a dozen different places in order to subdue his partner. The fact that officers were trained so that when they were faced with imminent lethal action they could neutralize the adversary by whatever means possible seemed to have slipped their minds. With Franks having a gun aimed at him and his already having been hit, Mason had reacted accordingly and had aimed above any possible vest protection. The headshots had been meant to kill.

The only person in the room that wasn't looking at him with abject hatred was a young woman sitting in front of a small stack of three ring binders. Just like everyone else, she was definitely looking at him, but with curiosity rather that loathing.

Mason estimated that she was in her late twenties/ early thirties. She had strawberry-red hair and sharp, almost chiseled features that were softened by a dusting of freckles on her cheeks. Judging by the pile of older murder books in front of her, he assumed that she was new to the

18

department and had been given the standard onboarding task of reviewing the older, open- unsolved cases.

The binders were where every note, document, photo, receipt and chronological log that related to each case were bound together in a cheap, plastic, three ring binder. Even though all such records were now computerized, most detectives, when looking back at older cases, still liked to reference the tangible documents and notes, rather that the data that had been transcribed and entered into the database by uninvolved administrative staff. It wasn't that they weren't accurate, they were. It was more that there was a subtlety and nuance to reading the old handwritten notes from the original investigators.

"Darby," Lieutenant Montez shouted as he stepped out of his glass-walled office. "New officers are supposed to check in with me on their first day."

Montez had been lieutenant even before Mason had joined the department. He had more than a passing resemblance to Cheech Marin but without the sense of humor and love for weed.

Mason was about to challenge the 'new officer' dig, but after reading the room carefully, decided to play along for the time being and followed Montez into the cramped room.

Mason was about to sit down in one of the cheap, leatherette guest chairs that had been there for as long as he could remember, when the lieutenant interrupted him.

"I'd prefer for you to remain standing. This isn't going to be a long meeting, and I have no plans to reminisce about the good old days. I was told that you were coming and that I was to incorporate you back into the department. That said, I was not told that I had to make your return a pleasurable event for you. You should know that I don't want you here and as I'm sure you've already noticed, the Ds don't want you anywhere near them either," the lieutenant said.

"I was told that I would have my old job back," Mason replied. "That means I'm a detective three. So long as I can work as I did before, I don't care what anyone else thinks."

"That right there is our biggest problem. You never cared what the others thought of you. There was always something a little superior in your attitude."

"Maybe I cared more than anyone else."

"You can put your fucking cross away," Montez snapped back. "Jesus needs the wood."

Mason said nothing as he met Montez's harsh stare.

"As you may already have assumed, it wasn't easy pairing you up with a new partner. Funny, isn't it, how you killing the last one seems to have poisoned the waters around here. The good news is that one detective did step forward. You don't know her. She started here a few months ago and so far hasn't been paired up."

"Why?" Mason asked.

"Probably because Detective One, Teri Grey, is the stepdaughter of the chief and nobody wants to partner up with some mouthpiece to the tenth floor."

"She's Ballsack's daughter!" Mason exclaimed, using the chief's less-than-flattering nickname.

"To be completely accurate, she's her stepdaughter from the chief's previous marriage."

"And Ballsack wanted her to be my partner?"

"I greatly doubt that," Montez replied. "I just felt that as nobody else wanted to work with her, it would be a slice of vengeful irony for me to assign her to you."

"Is this how it's going to be between us?" Mason asked.

"This is just how it is," Montez replied.

As Mason turned to exit the office, Montez added one last thought.

"Memories aren't always guaranteed to be that long. I get the feeling that at some point, when they all feel you've paid enough penance, things might just ease up."

Mason turned back to face the lieutenant.

"I hope you're right. Working cases with people that don't want me around won't be that productive."

"Thanks for reminding me. I'm keeping you off the roster for a while. The captain felt you should ease back into it slowly. You're going to work with Detective Grey on the open-unsolved backlog."

"Really? You're gonna bench one of your top solvers out of spite?"

"First of all," Montez replied, "you haven't solved a case in a year. Second, a detective is only as good as his support. I'm not sure how good yours is at the moment."

"That's a—" Mason started to say.

"And thirdly," Montez continued, "putting you on cold cases takes you out of the limelight. Remember, your return has started a media frenzy. You do not want to be working a current homicide case with the press hounding your every move. It wouldn't be fair on you, the vic or the department. After a while, they'll find something else shiny to jump onto. Until then, do some good with the open cases."

"How long is 'a while'?" Mason asked.

"How long do you think the public will give a fuck about you?"

"I'm kind of surprised that they still do," Mason replied.

"Really? A cop shoots another cop then sues the LAPD and the city for millions which he then gives to the victim's families, then, as if that wasn't enough, he even gets reinstated. It's a modern-day Robin Hood story."

"I didn't sue. We settled."

"As far as the public is concerned, it's all the same. You managed, in one year, to go from good cop to bad cop then back to good cop. Don't be surprised if Dick Wolf wants to make a movie of the week about you."

"How would he ever be able to find someone handsome enough to play you, Lieutenant?"

"Not a problem. Jimmy Smits is always getting mistaken for me. I may just let him take a shot at the part."

With anyone else, it would have been assumed that they were joking. As Montez had never shown any indication of his having a sense of humor, Mason knew that he was being serious.

"I'll keep that in mind when the studio calls," Mason said, as he again turned to leave the office.

"Oh, one other thing. You don't need to clean off your workspace up here. I arranged for you and Detective Grey to have an office so you two can spread out and get some work done."

"And keep us hidden away?" Mason suggested.

"That too."

CHAPTER 4

"You've gotta be fucking kidding me," Mason said after the duty sergeant led him and Teri down a flight of stairs, then along a bleak hallway to the first of six identical doors. "This is an interview room."

"Not anymore," the sergeant said, as he opened the door and turned on an overly bright, strip light.

The room had scarred, magnolia-colored walls, a grey vinyl floor and a six by four, dented, metal table taking up the entire center of the space.

"Remember, each of these rooms has an observation alcove so no hanky-panky."

"What's to stop anyone from coming down here and watching us work?" Mason asked.

"I think the real question is what would make anyone want to trapse down here just to watch you and Detective Grey? Actually, I can understand a few of the letches in vice wanting to check her out. But you – not so much."

"Are we allowed to make this dump look a little more professional?" Teri asked as she scowled at the room, ignoring the sergeant's misogynistic comment.

"So you do speak," Mason said.

"Only when I have something to say, like now," she replied, as she turned to face the sergeant. "Well?"

"I was just told that you would be working in this room for a while. No one told me about any modifications?"

"I'm not talking modification. I'm talking about a couple of desks and some light we might actually be able to work in."

"I got a few old desks from Parker. You can have two of those, though I don't know where you think you're gonna put them. That metal table is bolted to the floor. It'd take a construction crew half a day to get it loose and you'd end up with a destroyed floor. As for the lights... for obvious reasons, there ain't no power sockets in the room."

Teri gave him a questioning look.

"We don't want prisoners finding their own way to electrocute themselves," he explained.

As Mason looked on, smiling at her attempts to get help from the sergeant, Teri continued, "So how do we get electricity for the computers, our phone chargers... everything?"

"Beats me," he said as he rolled his eyes for Mason's benefit, before heading back down the hallway.

"He was helpful," Teri commented.

"The guy's been doing that job for over thirty years. I don't think he has much patience for any cop that can't find a way to help themselves."

"I don't need help. I just need a few basic office essentials."

Mason stepped into the room and looked at it, as if for the first time. He couldn't even count the number of hours he'd spent in that one, and other rooms just like it. On those occasions, however, his focus had always been on the perp, not the space itself.

"I agree with Wally about the table, we don't want to cause too much damage, considering our current status here," Mason said.

"What status is that?" Teri asked defensively.

"Unwanted."

"For you, maybe, but I just started here. I haven't done anything yet that would piss anyone off."

"You don't need to," Mason replied. "Your stepmother has been laying that groundwork for years."

"She's my ex-stepmother, and what does she have to do with what people think of me?"

"Seriously? You can't see the issue?"

"No I can't!"

"Just about every officer in the LAPD is sick to death of what they perceive as the new 'big brother' model that flows down from the tenth floor."

"So, what's that got to do with me?" Teri shot back.

"You're kidding? You really don't see the ethical conflict to you having been assigned to the Robbery Homicide Division?"

"No, I don't," Teri replied trying hard to keep her temper in check. "I reached detective level in Stockton then I transferred to LA."

"Just like that?" Mason asked. "Do you realize how hard it is to get into RHD? Highly qualified detectives wait their entire career to move here, and you managed it on your first try?"

"I'm getting the feeling that you think that, because Chief Balisek was my stepmother many years ago, I got some sort of preferential treatment?"

"Didn't you?" Mason asked.

"Far from it. I got the position because I had the best solve stats in Stockton. When I applied to come here—"

"Why exactly did you want to move down here?" Mason asked, interrupting.

"My grandparents live down here."

"I don't think I've ever heard of someone your age relocation to be near their grandparents."

Teri glared back at him.

"There's someone else," Mason suggested. "It must be someone important... someone—"

"Stop being a detective," she interrupted.

"Stockton is only five hours away, so it has to be someone that you want to be close to."

"You're wasting your time. There's nobody that—"

"It's a child," Mason continued unabated, as he closed his eyes in deep thought. "You have a child that's being raised by your grandparents." Mason scratched his head. "You gave him... it is a him, isn't it? You gave him up so you could focus on your career, but now, you either want him back or just want to be a part of his life."

"How the hell did you—?"

"He's around five now."

"Stop it!" Teri shouted. "You've proved your point that you're a good detective, but can we please leave my personal life out of it?"

"Wait," Mason said as he pretended to concentrate even harder.

"His name is... Doug... no, wait a minute... Craig. No, that's not right. It's Gregg!" Mason stated.

Teri took a step back then suddenly caught on.

"You dipshit," she said as she shook her head. "You checked up on me."

"Well, duh! I'm a detective. Would you seriously expect any less?"

"I guess not, but I'm impressed you managed to do it so quickly. I was only told about you being my partner an hour ago," Teri said, feeling some sense of relief that she hadn't been that easy to read.

"What do you think I was doing while you were in the lieutenant's office?" Mason asked, grinning.

"Most of that is public record, but that stuff about my kid is in my private HR file. How'd you get into that? You some sort of super-hacker?"

"Hardly," Mason replied. "I called Stockton and spoke to your lieutenant. Williams and I worked together on a case about five years ago."

"That didn't give him the right to blab about me."

"The part about the kid was the only thing he told me, and he only did that so that I would have a better idea how my new partner's mind ticks."

"Why is that important?"

"Some cops, especially the ones that have been around a while, don't worry enough that they might get taken down. Some even feel that living's not that important to them anymore. That's fine, except it can make some of them overly keen to charge blindly into a situation. I prefer a partner who's got something to live for and is going to think things through before doing something dumb."

Teri studied Mason for a moment.

"Okay. I guess that wasn't so bad," Teri said, smiling.

"He also told me why you left Stockton."

Teri's smile vanished.

"Want me to remind you?"

Teri glared at him without speaking.

"What'd I say?" Mason asked, still grinning.

"I can see that this is gonna be a match made in fucking heaven," she replied, rolling her eyes.

"Tell me more about you and Chief Ballsack."

Teri laughed. "Is that how she's referred to here?"

"Never to her face," Mason replied.

"If it makes any difference, she and I never got on for a second. The moment she started dating my dad, she began treating me as if she was my mother."

"Where was your mother?"

"She moved back east when my dad divorced her. I'm surprised you didn't somehow find that out as well."

"I didn't go that deep," Mason replied. "I do have one question though, if your mom is still around, why didn't you have her raise your boy?"

"For the same reason my dad divorced her. Soon after I was born, she started suffering from depression. People thought, or so I've been told, that she would get over it, but instead of getting over it or seeking professional help, she started self-medicating."

"Opioids?" Mason asked.

"Chardonnay."

"That doesn't sound that bad."

"If your mother drank a liter of Gallo before noon each day, you wouldn't say that. I guess she was what's called a 'functioning alcoholic', but to us, she sure as shit wasn't functioning as a wife or mother. Her mood swings went from anxious to adoring, to depressed to euphoric. The problem was, just like that *Forrest Gump* guy, we never knew which one we were going to get. Finally, one day, after waking from a booze-filled morning and the subsequent two hours of unconsciousness, she came stumbling out into our backyard, and screaming at the top of her lungs, 'go back to your own homes, you horrible little bastards.'"

"Little bastards?" Mason asked.

"It was my tenth birthday party and my dad had invited all my friends to a barbeque."

"That must have been a memorable day."

"It was. Especially the part when my dad packed her into our old Chevy and drove her straight to a live-in rehab center, before calling his lawyer and starting divorce proceedings."

"This may be a stupid thing to say, but I'm surprised that Ballsack wasn't an improvement, considering what you've just told me."

"That's the weird thing. She might have been a drunk and a terrible mother, but she was the only one I'd ever had and despite all her flaws, I still loved her."

"But not enough to have her raise your kid," Mason commented.

"Nowhere near enough."

"What did you mean about Ballsack treating you as if she was your mother? Isn't that a good thing?"

"Let me give you a good example. I had no idea that my dad had been seeing her or that it was starting to get serious. Then, one day, he tells me that we are going to dinner at PF Chang's and that a friend of his would be joining us. As soon as I heard where we were going, I smelled a rat. That was my favorite place back then, and we only ever went there when it was a celebration or for a serious talk."

"I used to love that restaurant," Mason said. "Best Moo Shu Pork I've ever had."

"So, we get there and about fifteen minutes later, my future stepmother shows up. She was wearing her full captain's uniform – she was only a captain back then – and practically marched across the restaurant. At first, I thought that we were in some kind of trouble until my dad jumped to his feet and kissed her. I wanted to crawl away somewhere and die. Every single person in the restaurant was staring at us."

"That's the bad part?" Mason asked.

"Not by a long shot," Teri replied. "She hadn't been seated for more than ten minutes when she leaned over and told me to take my elbows off the table. I looked at my dad for support and all he did was nod, then told me to do as she asked. She spent the whole dinner picking on me. 'Stop chewing so loudly. Sit up straight. I think you've had enough spare ribs.'"

"What a bitch," Mason said, trying to suppress a laugh.

"Are you serious?" Teri said, stunned at Mason's comment.

"If you had trouble with her micro-management back then, you're going to love working under her now."

"Great, but my point is that I was not placed here to spy on the department. The first time I'd spoken to her in fifteen years was during the interview process for this job, and guess what? I don't think she even knew who I was."

"First of all, I should warn you that she puts on that act all the time. She thinks it rattles the other person enough to put them off guard. Ballsack never, and I mean never, forgets a face or even a name. Besides, didn't you wonder why the chief of police wanted to meet a candidate? I've only met her a few times and one of those was cause she felt the need to threaten to have me killed."

"Great. What's the second thing?" Teri asked, while trying to get her head around what Mason had just said.

"I hope you realize that I'm the worst possible person to share details of your rocky relationship with the chief. I hope you weren't expecting me to be able to pass that on to everyone else, so they'd stop treating you like kryptonite. In case you haven't noticed, I am more of a pariah than you are."

"Oh, I knew that within five minutes of starting here. It's weird though. Everyone seems to hate you, but at the same time, when asked about some of the best case solves, your name came up... a lot."

"Great. So, I'm hated and respected at the same time. Hard to know how to navigate those waters."

"I suggest, very carefully," Teri replied. "From what I can tell so far, the squad are a decent bunch. Sure, there's a lot of ego and testosterone in the place—"

"That's sexist," Mason joked. "What about the female officers?"

"I was referring to the female officers. Those are some seriously hard women."

Mason laughed. "Look, why don't you go back up to the squad room and keep sorting through the cold cases. I have a few ideas about how to fix this space. Let's meet here tomorrow after the morning briefing."

"Can I help?"

"Not this time."

"What are you planning to do?" Teri asked.

"Sometimes, it's best not to ask too many questions," Mason replied.

CHAPTER 5

Teri arrived early the next morning and made her way directly down to the interview room, hoping to see if Mason had managed to do anything with the space they'd been assigned. As she approached room four, she heard loud cursing.

She opened the door and couldn't help but laugh at the sight of Mason, lying under the metal table, strapping a thick wad of cables and wires to one of the table legs with police-issue plastic flex cuffs. At some point, he had removed the two-way mirror from the alcove and had run power and ethernet cables from within that space.

Mason had also somehow procured a grey partition that he'd managed to bolt to the table with wood clamps, thus dividing it and creating two distinct workstations. Each had an angle lamp, a faux leather blotter, a widescreen monitor and a brand-new looking CPU. On a shared side table, the murder books that Teri had been working on were nestled between two bricks that were acting as makeshift bookends.

"How the hell did you manage to get all this stuff?" Teri asked.

"Some questions shouldn't be asked," he replied as he crawled out from under the table.

"Are we going to take some heat for any of this?" she asked.

"Let me let you in on a little secret. For the foreseeable future, I, and by association, you, have an ironclad get-out-of-jail-free card. They still feel guilty as hell about what they did to me and aren't completely convinced that I won't go after more blood. For the time being, we are completely bulletproof."

"I get your point, but maybe try a different term than bulletproof? Especially in our profession."

"Superstitious?" Mason asked.

"Just pragmatic."

"That'll wane after a few years in LA."

"I am impressed though," Teri said as she looked around the room. "However the hell you managed it, you did good. I feel I can actually work here now."

Mason smiled. "Let's get the briefing out of the way, then we can start putting our new home to good use."

*

The meeting was relatively brief. Overnight, there had been the usual violent interactions that happen in LA when the sun goes down, but most of those were already assigned or closed. There were a few additional APBs, and, of course, there was the latest administrative BS that rolled down from above. That morning, it related to the new requirement for two supervisors' signatures before incurring any overtime.

Though Lt Montez made the announcement as if he was completely in favor of the move, he knew as well as everyone else in the room that the new policy would be nearly impossible to follow, especially for the detectives in RHD. If they found themselves close to apprehending a perp, or were mid-interview somewhere off-site, there wasn't a chance in hell that they were going to stop and try to contact two supervisors so that they could continue doing the job they were assigned to do.

When the briefing came to an end, Montez asked that Mason and Teri stay behind. He pulled a couple of chairs out of the front row and gestured for them to sit.

"I hear you've made yourself comfortable in your new office space," he said, with a slow shake of the head.

"We had to do something," Mason replied. "There was no way..."

"That's not what I wanted to talk to you about," Montez interrupted. "I got a call from the tenth floor last night. You two have been given your first case."

"I thought we were supposed to be working on the unsolved cases?" Teri asked.

"You still are, but you've been requested to have another look at..."

"Don't say it," Mason said, hanging his head.

37

Montez smiled. "I think your partner knows where this is going."

"Well, I don't."

"We're about to get dumped on from a great height," Mason said to her.

"I still don't—"

"We're being given the Harter case," he replied.

"Why is that a problem?" Teri asked.

"Yeah, Mason," Montez said, still grinning. "Why is that a problem?"

"You know exactly why."

"I do, but maybe you should explain it to your partner."

"This is blatant retribution," Mason said.

"How is giving you such a prestigious and high-profile case a bad thing?" Montez said, trying to keep a straight face.

Mason turned to Teri. "Cynthia Harter and Pietro Ginetto were murdered in her home in 2007 after a party."

"I saw that one on a printout. What's so special about that case, other than the fact that it's still open?" she asked.

"Cynthia Harter was considered Los Angeles royalty," Mason explained. "She was a major donor to the arts, and California politics. She also had three ex-husbands, one of which is the current city controller."

"Okay. I get that she was important, but what's all that retribution stuff about? This sounds like the sort of case that could actually help both our careers."

Montez couldn't contain his laughter. "Do you want to explain it to her or should I?"

"Please," Mason said raising his hands in mock surrender. "You're the one who seems to be enjoying this the most. You should have the honor of giving her the backstory."

"I won't bore you with the details, as you will shortly be doing a deep dive within all the data sources anyway. In a nutshell, Ms. Harter had thrown one of her regular A-list parties and, as was the norm for her, chose one of the catering crew to join her once the rest of the staff and guests had gone home. That's as much verifiable information as we have up to that point. The next morning, when her housekeeper arrived, she found Harter and Ginetto dead in the master bedroom."

"Robbery gone wrong?" Teri offered.

"Nothing was taken or disturbed anywhere else in the house."

"COD?" she asked.

"That's where things start to get interesting," Montez replied. "Neither the detectives nor the coroner ever found a cause of death."

"That's not possible. There had to be some indication."

"Oh, there was an indication," Montez replied. "Ms. Harter's head was facing the wrong way."

"Wrong way?" Teri asked, confused.

"Her head was turned one-hundred and eighty degrees."

"Then there was a cause of death," she insisted.

"Unfortunately, it was found that she had died prior to the rearrangement of her neck and head."

"Well, it sounds pretty obvious to me. Ginetto strangled her until he broke her neck."

Montez grinned knowingly over at Mason.

"Her neck wasn't broken," Mason explained. "It was just… twisted."

"Still, it had to be Ginetto," she asserted.

"You would think. Only, in his case, his head had been removed entirely."

"How?" she asked. "Axe?"

"No," Montez said as he continued to study her features.

"Don't torture my partner," Mason said. "According to the coroner, his head had been pulled off."

Teri stared at him for a good few seconds.

"Pulled off?"

"Like a Ken doll," Montez interjected.

"You guys are pranking me, aren't you?" she asked.

Montez leaned forward and passed Teri a thin brown folder. She looked at it questioningly for a moment, then opened it.

Inside were a number of crime scene photos. The first one showed Harter. Her head was facing upward and her body downwards. Her green-grey neck looked like the threading of a giant industrial bolt. What Montez hadn't mentioned earlier was the expression on her face.

Even in death, the look of horror was not softened in the least.

Her amber eyes, now cloudy and unseeing, were wide open. Almost comically, her mouth had frozen open in an almost perfect circle. As far as Teri could tell from the picture, there was no sign of blood or any other injury, other than the corkscrew neck.

She slid that picture aside to reveal one of Ginetto, or at least, a portion of Ginetto.

Strangely, his lean, gym-honed body had not paled in death. His torso looked well-muscled, even though Teri knew that when rigor released its iron-like grip on his body, all the sculpting in the world wouldn't stop the rapid atrophy.

Where Ginetto's head should have been there was instead a jagged tear at the top of his neck. The white carpet had acted like a sponge, and absorbed what looked to be a large quantity of blood. It had turned the wool fibers dark, almost black, and in a stroke of horrific irony, the blood pattern had formed into the vague outline of a human head.

Teri had seen hundreds, if not thousands, of homicide crime scene pictures, many far gorier and more graphic than the ones she was holding, yet there was something about Ginetto's headless corpse that sent a shiver throughout her entire body. She took a deep breath, trying to ensure that neither officer noticed her reaction to the image.

She moved the picture aside. Below it was a photo of Ginetto's head. The small section of remaining neck was as jagged as the part still attached to his body. Teri tried to imagine which jagged sections between the head and torso would fit together to make a whole.

There was no way to read Ginetto's expression, as the decapitation and immediate death had caused his facial muscles to contort beyond anything that could have existed in life. It almost looked as if part of his jaw and cheek had melted, such was the force of the assault.

His eyes, however, were wide open and clearly showed a final moment of complete terror.

"It's obvious how they died," Teri stated.

"No," Montez replied. "That's the problem. It's not obvious at all. To this day, nobody has come up with an explanation of how two people ended up like that without any other signs of a struggle. There were no marks on either body, despite one head having been removed and the other twisted to face the wrong way."

"So, what did the coroner record as the cause of death?"

Mason and Montez replied together: "Unknown."

CHAPTER 6

"I still don't understand why you think that us getting this case is some sort of punishment?" Teri said, as she placed the photos back in the folder.

"Politics," Mason stated bluntly. "No one knows how many LA officials had their sweaty little paws in Harter's pockets. What I do know, is that every officer that has been involved in investigating her and Ginetto's death has been subjected to an untenable level of micro-management from above."

Teri looked over at Montez to see his reaction to her partner's claim.

He shrugged and gave a slight nod. "There might have been some interference from... how shall we describe them? Invested individuals?"

"Some!" Mason shot back. "I know of five officers that got dragged into that case and none of them are still part of the LAPD. In fact, none of them even live in Southern California anymore. I spoke to Higgs and Belmont after they got stuck with the case, and they both told me how the 'interference', as you put it, started day one and involved pressure from the mayor's office, the tenth floor, City Hall and even the state senate. Apparently, once assigned to the Harter case, it becomes open season for any public official to hound and harass the investigators."

"It can't really be that bad?" Teri said.

"I found Higgs sitting in his unmarked one night, right outside in the parking lot," Mason explained. "His head was bowed down and for a moment I thought he was sleeping, but as I got closer, he looked over at me, and it was obvious that he had been crying. I'm talking about a top homicide detective with over fifteen years with RHD. He'd seen more violence and carnage in a day than most people will see in their entire life, yet he always kept his shit together. At least, that was until he became the whipping boy for the LA political elite. Six weeks of that crap and they broke him."

"How could it have been allowed to get that bad?" Teri said.

"It was worse than bad," Montez said forcefully, surprising both of them. "Three weeks into the assignment, Higgs' daughter was getting married at some fancy place in Malibu. Halfway through the service, a uniformed officer turned up and tried to get him to turn his phone back on so he could take a call from an LA city councilman. Higgs refused, and basically told the guy to fuck off, which he did. Fifteen minutes later, five officers from the sheriff's department showed up with orders to detain Higgs and bring him directly to City Hall."

"I hope he refused," Teri said shaking her head.

"He didn't need to," Mason explained. "There was quite a large contingent of officers and brass at the wedding. They escorted the sheriffs out of the building and stood guard for the rest of the afternoon."

"Wow."

"It gets better. The councilman went crying to the mayor and Higgs ended up with a note in his file. Some bullshit about his having an unhealthy attitude when dealing with politically sensitive situations."

"Four weeks later," Montez took over, "on his fiftieth birthday and with a total of twenty-two years on the force, he stepped into my office and put his shield and gun on my desk and told me he was moving to Naples, Florida. I didn't know how serious he was being, so I suggested that he look into D.R.O.P., that way he could start getting a pension payment while also earning his full salary. You could only do it for five years, but I thought that maybe some extra money would help him to get over whatever was bugging him, and he would reconsider leaving."

"You knew exactly what was bothering him," Mason said. "The guy had a clean record, then some vengeful politician tried to throw his weight around, and when that didn't work, went out of his way to make sure that a black mark ended up in Higgs' jacket. I don't know if you're aware, but Higgs was one of the most loyal cops the LAPD ever had, right up until he got the full force of the BS avalanche that went with the Harter case."

"I knew," Montez replied.

"Then why didn't you help him?"

"I did. The mayor's office wanted him suspended. I found a way to get them to see reason."

"What was that?" Teri asked.

Montez studied each of them before responding, wondering how the pair would accept his answer.

"Linda Thatcher," he finally replied.

Teri shrugged, having no idea who that was. Mason, on the other hand, looked momentarily stunned.

"You called her?" he asked.

"No. I threatened to, if the persecution of one of my detectives didn't stop."

"I'd never heard this before," Mason replied. "Did Higgs know what you did for him?"

"Nobody but Ballsack..." Montez turned to Teri. "Sorry... Balisek, knew about my threat."

"You don't need to apologize to me," Teri said.

Mason took a deep breath and silently stared back at Montez. Things started to make sense. The lieutenant had been on a fast track to get a captain's slot in the LAPD, yet at some point, his rise had been halted and he had remained in his current position within RHD. Mason now understood that the lieutenant, by going to the defense of one of his detectives, had jeopardized his own career. His threat to call Linda Thatcher was a risky move. Thatcher, back then, had been the lead reporter for the LA Times crime desk.

46

The irony of Montez going to bat for Higgs, ruining his own career, then having Higgs retire a few weeks later was not lost on Mason. It explained a lot about the man.

As Teri and Mason made their way back to their office, she asked, "Who is Linda Thatcher?"

"She used to be the crime reporter for the LA Times."

"Wow. Dangerous threat."

"Very dangerous," Mason concurred as he opened their office door.

"We've had a visitor."

When they'd left the room, there had been five murder books on the table. They had apparently been removed. Sitting in their place were two binders: the combined murder book for Harter and Ginetto. In front of them was one of Chief Balisek's business cards. On the back were the handwritten words 'GOOD LUCK'.

"Looks like the interference has already begun," Teri said as she opened one of the plastic covers.

"It has. However, the chief has given me an interesting idea."

"Care to share?"

"Actually, no. I want to test the waters first before having you drown with me. I'll be back in a few minutes."

Mason left Teri wondering what the hell her partner was about to do that could in any way jeopardize her position.

Mason took the elevator to the tenth floor and made his way to the double doors that led to the chief of police's office suite.

Both of her assistants seemed to recognize Mason, though he was pretty sure he'd never seen either of them before. The older one of the two, a man in his fifties with what looked to be an Elvis-inspired hairdo, stood up and casually approached the door to the chief's office. It almost appeared as if he was positioning himself to defend her space should Mason make a move.

"The chief's not here," the man said.

"Don't lie. It's not a good trait within these walls," Mason replied. "I already checked out the garage and saw that her car and driver are down there."

"She walked to City Hall."

"No, she didn't. Please tell her that Mason Darby is here and wants to discuss the note she left me."

Mason waved the business card that had been on the table next to the Harter murder book.

Elvis hesitated a moment then knocked gently on the chief's door.

"Mason Darby is here to see you."

"Tell him I'm busy and to make an appointment like everyone else," she replied in a lowered voice.

Mason stepped to the door and peered through the partial opening.

"Instead of trying to destroy the career of your stepdaughter and me, how about giving us a chance to actually solve the murders?"

For a moment, Balisek glared back at him.

"Let him in," she said, resignedly.

CHAPTER 7

"I hope this level of insubordination isn't going to be a regular thing," Balisek said as Mason took the liberty of sitting in one of her guest chairs without being asked.

"Don't worry, I'll only abuse the privilege when it's important."

"Important to you, or important to me?" she asked.

"That will have to be determined on a case-by-case basis," Mason replied, smiling. "In this case, it's important to both of us."

Balisek just glared at him.

"I have a condition to Detective Grey and I taking on the Harter case."

Balisek snorted. "You don't get to give conditions regarding what cases you are assigned."

"Of course I don't, and I really hate to have to mention it, but in our contract, there was a very specific clause regarding abuse, retaliation and targeted harassment from my supervisors and from the tenth floor."

"How does the Harter case fall under any of those categories?"

"Please!" Mason replied, slowly shaking his head. "You and I both know the history of that particular case. You know about the interference, and you know that all investigations have ended up hampered in such a way that no progress has been made since the original investigation in '07."

"Go on."

"You sent me your card with the words 'good luck' on the back. How about we aim for something more than just luck? What if we found a way to let your assigned detectives actually treat the case with the respect it deserves, and maybe, just maybe, we might get results."

"What did you have in mind?"

"For the entirety of the investigation, I would ask that you mandate that any interested parties outside RHD have to go through your office. Officer Grey and I will be given new, unlisted cell phones, and the numbers will never be known to anyone other than those directly involved in the case. In addition, I would like to suggest that we be given secure rovers so that they too cannot be used for contact by those that have no business doing so."

"That's a big ask," Balisek opined.

"I'm not finished. I need you to stick to your guns and run interference for us. I don't care if it's the president himself, everyone has to go through your office for information. I don't want a three-ring circus like what happened to Higgs."

"Why should I want to put myself in such a compromising position?"

"Because you are the chief of police and as such, owe it to your officers to make sure that they can get on with their jobs, without the fear of political bullshit rolling downhill and burying them alive."

"What do I get out of this?" Balisek asked.

"Other than the reward of knowing you did the right thing? How about my word that Detective Grey and I will move heaven and earth to investigate the hell out this case and maybe actually solve the damn thing."

Balisek looked down at her desk for a good few beats before answering.

"Let me think about it."

*

"How'd it go?" Teri asked when Mason stepped into their office.

"I don't know yet. As soon as I do, I'll tell you."

Teri studied him for a moment then pointed to the open murder book in front of her.

"I've been comparing what's in here with what's on the database. So far, they seem to match."

"Is that a bad thing?" he asked.

"No, but what is, is that despite the size of the folder and the data file, there's hardly any meat on the bone. From what I've read so far, there was zero trace evidence."

"Someone literally got away clean," Mason quipped.

"Cute." She smiled. "Everyone who was in the house that day and even the previous week has been interviewed dozens of times, and their locations at the time of the murders were verified and alibis confirmed and investigated. Everyone was where they said they were and other than the two vics, were not in the house at the time of the attack."

"That's going to make for a fun investigation," Mason commented.

"I hope you don't mind, but while you were off doing whatever the hell you were doing, I checked on current ownership of Harter's old house. Turns out, it's for sale. It's on the market at twelve and a half million and we have an appointment to have a walkthrough with the realtor at one o'clock today."

"I should leave you alone more often," Mason joked.

"You would be amazed how often men say that to me," Teri said, not joking.

*

The house was on Cardwell Place, high above West Hollywood. Mason drove up the winding, ever-narrowing roads until they couldn't get any further. The street was a cul-de-sac. The second house on the left had belonged to Ms. Harter at the time of her death. The building was only set a few feet back from the road and, from the outside, didn't look like much.

It appeared to be a long, narrow, single-story ranch-style structure and looked charmless and dated. The only giveaway that there was more to the place than the lackluster exterior were the twin garage doors. Each looked to be two cars wide. Mason knew that any house that could manage four cars under cover up in those hills was bound to be in the higher price range.

"I was expecting something a little more extravagant," Teri said as she scanned the front.

"Something tells me that you should stick to your original expectation."

"You wouldn't know it from here," Teri replied.

"I think that's the point. An understated entry might just deter a random break in."

"I thought that Ms. Harter was all about show?"

"She was, but at the same time she was a woman living alone. Looks like she was smart enough to not advertise that fact."

"I noticed in the book that, even with all that money, she didn't have any live-in staff."

"I kinda get that," Mason replied. "If I was rich, I don't think I'd necessarily want to give up my privacy. I like the fact that she had everyone leave at the end of the day."

"Even though Harter being alone might have led to her being killed?"

"It was a party night. Time of death was estimated to be around two a.m. The last member of staff left at one-thirty.

I'm not sure that her privacy policy had anything to do with her and Ginetto's death."

Before Teri could say anything else, a gleaming black Range Rover pulled up in front of the house. As the two watched, a woman, who looked surprisingly like a younger version of Dolly Parton, carefully stepped out of the immense vehicle. Mason wasn't sure if she was exceptionally tiny or whether it was the effect of being dwarfed by the SUV.

With a purposeful stride, she approached the detectives. As she got closer, it became obvious that very little of her visible body had gone unaltered. With the sun illuminating her face, her skin looked more like plastic than living flesh.

Mason and Teri stepped out of their ride just as the woman reached them. As if by magic, two business cards appeared in her flawless right hand.

"I'm Leticia Gold. This is my listing," she said, as she distributed the cards.

Mason looked down at the fancy gold lettering on a slate-black background. The company name was Pure Gold Real Estate.

"Catchy," Mason commented.

"Has to be. It's all about the flare nowadays."

The two introduced themselves to Leticia, at which point she started with her scripted spiel.

"Though the original house was built in the fifties, it's been improved and remodeled a number of times. Just as a reference, back in—"

"Ms. Gold," Mason interrupted. "You don't need to give us the whole production number. Neither of us will likely ever be able to afford a parking space up here, let alone a house. If you don't mind, we're here to see the property as part of an unsolved case. We would like to start in the master bedroom, then be left to wander unaccompanied while we get a feel for the place."

"I'm not sure I can let you just wander. The seller was emphatic in stating that no clients could go unaccompanied within his home."

"We understand," Teri stepped in, "only we hoped that we could have a casual look without having to get a search warrant, which would of course have to be disclosed to the owner."

"I would prefer not to disturb him. He's in New York," Leticia replied with a sigh. "Just promise me that you won't... disturb anything. The owner is very fussy."

"We have no need to touch anything. As I explained on the phone, this is all in regard to a case from 2007. Though there's doubtless nothing left here from that time, we just need to get an idea of the layout and possible ingress points."

"I can guarantee you that all of it has changed drastically since then. Come. Let me show you."

Leticia led them to an unadorned, grey front door. Both Mason and Teri noticed that the handle had corroded over time and the paint had lost its sheen and was even flaking in a few places.

"I thought you said the owner was fussy?" Mason commented.

Leticia smiled and winked. At least she tried to wink. At some point during her journey to surgical perfection, her muscles stopped responding the usual way to the wink command. Instead of a crinkling of the skin between brow and cheek, all Mason got was a couple of rapid blinks from one eye before she used a worn-looking key to unlock the door.

Leticia stepped aside to let the two visitors enter the house.

Mason was ready to be wowed by the interior, but instead was completely underwhelmed. They were in a low-ceilinged entry hall with faux wood-paneled walls and cheap-looking laminate flooring. The only illumination came from a frosted dome light that seemed to have a number of deceased insects gathered at the bottom of the curved glass.

A number of Amazon parcels were piled against the right-hand wall.

"I'm impressed so far," Teri whispered to Mason.

Leticia stepped up to another poorly-maintained door and pressed her palm against what looked to be a black glass doorknob. A loud click let her know that the door was unlocked.

"Biometrics!" She started to open the door. "This is the part when you are supposed to be impressed," Leticia said as she tried to force her face to smile.

56

She swung the door wide and both Mason and Teri involuntarily gasped.

CHAPTER 8

Beyond the doorway was a white, marble-tiled atrium with a glass ceiling. Beyond that was a tinted, glass-enclosed escalator that angled down to the floor below. The left side, when activated, moved downwards, the right, up. Because of the glass ceiling and the angle of descent, once on the escalator, Mason was able to look out over the city with an unobstructed view.

As they alighted on the lower floor, Leticia turned to him. "Impressed yet?"

"Getting there," he replied.

"So, to give you an overview, this floor houses the living room, formal dining room, kitchen and two guest powder rooms. The next floor down is the master suite, and below that there are three guest suites."

"It only has four bedrooms?" Teri asked, surprised that twelve million didn't seem to buy that many rooms.

"There are two staff bedrooms on the top floor behind the garages, but other than that, yes, that's the lot."

"Was the escalator here in 2007?" Mason asked.

"No. That was added by the current owner, however, even with a stationary staircase, it was still extraordinary."

"Were you familiar with the house when it was owned by Ms. Harter?" Teri asked.

"I was the one who got the listing after her death."

"Lucky you," Mason commented.

"Also, there's a traditional staircase off of the garage lobby for staff and contractors," Leticia explained, ignoring Mason's remark.

"May we start with the master bedroom?" Mason asked.

The escalator only went down the one floor and they were forced to use the original, conventional staircase to descend to the next level. A marble-tiled landing led to a set of ten-foot tall, red-lacquered doors. A pair of waist-high, Chinese fighting dogs stood guard, one either side. Mason thought they looked like solid iron, but doubted that anyone would have gone to that much trouble considering the weight. He tapped one with his knuckles. They were iron.

Leticia cleared her throat.

"Sorry," Mason said having forgotten the 'no touching' rule.

Leticia opened one of the doors and stood aside so they could enter.

"Do you want me to stay?" she asked.

"If you don't mind, it's probably best if you don't. We're going to be discussing the orientation of the room in relation to where the bodies were found."

Leticia raised her hands in mock surrender.

"I don't want to hear any of that. I'll wait upstairs."

As soon as Leticia was gone, they stepped into the bedroom and Teri opened a new file she had created on her iPad. In it were photos of the crime scene she'd scanned from the murder book.

One look at the first picture against the room itself showed just how much had been changed over the years. When it had been Ms. Harter's bedroom, it had been lavishly furnished with antiques and expensive sculptures and paintings. The walls had been papered with thousand dollar-a-roll wallpaper depicting life-sized palm fronds. The carpet had been ultra-white, velvet pile. Lighting had come from a number of expensive-looking floor and table lamps.

The current owner had gone for stark minimalism. The walls and ceiling appeared to be covered in multi-colored, Jackson Pollock style, abstract paint squiggles. The sparse selection of furniture was transparent acrylic, including the bed frame. One entire wall was nothing but glass, offering a jaw-dropping view of the city below. As if the décor wasn't already strange enough, the floor appeared to be made of some sort of rubber and was dyed a dark red.

"It looks like a giant pool of blood," Teri observed.

"Funny," Mason replied. "I was thinking of doing the same thing in my place."

Teri rolled her eyes. "It's certainly a statement room. You'd think with that view they would have left things simple."

"They definitely didn't do that. I can't stop looking at the damn floor." Mason cringed. "I'd hate to get called out to a homicide in this room."

Teri studied the iPad. "I think the orientation photo was taken from here," she said, as she stood with her back to a wall next to the double doors.

Mason joined her and looked from the screen to the room.

"I think you're right. That means Harter's body would have been..." He walked diagonally a couple of paces to the left. "Here."

"I agree. So, Ginetto's body would have been just to the right of that spot, and his head another three feet closer to the foot of the bed."

The two spent a few minutes comparing each crime scene photo with the geography of the room. They then checked the walk-in closet and the enormous, black marble bathroom.

"This is a complete waste of time." Mason finally said what Teri had been thinking. "I was hoping there would be some vibe remaining, but the slaughterhouse décor has pretty much put paid to that."

"Ironically, when it actually was a slaughterhouse, the room would have been serene and tasteful," Teri commented.

Mason stepped to the open door. "Leticia," he called out. "Would you mind joining us for a minute?"

"Only if you've finished with your horrible pictures."

"We have."

Moments later, they heard her heels on the marble stairs.

"What can I help you with?" she asked as she reached the landing.

"Do you know if the glass wall was here in '07? The photos were all taken with closed drapes covering that side of the room."

"It was. I believe that the glass was put in in 2005. Isn't it spectacular! That alone adds at least two million to the price."

"Of course it does," Mason commented under his breath.

"You should see the room when it gets foggy. The floor looks like it's floating on air."

Teri looked down then crinkled her nose in distaste.

"Thank you, Ms. Gold," Mason said. "We're just going to check out the rest of the house, then we'll be out of your hair."

Mason and Teri went from room to room and continued to be astonished at, what they both felt, was surprisingly bad taste on the part of the current owner. The home had exactly zero charm left within it.

After twenty minutes, they met up with Leticia by the main entrance.

"I do have a couple more questions," Mason said. "Then I promise we'll be gone. From what we could see from the inside, there doesn't appear to be any access from the LA side of the house. Is that really the case or did we miss something?"

"You didn't miss anything. When it was remodeled in 2002, that owner made sure that no unwanted guests could climb up and get into the house. Ironically, a few years later, he was one of the producers of those *Purge* movies and I've heard it said that this house was the inspiration for the first one."

"I imagine you don't use that line when you're trying to sell the place?" Mason quipped.

Leticia stared blankly back at him, unable to process his sarcasm.

"Thank you," Teri said. "If you don't mind, we'll just have a look at the perimeter from up here before we go."

"Fine with me, but I doubt you'll find a way in other than through the secure entries."

"I hope you're right," Teri said with a smile. "Would you mind opening both garage doors while we do our check?"

Other than access through the garages or the front door, there was no other way into the house. The only outside area was a back deck with an infinity pool that was cantilevered out over a sheer drop of a good fifty to seventy-five feet depending which part you were standing on.

The nearest house was over a hundred feet away, so there was no access from a neighbor's roof. Both sides of the house had no opening windows, so that means of entry was also out of the question.

"Let's check the street below and see if Leticia was right about access," Mason suggested.

The first thing they discovered was that there was no street directly below the house. The nearest was Reppert Court, a tiny cul-de-sac which offered a distant view of the Harter house.

"The Gold woman was right," Teri said. "It's impossible."

Mason had to strain his neck just to look up at the house, deck and the sheer, rock promontory on which it was built.

"I doubt anyone got in from this side."

"If they didn't get in from the front, the sides or the back, that doesn't leave many options."

"Actually, it only leaves one. Whoever murdered them was invited to be inside that house."

CHAPTER 9

The traffic was brutal getting back to downtown LA. Sunset Boulevard had, as usual, gone into unexplained gridlock in the middle of the afternoon. They tried to go down Laurel Canyon, but police activity had closed the road one block south of Sunset. They finally made it to Cahuenga, dropped down to Wilshire, then managed to head east without too much traffic.

"Want to grab some food?" Teri asked. "You should probably be aware that if I don't eat something every three hours, I get grumpy."

"How do I tell the difference?" Mason replied.

Though he didn't see it, he received his second eye roll of the day.

"Do you like Mexican?" he asked.

"What's not to like?"

"Got any problem about eating off a roach coach?" Mason asked.

"Not at all, if it's a good one."

Mason checked his mirrors then braked hard and did a U-turn.

"It's Tuesday, right?" Mason asked.

"Has been all day."

Moments later, Mason took a right on la Brea, heading south, then turned onto Eighth Street.

Parked off to the right was a brightly-painted food truck with Leo's Tacos printed on the side.

"What's good?" Teri asked as the two approached the truck.

"Everything, but for a first timer, I would go for the carne asada taco with green tomato salsa."

After getting their order, Mason led Teri across Wilshire to Mansfield Park, a hidden patch of green off Orange Drive. They found an empty bench and tucked into their food.

"Oh, my God," Teri exclaimed. "This is amazing."

"I know. I don't know about you, but I'm personally loving this whole food truck revolution. It is getting hard to find one where the food isn't excellent."

"Keep searching. I'm sure you'll find something sub-par eventually," she replied, smiling.

"So, Ms. Grey," Mason said. "Tell me about yourself."

"I'm sure you've already investigated me."

"That would be unethical," Mason said as he wiped some hot sauce from his chin.

"You're saying you didn't even check my personnel file?"

"No! Of course I did."

Teri laughed. "What more do you want to know?"

"A personnel file is hardly a road map of a life lived," Mason pointed out. "For example, it notes that you have a child, but there's no mention of a current or prior husband or partner."

Teri finished her second taco then took her time wiping her mouth with a paper napkin, all the while keeping her eyes fixed on Mason's.

"It's not obligatory to share," he said. "But, if we are going to be umbilically connected for the foreseeable future, it's a good idea to get to know a little about each other."

"Gregg's father was my boyfriend," Teri said matter-of-factly. "We were both eighteen and after one particularly boozy night, we had unprotected sex."

"I'm guessing one of the swimmers managed to get through."

"Yup. The Michael Phelps of sperm."

"What was your family's reaction?" Mason asked.

"My dad was pretty cool about it, and let me know that he was behind me and would accept whatever choices I made regarding the child."

"That must have felt pretty good knowing your parents were on your side."

"My father was on my side. Ballsack however, spent every moment trying to persuade me to terminate. It got so bad that I started staying over at friends or at my grandparents when I knew that she would be home."

"What about your boyfriend?" Mason asked.

"What about him?"

Mason detected a coldness in Teri's tone.

"What did he want to do?"

"He wanted to marry me," Teri replied as she bit her bottom lip. "I obviously suggested we wait before making a decision on something that drastic."

"Maybe I'm missing something, but other that Ballsack, it sounds like you had some good support."

Teri took some time to clear up her lunch detritus before answering. As she looked into Mason's eyes, he could see that hers had welled up with tears.

"Hey," he said gently. "I didn't mean to bring up some shit that you don't want to talk about."

"I'm okay. I should talk about it. Maybe that way it'll help me find some... I don't know..."

"Closure?" Mason suggested.

"No. Not closure. I'll never get that. Maybe some basic level of acceptance would be a good start."

"You really don't have to tell me."

"Yes, I do," Teri said as she took a deep breath. "My dad and Russ, that was my boyfriend, decided to throw me a baby shower. Ballsack was, of course, against it and didn't lift a finger to help them."

"What about his parents?"

"They lived back east, and on top of some other stuff, his mother had a horrific fear of flying so, they rarely, if ever, came out to the west coast. Anyway, my dad picked up Russ from UCLA where he was a freshman in the art school. They planned to hit a bunch of party stores in Santa Monica. They got on the 405 freeway and from what I was later told, some asshole in a lowrider cut the car off. Russ, not knowing the rules in LA, reached out the window and gave them the finger."

"Oh shit," Mason sighed.

"Oh, shit, indeed," Teri said. "The lowrider braked and maneuvered next to my dad's car. One of the occupants lowered his window and fired an automatic weapon directly at my dad's side window. He, apparently, died instantly. Russ, on the other hand, survived almost a week before dying from the injuries he sustained when the car crashed into an overpass support column."

Mason sat in complete silence, for once not having a clue what to say.

"Now you see why my grandparents were my only option for raising Gregg."

"What about Russ's parents? I know they weren't local, but still…"

"They are born-again Christians and made it clear that the child was the result of sin and that if they were to take him in – their words, not mine – they would make sure that he was raised according to the teachings of our Lord. For obvious reasons, I didn't want the little guy brought up in that environment."

"Too religious?" Mason asked.

"Too fanatic."

"Man, that had to be a hard time for you.'

"It wasn't easy," Teri said, managing to force a weak smile.

69

"Subject change," Mason said.

"There's no need."

"What made you want to join the police force?"

"Actually, the answer to that is a continuation of the previous saga. After my dad and Russ died, I began obsessively following the investigation. I pestered the two detectives assigned to the case and, after a while, they started giving me unofficial, weekly briefings. I soon began to understand more and more about their process, and they in turn gave me more detail about the investigation than they probably should have.

"Once a month they took me out to lunch and let me pepper them with questions. I think they both started to feel some weird sense of responsibility for me. After constant pleading, they actually took me with them one morning and, even though it wasn't their district, showed me the area where it was believed that the gang members who had been in the lowrider that day lived.

"They explained how evidence, as well as word from a couple of CIs, had led them to focus on members of the MS 13 gang. They drove me down to South Berendo Street just west of Korea Town and pointed out a number of abandoned houses, and explained that they were believed to be what the gang called their 'destroyers', or places where they carried out their 'business' without being seen."

"That was brave of you to do that," Mason commented. He didn't mention how much he hated going down there even now, and he was a seasoned officer with some serious years under his belt. The place was a hell hole and from what he could remember from ten years earlier, it had been even worse back then.

"I don't remember feeling any fear. I don't think I fully understood what gangs like the MS 13 were really like. I was a valley girl from Encino and the closest I ever got to the gang scene was listening to rap. Anyway, two weeks after that little tour, and with a confirmed sighting of the suspected shooter entering one of the destroyers I'd been shown, the detectives, supported by SWAT, descended on the house. They cleared the ground floor without too much trouble, but a couple of gang members tried to shoot their way out from the first-floor landing. They lasted about five minutes.

"Once their bodies had been identified, it turned out that the two were the driver and the shooter from the lowrider."

"How'd that make you feel?" Mason asked.

"Wonderful. I felt as if a huge weight had been lifted from my soul. I know they say that vengeance doesn't satisfy the hurt, but I gotta tell you; it sure as shit satisfied mine."

"You're starting to scare me," Mason said, smiling.

"From that moment on I knew what I wanted to do with my life. I wanted to do what those detectives did. They brought tangible justice into the world."

"I hope by now that you recognize that that kind of tit-for-tat justice is a rare thing for us. Even if we solve a case, lawyers can undo all that good within a matter of hours in a courtroom."

71

"Oh, believe me, I know that all too well. But, in a weird way, that makes our job even more interesting. There are no slam dunks. We have to be one hell of a lot smarter than the people who commit the crimes and make sure that there is nothing for a bottom feeding lawyer to grab onto."

"Eloquently put," Mason said as he took one last sip of his Dr Pepper. "Do you mind my asking who the two detectives were?"

"Not at all. They both worked out of Santa Monica. You might have known them. Waits and Musgrove."

Mason's felt his stomach twist as an icy chill flooded his body.

"Fuck," he said.

"I know," Teri said, nodding. "My mentors ended up getting gunned down as retaliation for taking down the MS 13 destroyer."

"I remember that all too well. The LAPD response almost started another LA riot. Jesus, Teri, I'm sorry. That must have fucked you up."

"It did for a while. I even ran away to San Francisco, hoping that would somehow help me forget. Eventually, I rationalized that everything we do has a risk. As homicide detectives, they especially knew that. I ended up reasoning that Waits and Musgrove were both doing what they wanted to be doing and therefore died well."

"That's some pretty thin reasoning," Mason said, shaking his head.

"Most justifications in our job usually are."

CHAPTER 10

Once back downtown, Teri headed off to scavenge some office supplies. When Mason walked into their converted interview room, he immediately felt the warm glow of victory.

Sitting on the partitioned table were two brand-new cell phones still in their boxes. Next to them was a pair of police-issue Motorola radios, or rovers, as they were known within the force. They were the main means of communication for an officer in the field. Though detectives tended to rely more and more on cell phones, the rover was used when a more instantaneous connection with someone was needed. Being assigned a pair that could only be contacted by a limited few guaranteed some degree of autonomy from the political busybodies once they learned that the Harter case was being looked at again.

By the time Teri had returned from her pillaging mission, Mason had powered up the chargers for the rovers and plugged in the new phones.

"What have we got here?" she asked.

"A taste of victory," Mason said, grinning.

"Is this related to what you said earlier about saving me from drowning?" Teri asked.

"I didn't want any shit to roll downhill if my impromptu meeting with Ballsack went south."

"It obviously didn't, so maybe you should tell me what you're up to," Teri suggested.

"It's very simple," Mason replied. "I basically suggested to the chief that perhaps, for a change, this case should be allowed to be investigated without any interference or sideline hecklers. I requested that her office be the only point of contact by any interested parties and that you and I be given unlisted phones and alternate-channel rovers."

"And she went for that?"

Mason waved his hand towards the new phones and radios.

"Sure looks like it."

"You must have turned the screws pretty tight."

"I didn't need to. I may have reminded her about a clause in my contract with the department, but mainly I focused on her integrity and the possibility that we might just, if left alone, solve this mother."

"That would be great, but I'd feel a little more optimistic about that possibility if we could find even the slightest piece of usable evidence about how the perp got into the house."

"There isn't any, and there won't be. The place is a frigging fortress. I wasn't being flippant earlier when I said that the killer had to have already been in the house. That's a major factor. We've vastly reduced the odds of an unknown assailant and instead have narrowed it down to those on the guest list and the staff that were there for the party."

"That's one hundred and twelve possible perps," Teri said, shaking her head.

"No, it isn't," Mason shot back. "Thanks to the security sign in, we know that Ms. Harter was still upstairs at the party at one a.m., because that's when she told the caterers they could go when they'd finished packing up. If we eliminate anyone who was signed out before that time it will drastically cut the size of the list. If we also get rid of anyone incapable of having the strength to physically pull a head off, that should leave us with a much smaller number."

"Do you honestly believe that someone could pull a head off a human body? I mean, is that even physically possible?" Teri asked.

"I've seen an off-duty fireman lift the front of a Honda Civic off the ground after a kid got pinned under it. I think the right person with the right motivation..."

"Motivation?"

"There was no physical way that fireman could have lifted that car just by strength alone. He was driven by the fear that if he didn't lift that car, the boy would die," Mason responded.

"I doubt that sort of emotion was present in Ms. Harter's bedroom."

"Not that one, maybe, but there could have been an equal amount of anger or hatred within whoever killed the two of them."

"And you think being pissed off is enough to literally tear a head of a body?"

"I don't know. But I know someone who does. Why don't we swing by Mission Road tomorrow morning and have a talk with Alice Chang? If anyone can tell us if something like that is possible, it'll be her."

"Why not go this afternoon?"

"I'd like for us to try and reduce the list of names first. That way we will have some idea of…"

Teri was smiling at him as she shook her head.

Mason closed his eyes for a moment to run back his mind's recording of the last few minutes to see why Teri was giving him the headshake.

"Shit," he said as he saw the problem. "We need to know exactly what body type could even have the capacity to do such damage before we can eliminate people."

"Yup," she agreed. "I suggest we spend the rest of the shift thinning the list by getting rid of those who couldn't have had that amount of strength. People over sixty—"

Mason rocked his right hand in the air.

"Okay," she conceded. "Over seventy. Finding these people after all this time should be interesting," Teri commented.

"Actually, that might just be the easiest part of this investigation. Because the case has been reinvestigated so many times and is still listed as open, all witness contact info was current up until eighteen months ago, and they were supposed to notify RHD if they moved after that."

"Want to split the list in half?" Teri suggested. "That way we should be able to knock it out in a few hours."

"Sounds like a plan."

After three hours they had only managed to vet twenty four people. Two of which claimed to have had injuries that would eliminate them from a suspect list.

"I don't like the fact that we have to take their word for their having had a disability," Mason commented.

"We may not have to," Teri said as she studied the original interview chrono. "You know those numbers beside some of the names that we thought were something to do with the order they were interviewed?"

"Yeah. Was that wrong?"

"I found this folded in the front sleeve."

Teri passed the page across to Mason. He studied it briefly, then slowly nodded.

"Give me one."

"Mark Gilson. There's a number seven by his name."

Mason ran his finger down the numeric list and stopped at seven.

"Right leg in cast following bike accident. Verified with MD. Gibson incapable of aggressive action."

"Not exactly the correct procedure for such a notation, however, it's probably pretty rare to have to consider the mobility of that big a crowd. They came up with a pretty good way of keeping the chrono clean and clear."

"It would have helped if they'd left a note saying what they'd done," Mason griped.

"Maybe they assumed that any other detectives that had to go through the book would come across it," Teri suggested.

"What about all the subsequent times the case has been reviewed?"

"Same reason. They probably felt that if they could put the parts together, the next detectives who got the case, should be able to do the same."

Mason simply shrugged.

After noting the results of the calls and updating the injury data on a new chronological record sheet, they called it a day and rode the elevator down together.

"Want to grab a drink at the Formosa?" Mason asked.

Teri's heart sank. She'd hoped that Mason would be considerate enough to keep their relationship purely professional. Though she actually found him to be quite charming and with him reminding her of Luke Wilson, he wasn't that hard to look at, but that wasn't the point. She had learned when she was a rookie in Stockton that dating a cop was a bad idea, on a whole lot of levels.

The obvious issue of a break-up with a co-worker, while bad enough in a normal office environment, was doubly worse in the force. Teri had briefly dated a detective from the burglary division until his raging jealousy became too much to deal with. They'd been going out for less than a month when she'd told him she was done, but the guy's reaction was epic. He spread horrible rumors about her within the squad, and on one occasion, when she had to rely on some background from a number of previous burglaries, he'd intentionally given her bad information which had ended up putting her and her partner at risk.

That was her first and last time dating a fellow officer.

Mason sensed her discomfort.

"You look perturbed," he said. "I just thought you'd be coming to Mangler's retirement party."

Mangler was the nickname given to Harry Maglour. He earned the name after a foot chase early on in his career, when a perp, while trying to get away, ran headlong into the rear of an LA sanitation truck and somehow flipped inside the back just as the scoop was lifting trash into the holding area. The guy was a complete mess, with most of his bones either broken or bruised. The moniker was almost too easy a fit, but it stuck throughout Maglour's twenty-three years on the force.

"I'm sorry," Teri said. "I thought you were—"

"Putting on the moves?" Mason asked, smiling. "You can relax. I learned a long time ago not to shit where I eat."

Teri felt as if a huge weight was lifted off her shoulders.

"It's nothing personal," Teri said. "I just live by the same rule."

"Good. Now that's out of the way, let me try again. Do you want to meet up at the Formosa for Mangler's retirement party? Separate cars, of course."

Teri smiled.

"Sure. Why not."

CHAPTER 11

Teri had never been to the iconic West Hollywood restaurant and was unprepared for the visual shock as she walked inside. Located on the corner of Santa Monica and Formosa, the restaurant had opened in the late 1930s as a watering hole for the actors and crew working next door at the Samuel Golden Studios. Despite its storied history, its bright red, Chinese-inspired interior took some getting used to.

Mason had suggested that Teri get there a few minutes before him so that she wouldn't be seen to be arriving with the department pariah.

"You're my partner," she replied. "We walk in together or I don't walk in at all."

They could hear the din from inside the restaurant before they even passed under the gaudy, green, neon entry sign. If there was one thing about cops, when letting off steam, they were a noisy bunch.

Mason held the door open for Teri. The noise faltered for a moment, then started to rebound until the revelers saw who else was joining the party. By the time Mason had stepped though the small entry lobby, the room had gone eerily quiet.

"Look what the fucking cat dragged in," a voice said from somewhere amongst the crowd.

Mason started to wonder if his turning up was a good idea after all. He was not one to avoid confrontation, but at the same time, he didn't want to screw up his mentor's retirement bash.

Before he could decide what to do, Mangler pushed his way through the herd and walked right up to Mason. He grabbed him by the shoulders and pulled him into a bear hug. After a moment, he released his grip then, with his arm around Mason's shoulder, he turned to face the onlookers.

"Attention, you fuckwits!" he boomed. "This man saved my life when he was still a boot, and I was his training officer. He's a friend and a man I was proud to call partner. If any of you dickheads have a problem with that, then fucking leave. This party is about me, not you. So, keep drinking, have a good time and keep your bullshit prejudices to yourselves. We clear?"

There were some murmurs from the group.

"I said, are we fucking clear?" Mangler shouted.

There was millisecond of silence then almost as one, the other officers shouted back, "As fucking crystal, sir!"

Per Mangler's instructions, the party kicked back into gear. Mason seemed to almost be welcomed back into the fold, but he knew that they hadn't forgotten or forgiven him in any way. They'd just put their feelings on ice for the night.

Though Teri was not the only woman at the party, she was the only female detective in the RHD who'd shown up. There was one from Gang Homicide and two from Vice that she'd seen in passing, but Teri had already picked up on the fact that there seemed to be little interaction between the different departments, despite them being in the same division.

After two beers, she'd had enough of the testosterone-fueled bravado. She couldn't fully understand why men who'd already put their lives on the line every single day, felt the need to try and outboast each other with one crazy takedown story after another. In her eyes, they had nothing to prove. In theirs, however, there was some deep need to prove their worth every single minute, even during downtime.

Teri caught Mason's eye and gestured that she was going to head out.

He nodded knowingly and mouthed, "See you tomorrow."

When the valet pulled up in her vintage, faded-yellow Alpha Romeo Spider, she pulled into the line of late commuter traffic and made her way towards Laurel Canyon. As it was past seven, the traffic into the valley had thinned out. The winding road that connected LA with the San Fernando Valley should have been a fun drive, especially in Teri's sports car, but lack of maintenance of the road made avoiding potholes the main priority.

Once she reached the valley floor, she turned left just after Ventura Boulevard. After a few hundred feet, she pressed her gate opener that was clipped onto the sun visor, then drove into the parking area that serviced the ten condo units which sat directly above it.

Teri had managed to put a down payment on her unit from some of the inheritance she'd received after her father's death and had been saving, ever since. Nobody would call her condo grand, but to her it was a place of safety and quiet after days spent in the stressful environment of the RHD.

The townhouse was two stories with a living room, kitchen and dining room on the first floor and a bedroom and bathroom on the second. The whole place was less than eight hundred square feet, and would have looked cramped, were it not for the high ceilings and sliding glass doors that looked onto what was laughingly called the Studio City River, but was, in fact, a storm run-off canal. It did, however, have dense eucalyptus trees planted on either side of the concrete lined waterway which gave it something of a country feel.

The moment she walked into her tiny entry hall, Cheesecake, her four-year-old rescue cat, appeared as if by magic, and began extensive head butting of Teri's calves.

"I'd be grateful for the attention if I didn't know that you're just after some food," Teri said as she scratched the tabby's head.

After putting down a bowl of Fancy Feast, Teri grabbed a beer from the fridge and sat outside on her poor excuse for a patio that was little more than a flat area of roof just off the bedroom. It was just starting to get dark, but there was enough light for her to see what remained of her four miniature orange trees that she had planted in massive, fake terracotta pots only three months earlier.

Teri had followed the nursery instructions as well as every YouTube video she could find on how to care for a potted citrus tree. It didn't matter. Within weeks, the rich green of the leaves changed to yellow and then brown. She at first wanted to get rid of their remains, but decided that as they were already dead, they needed no more care and would remain as a reminder to her that, just as at work, she couldn't save every life.

Teri had a fitful night's sleep, during which she had a recurring dream that she was inside the Harter murder house and was stuck on the escalator as she tried to climb the descending steps to get away from a rising pool of blood that had already consumed half the treads.

At five-thirty, Teri gave up any attempt of falling back to sleep. She had a quick shower, threw on some clothes and headed to work early so she could spend some serious time with the murder book.

Even at six o'clock in the morning, Laurel Canyon was already snarled with morning commuters. Instead, Teri took Ventura Boulevard until it became Cahuenga, then, once through the pass, turned left opposite the Hollywood Bowl and wound her way down to Franklin. From that point on, she weaved through side streets all the way to headquarters.

Once in the building, she decided to skip coffee and go straight to her shared office so she could at least get an hour or so of peace before the day got in her way. Teri opened the door to their private interview room and was amazed to see Mason in grey sweats, with volume one of the murder book open on his lap.

"Morning," he said distractedly.

"I didn't expect to see you here this early. I was hoping to catch up on some reading," Teri said.

"Don't let me stop you."

"I don't have much choice. You're holding the book."

"I've been here since four," Mason said as he closed the cover and held out the binder. "Here, you have a turn while I shower and change."

"Why so early?" Teri asked, as she reached over for the book.

"I don't know if it was those spring rolls last night or what, but I couldn't seem to sleep. I kept having weird dreams about the Harter house."

Teri gave him a concerned look. "Ditto."

"That's a little weird, then again, that was a seriously strange place."

"No argument here."

"I thought we'd head over to see Chang at about nine. That okay with you?"

"Does she know we're coming?" Teri asked.

"God, no. That would give her time to find an excuse to sneak out and avoid seeing me."

"Why would she do that?"

"We may have had a little thing going before I got suspended, then fired."

"I thought you were engaged?"

"I was."

"And you cheated with the coroner? That's a little kinky," Teri said, grinning.

"Not quite," Mason replied. "The coroner was my fiancé. Then like everyone else in this building, she dropped me the second I was accused of killing my partner. I haven't actually seen her since."

"And today's the reunion? Oh, this is going to be such fun."

"You have a mean streak, don't you?"

"You have no idea."

CHAPTER 12

Teri had seen a good number of murder books since becoming a detective, but had never seen a chronological record that was anywhere close to being as long as the one in the Harter/Ginetto binders. The chrono was where detectives noted the timeline of every action and interaction that occurred during the investigation.

Usually, the witness interview reports ran to as many as ten to twenty pages. Because of the number of witnesses and the recurring cold case re-investigations of the Harter case, the chrono managed to fill over half a binder.

Teri focused on the initial reports from the crime scene. The two detectives assigned to the case were Kyle Washington and Trevor Plassel. Both were veteran homicide detectives, and from what Teri could see in the reporting, were thorough and professional.

Following a 911 call from Ms. Harter's housekeeper, a patrol car had been dispatched and arrived on the scene at five past nine in the morning. The uniformed officers could tell immediately that the deaths had not been the result of 'natural causes', and because of the A-list nature of one of the vics, the duty sergeant contacted RHD directly, knowing full well that the brass would assign it to them anyway.

Teri read their report with a careful eye, to see what might have been omitted due to the celebrity of the deceased, but could find no holes whatsoever. She again looked at the crime scene photos, but tried to supplant the images into the red-floored room she had visited with Mason.

Even though Teri was hardly what could be called a veteran homicide detective, she still considered herself to have the all-important gut feeling that good investigators seem to develop over time. She was used to viewing murder scenes, and always managed to get a good sense of how the final moments had played out.

Despite having walked the crime scene, and repeatedly looked at the photos of the Harter house murders, she wasn't feeling anything at all. The bodies, one with a corkscrewed neck, the other, sans head entirely, seemed almost unreal, as if she was looking at a staged death in a low budget horror movie.

She knew by the blood and the torn flesh that the photos were undoubtably authentic and that the disconnection from the crime was coming from her. The problem was that at any other murder scene, she had been able to work out roughly where the perp or perps had been standing in relation to the body or bodies, and could choreograph the movement of all parties leading up to the point when the victim or victims no longer moved.

"How are you doing?" Mason asked as he walked in.

His greying hair was still wet, and his white shirt had damp spots where he hadn't dried off properly.

"I can't get my head around this one," Teri said.

"That's why we are heading off to see Chang. Maybe if she can shed some light on just exactly who or what could cause such catastrophic injuries, maybe it will help us to lock into what we need to be looking for."

"I hope you're right."

*

They drove down First Street until North Mission, then turned left. Mason assumed that it was Teri's first time at the LA Coroners as the cold cases she'd been working on were too old to require an in-person conversation with anyone in the Medical Examiner's office. However, when he glanced across at her, he saw that Teri had noticeably paled.

"You okay?"

"Fine," she replied in barely more than a whisper.

"Fuck," Mason exclaimed as he pulled the car to the side of the road. "You've been here before, haven't you?"

Teri nodded.

"Don't tell me they had you ID your father?" Mason asked.

Teri turned to face Mason. "I was the only one available who knew him by sight. My grandparents were off somewhere, hiking in the wine country."

"That must have been rough."

"It was probably the hardest thing I've ever had to do in my life. The only good side was that the two detectives that ended up befriending me were there at the same time, and made it a point to introduce themselves and give me the kid glove treatment."

"I'm sorry. If I'd known, I would have come alone today."

"That wouldn't be fair on you. Don't worry about me. I know how to raise my defensive barriers. Let's keep going."

"You sure?"

"I'm sure."

Mason pulled back into traffic and moments later pointed out the building's oversized LED screen with rolling text asking people to not drink and drive. He informed Teri that the sign itself was so distracting to passing motorists that there had been a number of accidents right out front as people tried to read while maneuvering through traffic.

Mason drove to the back, where the coroner vans parked, and unloaded.

"This way we don't have to walk half a mile to get to the autopsy rooms," he advised.

"How do you know she'll be there?"

"She usually is. If not, she has a small 'day office', as she calls it, right down the hall."

"She has two offices?" Teri asked.

"Yup, one fancy one on the third floor for formal business and politicking, and a little one near the cutting rooms,

91

where she can take a break between autopsies and check over her notes."

Mason walked through the van loading area and waved at a uniformed cop that looked to be well past retirement age.

"How are you doing, Hal?" Mason called out.

"Well, look what we got here!" the man said with a smile. "I heard they let your scrawny ass back in."

"They missed me too much," Mason replied.

"Shame you didn't miss your partner," Hal said, still smiling.

Mason stopped in his tracks and looked over at him with a hurt expression.

"Too soon?" Hal asked.

"A little. Jeez, Hal, gimme a few weeks before you start pelting me with your wisecracks."

"Noted."

"Hal, this is my new partner, Teri Grey. She just joined RHD."

"Welcome. Hope you do better than the last one."

"Hal!" Mason feigned shock.

"Still too soon?"

"Nice to meet you, Hal," Teri said.

"In all seriousness, you could've done a hell of a lot worse. There're days when Darby here seems to actually know what he's doing."

"Good to know," Teri replied.

"Is Chang down here?" Mason asked.

"She was about fifteen minutes ago. Here to ask her if she'll take you back?"

Mason shook his head and led Teri through the dock and into the building proper.

"Isn't Hal a bit old to still be in uniform?" Teri asked.

"When there's no controversial guests in the morgue, they use retired officers as security. They started that about ten years ago after there was a public outcry about the coroner having active police officers as security when they should be out solving crime. Apparently, LA residents didn't understand why dead bodies got better protection than living ones."

"Not a bad question."

"One that the city didn't have an answer for, hence retirees like Hal."

As they stepped into a bright-white corridor, they both smelled the powerful aroma of bleach mixed with decomposition.

"Hopefully we can find Chang somewhere other than in the autopsy room, otherwise we are gonna stink all day," Mason commented.

"I don't know, I've found that the smell sometimes helps perps be a little more forthcoming. Probably something about sensing their own destiny."

"What the hell are you doing here?" a voice boomed from further down the hallway.

"Ah, the dulcet tones of my lovely ex," Mason whispered as he forced a smile.

93

"I heard you were on cold cases," Chang said. "Why come here and bother me?"

"Maybe I just wanted to see you," Mason suggested.

"That was very unilateral of you."

"Teri, I'd like you to meet my partner," Mason said, ignoring her comment. "Alice Chang, this is Teri Grey. She joined RHD a few months ago."

"You poor thing. I can't believe you agreed to team up with him?" Chang said.

"I wasn't actually given much of a choice, but so far, we seem to be clicking," Teri replied.

"Wait until you get to know him better, then we'll talk," Chang shot back.

"We're here because we need some expert guidance about the COD on a cold case we're working on," Mason advised, ignoring the last barb.

"Which one?" she asked.

"Harter/Ginetto."

Chang burst out laughing. "Wow, the brass must really be happy that you're back. That one's a career ender."

"I know, but I'm hoping we get given enough rope to actually work the case."

"If precedent is anything to go by, that won't happen, but let's pretend that it will. What do you need to show me?"

Teri held out a file with copies of the crime scene photos.

"You do know that I've seen these a number of times?"

"You told me about that when we were still speaking to each other."

"We're speaking now," Chang pointed out. "Why don't we go into the autopsy room so I can look at them under a magnifier."

"Any chance of not going in there?" Mason asked.

"Don't be such a pussy," Chang said as she walked towards a set of double doors.

Mason sighed and followed her. Teri smiled to herself then joined her partner.

The autopsy room was a model of efficiency and sterility. There were eight work areas, each with a stainless-steel autopsy table, a workspace with a desk and chair and a utility sink. Everything gleamed under ultra-bright, LED lighting. At the end of the room, two stations were in operation.

Despite the hyper-cleanliness of the place, nothing could fully mask the smell of decomp. Even the massive industrial extractor fans weren't enough to take away the pervasive and gag-inducing aroma of death.

Mason removed a mini tub of Vicks Vapor Rub from his pocket and put a smear of it under his nose.

"Want some?" he asked, holding it out to Teri.

"Doesn't bother me that much," she said as she shook her head.

Chang sat in the desk chair at the first workstation and looked up at the two detectives.

"Let me see them."

Teri handed the folder to her. Chang looked at each one for a moment before looking from Mason to Teri. "What do you want to know?"

"Any chance of a couple of chairs for us?" Mason asked.

"Nope. Too busy. Just ask your question, I'll answer it then I can go back to my hating you."

Mason sighed.

"The injuries. Is it actually possible for a person to inflict that sort of damage?"

"Possible... yes. Likely... not very. The point where the cranium meets the spine is not that strong, however, the shoulder and neck muscles are. That said, a seriously strong individual could possibly pull the head off the body, especially after tearing the ligatures by twisting the skull repeatedly."

"So, it is possible?" Teri asked.

"Theoretically. However, for someone to do so without leaving any other signs of injury or bruising is impossible. The attack would have to have been frenzied and time consuming. There's no indication of either being the case."

"So, what could have caused such damage?" Mason asked.

"That's why it's still unsolved," Chang said. "It had to be a human yet, it's almost inconceivable to imagine just what that person would have looked like. For a start, to have the leverage to tear the head off, the person would had to have been at least seven or eight feet tall. Either that, or he or she had supernatural strength.

"Have you ever encountered such a person?" Teri asked.

"Nope. And I gotta say, I sure as hell hope that I never do."

CHAPTER 13

"You realize that, thanks to your ex's description of what a person would have to look like, none of the guests or staff at the party are going to fit?" Teri said as she drove the unmarked back to headquarters.

"Actually, she said they'd have to look like that *or* have superhuman strength."

"So, we're looking for a Marvel character?" Teri joked.

"We don't need to go that far. There's a number of drugs out there that are known to cause violence and increased strength. It used to be PCP, but now the big ones are Bath Salts and Flakka. A couple of years ago we were called out to The Grove where some guy was ripping out movie seats from the theater with his bare hands. They were metal framed and bolted to solid concrete. He'd snorted some Flakka and got upset when his phone fell between the seats, and he couldn't find it. It took eight officers to subdue the guy. Maybe that's what we should be using as our search criteria."

"You want to filter out everyone who was high at a Hollywood party in 2007? I'm gonna guess that that's just about everyone. You saw in the autopsy for Harter that she was on E that night and she was in her sixties."

"Don't be ageist," Mason replied. "Drugs are fun for all ages nowadays."

"You're a great help."

"You know what I would like to check out? Whether there were any unusually violent exchanges at other A-lister parties around that time. I checked the book and from what I could tell from the chrono, nobody else has looked into that."

"When you say A-list parties...?" Teri asked.

"I'm talking Hollywood Hills, Bel Air, Beverly Hills, Holmby Hills and Brentwood. Those are the places that are least likely to end up with people tearing each other in half. At least, not on a regular basis."

"That's a cheerful overview of greater Los Angeles," Teri said as she pulled into the underground parking area that served LAPD headquarters.

Once back in their office, Teri continued to sort staff and guests with a new emphasis on the possible use of violence-inducing drug use. Mason, meanwhile, began searching the LAPD site using the terms 'violence', 'homicide', 'party', the years '2005 – 2010', and added the ZIP codes for all five of the target areas.

"Holy shit," he said as his screen began to populate with potential matches.

"You found something?"

"I've got three hundred hits already and it's still searching."

"I think that the term 'violence' is too broad," Teri suggested. "Even a run-of-the-mill drunken punch-up is going to show if it was reported, and considering how litigious you Los Angelenos are, that could mean most of them."

"What do you think, replace violence with severe injury?" Mason asked.

"Add death, then try it and see."

Mason made the changes. Within seconds he got sixty-three hits.

"That's better," Teri said as Mason showed her the screen. "Still a lot though."

"Some of those are going to be legitimate accidents."

"Why would police be called out for an accident?" Teri asked.

"In LA, if an A-lister calls for police, even if it's because someone tripped and fell in the pool, a black and white will almost always get a call out. It's a shit system, but precedent shows that when the head of a studio or TV station calls for a cop and doesn't get one, the dispatcher will end up having to explain his or her actions to either the tenth floor or to City Hall."

"I'm surprised people haven't complained," Teri said.

"People complain all the time when they can't get a patrol car out to a home invasion, yet some soap star manages to get one because a neighbor's party is too loud. The fact is, this is Hollywood, Ms. Grey, not a freakin' democracy. Money and power rule the roost."

Teri shook her head as Mason did another search, but this time added the term 'accident'.

"There were eighteen legitimate accidents for which a car was sent," she advised. "That still leaves forty-five cases."

"Now we do the master cull. Have any of those cases remained open?"

"Nice," she said with a nod to Mason.

"It's a long shot, but what the hell."

"Wow," Teri said, surprised. "There's two."

"Homicides?" Mason asked.

Teri nodded.

"See if both have electronic files."

After a moment, she responded.

"They do."

"Names?" Mason asked, as he grabbed a piece of paper and a pen.

"Groppel, H and Whitlough, P."

Teri then spelled out each name as Mason wrote them down.

The two spent the next fifteen minutes on the LAPD database reading up on the two cases.

Groppel had been a healthy man in his late forties. On Friday, April 4, 2008, he had attended a friend's birthday party at a lavish mansion in Bel Air. Once the party started to wind down, Harry Groppel had decided to have a little meander through the eight-bedroom house. A few guests saw him nosing around the second floor and would normally have said something to the host, however, Harry was the president of Mogul Pictures and was thus considered unlikely to be casing the place for any nefarious purpose.

The host found Harry dead at three o'clock in the morning in the lobby of the upstairs VIP guest suite. The initial belief was that Harry had died of a massive heart attack. While the heart was indeed the issue, the coroner found that it appeared to have been crushed by some massive force.

Despite his findings, there was no sign of any external injuries that could, in any way, account for the damage inside. The death certificate listed the COD as heart failure, but with a note that the circumstances were unlikely to have been the result of any natural occurrence. The case was briefly placed in the hands of RHD. As there was no sign of external violence or a struggle, the investigation was brief and unenlightening. The murder book remained in the unsolved archives in Westchester, near LAX, but there was no record of there having been any subsequent investigation.

Pamela Whitlough had been fifty-four on Saturday, September 25, 2010. She had been at a private party at the iconic Sunset Tower Hotel. There had been eighty-three guests at the event, all of whom were there to celebrate the sale of Pamela's latest best-selling novel, *GLAM,* to Mogul Pictures for what was reported to have been an eight-figure sum.

It wasn't until all of the guests had left, and the night staff checked the pool area for any glassware that may have been left outside, that they saw something odd at the bottom of the pool. At first, they thought that a towel had somehow ended up stuck there and was being held in place by the suction of the cleaning filter.

Once the crew turned the pool lights to full, they recognized the foreign object as being a body.

The initial COD was thought to have been accidental drowning, and once the coroner was able to examine her more closely, he found that there was, indeed, water in her lungs. Her body showed no bruising or damage and she appeared to have been in perfect health prior to death.

For some reason other than some sort of Hail Mary hunch, the coroner had the water in her lungs analyzed and compared it with a sample from the pool.

They didn't match. The pool water had all the usual chemicals and chlorine, however, the water in her lungs was remarkably clear of any impurities. It had some specific trace elements which, when compared to the bottled water that was available at the Sunset Tower, he found was a match with the French spring water, Evian.

As hard as it was for the coroner to understand how it could have happened, there was little doubt as to her COD. Pamela Whitlough had drowned as a result of her lungs being full of twelve-dollars-a-bottle mineral water.

The case was immediately picked up by RHD, who began the investigation with the natural assumption that she must have died somewhere other than in the pool, and had then been submerged in it later to cloud any investigation.

Further, there was no sign of a struggle and none of the guests or staff remember seeing any altercation involving the victim, or her being placed in the pool.

After six months of exhaustive investigation with minimal evidence, the two assigned detectives, working closely with the office of the medical examiner, could find no explanation for her death. Both detectives made a note that three of the guests, all of them executives at Mogul Pictures, had also been at the Harter party years earlier.

While the Harter killings remained as close to active as a cold case can be, Whitlough's didn't rate the same attention, even with her fame as a best-selling writer. The reason was simple; Harter, even in death, wielded real power in the city, thanks to the millions she'd given to various campaigns. Whitlough, on the other hand, had never donated to anything. She also had a reputation with the LAPD of trying to use her fame to get herself out of DUIs and public intoxication charges. That hadn't worked when she was alive, and certainly hadn't worked after she was dead.

Despite extreme pressure from her family, friends and readers, the case remained unsolved, and her murder book was eventually sent to Westchester for archiving.

CHAPTER 14

"Well?" Mason asked as he finished reading the electronic case files.

"Three A-list parties and four deaths that couldn't be explained," Teri said. "How was the connection never made?"

"I think it was, in a way. In Whitlough's case, one of the detectives noted that the staff and guest list had been compared to the Harter and Groppel homicides."

"I would hope so," Teri replied.

"While it was a sound decision to do so, it didn't pay off. There were three movie execs at both the Harter and Groppel parties, but they had left both events long before the murders took place. Other than them, there were no matches in any of the three lists."

"Isn't that a little unusual?"

"Not really. These weren't what you'd call massive gatherings. People, and therefore their parties, have different cliques."

"So, what's next?" Teri asked.

"How about an early lunch? Then we can get back to contacting the remaining names from the Harter party."

"Sounds good."

"Where do you want to eat? Musso and Frank?" Mason asked, with a straight face.

"God no. Way too stuffy. How about something in Chinatown?"

"You into Dim Sum?" Mason asked.

"Does the Pope shit in the woods?" Teri replied, grinning.

"Let's go to CBS Seafood. It's only a two-minute drive to Spring Street."

"We could always walk," she suggested.

"You're in Los Angeles now, walking is what you do on a treadmill or with your dog."

"There's one thing you should know about me before we go," Teri said, her voice suddenly serious.

"What's that?"

"I'm not eating chicken feet."

"That's their specialty."

"I don't care if it's the best chicken feet on the planet. It feels like you're eating slime and the taste makes me gag."

"Ever thought of doing restaurant reviews in your spare time?" Mason asked.

*

Even though Teri had driven around downtown LA a lot since join RHD, she was still stunned at the dramatic change

105

a couple of blocks could make. You could be amidst luxury condos and hotels, then turn a corner and come face to face with what could only be called urban blight.

There were parts of downtown where, despite the city's best effort to stop it, the homeless had basically taken over. When she had first moved back down to LA and seen the conditions within the camps and shelters, she went to a local bakery and bought fifty dollars' worth of bread, thinking she was about to do some good. She had pulled up in front of the Los Angeles Mission with the intention of giving out the loaves and rolls that filled a shopping bag.

The moment her car had stopped, people had begun appearing from the shadows. Their vacant, yet desperate eyes had reminded her of B movie zombies. Within seconds her car had been surrounded, and she suddenly feared for her own safety if she opened her door. Instead, she had lowered her window and had begun passing out bread to one person at a time. Suddenly the crowd surged towards the opening, and before Teri knew what was happening, arms had reached into the car, grabbed the shopping bag and pulled it out.

Teri had watched in horror as people literally fought over the bread. By the time she had closed her car window, all that was left of her 'good deed' was a torn, canvas shopping bag and a few crumbs on the filthy sidewalk. There had been no sign of the homeless horde that had been there only moments earlier. They had simply vanished back into the shadows.

Teri was concerned when they pulled up in front of the restaurant. The freestanding stucco building did not exactly exude an air of 'fine dining'.

"It gets better," Mason commented, picking up on his partner's concern. As he opened the door to let Teri enter, a waft of Chinese spices and roasting meats greeted them, as did the polished wood and crisp white tablecloths.

As soon as Mason walked inside, the owner, an elderly Chinese man in a black vest and starched white shirt, raised his arms in the air and shuffled over to him.

"Detective Darby," he said in a heavily accented voice. "Where you been? You gone too long."

Mason knew full well that Henry Chow knew perfectly well what had happened to Mason and chose to pretend that he was not aware of any such occurrence.

"Just a little break," Mason replied. "But I'm back now, that's all that really matters."

Mason gestured to Teri.

"Mister Chow, this is my new partner, Teri Grey."

"You too pretty for a policewoman. You should be on TV," Henry replied as he led them to a table in the far corner.

Teri smiled, all the while checking out the other diners. The first indication that the food was going to be good was that at least half the tables were occupied by people of East Asian descent. The other clue was that there were a good number of cops dotted around the room, interspersed with some hard-looking Hispanics and African Americans. The cultural melee was not a natural mix, yet in LA the few locations that seemed to be accepted 'neutral' grounds could be counted on for good, reasonably priced food.

Mason ordered an astonishing amount, including chicken feet in black bean sauce.

"I told you I can't eat that," she reminded him.

"I know, that's why I only ordered for myself."

Shaking her head, Teri ordered Chicken Lo Mein and stir-fried vegetables.

"That's all you're going to eat?" Mason asked.

"I like to eat human-sized portions."

"There's a trick to eating here. Always order enough for at least two, then you're set for leftovers at home for the rest of the week."

"I take it you don't cook?" Teri asked.

"No, I cook. I just don't cook well enough to enjoy eating it."

Teri laughed.

While waiting for their food to arrive, Teri asked, "I gave you my abridged life story last time we ate. What about yours?"

"What about it?"

Teri gave him a lengthy dose of stink-eye.

"You know about my life," Mason eventually replied.

"I know about the last year or so, but I would like to think that there is more to you than one hiccup."

"Hiccup! I killed my partner," Mason threw back.

"No. You killed the Runyon Park Strangler, who just happened to be your partner."

"Same thing."

"No, it's not," Teri insisted. "If a perp draws down on you, what do you do?" Teri asked.

"I see where you're going, but Jesse wasn't just another suspect, was he? I should have aimed for something a little less vital than his head."

"Is that how we are trained?"

"No, but to be fair, there's no training that covers drawing our weapon against someone we know."

"Was he going to shoot you?" Teri kept on.

"What do you mean, was? He did shoot me."

"Then you did exactly as you were supposed to do. A shooter is a shooter is a shooter. I don't care if it was Santa Claus. If he was about to draw down, or worse had already fired, there's only ever one option."

"Our food will be here in a minute," Mason replied. "Can we please change the subject?"

"Not quite yet. I have one more thought to add to the pot. Say you'd somehow managed to disable him with a trick shot to the knee or something, then what? Your partner would have ended up crippled and on trial for the murder of nine young women. Even though he might have once been your friend, he had turned into a monster. His life would have been spent in courtrooms and solitary confinement at some supermax prison. In a weird way, didn't you do him a favor by ending things there and then?"

"That's bullshit," Mason replied.

"Is it?" Teri answered. "If you feel so bad about what you did to your partner and best friend, ask yourself; didn't I actually help him? Maybe you should stop feeling so sorry for what you did to Jesse, and instead, quietly give yourself the praise that you're due. You saved the city from one of the worst murderers in decades and, at the same time, saved your pal from a lifetime of torture."

Before Mason could reply, plates and bowls of steaming hot food were placed in front of them. Mason waited until the two waiters had left before saying anything.

"Do you have any idea what I've been going through for the last year? I ended up speaking to so many lawyers and head doctors you wouldn't believe it, but you know what really pisses me off?"

"What?" Teri asked, as she emptied half the serving bowl of Lo Mein onto her plate.

"Not one of those dipshits thought to tell me what you just did. Not one of those fuckers!"

Teri watched Mason as he systematically filled his plate from the small armada of serving platters.

"I hope you learned something today," Teri said, almost casually.

"What?"

"Next time you get yourself in that much shit, there's only one person you should trust enough to give you the right advice."

Mason initially glared back at her, then his features softened.

"So, what did you do before you became a cop?" Teri asked.

"I surfed a lot."

"What else? Where'd you go to college?"

"I didn't. After high school I travelled around the country for a while, then my dad started putting pressure on me to follow in the family business."

"What business was that?"

"My dad and grandad had both been cops and had hoped that I would automatically follow the same path. The problem was that I didn't want to. I couldn't think of anything worse than working in LA as a policeman."

"Why?"

"Ironically, because of being a policeman's son. I grew up in cop world and heard too many testosterone-fueled stories of takedowns to ever want to work with those people. They all carried their own dark clouds with them wherever they went. I knew, even back then, that what they'd seen and done would screw up just about anyone, but what I saw in those guys was something else. There was a darkness inside them that no amount of Jack Daniels was ever going fix. I just didn't want that sort of life."

"What changed your mind?"

"Nothing. I still don't want that for myself. Do you mean, why did I decide to sell my soul? That's because my dad did one good thing for me. He managed to get me a summer gig as a volunteer helping out in RHD. Most of the time, it was mind-numbingly boring stuff like filing or running errands, but every so often, when the detectives were short-handed, I would help coordinate interviews, and sometimes they even had me go through murder books looking for some specific name or place. After a while, they saw that I was more than some cop's dumb kid and I got to sit in on case meetings so I could watch and learn."

"I take it you liked what you saw?" Teri asked.

"Hook, line and sinker," Mason replied. "At the end of the summer, the lieutenant helped me apply to the academy and promised he'd hold a place for me in the department."

"You went from the academy straight to Robbery-Homicide?"

"I thought that's what he meant too, but no. I found out, pretty quick that there was no fast track to getting a gold shield. Despite my earlier stance of never wanting to be a cop, I ended up being a patrol officer, then, after a couple of years, I applied and got my sergeant stripes. It was five years before I finally made detective one and that was in robbery."

"So, you got to RHD pretty fast yourself," Teri commented.

"Nope. I was assigned to robbery in Hollywood."

"Sorry." Teri grimaced.

"No shit," Mason shrugged. "I felt like I'd been promoted downward. But, by then I already had a pretty good idea of how the system worked and kept my head down for a few years and did some good numbers. Then, one day, I got loaned out to RHD to liaise on a double murder that seemed to dovetail with a couple of burglary cases I was working on. Without blowing my own horn, I was the one who ended up putting all the pieces together and pointed the homicide detectives in the right direction. Amazingly, the detectives gave me full credit and I ended up with a solved homicide in my jacket. When a position opened up a year later, I applied and remember that lieutenant I mentioned? He put me on the shortlist and, by some fluke, I got the gig."

"So, tell me," Teri said as she moved the Lo Mein dish closer to her, "has the job darkened your soul?"

"In a way, yes. Of course, it has. Nobody can do what we do and see what we see and not be tainted by it. I just rationalized that we are like zookeepers. We love the animals and try to make sure they stay safe and healthy but at the end of the day that requires shoveling a whole lot of shit."

"That was deep," Teri commented.

"Sometimes depth can be comforting."

"Have another chicken foot," Teri suggested as she rolled her eyes.

CHAPTER 15

Once settled back in the car and surrounded by a cacophony of aromas coming from Mason's oversized doggie bag, Teri nudged her partner with her elbow.

"If It's any consolation, you don't come off as having that dark a soul."

Mason smiled. "You can deduce that from two days together?"

'I'm good at judging people, whether they want to be judged or not."

"I believe it. I can already tell that you have a certain bullheadedness in your DNA makeup."

"Isn't that a prerequisite to being a successful detective?"

"To a degree," Mason replied.

"Are you suggesting that I'm too pushy?"

"I don't know yet. The jury's still out, but..."

"Uh oh. There's a but."

"I was gonna say that, judging by your record in Stockton, and what I've seen so far, you seem to know what you're doing. I don't mind persistence if it's used in good faith."

"What do you mean by good faith?" Teri asked.

"A cop being persistent in getting info from a perp or witness is a good thing. A reporter being persistent so he or she can write a smear piece just to satisfy their own ego, is a bad thing."

"You sound like you're talking from experience," Teri suggested.

"Did you read any of the crap that the papers were saying about me in the early days after I shot Jesse?"

"I was still up north, so I'd have to say no."

"The worst was from some new guy at the *Times*. I sat with him for almost four hours, opening my heart and soul with the expectation of an honest and un-biased article."

"I take it that's not what was printed?" Teri asked.

"It was not. I was made out to be some sort of trigger-happy vigilante suffering from depression and job burnout," Mason answered.

"And were you?"

"Considering the situation, I was certainly a little down at the time of the interview, but how he got 'burnout' and 'vigilantism', I'll never know. The amazing thing was, that a day after the article was published, the jerk called me to see how I liked the story."

"Did you give him your honest appraisal?" Teri asked, cringing.

"Let's just say that I think I managed to get across that I was a tad unhappy."

Teri laughed. "I bet he never called you again."

"There wouldn't have been a point. For some reason he moved to Chicago," Mason replied, matter-of-factly.

*

Once back in the office, they resumed sorting the Harter party attendees into three tiers: N/A, unlikely and re-interview.

While finalizing the lists, Mason noticed something surprising. There was one name on the Harter list that showed as never having been interviewed. On a hunch, he checked the two electronic files for the Groppel and Whitlough cases.

"That's weird," he muttered to himself.

"Having a reaction to the chicken feet?" Teri asked from behind her monitor.

"Come over here and look at this," Mason said, ignoring her jibe.

Teri stayed in her chair, but foot-shuffled it around to Mason's side of the interview table.

"What ya got?"

"Check out the guest marked as 'party entertainment'."

"On which list?" Teri asked, seeing that Mason had all three guest lists up on his screen.

"All of them."

Teri took a moment to study the interview data from the three homicide cases.

"Okay, so, on the Harter list, there was a guy called Ray Spirito. On the Groppel list, it was someone called Adam Parition and at the Whitlough event the entertainment was apparently provided by someone called Garry Houl."

"See the problem?"

Teri studied his screen more closely.

"Wow! None of them was ever interviewed," Teri said as she turned to face her partner. "That's an awfully strange coincidence."

"I don't believe in coincidences. Certainly, not in a murder investigation."

"Maybe nobody bothered cause they all appear to have left the parties way before the TODs."

"They interviewed everyone else," Mason commented.

"I'll order the murder books for Whitlough and Groppel from storage. We should check if anything was missed when the data was transcribed onto the server."

"Sounds like a plan."

"One other thing. I'd like to visit the other two sites, The Sunset Tower and the Bel Air house."

"The hotel should be easy, why don't you take that one...?"

Mason noticed Teri's stern expression.

"I suggested you take the hotel, not because it would be easier, but because the Bel Air house was bound to be complicated. They usually are up there. Something to do with all the owners either being billionaires or wannabe billionaires. It's never straightforward. I just thought as I've had experience wading through the elite bullshit, you'd make more headway with the non-political target."

"Good recovery," Teri said, smiling.

Teri contacted the Sunset Tower and was advised that the ballroom was hosting a private function that afternoon and evening, but that they were welcome to come by any time the following morning.

It had taken Mason almost an hour to find contact details for the current owner of 127 St Cloud Road in Bel Air, but when he tried to call the given number, it was out of service. He was about to call the property management company who'd provided the details back, when Teri interrupted his train of thought.

"You're not going to believe this," Teri said from behind her monitor. "127 St Cloud is for sale."

"Great. Another coincidence."

"It gets better. Guess who has the listing?"

"Don't tell me. Leticia Gold?"

"You got it. Want to see if I can get us a viewing this afternoon?" Teri offered.

"Might as well. We're kind of on pause until the murder books come over from Westchester."

*

Even though it was only just past three, the LA traffic was already in evening rush hour mode, clogging the freeways like cholesterol in the city's arteries. An accident on the 10

118

meant they had to take surface streets which used to be a great alternative if you knew the rat runs. Unfortunately, ever since the Waze app, every Los Angelino was able to navigate the lesser-used roads and alleys, resulting in there no longer being any 'secret' ways to traverse the city.

After almost forty-five minutes, they made it to Fountain Avenue and stayed on it until it dead-ended at La Cienega. They dropped down to Holly Drive then did a diagonal dash to Sunset. Teri was still new enough to the job to find the iconic street fascinating. Mason, on the other hand, thought of Sunset as just another log jam and dodged down Doheny so he could continue the trip west on the Beverly Hills side streets.

Teri would never consider saying so, but was impressed by the way Mason seemed to know how to avoid every single stop sign or light. Because of the strict speed limit enforcement within Beverly Hills proper, few people chose to use the residential area as a short cut. The police were usually omnipresent, and the fines were exorbitant.

Mason had no such qualms and kept his foot hard on the pedal the whole way through the maze, only slowing down at a few junctions where the roads had been built with deep rainwater runoff gullies. He had learned early on that trying to cross those dips at speed usually resulted in costly damage after the police vehicle bottomed out.

After re-joining Sunset Blvd at Whittier, they arrived at the Bel Air gates five minutes later. It was Teri's first time in the iconic neighborhood. It was one of the wealthiest enclaves on the planet and its six and a half square miles contained some of the most lavish homes in the world. The cheapest property went for well over a million, the most expensive could top the one hundred million mark.

Despite being excited to actually see some of the wealth displayed as bricks and mortar, Teri soon realized that most of the homes were hidden from the street. All she could see were ornate walls and dense vegetation.

Mason turned onto St Cloud drive then pulled up to an impressive pair of wrought iron gates. He was about to push a 'talk' button mounted on a curved steel pole when the barriers separated, permitting access onto the property.

"It's hard to believe that people actually live like this," Teri said as they drove up the curved driveway, surrounded on both sides by manicured cypress trees. "It's like a completely different city."

"More like a completely different universe," Mason replied.

Once through the final bend, before arriving at the forecourt, they both got their first glimpse of the house. It looked like an English Tudor mansion that had somehow been transplanted in California. Though LA is dotted with faux English architecture, 129 St Cloud looked like the real deal, right down to the ivy-covered walls and small leaded windows.

Mason pulled up next to Ms. Gold's massive Range Rover, and before either of them could alight from their grey, police issue Ford, the front door opened and Leticia appeared, waving.

"Isn't this remarkable?" she said as she gave Mason then Teri a double-cheek, air kiss.

"It's a little out of our price bracket," Mason mumbled.

"Not the house, silly. Isn't it remarkable that I'm showing you the interior of yet another potential murder house!"

"It's almost as if you and the murders are somehow connected," Teri said, straight-faced. Normally, she wouldn't toss around such an unnerving quip, but there was something about the diminutive realtor that got on her nerves.

Leticia's fake eyelashes fluttered madly, and for a moment it looked as if she was going to go into a full theatrical swoon.

"My partner was just kidding," Mason said, suppressing a smile.

Leticia shook herself as if trying to reboot her psyche, then gestured towards the open door.

"This time you're in luck. The house is still furnished and decorated just the way it was in 2008."

"Isn't that a little unusual?" Teri asked.

"Yes, however, considering the house was literally brought over here from England, together with all the original furnishing, no one so far has considered changing a thing."

"How do you move a whole house all the way from England?" Mason asked.

"Stone by stone," Leticia replied.

Mason scanned the front of the house.

"Still, to have kept the same interior even after the murder?"

"Especially after the murder," Leticia answered. "It's funny, but in LA, when something gruesome happens in a house like this, which already looks as if it could have a few ghosts of its own, people want to keep it just the way it is. When we get a listing on a newer stigmatized property, the first thing everyone wants to do is to somehow decorate away any of the morbid history."

"Why?" Mason asked. "I would have thought that an older house like this, where someone died unnaturally, would benefit even more from a complete overhaul and face lift."

"I know, but when you consider that this style of house in the thirty-to-fifty-million-dollar range is usually bought as a second or even third home, a dark history is often a plus. The people who buy the higher-priced homes tend to have quite a basket full of eccentricities. A house like this, with its own quirks, fits the bill perfectly for the right buyer."

"May we have a look?" Teri asked.

"Of course," Leticia said as she stepped through the doorway. "If you see any objects move by themselves, don't worry. It's just the house being playful."

Teri froze in place.

Leticia poked her head back outside and grinned.

"Just kidding. There. We're even."

As they entered the home, Teri looked back at Mason and mouthed, "I hate her."

CHAPTER 16

The entry hall was a celebration of gothic excess. Dark woods, insufficient natural light and a massive, carpeted staircase with heavily carved wooden balustrades and newel posts all made the space look like something from an old Hammer movie. Leticia led them off to the right, into a room straight out of an Agatha Christy mystery. The room was big, yet had an unusually low ceiling. One entire wall was taken up with a massive Inglenook fireplace. Heavy chintz furniture was surrounded by gleaming walnut tables and chairs.

"This is the grand salle," Leticia advised. "Isn't it delightful?"

Teri felt that it could have benefited from more modern décor and bright lighting, but kept the thought to herself.

"It's gorgeous," she lied.

"Would you mind if we went straight to the guest suite?" Mason asked.

Leticia looked disappointed to not be able to give them her full tour experience and stepped back into the entryway and headed up the stairs.

Teri rubbed her hand on the dark red carpet, then looked up to the landing.

"Will Rhett Butler be joining us?"

Leticia giggled. "It is a bit much, isn't it, but say what you will, it's all original."

Leticia led them up to a low-ceilinged hallway, then stopped at a pair of closed mahogany doors.

"This is the VIP guest suite," she said as she opened both doors, revealing a sizeable entry lobby. "I assume that you would both like me to make myself scarce?"

"If you wouldn't mind," Mason replied before Teri could respond.

"I'll wait downstairs. Are you going to want to check out the rest of the house afterwards?"

"You're getting to know our routine too well," Mason said, smiling.

Teri's produced her iPad and opened the digitized version of the Groppel murder book. She clicked on the crime scene photos and held it out so Mason could see it as well.

"That's the table," Mason said, pointing to the wall on the left where an antique half-moon table stood beneath a vintage painting of a fox hunt.

Teri looked at it, then at the image.

"Yup. That means that Groppel was found lying here with his head next to the right front table leg."

"Odd place to be attacked," Mason commented. "Why not in the suite itself?"

Teri stepped forward and opened the inner door. The moment she released the catch, the door flew open, and the pair were almost knocked over by a gust of icy wind.

"What the fuck?" Mason said as he stepped into the suite.

It looked as if a tornado had gone through it. Furniture was upended. Papers and linens were interspersed and strewn across the room. At the far end, two floor to ceiling windows were wide open, and judging by the nearly horizontal drapes jutting out into the open air, it was clear that was the point of origin of the wind.

"Leticia?" Teri called downstairs.

"Coming," she replied, two moments before appearing in the lower entry hall.

"You should see this," Teri said, gesturing towards the suite.

Leticia trotted up the stairs then gasped as she walked into the room.

"Not again," she said shaking her head in frustration. "These old windows won't stay latched and even the slightest wind seems to force them open."

"I hadn't noticed that there was that much wind today."

"Trust me," Leticia replied. "there's always wind this far up the hill. It seems to come off the ocean then speed up as it whips through Bel Air."

Mason studied the chaos in the room. "Are you saying this has happened before?"

"A couple of times. The last one was when I was showing the property earlier in the week. It was the second showing to a very interested couple, and just as they seemed ready to talk turkey, the wind came up and did the same thing."

"I take it the buyers lost interest?" Teri asked.

"Yes, they did, but not because of the wind. The husband was a professional basketball player, obviously I can't tell you who, but suffice to say, he was almost seven feet tall and decided that, as quaint as it was, the low beamed ceilings and his height just weren't going to mix well."

"There's not much point in checking out the suite in its current condition, do you mind if we mooch around the rest of the house and grounds?" Mason asked.

"Of course. I'd better call the cleaning service to come back and straighten up this mess," Leticia said, rolling her eyes.

Mason and Teri poked around the other bedrooms and bathrooms, but didn't find anything untoward or of interest. They returned to the ground floor and slowly walked through every room.

"The house is like a rabbit warren," Mason said. "There are so many weirdly interconnected rooms that it would have been hard to know who was here and when anyone left."

"The only security was at the gate, and they did check all cars and people in and out," Teri reminded him. "There's also the fact that a number of guests remember seeing Groppel head upstairs, but according to their statements,

126

none of them noticed anyone else follow him up there, nor did anyone else come down."

"Is there any other way to get up to the VIP suite?" Mason asked.

"When they rebuilt the house here in Bel Air, they decided not to keep the original servant's staircase at the side of the house. That way, they could expand some of the rooms. Is that a problem?" Leticia asked.

"I was hoping to prove that the butler did it, but with no secret way to get upstairs, that might not have been that easy."

"Then there's the fact that they didn't have a butler," Leticia replied, dead serious.

"Let's check the grounds," Teri suggested.

They spent close to an hour walking the perimeter of the property, most of which was concealed by ten-foot-high walls of dense Nerium oleanders.

"Even if someone could get to the property line, I don't see how they could get through the trees," Mason declared. "That said, I guess if someone really wanted to sneak in, they could, but not without waging a serious war on the foliage. They would doubtless have had the battle scars to prove it. I don't see someone coming in that way then casually mingling with the guests, do you?"

Teri shook her head.

"That just leaves the gate security."

"According to the original investigation, there was video of everyone who came in or out. The original detectives watched it and wrote that they couldn't find anything unusual and were able to tally every name with every guest or party staffer."

"We should probably have a look at it," Teri said. "If nothing else, we might get to see one of the elusive entertainers that nobody has interviewed.

"Worth a shot," Mason said, as he started back towards the house. "I'll order the video sent up. Will you check with the original team and see if they, by any stroke of luck, created some sort of log that showed the name of each person against timecodes?"

"Why do you think anyone would have ever gone to that much trouble?" Teri asked.

"Because that's what I would have done." Mason shrugged.

The traffic heading back downtown was even worse. It didn't matter what routes Mason tried, they were all clogged with lemming-like commuters who seemed to spend way too much time trying to head west in the morning, then east in the evening.

It took over ninety minutes to traverse the city. By the time they reached 100 West First Street, it was gone six.

"Want to check on the status of the murder books while I see if I can find the video footage from the gate?"

"Sorry. I have plans," Teri replied, feeling strangely guilty.

"No sweat. All I've got planned is to reheat some of that Chinese food for dinner. That is, as long as the scavengers haven't been picking at it all afternoon."

"I thought you left it in the squad room fridge?"

"I did. One thing you need to learn about this place; you may feel that you can trust your life to your fellow officers – and you can – but don't for a moment ever think that anything you leave in the fridge is safe. I've seen an entire birthday cake that the lieutenant bought for his wife vanish within minutes. There wasn't even a crumb trail."

"I'll remember that," Teri said as she headed to her car.

After a few steps, she stopped and turned back to face Mason.

"I'm going to see my kid tonight. It's a once-a-week thing and I really don't want to miss it."

"That's gotta be tough."

"It is. Enjoy your leftover chicken feet."

"I always do."

When Mason reached their repurposed interview room, he was surprised to see that the two requested murder books had been dropped off, something that would normally have taken days. He was tempted to start reading through them, but instead, spent a couple of hours writing up what they'd accomplished that day, as well as researching where he might find the gate video from the Bel Air party.

He ended up calling the lead detective on the Groppel case. Peter Archer had retired five years earlier and had spent the subsequent years slowly drinking himself into blissful oblivion.

"Archer," Mason said as he heard the call connect.

"Fuck. Mason Darby," the slurred voice boomed through the phone speaker. "To what do I owe the honor of speaking to my favorite cop killer?"

Mason had hoped that he'd catch the ex-detective between drinking binges, but realized that since the last time they'd talked three years earlier, there probably weren't any breaks in the cycle anymore.

"You sound good," Mason lied.

"You're full of shit," Archer fired back. "What do you want? You're fucking up my evening mellow."

"Remember the Groppel case?"

"I remember all the fucking cases. Why do you think I have to drink?"

"It's been reopened. It has some similarities to another cold case."

Archer laughed. Within seconds it turned into a phlegmy cough.

"I heard they dumped the Harter case on you. Good fucking luck."

Mason was curious how Archer could still maintain some sort of data exchange with the department, but he obviously did.

"I'm looking for the gate video from the night of the party."

"Why the fuck should I help you?"

"Maybe clearing a case you couldn't close might help with the nightmares," Mason suggested.

"How do you know about my nightmares, you fuck?"

"Because we all have them. Any cop that doesn't wake up screaming occasionally either doesn't give a shit, or, is a budding sociopath. Are you going to tell me where the video is or not?"

"I thought you were supposed to be some sort of super cop," Archer slurred. "You'd think that a super cop would know where to look."

"Forget it," Mason said as he held the phone out to end the call.

"Wait," Archer shouted. "What's the first thing you learn both in the academy and then as a rookie detective about evidence?"

"Chain of custody," Mason replied.

"Not that. Isn't there somewhere that you're supposed to keep a note about any evidence in a murder case?"

"Look if you're just gonna..." Mason started, then the penny dropped. "Got it. Thanks Archer."

"Fuck you, Darby."

The call ended.

Mason looked down at the scarred metal tabletop, wondering what the hell was wrong with him. After a moment, he reached over and grabbed the Groppel murder book. He flipped through the layers of clear plastic sleeves until, near the end, he found that one of them held more than just a sheet of paper. Two DVDs were rubber-banded together around a couple of folded pieces of paper. Mason removed the band and unfolded the sheets.

131

"Fuck," he said to himself as he saw what was written. It was a timecode log to use with the DVDs to match the details of every single person that arrived or departed 127 St Cloud on the night of the party. Mason couldn't believe his own stupidity to have not checked the book before calling a retired cop, especially a good one, who now spent every waking moment trying to forget his entire twenty-two years in the force.

CHAPTER 17

After a frustratingly slow drive down Wilshire Boulevard, Teri turned right on South Sweetzer, then right again onto Orange Street, and pulled up in front of her grandparent's duplex. Though the area was still a little iffy, gentrification was slowly moving south and would soon envelope the entire neighborhood. As another bonus, wealthy gay couples had started buying the duplexes as they came on the market and restoring them from the ground up, adding to increased values and a more stable demographic.

Freeda and Bobby had bought their property in the nineties, and had lived in the bottom unit ever since. They rented the upper half and made enough to see them happily into retirement with some degree of fiscal stability.

As Teri approached her grandparent's home, she heard the deep bass of loud hip-hop music filtering out of one of the other houses or apartments.

As soon as she rang the doorbell, Teri heard the frantic barking of their rescue dog. Tito was a Heinz 57 variety as far as breeds went, but when it came to personality, the little guy was best in class.

Bobby, late sixties, long white hair and wearing a worn dress shirt over faded blue jeans opened the door, causing Tito to do his ridiculous two-legged 'happy dance' in the entry hall.

"You're early," Bobby said, embracing his granddaughter in a Calvin Klein's Obsession-infused hug.

"I don't know how," Teri replied. "It took forever to get from downtown."

"Beer?" he offered.

"Where's Gregg?"

"Still in the bath. Freeda is in there with him trying to get him to wash his hair."

"Why don't you have one and I'll have a few gulps?" Teri suggested.

"I will never understand why you don't want your son to see you with a drink," Bobby said as he headed into the kitchen.

"If you saw as many messed up homes where kids have watched their parents drink themselves either to death or violence, you'd understand. Then of course, there was my mom… your daughter. She was hardly a good example of happy homebuilding through alcohol consumption."

Bobby nodded as he closed the fridge door.

"Shit. Sorry. I don't know why I said what I said."

"No biggie. Shall I go out back?" Teri asked, always enjoying the organized chaos of the lush plantings that made up their small garden.

"We're having some work done, so let's stay in the front room," Bobby answered as he appeared with a frosty mug of what Teri knew to be Miller Lite.

Teri followed him and sat in one of the two matching floral-patterned armchairs. She immediately heard the same loud music she'd noticed outside, but it was now muffled and seemed to be coming through the living room ceiling.

"What's with the music?" Teri asked, pointing upwards.

"That's just Emanuel. He likes to play a few tunes when he gets home from work."

"I though the upstairs unit was rented to the Hardings?" Teri asked.

"They ran into a little financial trouble and very kindly saved us the bother of finding a new tenant and managed to sublet it to Emanuel."

"The Hardings were your tenants. They're not allowed to sublet. If they couldn't afford the rent, they can't just shove a stranger up there. This is your home."

"It was all done and dusted before we even knew what was happening."

"What does Freeda have to say about it?" Teri asked.

"She's resigned herself to the whole situation. It's no big deal, really."

"It is if this Emanuel guy is going to blast music right into your home. Tell him to turn it down."

"I will," Bobby assured her as he held out the mug of beer.

Just as Teri reached for it, thunderous footfalls could be heard approaching from the back of the house.

"Mommy!" Gregg said as he charged into the living room.

Teri jumped to her feet, ignoring Bobby's outstretched arm. Gregg threw his freshly bathed and pajamaed body up in the air, trusting that his mother would catch him.

She did.

*

After a frustrating search of the squad room, Mason finally found the old DVD player under copies of ancient reverse-directory phone books that had been used prior to the modern, online alternatives. Though basically useless, they were kept as some sort of nostalgic reminder of the 'old' ways. The fact that they were scattered on top of a digital technology, that was itself on the way out, seemed somewhat fitting.

Mason watched the first DVD showing the various guests arriving for the Groppel party. He stopped at various points and compared the name on the time log to the image on the screen. After the first hour of footage, he fast-forwarded the video to one specific time code. The one associated with the name Adam Parition.

Next to his name were the words 'party entertainer'.

Adam looked to be in his mid to late fifties, had long dark hair and a prominent curved nose. Mason couldn't help

136

feeling that the man looked a little like the bad witch in *The Wizard of Oz*.

Mason reviewed the notes in the recently delivered murder book to try and find mention of what exactly the guy did to entertain the party guests.

Much to his surprise, there was no such revelation. Usually, such information would be noted either by the detectives or be mentioned within the witness interviews. After speed reading through countless guest statements, he couldn't find one reference to what exactly the entertainer did.

Tired and disheartened by how little he'd accomplished despite staying late to knock a few more bricks out of the wall, Mason realized that he was hungry.

It was past eight, and the department was quiet. It was that miraculous time between the busy, but controlled, chaos of the day shift and the darker, more insidiously dangerous lunacy that began around eleven and continued through the wee hours of the morning.

Mason walked through the quiet department and was surprised to find no other detectives roaming the halls or agonizing over crime scene notes. He felt saddened that budgetary constraints aimed at pacifying the police 'de-funders' had put an end to the iconic image of detectives burning the midnight oil.

Once in the parking garage, Mason pressed his car key-fob so it would flash the vehicles headlights and give a short beep. He had come in so early and been so anxious to get to the murder book that he had no idea where exactly he'd parked his car.

Just as he reached the Jeep, Mason sensed someone approaching him from the shadows. He instinctively dropped his key fob and started to reach for his FN 509 handgun, the model mandated by the chief to be used by all Los Angeles police officers.

"There's no need for that," a voice replied, just as the speaker emerged from behind a support pillar, revealing his expensive suit, his greying hair and false, overly white smile. "Michael Gainbury," the man said, offering his hand to Mason.

"What do you want?" Mason asked, his hand still on the butt of his gun."

"We haven't met, but I'm the deputy controller for—"

"I know who you are," Mason interrupted.

"I was wondering if I could buy you a drink?" Gainbury asked.

"Why?"

"I just wanted to touch base with you regarding one of your cases."

"Talk to the chief. She's the liaison for any updates."

"I know that's the prescribed protocol, but I thought that maybe you and I could open a line of communication so that..."

That was as far as he got before Mason drew his weapon and, pointing it towards the ground, held it by his side.

"Sneaking up on someone in a dark parking lot can be dangerous. I could mistake you for some punk trying to take a cop down as some sort of gang initiation. I would then almost certainly have to use lethal force to stop such an assault."

Gainbury laughed nervously and gestured down at his expensive wardrobe.

"Do I look like a gang member?"

"That's the problem, I couldn't tell in the dark. If only you had stepped into the light."

"Are you threatening me?" Gainbury asked, his voice noticeably shaky.

"No, of course not. Just pointing out how dangerous it can be to sneak up on an armed police officer in a dark garage. My suggestion is that you go through the proper channels in future. Just to be safe."

"I will, but now that I'm here..."

Gainbury heard the distinctive sound of Mason's gun being cocked. One look at the detective's face was enough for him to back away.

"Sorry to have bothered you."

"No bother at all," Mason replied as he retrieved his fob, opened the car door and got in.

*

During the entire time that Mason had been a cop, the simple act of getting in his car and driving home had seemed

139

like second nature. Since the charges, his firing and the long, dark year that had followed, the simple act now felt entirely foreign to him.

Though Mason could have taken the LAPD for five times the amount he'd asked for, the fact was, he had no interest in wealth. Since receiving his two-million-dollar payout he'd only bought two expensive things, though neither of which were what anyone would consider a luxury item. He'd bought a three-year-old Jeep Cherokee and a tiny, two-bedroom shack tucked away near the top of Beachwood Canyon.

Having only just moved into the cabin-like structure, Mason had yet to start any serious restoration projects, even though the house didn't have heating, air-conditioning, double glazing or even a proper kitchen.

It had been built in the sixties by a small hippy commune that wanted to camp in the hills, but have a central structure for meals and meetings. After the last of them had abandoned the place in the late nineties, it had been used as an 'off the books' rental for almost twenty years, as none of the subsequent owners had any interest in spending the money to bring the place up to code. If it had a view of the city as some of the nicer houses in the canyon did, then maybe there would have been some interest. Number 206 however, was a small quarter-acre lot that had a two hundred and seventy degree view of the surrounding hillside, but little else.

Unlike the average Los Angeles buyer, Mason had zero interest in looking down at the city. He had spent too many years working its dark streets and alleys to find any beauty in its unwieldy expanse.

Mason had always wanted to live in one of the Hollywood Hills' canyons, despite the ever-present threat of fire, flood and quake. Beachwood had always been his favorite as it was one of the very few that wasn't a commuter's conduit between LA and the San Fernando Valley.

Mason had yet to get to know his three neighbors in the cul de sac. In fact, he had so far only ever seen one of the residents. He was a guy in his fifties who was overweight and was always tinkering around with his house. He appeared to be renovating it by himself, and from Mason's perspective, not doing that good a job of it.

The man's latest project was to replace the original, flammable, roof shingles with something a little safer. The previous week, he had single-handedly stripped the roof down to the rafters, then spent two days covering the entire building with two enormous blue tarps to keep out the weather.

Though the noise of the guy hammering and sawing was a continuous auditory backdrop, Mason still preferred that sound to the cacophony that existed down on the flats of the city.

Mason removed the paper bag containing his prized Chinese leftovers from the car and crossed his gravel drive to his new front door. That was one improvement that couldn't wait. At some point during the house's checkered past, the front door had been replaced with a cheap interior door that, over the years, had swelled, expanded and warped according to the seasonal changes. By the time Mason heard about the property, the portal hardly fit the frame and was only kept in place with rope and zip ties.

"Fuck," Mason cursed as he unpacked the plastic containers.

He'd briefly checked the contents at the station but now, able to fully view what was inside the cardboard containers, he could see that the six spareribs that he'd been especially looking forward to had not only been pilfered, but the cleaned bones had been carefully placed back in the square box.

Considering the current sentiment towards him, he counted himself lucky that they hadn't vandalized everything. Mason filled a plate with his culinary treasure, then set the microwave to three minutes on high. As the timer counted down, Mason grabbed himself a beer from the ancient and oddly vocal fridge. For twenty-four hours a day it made a series of different mewling sounds that permeated the whole house. When Mason had first moved in, he thought there had been a wounded animal nearby, and was greatly relieved that it was only the appliance that seemed to be in such a state of abject misery.

Mason fired up the only luxury item in the house, a fifty-two-inch LG TV and selected Netflix from the remote. Unlike the literary detectives that let jazz or classical music wash away their inner, tortured anguish, Mason liked to watch movies. Everything from black and white classics to the

Marvel multiverse. The one thing he wouldn't watch were crime dramas. It wasn't because of some sort of moral or professional taboo against the genre, rather he simply felt that he'd been there, and most certainly, done that.

Mason, in a quest to have access to any movie he could think of, had a subscription to every streaming platform he could find.

That night, the mood hit him to watch one of his old favorites, a classic with Cary Grant, where he is forced onto a deserted island in the Pacific during World War 2 so that he can report on any enemy aircraft sightings.

After devouring a good quantity of the Chinese leftovers and reaching the part in the movie when Leslie Caron hides all his bottles of whiskey, Mason heard a scratching sound coming from the back door. Smiling, he paused the movie and went through to the kitchen, grabbing the two spring rolls that he'd already cut up into small pieces.

Mason slowly opened the back door and as usual, saw nothing outside. He threw one of the treats onto the weed-infested patio, then closed the door again. He counted to thirty and re-opened it.

The treat was gone.

Mason threw another one. The game went on for another ten minutes then, a thin and obviously nervous coyote stepped out of the undergrowth and stood staring at him. Despite its thinness, its coat was full and predominantly sandy brown. The only exception was its left back paw, which was black.

"Hi, big fella," Mason said in little more than a whisper, as he gently tossed another treat only a couple of yards away from the house.

The coyote kept its eyes rivetted on Mason, then, after a couple of minutes, and in a partial stoop, it approached the piece of food. Still watching Mason, it lowered its shaggy head and gently picked up the morsel. Once firmly in its mouth, the animal spun around and vanished up into the verdant hillside.

Mason smiled to himself as he closed the back door. He knew full well that every neighbor in the canyon would be in his face if they found out that he was feeding a coyote, but the one he'd just fed had approached him first, and in a weird way, Mason felt that the two shared a common trait.

Both were scavengers and both were out for blood. The only difference was that Mason was paid to do the hunting.

CHAPTER 18

As Mason and Teri carried out phone interviews with the guests and staff from all three parties, three things became apparent. Nobody was aware of their having seen anything untoward during the events, the description of the 'entertainer' matched the images from the Groppel video, and everyone they spoke to flatly refused to disclose exactly what it was that Victor Spirito, Adam Parition and Garry Houl did to entertain the guests.

No matter how they phrased their questions, none of the interviewees were willing to give any details about the entertainment, until a Mexican bartender, who was clearly conflicted about what he should and shouldn't say to the police, produced the only tangible piece of new evidence. Despite his obvious lack of trust for the two detectives, Javier agreed to come into the station, and reluctantly produced a folded piece of paper from his worn backpack and slid it across the table.

The document was short, but highly specific. It was a non-disclosure agreement between, in Javier's case, him, having been part of the support staff for the Groppel party, and Adam Parition... AKA, the entertainer.

"The paper, it says I can't talk about the show, but it doesn't say I can't tell you about having to sign that."

Javier reached over and tapped the NDA.

"Is that true?"

"We're not lawyers, but that seems to be about right," Teri replied.

"We don't want you getting in any trouble here," Mason added. "Maybe you could, without being specific, tell us at least what type of act Mr. Parition put on. I mean, was it magic, music... what?"

Javier looked to the officers across from him, then down at the sheet of paper.

"I can't tell you."

Mason sighed in frustration.

"Is not because I don't want to. It's because I don't know. We all had to sign one of these." He gestured to the contract. "Then, about fifteen minutes before it started, all the staff were shut out of the main room. That's why I don't know what the man did."

"Could you hear anything?" Mason asked.

Javier looked down at the document and shrugged.

"Let's try this another way," Teri said with a reassuring smile. "Could you hear the guests in the room?"

Javier nodded.

"Were they laughing, singing... what?"

146

"No," Javier replied. "They were… I don't know the word… gritando."

"Screaming?" Teri said, surprised. "What type of gritando? Happy, excited…"

"No. Not like that. The people… the people in that room… they were scared. The screaming was the kind you hear right before death."

*

After unsuccessfully trying to get any other information from Javier, they thanked him and reassured him that nothing he had said would ever be shown to have come from him.

Both could tell that no matter what they said to the guy, he was never likely to stray far from the shadows until he'd managed to get his green card converted to citizenship. Javier knew that it had become all too easy to be targeted and returned across the border, even when legally in the country.

"What do you make of that?" Mason asked.

"I think the guy was pretty scared himself."

"Yeah, but what do you think it meant that this Adam Parition was causing a room full of monied white people to be screaming?"

"I think that Javier just did us a huge favor. There's only one kind of show that can make people gasp and sometime scream," Teri commented.

"Opera?" Mason said, grinning.

"Besides that," Teri replied, shaking her head.

"So, what then?" Mason asked.

"I'm putting all my chips on magic," Teri replied. "Now that we've got a possible genre, it should be easier to track down the illusive showman."

"Before we head down that road, fancy giving the Sunset Tower another try?"

"Every time I've called, they've had another booking or rehearsal. Let me try them now."

Teri was on the phone for less than a minute.

"If we can get there in forty-five minutes, we can check the place out before a bar mitzvah starts at three."

"Nice."

"They rented out the ballroom. That's gotta be an expensive little party for a thirteen-year-old kid," Teri commented.

"Not in Los Angeles."

*

After managing to avoid the worst of the traffic on the way to West Hollywood, Mason and Teri pulled under the elaborate, deco-era portico of the Sunset Tower. They were introduced to the assistant manager, who quickly offloaded the pair to the event services director.

Inga Civalla, late thirties, blond and stocky, was intrigued about the old case and was more than willing to show them the event space and infamous swimming pool. Its notoriety had originally been earned when Madonna chose to sunbathe topless in view of all the other guests. However, since the body of Pamela Whitlough had been found at the bottom of the lagoon-style pool, Madonna's tits held little interest in comparison to an unsolved murder.

Inga led them down a red, velvet-lined hallway to a pair of double oak doors. She theatrically opened them both at the same time so the officers could get the full impact of the event space beyond.

The room was massive, not just in length but also in height. It was easily two stories tall, with carved stone pillars and half-moon uplighters dotted along the gilded walls. Staff members were busy giving the place a few finishing touches before the Hershel bar mitzvah began in less than ninety minutes.

The Hershel's private event planner zeroed in on the two officers and, after taking one look at their off-the-rack clothes, told them that whatever their reason for being there, they had to leave immediately as he had the room booked all day.

Mason showed his ID and explained that they just needed to have a quick look in regards to a cold case they were investigating.

The planner waved them away as if they were little more than a bad smell.

"You'll just have to come back another time," he said, as he sashayed back towards what was obviously the head table for the young prince and his family.

Teri got in step with him then, putting an arm around his waist, whispered something in the man's ear.

The planner stopped in his tracks and looked back at Mason, then at Teri. He'd somehow lost fifty percent of his fake tan.

"Oh, all right! But try not to get in the way."

As Mason watched the little man tear into a couple of waiters for not having placed the glasses in a perfect line, he asked Teri what exactly she'd said to the man.

"I just told him that we wouldn't be long, but if he was adamant about us not being here, we'd be happy to leave, however, a forensic team would then have to be immediately brought in and would doubtless take at least four to five hours to tear the room apart."

"Isn't that an abuse of police power?" Mason asked, grinning.

"Not if the pretentious little shit was asking for it."

Mason laughed before he could stop himself as Teri produced her iPad and opened the crime scene photos from the 2010 murder. She held the tablet up so that both of them could see the current room in comparison with the photo.

"Am I going nuts or does the room look substantially bigger now?" Mason asked.

"Your sanity is still secure... I would imagine," Inga, who was standing off to the side, said. "The wall panels are actually suspended from above and can be repositioned, depending on the size of the event. For the Whitlough party, the space would have been almost half the size you see today."

"That's impressive," Teri commented. "I don't think I've ever seen anything quite like it. I mean, I've been to conference halls that can do that, but nothing this grand."

"When the hotel was remodeled in 2009, the owner hired a Broadway staging company to design the room. They wanted every party here to be memorable."

"They sure as hell got their wish with Pamela Whitlough's bash," Mason said. "It's right up there with John Belushi's last night at the Chateaux Marmont."

"Yes, but the Marmont doesn't have a ghost," Inga pointed out.

"And the Sunset Towers does?" Mason asked, having zero belief in anything beyond what his eyes could see.

"I've never seen it myself, but ever since the remodel, there have been a number of sightings. We're even listed on hauntedhotels.com."

"You must be very proud," Teri joked.

"Whether there's any truth to it or not, we get almost twenty percent of our guests from that site and others like it. Staying in a haunted hotel has become big business. We do a two-night Halloween package that starts at $1500."

Mason shook his head at yet another way the City of Angels had found to wring every last dollar from its naïve visitors.

"I've seen enough in here," Mason said as he turned to Teri.

"I agree. It's literally a completely different space to the one in the pictures."

"Ready to see the pool area?" Inga asked.

She led them to the far side of the event space, then seemed to notice something amiss about a set of massive bi-fold doors. Inga started to reach for a switch on the nearest wall when, suddenly, the planner could be heard screeching from somewhere behind them.

"Don't open the doors, you simpleton! Have you noticed the wind out there? Do you have any idea what that could do the decorations in here?" he said as he leant against the wall, protecting the switch from Inga's touch. Unfortunately, he leant against it with a tad too much force and the seals between the reinforced glass frames hissed just before the folding doors began to retract.

The result was instantaneous, though not exactly what Mason or Teri imagined would have happened. Instead of a massive gust of wind causing havoc within the event space, the opposite occurred. The wind beyond was whipping by the opening, from left to right, resulting in a momentary vacuum from within.

Almost every table within twenty feet of the doors was instantly cleared of anything that didn't have serious heft. Glitter, streamers, placements and even the floral arrangement went airborne and ended up strewn across the flagstone patio and stone steps.

The planner slid down the wall in a theatrical display of mock tragedy as Inga opened a concealed doorway that led into the kitchen.

"I'll have you fired for this," the planner screamed from the other room.

Inga ignored the man.

"You don't seem worried," Teri commented.

"I'm not. I was reaching for the switch because I noticed that it wasn't in the safe mode and wanted to secure it. The fact that that officious creep managed to activate it himself is hardly my concern. Let's go this way."

Inga approached a pair of doors that were used for drink and food service for the patio and pool area. The first thing they noticed was the wind. Los Angelinos can recognize a Santa Anna just from the warmth and dryness. Some even swear that they can smell the acridity of the desert floor from which the wind was spawned.

The problem was, the wind they were feeling was unnaturally cold and, if anything, smelled mainly of diesel fuel.

"Sorry about the mess," Inga said, straight-faced, as she scanned the detritus that had escaped from within the hotel onto a used-brick pathway.

She led the pair to the very back of the hotel where the pool and surrounding stone terrace appeared to be perched precariously above a sheer drop.

"I don't remember there being any wind when we pulled up outside," Mason said as he buttoned his suit jacket.

"It never reaches the front. It rises up the hill from the flats below. It's something to do with the colder air up top and the heat from the city below. It does this a lot. The hotel has to spend a small fortune on heat lamps just so the guests can enjoy their sundowner cocktails out here."

"Do you mind if my partner and I nose around out here for a while?" Mason asked.

"Is this where you compare the gruesome pictures to the real thing?" Inga asked, wide-eyed.

"You seem to know the routine," Teri commented.

"Though the one you're investigating is the most famous case for the hotel, there have been quite a number of other crime scenes photographed here."

"Hopefully no other murders," Mason added.

"Actually, there have been three murders, two unexplained deaths and nine suicides. Not bad in eighty-seven years," Inga recited with a smile. "I'll wait for you in the lobby."

"Why do you know all that?" Teri asked.

"For when I give one of the hotel's haunted tours."

"I presume the hotel charges extra for that?"

"Seventy-five dollars per person," Inga replied, with what sounded like pride. "Now, try not to scare away the guests," Inga said, dipping her head toward a couple that were huddled at one of the tables, trying desperately to sidle up closer to the nearest heat lamp.

CHAPTER 19

"That was weird," Mason said, once Inga had re-entered the hotel.

"What's weird are the morons that cough up all that money for the rooms and the tours," Teri replied.

"I take it you don't believe in ghosts?"

"If I ever see one, I'll start believing in them, but so far, I put them in the same catalogue as little green beings from outer space, sea monsters, and men that remember to put down the toilet seat after peeing."

"I put the seat down," Mason replied, though not sure why he felt the need to declare his innocence.

"Great. That makes one of you," Teri said as she approached the side of the swimming pool.

It was meant to look like a tropical waterfall cascading into a secluded and inviting rock pool. Boulders were dotted along the 'naturally' uneven edge. The bottom appeared to have been painted black or maybe dark blue. At one end, a thin stream of water gently frothed down from a fifteen-foot cliff.

"This looks like something from Vegas in the seventies," Mason commented.

"Yeah, but in Vegas, this would have been inside one of the cheesy penthouse suites."

"You sound like you speak from experience," Mason remarked.

He received yet another eye roll.

"I'm amazed that they haven't turned this into one of those infinity pools. It would be perfect right on the edge of a hill like this," she said as she approached the rim.

"I can't see the bottom," she observed.

"That would explain why nobody initially saw the body."

Teri swiped to an image that looked as if it had been taken from almost exactly where they were standing and was focused on the bottom. A dim light set in the side of the pool had offered just enough illumination so that the ghostly image of a body wrapped in a couple of hotel towels was visible.

Even in still photos, the edges of the fabric appeared to have been wafting on some invisible current, almost as if some unsecured death shroud was caught up in a light wind.

"It's a good job this happened at night," Mason observed. "Without that pool light, they'd never have seen her."

"I'd still like to know how she got in there while the party was in full swing inside. Someone must have seen or heard something."

"You read the interviews. Nobody even noticed she was missing."

"How is that possible?" Teri asked. "I mean, it was her party. I could understand if..." She stopped, having noticed her partner's focus change as he turned back towards the path leading to the ballroom. "What?"

Mason sighed. "I had a thought. What could have happened at some point during the party that would have distracted everyone enough so that nobody noticed that Pamela had disappeared?"

"Shit," Teri said, shaking her head. "The show! Obviously, it must have been riveting enough to have kept all eyes on whatever the act was. I don't suppose there was anything in the murder book about what the entertainment actually consisted of?"

"There was no mention. Probably because this Gary Houl guy left well before the body was discovered," Mason replied. "The only thing that the planner mentioned was that Gary had been in the room well before showtime and seemed to have been treating himself to more than his share of food and drink."

"Yet no mention of what the guy did. That remind you of anything?"

"Yup. Same thing with the Groppel murder. Is this a new thing, that entertainers lock everyone into a non-disclosure agreement before each show?"

"I know one way of finding out," Teri said, grinning as she turned to Inga who was standing on the top patio looking at the view.

"I don't suppose any of the staff from 2010 still work here, do they?" Mason asked once they'd climbed back up to the top level.

"The only one I can think of is old Barney Fisher. He's been working here since way before that," Inga said after consulting a staff roster from her event contact list.

"Is he here today?" Mason asked.

"You were standing next to him in the ballroom," Inga advised. "Let me send someone to get him. I don't think I want to interrupt that douchebag planner again."

A short time later, Barney shuffled over to where the three were sitting in the front lobby.

"Am I in trouble?" Barney asked bluntly.

"I don't know," Mason said, getting to his feet. "What have you done?"

"Nothing in about forty years, but before then I was something of a wild man."

Teri also stood and after taking a close look at the guy, couldn't quite see much of the 'wild' left in him. Barney had to be in his mid to late seventies, was slightly stooped and obviously spend a lot of time trying to wrangle the last few hairs on his head into some sort of order.

Mason tried not to smile. "I understand that you were working here back in 2010?"

"I was, and I told the detectives back then that I had no idea what happened to the woman?"

"I don't doubt that," Mason said in as calming a voice as possible. "We were wondering if you can remember anything about the entertainment that night. I believe the performer was a man named Garry Houl. We are just curious about what exactly this Mr. Houl does... or did."

"I have no idea," Barney replied.

"Some of the staff must have seen the show," Teri pointed out.

"None of us saw a thing. We were all asked to leave the ballroom and sign some piece of paper that said we would be sued if we ever talked about the entertainment or about Mr. Houl."

"You were forced to sign a non-disclosure agreement?" Mason asked. "Didn't you find that a little strange?"

Barney laughed. "Not in this town. I've probably signed over fifty of them since working here. You'd be amazed at how many wealthy celebrities don't want details of their goings-on to leak to the press, or whatever they call it today? Oh yeah, the media!"

"So as far as you know, none of the staff saw the show?" Mason continued.

Before Barney could answer, Teri opened the video file from the security gate at 127 St Cloud, in Bel Air. She held it out so Barney could see the screen, then pressed play.

"Is this the entertainer?" she asked.

The waiter looked half-heartedly at the screen then suddenly blinked rapidly.

"Do you recognize the man in this video?" Mason asked.

Barney shook his head while lowering his gaze to the floor.

"Mr. Fisher." Teri lowered her voice conspiratorially. "We are investigating three murders, and it is possible that this man was present at all of them. I should advise you that the law does not accept a non-disclosure agreement in lieu of evidence in a murder investigation."

Barney looked up at Teri, and she couldn't miss the look of fear in his eyes.

"I don't want to get in any trouble," he whispered.

"You won't," Teri said.

Barney stood silently for a few seconds, then sighed loudly. "That's the guy who put on the show. None of us ever saw what exactly he did, but I'll tell you one thing, he was one rude sonofabitch!"

"Thank you, Barney," Teri said. "Also, whatever you're still running from is, I'm sure, long in the past. You can stop looking over your shoulder."

Barney nodded and mouthed a silent thank you before heading back towards the ballroom.

Mason waited until Inga was out of earshot. "What the hell was that about?"

"It was the way he asked if he was in trouble. It's like he's been expecting something to resurface, and for a moment, he thought we were it. I ran him through the database while we were talking. He did some serious time in the late seventies."

"What for?"

"It seems that Barney was, and I assume still is, gay. I only looked at the summary, but it seems some dickheads tried to beat him up in West Hollywood and Barney got a good punch in; a kid hit his head on the curb and died. He got man slaughter one. Fifteen years."

"And somehow got this job once out of the joint," Mason said. "No hotel owner was going to hire some guy with a federal rap, so how did he even get a job?"

"No idea, but it sure explains why he's been working here for so long," Teri opined. "He was probably convinced he'd never get another one."

"I wonder if—"

Before Mason could finish his thought, his phone began making chirping sounds. He checked the screen.

"Ballsack wants us back at the station ASAP."

"You're sure she wants both of us?" Teri asked hopefully, only one second before her phone started quacking.

"That answer your question?"

CHAPTER 20

Mason and Teri were waved into Balisek's office the moment they entered the suite.

"And so it begins," Mason said.

"I have no idea what you're griping about, but I thought you both should know that there's been another murder with some worrying similarities to the ones you're currently investigating," Balisek said, ignoring Mason's remark.

"You're assigning it to us?" Teri asked, trying not to show the surprise she was feeling.

"No, of course not. I am hardly going to put my most controversial officer on a case like this."

"A case like what?" Mason asked.

Balisek took a moment to study the pair.

"Why don't you sit down?"

"Will we be here that long?" Mason shot back. "Especially as I'm so controversial."

"Just sit down and shut up for once... please."

The pair sat.

"Patrol officers were called to 2648 Loma Vista Drive early today. It would appear that there had been some sort of A-list party that ran well into the night. This morning, the butler—"

"Butler?" Mason interrupted. "Seriously?"

"I couldn't make this stuff up," Balisek replied. "Anyway, the owner of the house was found unresponsive in what the uniformed officers referred to as a 'basement torture chamber'."

Mason was about to interject again, but Balisek held up her hand for him to keep quiet.

"The owner was found inside an antique torture device. He apparently collected them."

"What sort of device was it?" Teri asked.

Balisek consulted some handwritten notes. "It was something called an iron maiden. According to the butler, his employer had purchased it at Sotheby's earlier in the year."

"Can I assume that the device was closed?"

Both Mason and Balisek gave Teri a surprised look.

"I used to be fascinated by some of the darker punishment techniques used in the Middle Ages," she explained.

"Nice," Mason said, raising his eyebrows.

"Perhaps you can fill us in on exactly what this device looks like?" Balisek asked. "I haven't seen any of the crime scene photos yet."

"It's a hollowed-out wood or metal figure of a woman... a maiden, usually a noble one. The front of the thing is hinged, and swings open far enough so that a person can

163

stand inside. Needless to say, this was rarely voluntary. Most people who were sentenced to the iron maiden had to be restrained, then chained within the device. Once secure inside, the hinged door was slowly closed and sealed. I should mention that the door was covered in long, jagged spikes that pointed inward."

Balisek looked as if she'd just smelled something unpleasant. Mason on the other hand didn't seem to be the least bit fazed.

"If the owner was shut in this metal woman thing—"

"Iron maiden," Teri corrected him, shaking her head.

"If this iron maiden thing was closed," Mason continued, "how did the butler know he was in there?"

"It seems that the owner liked to unwind after a long evening by sitting alone in the basement while listening to gothic chants."

"Holy shit," Mason blurted out. "Who the hell is, or was, this guy?"

"This morning, after not finding his employer in bed as usual, he searched the house, including the basement."

"That still doesn't explain why he thought his boss had been shut in the Def Leppard thing."

"Iron maiden," the captain shot back. "Apparently, the device is not particularly watertight and the floor surrounding it was covered in congealed blood."

"Who's the vic?" Mason asked.

"Gilberto Tamacini."

"The opera singer?" Teri said, shocked. "I took my grandparents to see him at the Hollywood Bowl just last month."

"I hope you saved the ticket stubs," Balisek commented. "They've just become collectables."

"So why call us into your office to announce that we aren't being assigned this new murder, or at least, what we assume was a murder."

"I wanted you both to hear directly from me that I'm reading you into the investigation. You will remain primary on the other three unsolved cases, but for the Tamacini case you will act in a consulting roll to the lead detectives."

"Why us?" Mason asked.

"Because we have another unexplained death during an A-list party. While the investigation is in its infancy, I thought it best to have you both in the loop. If it does indeed turn into another mystery case, it will likely dovetail into your current investigations. The detectives are expecting you up at the Loma Vista house."

"And who are the lucky pair?" Mason asked.

"Hardwick and Simmonds."

"Of course," Mason said, shaking his head.

"Why of course?" Balisek asked. "They're the best closers we have."

"They're only the top closers because you keep giving them the highest profile cases. A rookie straight out of the academy could have solved half of those homicides with the amount of support and unlimited funding they keep getting."

"They get the funds and support because they solve the cases," she insisted.

"And I suppose it doesn't bother you that the pair of them spend more time on talk show sets than they do running down leads. You've basically created a culture where the best cops get buried under the workload of your two favorites."

"Careful, Darby." Balisek's voice had taken on a dangerously hard edge.

"I assume that there is a media blackout on this case?" Mason pressed on.

"Naturally."

"Then I'll bet you a steak dinner for two at the Palm that Harddick and Simpleton find their way onto one of the local, if not national, news shows tonight," Mason said, using the pairs' unflattering monikers.

That one struck a nerve with the chief. Mason could see Ballsack's telltale twitch develop under her right eye. He also noticed the way she placed her chin on one palm with her index finger pointed up under the same eye, in effect, hiding the muscle tremor.

"Can we maybe talk a little more about what our responsibilities are on this new case?" Teri asked, hoping to lighten the mood in the room.

"I'll take that bet," Balisek said as she got to her feet. "Your lieutenant will give you the formal assignment notification, as well as what will be expected from you both. In the meantime, I suggest you make your way to Loma Vista so you can check for any similarities with the unsolved cases."

As the two turned to leave, Balisek asked Mason to stay. Both stopped in their tracks.

"Just Mason," Balisek clarified.

Teri shot her partner a concerned glance, then stepped out of the office.

"What the hell did you say to Gainbury? I've had the city controller tear me a new asshole."

"Maybe a second one might be useful," Mason remarked.

Balisek shook her head like a disappointed schoolteacher. "You've managed, against all odds, to get your job back. Why jeopardize that?"

"The guy came out of the shadows in the parking structure. He wanted in on the information loop for the Harter case. I told him that he should be more careful and that a guy could get hurt sneaking up on an armed officer like that."

Balisek looked stunned. "You're sure he asked for info about the case?"

"One hundred percent."

"That cocksucker!" she exclaimed. "He told his boss that he was minding his own business and that you approached him and then threatened him for no reason."

"That would now make him a 'lying' cocksucker," Mason replied.

"Thank you, Darby. I'm sorry that happened. I gave strict instructions to everyone in this building and City Hall that you and Grey were off limits."

"What are you going to do now?" Mason asked.

"Once you're gone, I am going to call the controller back and give him his own orifice replacement."

"I won't keep you then," Mason said as he headed for the office door.

Before Mason was even out of the suite, he heard Ballsack shouting for her assistant to get the LA controller on the phone.

*

Loma Vista was Beverly Hills' first formally planned development. Whereas most of the city was built one house at a time, in the late '50s a successful developer named Paul Trousdale managed to buy up a huge chunk of what had previously been part of the Doheny Ranch. He then set about carving up a swath of the Santa Monica Mountain foothills into what, by Beverly Hills standards, were relatively small, graded lots.

He built a few modern – for the '50s and '60s – single-story ranch-style homes, many with the latest craze, a Hawaiian pitched roof. The place took off. Within only five years, half of the lots had been sold and many already had homes built on them.

2648 was on the lower, south facing part of Loma Vista Drive and was definitely one of the grander ones, even though you wouldn't know that from its exterior. Mason had been in a few of the Trousdale homes over the years and knew not to judge them by their modest exteriors.

"Holy shit," Teri said as she walked into the entry foyer after they both signed into the crime scene.

Even though most homes adhered to the single story policy within the estate, that didn't mean rules weren't bent in order to attain as much 'wow' impact as possible.

The entry was at least twenty feet tall. Even the double bronze-inlayed front doors were over fifteen feet. Italian marble tiles gave way to plush, white carpeting as they were led by a young, uniformed officer through the living room to a small utility hallway leading to the kitchen and staff quarters.

Another cop stood vigil next to an open door leading to the basement.

"Sorry, Detectives," he said, almost embarrassed. "The room's at its maximum already. Can you hang on while I see if I can get a few people to relocate?"

"Not a problem," Mason replied, having expected a crowd. When a celebrity, especially one as big as Tamacini (no pun intended even though the tenor did top the scales at over 300lbs), it always attracted way more investigative interest than a nobody from nowhere.

After a short wait, Detective Larry Hardwick emerged from the basement and looked directly at Teri, intentionally ignoring Mason. Hardwick was a big man and most of it was fat. Back in his youth, he'd been a running back for Hoover High School in Alabama, but he'd never had the drive to put in the work. He even managed to fumble what could have been the winning play in the county championships. After that, Hardwick spent more time smoking pot than training, and was eventually dropped from the team.

At some point, probably because of his love of beating up anyone smaller than him, he chose law enforcement as his career. Over the next twenty years, his muscles deteriorated about as fast as his hairline, leaving him with a bloated belly and a poor attempt at a combover.

"Still alive?" he said, as he openly stared at the top button of Teri's blouse. "Not all of his partners can say that."

"Yo, Harddick," Teri replied. "My eyes are up here and from what I've heard, if you'd been the one who'd had to face off against the Runyon Canyon Strangler, you would most likely have pissed yourself and crawled off into the dark, then gone on TV and taken credit for catching him."

Hardwick's jaw dropped open. Teri had gone out of her way to be a team player once she arrived in LA, and even despite the believed nepotism from on high, she'd shouldered the never-ending jibes with a stoic disregard. This was a watershed moment for her.

Hardwick desperately tried to get his sluggish brain to produce a suitable comeback, but after a night on Heradura Gold, the gears were reluctant to engage.

"Bitch," he retorted eloquently.

"You always were something of a wordsmith," Mason said as he squeezed past him and headed downstairs. Teri followed him, but after glancing back up, was amazed that Hardwick was clearly checking out her ass.

170

"I didn't say you two were cleared to go downstairs yet," Hardwick called after them.

"With you upstairs, there's plenty of room for us down here," Mason replied. "Thanks. We'll let you know when we're finished."

For a moment they thought that Hardwick was going to come down after them, then heard the officer on door patrol clearly tell him that he'd have to wait as the basement had reached his limit.

As they entered the maestro's torture chamber, they could distinctly hear the detective reaming the young man. Both smiled when they heard the officer offer to call the captain if the detective wasn't happy with the orders he'd been given to ensure both safety and crime scene integrity.

The room looked like it had had been copied from an old Frankenstein set. Mason was pretty sure that that was more than just coincidental. When you live in a town filled with struggling set designers and carpenters, it's not that hard to have a room, or indeed an entire house, made to look like something from one of your favorite movies.

The walls had been made to look as if they came from a medieval castle. The floors and ceiling were painted black and each torture device, and there were many of them, had its own spotlight, giving the place and even more sinister feel.

There were over a dozen techs and officers in the basement and most of them were focusing their attention on the device and the corpse within it.

"Look what the cat dragged in," Alice Chang said from behind a face mask and hooded, forensic boiler suit.

"It must be a big deal when they drag you out of your lair," Mason shot back.

"I can see that you both still have that magic spark," Teri said sarcastically. "Anything unusual besides a dead guy in a four-hundred-year-old torture device?"

"Actually, yes. When my team clears out, you can get closer to the body. You'll notice the scratches and bruises all over his face and hands."

"Maybe that's normal when you die in one of those things," Mason suggested.

"Maybe, but as bruising and oozing ceases when your heart stops beating, it means that they happened antemortem."

"Okay, that's a little weird. Are you suggesting that he was fighting someone before getting shut inside that contraption?" Mason asked.

"Maybe, but wait, there's more." Chang stepped closer to the pair. "Judging by the blood around the inside handle..."

"The what?" Teri asked, shocked. "Why would there be a handle inside the iron maiden? It wasn't meant to be self-activated. These things were controlled by the torturer not the person being tortured."

"You're right, but for whatever reason, this one had a handle on the inside of the door, and judging by the blood on it, plus the scratch marks and damage to the victim's fingernails, I'd say he not only closed the thing on himself, but put up one hell of a struggle to do so."

"What the hell would make someone do something like that?" Mason asked.

"I don't know, but by the expression on the guy's face, he was scared as shit over something. I think he jumped into the maiden to save himself from whoever else was down here last night."

Mason stepped past some of the peripheral personnel and stood facing the iron maiden. Tamacini was still in situ, awaiting the okay from the coroner to remove the body. Teri stepped alongside and gasped as she saw the horror within the torture device.

The tenor had been a big man, both in height and girth. It was obvious that the iron maiden had not been constructed to fit anyone in the triple-X size range, as obesity was rare in the Middle Ages. A couple of plagues, countless famines and the shortage of food even in the good times made for a generally slender population.

Despite his size, Tamacini had somehow managed to squeeze himself into the frightful contraption. Mason, at first, thought that he'd been wearing a dark red waist coat, until he spotted its true yellow color at the edges. The red had come from the dozen puncture wounds as the hinged front had been pulled or pushed closed, forcing the iron spikes that were welded to the interior of the door to penetrate from his clavicle to his waist.

As Chang had said, his face, even in rigor, was a mask of sheer terror.

CHAPTER 21

The following morning, Teri and Mason met up with Hardwick and Simmons to review the data and see if any aspect of their case dovetailed with the three unsolved cases.

"I'm not sure anything does," Mason said, as he cringed watching Hardwick consume an entire donut in one bite. "So far, your case looks like a run-of-the-mill VIP homicide. I still don't get Tamacini shutting himself in that device, but I'm not sure what else syncs with our investigations."

Teri, who had been reading some of the crime scene notes, including a brief description of the party theme and the guests, chimed in, "This is a little weird. It says that the party was to celebrate the end of Gilberto Tamacini's highly successful concert tour."

"What's strange about that?" Simmonds asked.

"Apparently they were treated to a very special show."

"Again, not that unusual."

"But so far, nobody has been able to track down the performer. It's like he vanished right after the show," Teri said, concluding her point.

"Does it show his name?" Mason asked, as a thin coil of ice started creeping up his spine.

"Yeah. The guy was called Paul T. Ergest."

"Has anybody run that name?" Mason asked.

Simmons nodded. "Yeah, we had the name run and there doesn't appear to be any such person in LA or even California for that matter."

"Maybe he was brought in from Vegas?" Teri offered.

Both Simmons and Hardwick stared back at her like deer in the headlights.

"Don't worry," Mason said. "You're both swamped at the moment. We'll run the Vegas check. In fact, we might as well go national, so there's no surprises later on. Oh, also, would you mind if we took a crack at the butler? I want to see what he remembers from the show."

Hardwick replied, his mouth full of food, "We already spoke to him, but go ahead, waste your time."

"Thanks. I'll let you guys know what we find."

"Since when do you volunteer to take work away from that pair of saggy dicks?" Teri said as soon as they were in the elevator heading down to their converted interview room.

"I just know them too well. I thought it best that we do it, so it gets done right."

Teri nodded, finding no cause to challenge her partner's assertion.

Mason opened their office door and saw a plain white envelope leaning against his computer monitor.

"What's that?" Teri asked.

"No idea," he replied as he forced his finger under the flap and tore it open. "God, I hate always being right."

"Let's say that's even half true, what have you done this time?"

Mason held out a piece of Balisek's personal stationery. On it was written:

They were on KTLA late news last night. I will deal with them.

I have instructed the downtown Palm restaurant that I will be picking up the tab for the two of you to have dinner.

Don't make me regret it.

"I hope you enjoy it," Teri said, not really understanding the value of a free dinner at one of the city's most popular and expensive restaurants.

"It's not just for me, you're my plus one."

"I don't know," Teri replied, feeling that same unease left over from Sacramento.

"Let's go early one night and call it an extension of work. We can review the case files while seeing how much lobster and steak two police colleagues can consume at one sitting. In fact, if we go as early as six, I bet we could even get in tonight."

"As a colleague, I accept."

"Will there be some point when you might actually believe that I have no interest in you in any other way?" Mason asked.

"Now I feel offended," Teri said with a smile. "Want me to call the butler?"

"Do you know how pompous that sounded?"

"I wouldn't know," she replied. "I usually have my chambermaid contact him for me."

*

After a sandwich lunch, eaten at what they laughingly referred to as 'their desk', Teri and Mason headed back up to the Trousdale Estates. As the place was still an active crime scene, Edgar Groves, AKA the butler, refused to leave the premises for even a second, convinced that the police would almost certainly destroy the place without his watchful eye. Hardwick and Simpson had tried to have him removed, but after a call to the mayor, a close friend of the deceased singer, Groves managed to persuade him that with Tamacini gone, just about any item in the house had become a collector's piece. He had also, right in front of the two detectives, stated that he had no faith that items wouldn't be stolen if he were not permitted to remain within the house. The mayor agreed.

Instead of Loma Vista Drive being filled with police vehicles, they'd been replaced by countless news vans from around the world. Like vultures, they had waited until the bulk of the police horde had departed before trying to get closer to the murder house and feast on what was left on the proverbial carcass. There were so many of them that they were tailed back to within spitting distance of Sunset Boulevard.

With his employer dead, Groves hadn't bothered to dress in the dark suit he'd been wearing the previous day and for the nine thousand, one hundred days before that. Instead, he was wearing a pair or Khaki pants and a dark blue, long-sleeved Polo shirt. Now in his late fifties, he still looked fit, and from his ramrod-straight stature, Mason assumed he had some sort of military background.

"Thanks for seeing us," Mason said as they entered the house.

"I didn't realize I had a choice," Groves replied with a forced smile. "Why don't we go to the study? We might actually get some privacy there."

Mason and Teri followed him down a book-lined hallway and stopped at a pair of polished walnut doors.

"This was the maestro's private office. It was the one place he felt safe from the world."

"Are you saying that he thought he was in danger?" Teri asked.

"Not specifically, but when you are one of the greatest performers in the world, it's amazing how many of his followers believed that they were entitled to more than simply seeing him in concert or listening to him in the privacy of their own homes."

"Have there been instances of people trying to break in here?" Mason asked.

"Here, not so much. In his home in New York, there was an attempt on his life a few years ago when someone thought they'd pay him the same tribute as was paid to John Lennon. Obviously, he failed. Apparently, his 3D printed firearm had been misassembled. There have also been a number of break-ins at his London home as well, but all were attempted while he was elsewhere."

Groves opened both doors wide, revealing the study beyond.

"Jesus," Teri said, before managing to catch herself.

"Grand, isn't it?" Groves said with a forced smile.

Mason stood at the entrance and tried to take in what he was seeing. The house from the front looked to be no more than about two thousand five hundred square feet. Clearly, that was wrong, by a factor of at least three.

The study, which he'd imagined would be a small room with a desk and maybe a sofa if there was space, was the complete antithesis. It was roughly fifty feet square with a fifteen-foot ceiling. Two entire walls were filled with rich mahogany, back-lit bookcases filled with vinyl albums, CDs, programs and books. The other two walls, with the exception of the windows and the entrance door, were covered in posters and printed memorabilia from the maestro's long and successful career.

In the center of the room were two dark-brown, leather, Chesterfield sofas. Between them was what looked to be an ancient, carved, wood door that had been topped with glass and made into a coffee table.

Groves gestured for the detectives to be seated. Once they were, he asked if they wanted any coffee or beverages.

"Why don't you sit and relax," Mason suggested. "You're off the clock."

"Permanently," Groves replied with a sigh before looking from one to the other. "What can I do to help you?"

"As I said on the phone," Mason explained, "we are investigating three unsolved cases that have similarities with this one, presuming that the coroner and the forensic team do confirm that Mr. Tamacini's passing was a homicide."

"Can there be any doubt?"

"There wouldn't be if it wasn't for the handle on the inside of the device," Teri said.

"Ah, that bloody thing," Groves replied, before realizing quite what he'd said. "When I said bloody, I meant bloody as in the English swearword sense, not that the handle was actually bloody... which of course it was. Oh, for heaven's sake, if I don't shut up, you'll be taking me away in chains at this rate."

"Not quite yet," Mason said with a smile. "I would, however, like to hear the backstory to your 'that bloody thing' comment.

"As you've seen, the maestro has quite a collection of torture devices, all of which come from the Middle Ages. When this one came up at auction at Sotheby's, he snatched it up and had it shipped over here. To be quite honest, I couldn't understand why he didn't save the money and keep it in his London house. It turns out he wanted it in Los Angeles because of the heightened interest in the macabre that exists here."

"I wasn't aware of that," Mason commented.

"Oh, yes. Anything to do with torture and any other aspect of the dark arts..."

"Dark arts?" Teri interrupted.

"That's the colloquial term for everything from voodoo to devil worshipping."

"Did the maestro engage in any of those?" Mason asked.

"No. Not really. However, because of his collection of torture devices, plus his global celebrity, he did tend to attract some very wealthy and very odd friends."

"Define odd," Mason said.

"That's a pretty broad spectrum on the West Coast. Suffice it to say that some of his regular guests dabbled in S&M, witchcraft, that sort of thing."

"How do you dabble in witchcraft?" Mason asked.

"I am delighted to say that I don't really know. Other than an excess of dark clothing and rather severe makeup, I don't believe any of them could cast any spells or bewitch each other, except maybe in the old-fashioned sense."

"Let's go back to the handle and the reason why he had it added."

"Simple. He had a handle installed on the inside as a Halloween gag. The device was placed out in front of the house, and a fake skeleton was positioned within the thing.

The maestro had someone from one of the studios rig up a gizmo that made it look as if the skeleton, its hand glued to the handle, was opening and closing the front of the iron maiden. In effect, repeatedly torturing itself."

"The kids must have loved that," Teri commented.

Just as she was about to ask something else, both her and Mason's phones alerted them to a new text.

Teri retrieved hers while Mason continued.

"I know you were already asked this, but is there any reason whatsoever that Mr. Tamacini would have intentionally closed the device with himself in it?"

"Absolutely not. He was an extraordinarily positive person. I honestly can't remember him being despondent, other when his long-time friend, Pavarotti, passed away."

"The text was from Hardwick," Teri interjected. "The blood on the handle was from Tamacini."

"How horrid," Groves said, and he closed his eyes for a moment.

"I guess that means he was holding onto it," Teri said.

"Yeah, Mason replied. "What it doesn't tell us was whether he was trying to close it or hold it open."

CHAPTER 22

Groves asked for a short break so he could get his emotions in check. He suggested that his making them some coffee would probably be the most calming activity he could undertake.

Ten minutes later, Groves was back with coffee and a plate of oversized chocolate chip cookies.

"They look good," Teri observed.

"They are. They're my own recipe. Well, that's not completely true. They are the recipe I created after the maestro challenged me to make a biscuit containing his favorite ingredients. These are made with dark chocolate, raisins, macadamia nuts, coconut, molasses and orange zest."

Teri looked dubious as she bit into one. "Oh, my sweet Jesus! I think I just found Valhalla!"

As Groves slowly lowered the strainer into the glass cafetiere, Mason resumed the interview.

"Was there anyone unusual on the guest list last night?"

Groves chuckled. "The better question should be, was there anyone who wasn't unusual? The answer would be a far smaller number."

Mason gave him a patient smile.

"I can't think of anyone that particularly stood out. No. That's not accurate. One man was memorable, but not because of any idiosyncrasies, more because of his abruptness and confidentiality requirements."

A tiny butterfly fluttered deep in Mason's gut.

"Could you elaborate on that?"

"Ironically, no," Groves answered. "At least, I can't expound on the show or about any specifics of the man."

"Are we talking about the entertainer?" Teri asked.

"Yes. Sorry. I probably should have made that clear. The moment he arrived, he made everyone sign a non-disclosure agreement, including the maestro himself. In his own home, mind you. And as if that wasn't bad enough, everyone had to leave their phones in the hallway."

"I don't have a copy of the guest list with me. Do you happen to remember his name?" Mason asked, even though Hardwick had already given them the name back at HQ.

"I doubt that breaches the agreement," Groves said, nodding. "His name was Paul T. Ergest."

"Can you tell us exactly what his show consisted of?" Mason asked.

"That, I know I can't divulge."

"Did you see any part of the show?"

"Yes," Groves replied hesitantly.

"Are you able to tell me if it was at least entertaining?"

"I suppose that won't matter. It was quite extraordinary. If I may be so bold as to suggest, perhaps if you spoke to Mr. Ergest himself, he might be willing to explain what he does."

"We will when we find him," Teri said. "If it's the same performer who was at three other murders, he uses a different alias for each party."

"How extremely odd," Groves replied. "Would I be permitted to see the names he's used, just in case one of them crops up on the HSG?"

"What's that?" Mason asked.

"Just a little informal gathering of my fellow colleagues in Beverly Hills and Bel Air. HSG stands for household staff grapevine. We often compare notes when it comes to bad guests and especially bad parties."

"Your last one certainly qualifies," Teri said as she produced her iPad and pulled up the other names of the performers.

Groves read them to himself a few times then started to hand the tablet back to Teri. A thought struck him.

"Would you mind adding our performer to the list?"

"Why?" Mason asked. "What have you seen?"

"Please. Humor me."

Teri took the iPad and added Paul T. Ergest to the list.

"Now read the names slowly, out loud," Groves suggested.

Teri glanced over at Mason who simply shrugged.

"Okay. This is a little weird, but, what the hell. Ray Spirito, Adam Parition, Garry Houl and Paul T Ergest."

Groves looked to the detectives, waiting to see if they'd seen the connection.

"I don't know what I'm supposed to see here," Teri stated.

"Let's focus on the first name only. I think that if you crack that one, you'll see the others."

"We're not here to play games," Mason said firmly.

"But I think you have to. Clearly the man you are looking for is playing one. Please. Try the first name out loud."

"Ray Spirito," Teri said with slow enunciation.

"Try again but run the names together," Groves said.

"Rayspirito. Rayspirito. Rayspirito."

Frustrated, Mason cut in. "Mr. Groves, I have to ask you to please..."

"One more. Go to the last name and do the same thing."

Teri sighed and said, "Paul T. Ergest."

"Run them together."

"Paulteergest. Paultergest. Fuck! Poltergeist."

Groves beamed back at her. "Well done. Now go back to the first name."

Teri studied the name for a few seconds then lowered her head to her hand. "Raise Spirit. He added the O for effect."

"Now try the last two. I'll give you a hint. Use the first name initial only."

Teri studied the names Adam Parition and Gary Houl.

"Holy shit," Mason said. "Ghoul and Apparition! Add those to Poltergeist and Raise Spirit and I think we can hazard a guess at what exactly our mysterious friend offers the partygoers. He must perform some sort of séance. Am I close?" he asked, looking to Groves.

"As I can categorically state that you came to that conclusion on you own, I don't think I would be breaching the NDA by simply nodding my head."

Groves nodded his head.

"One last thing," Teri added. "While you're in a nodding mood, have a look at this."

She loaded the picture of the performer from the Bel Air party.

"Was this the man?"

Groves nodded for a second time.

*

Once back in the car, Mason pulled over next to the old Greystone Mansion, the iconic ex-home to the Doheny dynasty.

"What's the matter?" Teri asked.

"I don't know. I feel like we just had some sort of break, but at the same time, I don't know what it means. We seem to be getting drawn into investigating the performer even though we know that he left each of the parties significantly before the TOD. I don't want us getting into an investigative rut just because some nut job happened to be at all four events. I'll bet you that I can find one creepy clown that's been at dozens of children's birthday parties."

"Maybe, but those parties didn't result in four dead bodies," Teri replied. "Besides, he's not just some nut job. He's managed to integrate himself into the highest echelon of LA society."

"Then why the name changes? How could someone, who is obviously extremely popular in the wealthy circles, get business when we can't even find him? All the names are fake, yet he is, I assume, still getting gigs and has so far avoided being interviewed after five murders. How is that possible, unless it's not the same guy?"

"Obviously it's the same person and we know why he was never interviewed. It was because of the dumb stage names," Teri said. "Nobody connected the dots."

"Including us," Mason pointed out. "Some butler takes one look at the list and sees the connection."

"To be fair, he knew what the guy's act was. Without that tiny piece of information, I don't think he would have zoned in either. We sure as hell didn't."

"The big question is whether any of this is remotely important. The only concrete fact we have is that he wasn't there when the murders took place. That's the same reason why the original detectives didn't spend too much time trying to locate him."

"Still, he should have been interviewed."

Mason nodded. "I agree, but we will have to find him first. Why don't we re-interview the short list and see if anyone feels like telling us about just exactly what the guy does that makes him so popular?"

"What about the people that either haven't yet hired him, or didn't go ahead with a booking? If the guy is in big demand by LA's A-listers, people must know about him."

"They might even have seen him at another party," Mason suggested.

"That wouldn't help. If they'd already been at one of his events, they'd have signed the NDA. We need to find someone who has heard about him, but never experienced him in person and therefore never signed an NDA."

"Okay, I get your logic," Mason said. "But if nobody who's seen him can ever talk about him, how do the uninitiated hear about him?"

"I would bet you that somewhere in the one percenter's code of ethics, they feel exempt from something as insignificant as an NDA so long as they only talk among themselves. I will bet you that if we find the right conduit to the right people, we can get them talking."

"And exactly how in hell are we going to do that?" Mason asked.

"I just might have the first piece of the puzzle."

"What is it?" Mason asked. "What can I do?"

"Driving would be a good start."

Mason smiled as he put the car in gear and headed towards Sunset Boulevard.

CHAPTER 23

Teri directed Mason to her grandparents' home on Olive Street, one block north of Wilshire.

"Want me to wait out here?" he asked as he pulled up in front of the cheerful duplex.

"No. You should meet them. They are very special and, as you well know, we don't get to rub shoulders with that many good people anymore."

As they got out of the car, Teri immediately heard thumping music coming from the upper unit. If anything, it was louder than the last time she'd been there.

"Sounds like a party," Mason commented.

"It's not. It's an illegal subletter; some guy called Emanuel. I wanted to speak to him the last time I was here, but my grandparents didn't want to get me involved."

"Why don't you go talk to them and I will have a little chat with him? I'll make out that a neighbor down the street complained. That way you're kept out of it."

"Thank you, but go easy. It'll probably take a while to legally get rid of him, so we don't want to cause an even greater rift between the parties."

"I could convince him to leave today, if you like?" Mason offered, smiling.

"Let's just stick to lowering the volume for the time being."

Mason shrugged, then headed for the outside stairway that led up to the rental unit. Teri watched him climb to the top then knocked on her grandparents' door, causing Tito to frantically whine and scratch at it until Freeda opened it. Despite his great show of wanting to get at Teri, once she was inside, Tito chose to roll onto his back and do a weird shimmy-wiggle waiting for someone, anyone, to rub his belly.

"Teri," Freeda exclaimed happily once she saw who it was. "This is a surprise. Gregg's at school. If I'd known you were—"

"I didn't even know myself until a few minutes ago. My partner and I are hoping that you might be able to help us out."

"You have a partner!" she gushed. "I knew you'd eventually find the right—"

"Not that sort of partner. He's the detective I work with. I told you about him last time."

"Oh well," Freeda said, bitterly disappointed. "You'd better come in."

"I can hear that your tenant didn't take to heart your request for him to turn down the music?"

"Yes. Well, he's a young man. Maybe it's us that are the problem. We stopped liking loud anything a decade ago."

As Teri entered the house, she took Freeda's hand in hers.

"You two are definitely not the issue. That noise would be too much for anyone."

Once in the living room Teri could hear the bass as clearly as if it was being played live a few feet away from her. She listened intently for a few moments and could make out Mason's voice somewhere in the background. It wasn't raised, but he was using his *don't fuck with me* tone.

"Would you like a cup of tea?" Freeda asked, having to raise her voice above the din.

"No thank you," Teri replied in a half yell.

The blaring bass stopped. The living room suddenly seemed overly quiet, despite the sound of footfalls on the outside stairs.

"That'll be Mason," Teri advised as she made for the front door.

"Everything go all right?" she asked in little more than a whisper as Mason reached the doorway.

"Fine. The guy definitely comes across as a hard case, but I convinced him that by being a good neighbor he would most likely see a great deal less of me."

"Did you threaten him?"

"Of course not. We just came to a bilateral understanding, is all."

Lisa studied his features, looking for any tells that he was lying through his teeth. Thankfully, she saw none.

"Mason, this is my grandmother, Freeda Woods."

Mason gave her his best smile as he gently shook her hand.

"Pleasure, ma'am."

"Ma'am!" Freeda cooed. "I haven't been called ma'am in years."

"He's got some old-fashioned manners when he feels like it," Terri said.

"So, what can I do to help two of Los Angeles's top detectives?" Freeda asked.

"Are you still in touch with Debbie Cohen?" Teri asked.

"Absolutely. In fact, we have a standing lunch once a month at Spago's in Beverly Hills."

Teri looked surprised.

"Don't worry, honey. She pays."

"Is she still an A-list party planner?" Teri asked.

"Most definitely. In fact, most of the lunch conversations revolve around the craziness of some of her clients."

"I can imagine." Teri smiled knowingly. "We were wondering if you could introduce us to her."

"I can just give you her number. I'm sure she won't mind."

"I think a personal introduction would be better in this case."

Freeda looked concerned. "Why? What has she done?"

"Absolutely nothing," Teri replied. "We just want to pick her brain about some aspects of her party planning."

"I don't see any problem with that. I have an idea. Our next lunch is in two days. Why don't you two join us?"

"Spago's is a little beyond our budget," Mason chipped in.

"I can guarantee," Freeda replied, "that Debbie will insist on picking up the tab. The woman is richer that Croesus and quite frankly, doesn't often get the chance to share any of it. Want me to call her?"

*

"So, what did you really say to Emanuel?" Teri asked the moment they were back in the car.

"I simply mentioned that someone who's already on shaky legal ground just by living in the Wood's unit may want to keep something of a low profile."

"And that was enough to get him to turn off the music?"

"Not exactly," Mason replied. "His response was that if I knew what was good for me, I'd get the fuck out of his home."

"Charming. You really do bring out the best in people."

"Don't I? Anyway, not wanting to escalate the situation, I again suggested he lower the music rather than my having to keep coming out here every time a neighbor complained."

"What did he say to that?" Teri asked.

"Nothing. He just smiled at me."

"What did you do?"

"I just stared at him until he finally turned down the music."

"That was it?"

"Pretty much. I gave him a big smile and left. You told me to be on my best behavior and I was."

"Do you think my family is in any danger?" Teri asked.

"I doubt it. I think the kids a punk with an attitude. He's definitely got the bully gene, but I don't see how he'd benefit from getting aggressive with his landlords."

After almost an hour-long drive back to headquarters they weren't in the mood to dress up for a fancy dinner at The Palm, so decided to postpone the night out and call it a day. Mason dropped Teri off so she could retrieve her car, then headed north.

Mason couldn't deny that there was something almost magical about being able to leave the dense chaos of the city in his wake as he crossed Franklin and wound his way up into the heavily wooded foothills.

Even when he saw the note pinned to his door, his mood wasn't dented. In fact, he'd been expecting something along the lines of the handwritten scribble for weeks.

It simply read, 'Don't feed the wildlife, asshole. Think of your neighbors.'

Mason laughed to himself. The Hollywood Hills were knee deep in coyotes. His throwing a few scraps wasn't going to change a damn thing. If his upset neighbor thought that by doing so, his dog or cat was in more danger that it already was, he/she was greatly mistaken. A fed coyote was far less likely to go after a chihuahua or whatever when starving, than after having already eaten.

Mason realized, as he turned on the living room lights, that all the thinking about wild animals and food had made him ravenously hungry. Despite there being some Chinese food left in the fridge, Mason had an urge for something with a little kick. Though the wildlife that surrounded his rundown little home could forage and kill whatever they needed to survive, Mason opted to have Uber Eats bring the food to him.

While waiting for his dinner, Mason decided that a comedy was the best plan for the night and went for one of his favorites.

Just at the point when Vince Vaughn and Owen Wilson manage to finagle their way into a Washington DC A-list wedding, Mason's doorbell rang.

A white guy in his forties stood on the stoop holding a bag of Indian food, its rich aromas enveloping Mason. He gave the man a five-dollar tip, then noticed that the guy was driving a newer-looking Mercedes AMG.

As Mason watched him drive off, he wondered what life drama had forced the guy to have to moonlight and deliver food. Then again, he knew that there were those who would prefer to starve rather than be seen driving something cheap and efficient in Los Angeles. Thus was the culture in a city where a person's entire being was initially judged by what they were driving.

Mason opened a liter bottle of Kingfisher (an Indian beer he kept for Indian food nights), and served up the chicken vindaloo, lamb saag and pilau rice. He placed a piece of naan bread on the end of his plate, then carried the feast to the coffee table and took the movie out of pause mode.

He wasn't planning to give the coyote any food that night as he didn't think it was a good idea to share his highly-spiced curry with a canine that wouldn't be prepared for that level of internal heat. Despite his plan to hold back on that night's treats, he heard the familiar scratching at the door just at the time that Vaughn was being seduced by Isla Fisher.

Mason paused the movie and headed for the kitchen, hoping he had something that would serve as a suitable tidbit for his new friend. The Chinese leftovers were mainly rice and noodles, which he doubted was on a coyote's favorite food list. After a more in-depth search, he came across a box he'd shoved into the utility room. Before the phone call from the chief resulting in his return to work, he'd had to resort to doing a lot of his shopping at the dollar store.

Much to his surprise, he'd found that it was feasible to buy a week's worth of food for twenty bucks. Sure, canned goods made up the bulk of the menu, but he soon came to enjoy devilled ham, canned chicken and his favorite, beef stew.

When he moved to the canyon, and money was no longer an issue, he didn't particularly feel like continuing with the routine, but at the same time, couldn't quite bring himself to get rid of the cans that remained on his shelves.

Mason rummaged through the box and found a couple of cans of chicken. There were also quite a few beef ones, but considering how much he'd looked forward to those during the bad times, he felt nostalgically reluctant to share those with the local wildlife.

He pulled the ring tab on one of the cans, then slowly opened the back door, expecting the coyote to have vanished into the overgrowth. Mason was surprised to see the canine standing in plain view at the end of the patio. As any interaction to date had been initiated without it being in the open, Mason wasn't quite sure how to proceed. He was inclined to just leave the can and step back inside, but the idea of the coyote somehow injuring itself on the sharp edges made him choose a more refined method.

Mason gave the coyote a pointless 'wait there' gesture then stepped back into the kitchen. He retrieved a chipped plate from the draining rack by the sink, then emptied the contents of the can onto it.

Once back outside, he was momentarily surprised to see that the canine had taken a few steps closer to the back door. It suddenly dawned on Mason that standing alone in the hills, facing off with a wild animal while holding a plate of food may not have been the smartest thing to do.

Mason stopped moving and stared at the animal to see if there was any indication of likely aggression. All he saw was curiosity in the coyote's eyes. That and the rapid breathing that often comes with stress.

"I'll just leave this here for you," Mason said, in little more than a whisper.

Mason then lowered himself to his haunches and placed the dish of food on the patio. The coyote didn't move until Mason was safely back in the house, at which point it crept cautiously over to the plate.

Mason turned off the kitchen light, hoping that his position at the window would be invisible from the outside. The coyote sniffed the air above the dish then, without warning, began wolfing down (literally) the chicken pieces. At one point, the animal stopped, raised its head, and stared directly at the glass panel in the back door.

Mason had no idea if the creature could actually see him, but it certainly looked that way. In fact, it appeared as if the animal was staring straight back at him.

Finally, it resumed eating as Mason watched.

Once finished, the coyote again stared up at the glass pane. Mason, not exactly sure why, slowly reached for the light switch and flipped it on. At that point there was no doubt that he'd made himself visible, yet the coyote didn't shy away or indeed, seem the least bit afraid.

For the longest time, the two stared at each other, neither moving so as not to spook the other. After a good few minutes, the coyote stepped up to the door and raked one paw down the wooden surface before turning and running off into the hills.

"See you tomorrow, Wolfy," Mason said into the night.

CHAPTER 24

Just as Teri and Mason settled down in their office, coffee at the ready, his personal phone started playing Elton John's *The Bitch is Back.*

Teri gave him a questioning look.

"It's Alice Chang," Mason advised as he answered the call.

After a short, one-sided conversation, Mason disconnected the call.

"We've been summoned," he advised.

"Why the call to your personal phone?" Teri asked.

"For the same reason we have to go to her. She doesn't trust the department phones. Considering Tamacini's celebrity, she doesn't want any information ending up on the news or worse."

"What could be worse?"

"TMZ."

Chang was waiting for them in the autopsy suite. Instead of multiple bays being in use, only the farthest one from the door was active. Clearly another attempt at keeping the lid on anything and everything to do with the maestro's post-mortem.

Chang was carrying out the autopsy alone, another clear indication of just how paranoid she was. Normally, that would have been frowned upon, however, since the coroner's office had begun springing leaks eighteen months earlier, she was doing everything possible to mitigate the problem, at least in the case of Tamacini.

Teri and Mason stood a short distance from the table and watched as Chang weighed an extraordinarily large liver that she had just removed from the body.

"What took you so long?" Chang commented.

"Is that a normal-sized liver?" Teri asked, clearly revolted.

"It is for someone who drank and ate as much as our friend here."

"Is that what you wanted to tell us?" Mason asked.

"No. I thought you might like to know my findings before I send them to Harddick and Simpleton. I confirmed that the injuries, with the exception of those caused by the iron maiden's spikes, occurred antemortem and were definitely not self-inflicted."

"So, it is a homicide," Mason said. "Please tell me that there was some trace evidence in the wounds?"

"There was," Chang replied. "Only you're not going to want to hear the next part."

"Try me."

"I found some foreign matter in the deeper facial lacerations. I, of course, assumed that the attacker had accidently left some trace from his or her hands or nails."

"And did they?" Mason asked.

"That's the other reason I didn't want to say anything over the phone. It's not just that I didn't want it getting out. I also didn't want people thinking I've lost my mind."

"People thought that about you when you agreed to marry me," Mason joked.

"And to a point, they were right. But what I'm about to tell you is way beyond that level of crazy. I'm talking straightjackets and padded walls."

"This doesn't sound good," Teri commented, still unable to take her eyes off the grotesquely large liver sitting in a stainless-steel surgical dish.

"So, when I was cleaning out the wounds, I found what I initially thought was sand, but after checking it out under the scope, I could see that it definitely wasn't that. I put as much of it aside as I could, then continued with the postmortem. As I worked on some of the other lacerations, I found more of the stuff, so I decided to put a sample in the mass spectrometer."

"And?" Mason asked, wishing his ex would get to the point.

"And, I had to run it two more times with different batches of the matter as I assumed that I kept getting a faulty reading."

"But it wasn't faulty?" Mason suggested.

"No. It was not. What I found in the wounds were particles of fingernails."

"That's good, isn't it?" Teri asked. "I mean, if there was any DNA in them, we can—"

"There was no DNA," Chang almost barked back at her. "That's the thing. The keratin itself was completely desiccated. There was no way to recover any DNA because of the extreme deterioration of the nail particulates."

"How can that even happen?" Mason asked.

"It can't. It'd take over a hundred years after death before a fingernail could even begin to deteriorate to that state."

"So, what's your explanation?" Teri asked.

"My guess is that whoever assaulted the victim used either a mummified hand or maybe even some derivative of the old, ritualistic hand of glory."

"I know I'm going to dread asking," Mason said. "But what the hell is a hand of glory?"

"Around the same time as the witchcraft burnings, there was a charming little ritual whereby the right hand of a newly hung thief (left if he was a lefty) was removed from the body and then, by various different, but uniformly horrid means, was preserved. It was traditionally kept on show as a warning to others. Over time, they became sought after items for use in voodoo and other rituals. Nowadays, they are collector's items. There are a number of glory hands on exhibition at galleries around the world."

"And you think that one of those hands could have been used to inflict the wounds?" Mason asked.

"I'm clutching at straws here," Chang admitted. "All I'm saying is that nail fragments from a long-deceased individual were found within the lacerations. Beyond that, I'm not prepared to give a definitive rationale as to how they got there. I'll leave that to you detectives."

"But at least we know they were human, right? Mason asked.

"I know it was from some sort of nail or possibly talon, but whether it was human... I can't tell you. The deterioration was too far along."

"One last question," Teri said, finally able to tear her eyes away from the oversized liver. "If we are to accept the fact that Tamacini closed the device on himself, knowing full well that that it would kill him; why would someone choose certain death, versus the possibility, no matter how remote, that he could have somehow survived the attack?"

Mason nodded his approval of the question.

"That, thankfully, is not my area of expertise, but if you want an opinion without any evidentiary support, I'd have to say that whoever or whatever was attacking him was more frightening than a quick death within the iron maiden."

"I know you said that it was only an opinion, but it's still kind of a stretch, isn't it?" Mason asked.

"Yes and no," Chang replied. "I have no proof about his choice of life or death, but I do have something that clearly showed just how terrified he was nanoseconds before the spikes pierced his body."

"I thought they were the cause of death?" Teri said.

"So did I, until about an hour ago. I had assumed from the get-go that the perforation in his right ventricle was the COD and was caused by one of the spikes. It wasn't until I lined up the entry wounds on his chest against the damage within his body that I realized that here was no entry point anywhere near the heart. I then did a full aortic dissection and found something most unusual. Let me show you."

Chang turned to a refrigerated storage unit.

"How about you just explain it?" Teri suggested.

"It's easier to point out the damage, but if you prefer, I can just tell you."

"Thank you."

"What I found was highly unusual. First of all, I need to make it clear that, despite his obesity, enlarged liver and various other damaged organs, his lungs and heart were in surprisingly good shape."

"But?" Mason voiced.

"But, just a few seconds before the spikes did their worst, Tamacini's heart ruptured."

"What exactly does that mean?" Teri asked.

"Basically, it exploded," Chang replied.

"Like a heart attack?"

Chang gave her a condescending shake of the head.

"A heart attack occurs when the heart stops receiving a supply of blood either through a blockage or vascular tearing. The heart muscles themselves rarely, and I do mean rarely, simply rupture. The only natural cause would be if the heart suffers a myocardial rupture following an infarction. The chamber walls could then have been sufficiently weakened to cause a breach."

"But that's not what happened to Tamacini?" Mason asked.

"Absolutely not. This wasn't a tear or rupture. The right ventricle actually exploded."

"So what can cause that?" Teri asked.

"The only known instances of that degree of damage that wasn't caused by massive external trauma, were deemed to have been the result of a massive surge in blood pressure brought on by extreme anxiety."

"Are you saying what I think you're saying?" Mason asked.

Chang smiled as if knowing just how complicated she was making things for her ex.

"Yes. Tamacini literally died of fright."

*

"What do you think?" Teri asked as soon as they exited the building.

"I think my ex-fiancé has a very dark side," Mason replied.

"To be fair, doesn't that kinda come with the job?"

"The job is to somehow cope with the everyday horrors that a coroner has to face. Taking pleasure in them is a whole different ballgame."

Having reached the car, Mason tossed the keys to Teri.

"You drive. I need to digest what she just said."

"What? You don't believe her?"

"The opposite. The problem is that I do believe her."

"Why is that a problem?" Teri asked as she slid into the driver's seat.

"Because it means that we are now potentially looking for someone who may be into ritualistic killings. Maybe even a modern-day practitioner of voodoo or something along those lines. Even worse, this person isn't leaving any trace evidence behind."

"Except for the fingernail residue," Teri pointed out.

"I don't consider that as trace we can use. Antique nail particles could have come from anywhere. You heard her. Whoever killed Tamacini could have got hold of one of those glory hands. While it's definitely something we need to check out, it doesn't, as far as we know, fit in with the other three cases."

"I disagree. It's the fourth person who's died after or during an A-list party at which the same performer, one that can't be traced, puts on some sort of show that necessitated, at least to him, that everyone sign a non-disclosure agreement. The cases are all exactly the same. All that's new is that particulates were found in wounds that were deemed to have not been the cause of death."

"That's my point," Mason insisted. "The previous three cases were homicides. This one is not. In fact, though gruesome, it looks to have been a suicide."

"Not if Chang is right and Tamacini died because an episode of severe anxiety brought on by the attack. Maybe it's not murder one, but it's still a homicide."

"That's for the DA's office to decide."

"Come on, Mason. Judging by the severity of the attack, if Tamacini hadn't gotten into the device, the perp would have almost certainly killed him."

"I'm as much of a fan of the movie *Minority Report* as the next cop, but in the real world, we have to follow the facts, not try and suppose a 'what might have happened if,' scenario."

"So, you're saying you don't think this case is related to the other three?" Teri asked.

"I'm not saying that at all. All I said was, this one is different. There were no visible wounds on Groppel, Harter or Whitlough."

"No visible wounds?" Teri shot back. "Harter had her neck corkscrewed around one hundred and eighty degrees, and as for her little toy boy—"

"Obviously they were mutilated, but not mauled the way Tamacini was."

"They all ended up dead."

"But the MOs don't match. You know as well as I do that serials follow the same path every time. Maybe there's a little variation, but the COD is always the same. These cases all seem to be tied to one guy, yet the homicides themselves are all different. I wish we could speak to that damn performer. It's driving me crazy that his name, or rather his stage names, keep coming up even though he wasn't present at the TOD for any of the vics."

"Maybe not, but he's almost certainly involved. To be at one or two of the sites would have been an odd coincidence. To have been at all four is not," Teri insisted.

Mason and Teri's police-issued cells both chirped at once. Mason, his hands free, retrieved his from his jacket pocket and checked the screen.

"What's going on?" Teri asked.

Mason took a moment to read it.

"Seems things have taken an even weirder turn. Leticia Gold just witnessed a murder."

"Where?"

"Back where this all began," Mason said.

"The Harter House?"

"The Harter House."

CHAPTER 25

By the time they reached the access road to Cardwell Place, crime scene tape and sawhorses blocked the cul-de-sac. The same young officer who'd been signing people in and out of the Tamacini property was assigned to barrier duty. He recognized Teri and Mason and noted their entry time, before waving them through.

"You're getting all the glamour assignments, aren't you?" Mason said after lowering his window.

"Hey, better than traffic duty. This way I'm at least close to the show."

As Teri drove between the barriers, Mason closed his window.

"I don't like rookies thinking that a homicide is a show. There's nothing entertaining about it."

"Relax, gramps. I think he was using show in the baseball sense as in 'the show' being the major league. Besides, a homicide trumps just about any other call out."

The cul-de-sac already had three black and whites, as well as a couple of unmarked Fords. Out in front of the Harter house, Leticia Gold's oversized Range Rover was being examined. Mason sighed as he recognized a new-looking BMW with government plates.

"Your mom's here," Mason jibed.

Teri parked as far from the Beemer as possible on the narrow road, as if subconsciously wanting to avoid any close proximity to her stepmother. Whatever the reason, it didn't work. As the pair approached the front door, Balisek came striding out of the house, wearing a full sperm suit, as the white crime scene PPE outfit was affectionately called. Once she removed her hood, her Elvis-haired assistant appeared and began taking cell phone shots of her.

"Perfect timing," she said as she veered towards Mason and Teri and lowered her mask, causing Elvis to take an additional flurry of pictures.

Before she reached them, another unmarked passed through the barrier. The windows were down, and Mason could clearly see the grinning faces of Hardwick and Simpson.

"Really?" he said to the chief. "You brought in those clowns? This one is definitely ours. This house is linked to all three of the open cases we're working on. Giving it to that pair of—"

"Before you say something truly inappropriate, you might want to dial back the bullshit," Balisek said. "I called them here purely for information sharing. The same way I read you into the Tamacini case. So, if you wouldn't mind holstering your attitude for a few minutes, I'll show you what we've got so far, but you'll have to put on your scene suit as forensics haven't arrived yet."

After donning their white unitards and masks that were kept in a go bag in the car, Teri followed Balisek back into the house, while Mason took a moment to scan the surrounding area before joining the other two. Balisek led them down the glass-enclosed escalator and stairs and then down another floor to the master bedroom, where Harter and Ginetto had been found.

"The vic was killed in the same room as Harter and Ginetto?" Teri asked, somewhat shocked.

"She was," the chief replied, having reached the double doors. "There's a taped 'safe' perimeter just inside the door. Don't go beyond that."

Teri and Mason stepped through the doorway and immediately understood Balisek's somewhat odd statement. A woman's body was roughly fifteen feet from the door, while her head was at least ten feet further on. The shiny red floor made it impossible to see exactly what was floor and what was blood.

"Jesus Christ," Mason muttered.

"The medical examiner has just left, and the forensic team have been told to bring standing UV floodlights so that we can differentiate what's red lacquer and what's—"

Balisek didn't feel the need to finish her sentence.

Teri and Mason walked up to the edge of the semi-circle of police tape and studied the scene. Even without being close to the vic, they could tell from her body position that she'd been severely beaten. Her legs were splayed at an impossible angle and her arms appeared to have been bent the wrong way at the elbow joint. The woman looked to have been wearing a Chanel suit, which was now little more than a bundle of torn, light blue material.

The woman's head had come to rest against a bedside table, facing away from the door.

"How long before we can get closer?" Mason asked. "I want to see her face."

Balisek reached into her suit and produced a giant-sized iPhone. "The responding officer thought to take a picture before access became limited."

She swiped to a zoomed-in photo of the victim's head. From the angle, it appeared as if she was looking right up at the camera. Other than the jagged tears to the flesh where the head had been removed from the neck, there didn't seem to be any other injuries to her face.

What there was, however, were her eyes. They were open comedically wide. Her excessive use of makeup made her last terrified expression look almost clown-like.

"Who is she and what was she doing here?" Teri said. "Was Leticia showing her the house?"

"We don't know. Before she went gaga, Gold apparently said something about the woman being a cleaner, but I don't see how that fits."

Mason and Teri both looked curiously back at Balisek.

"That little Chanel number sells for over five K. Not your average maid's outfit."

"Can we talk to Gold?" Teri asked.

"She's in the kitchen. According to the patrol officer, she was lucid for a few minutes then started screaming the house down. The medic had to dose her up on Ativan. I'm not sure what you're going to get out of her."

"Without being able to fully examine the bedroom, we're wasting our time down here," Teri commented. "Let's go see her."

"I'm going to check outside for the forensic team, then I'll head back downtown." Balisek said as she trotted up the marble staircase ahead of them.

Once they could see that the chief was on the escalator heading for the top floor, and therefore out of hearing range, Mason spoke.

"Someone please tell me why she insists on turning up at the crime scenes. All she does is slow things down."

"That's not fair. She probably thinks that she's helping. I'm not even sure she is slowing things down."

"The only reason she turns up is to be photographed in situ so that the public will think she's a hands-on investigator. As for her slowing things down, I can prove it. Assuming she'll have left here in a few minutes, start counting down now from seventeen minutes."

"Why?" Teri asked.

"Just do it."

Teri opened her phone's clock function and set the timer for seventeen minutes.

Leticia was sitting in a small breakfast nook, situated at the south facing side of the massive kitchen. A paramedic was kneeling next to her, measuring her blood pressure.

"Leticia," Mason said, forcing a smile. "You seem to have had quite a morning."

Leticia looked up at him with stoned eyes. It took a good few seconds before some sign of recognition landed on her enhanced features. Normally, she tried to never be seen without her hair and makeup being as close to perfect as science would allow. The woman who stared up at Teri and Mason looked like something out of a low budget horror movie.

Leticia's smeared makeup couldn't hide her extreme pallor and her usually perfect hair now resembled a bird's nest. Just like the body down in the master bedroom, her clothes were torn and covered in blood.

The paramedic seemed to know exactly what Mason was thinking.

"The blood's not hers."

Mason nodded as he and Teri sat across from them.

"I know that you must be in shock at the moment, but we were hoping you could tell us what exactly happened?"

Leticia looked back at him as if he'd asked her to recite a Diophantine equation. Mason looked questioningly to the medic.

"She goes in and out."

"Leticia?" Teri said as she reached across the table and gently took her hand.

Leticia jumped slightly, then stared at Teri and her hand as if trying to work out exactly what she was looking at. After a few seconds she slowly raised her head and looked right at Mason. For a millisecond he thought that she was trying to smile, then she began screaming.

CHAPTER 26

Mason and Teri waited until an ambulance drove off with Leticia inside. Even with the doors closed, they could still hear her bloodcurdling screams as the vehicle sped towards the UCLA Neuropsychiatric Hospital in Westwood. Just as the ambulance vanished from view, a grey van appeared around the corner.

"Forensics are here," Mason said. "Check your timer,"

Teri looked down and saw that it had only twenty-one seconds to go. "I don't understand."

"Every time Ballsack shows up at scene before the forensic crew, they get word and find somewhere to park until they hear that she's gone," Mason explained.

"But why?"

"Because the moment she arrives, she starts micromanaging the scene without any understanding as to why and how things are done the way they are. The techs have learned that it's better to wait until she's gone before they arrive. It's not out of spite. It's just their attempt to not have her screw up the process or even the crime scene."

Teri shook her head in mock sadness.

"What, are you developing a fondness for your dear stepmom?"

"Hardly," Teri replied. "I'm always amazed how you boys will find a million ways to avoid direct confrontation with the brass."

"I don't know how things worked in Stockton, but direct confrontation with the chief here in LA usually results in six months on the night shift in South Central."

"I can't believe that's true."

"Please, believe it," Mason said. "I don't want to lose a partner I'm just getting used to."

"From you, I'll take that as a compliment," Terri said, before heading back towards the house.

*

Four hours later, five CSIs were finishing up the first stage of their forensic evaluation of the scene. Once they'd assembled the two industrial UV lighting rigs, they were able to clearly see the blood pool on the floor, as well as whatever hard-to-see spatter may have been evident elsewhere in the room. Under the UV lights, the floor remained deep red, while the blood-spattered areas glowed bright blue.

There was a lot of blue. It was obvious that, when the victim's head had been severed from her body, she had either been standing or was propped up, as the arterial spray seemed to have jetted directly upwards for a good

219

few seconds. After that, it appeared as if her body, probably close to being fully exsanguinated, had been swung in a circle, sending splatter to all corners of the room to mingle with the wall art.

By the time Teri and Mason were allowed back into the room, the CSIs had moved on to the master bathroom.

"Want the UVs left on?" one of them asked.

Mason took one look at the carnage in the room and replied in the affirmative.

"Did you find any ID on the vic?" he asked.

"No ID, which isn't unusual for a woman as it's probably in her handbag somewhere, but also no jewelry, watch... nothing."

"Which is unusual," Mason commented.

"Actually," the tech replied, "it's a first for me. One of the other techs said that it was as if she was either robbed or about to have an MRI. I haven't had the pleasure, but I gather that because of the magnetic field, you have to remove absolutely anything that's metal."

"Thanks," Mason said, not sure of what to make of the guy's comment.

They didn't spend too long in the room. It was unlikely they would spot something the CSI's had missed, but it had happened.

Finding nothing, they headed for the hallway when Teri stopped at a white chest of drawers.

"What you got?"

"There's some ash residue on the top here."

"Cigarette?"

"I don't think so."

"Did you guys see the ash on top of the chest of drawers?" Mason called after the techs.

"Sure did," a woman's voice responded. "There was a smudge stick in a bowl. We bagged everything."

"What's a smudge stick?" Mason asked as he rubbed some of the remaining ash between his fingers.

"It's like incense but made of white sage," the voice replied. "People use it to ward off evil or cleanse a home."

"If it's supposed to clean the house, why leave a bunch of ash behind?"

Teri laughed. "Not that type of cleaning."

The tech appeared from the bathroom, still wearing the full sperm suit and face mask. She approached the pair and looked at the remaining ash.

"It's used by spiritualists to rid a house or building of an unwanted spirit."

"And you think that's what it was used for here?" Mason asked, surprised.

"I don't know what else it could have been doing here," the tech replied, before turning to Teri.

"You're new," she said. "Welcome. I'm Patty Gainer."

Teri, also still fully suited up, looked into Patty's turquoise eyes and felt a gentle shiver run down her spine.

"Thanks," Teri answered, her voice a tad raspy.

Even through the mask, Mason could tell that Patty was grinning.

"See you around," the tech said as both Mason and Teri watched the white, shapeless form of the CSI head back to the master bathroom.

"Ahh," Mason said. "You've made a friend."

Teri ignored his comment. "I've had an idea. Come with me."

Mason followed her out of the front of the house and into the cul-de-sac. She then made straight for the cop at the barrier.

"Long day, huh?" she said, lowering her mask. "The cars in the cul-de-sac that aren't ours, did anyone check out who they belong to?"

"First thing I did when I got here," he replied as he consulted a small black notebook. "The Chevy at the end belongs to the maid in the blue house. The white van belongs to a plumber who's working in the same house. The convertible Audi is owned by a woman in the house with the huge front wall. The black Range Rover belongs to—"

"I know that one," Teri interrupted. "That just leaves the Jag SUV."

"That's the only one we can't assign to one of the properties."

"Did you run the plates?" Mason asked.

"I did. It belongs to… a Phyliss Brimmer. She has a Beverly Hills address."

"Give it to me," Teri asked, opening her iPhone notes app.

"1721 North Camden in Beverly Hills," he recited.

"Thank you, Officer Applett," Teri said after checking his name tag.

Teri opened the DMV link on the LAPD site and ran a trace on Phyliss Brimmer at the given address. Within moments, a current driver's license appeared on the screen. Teri enlarged the photo then stood next to Mason so he could see the image.

"What do you think?" she asked.

"It's hard to tell with the fear and the trauma from the mutilation, but it could be her," Mason said.

Teri took another look at Phyliss's DMV data and found a cell phone number. She dialed it and waited while it connected. Moments later, a muffled, old-style ringer could be heard in the cul-de-sac. They walked towards the Jaguar, and were able to determine that the ringing was coming from within the vehicle.

"Shit," Mason said. "There was something on the kitchen counter."

"What?" she called after him.

Mason ran back into the house and returned to the kitchen. Sitting next to a wireless Bang and Olufsen phone was an ornate brass bowl. In it was some spare change, a few business cards and a couple of key fobs. One of them held the Jaguar logo.

He grabbed it with his gloved hand and dropped into a see-through evidence baggie.

"Find what you were looking for?" Teri asked as Mason reappeared.

Mason grinned as he pointed the fob at the car and pressed the activation pad through the plastic baggie. There was a beeping sound, and the interior dome light came on.

"Clever boy," Teri said as she approached the SUV.

There was nothing of interest within the car, in fact it was surprisingly tidy. It wasn't until they examined the cargo area and lifted the black fitted carpet that they struck gold.

Next to a full-sized spare tire (a costly extra), there was a storage area designed for a custom tool kit. Instead, in the utility well, there was a Gucci Handbag, a cell phone and a folding, leather, zippered carryall.

Teri chose the handbag while Mason reached for the case. After replacing the protective carpeting, Teri emptied the contents of the extravagant accessory onto the dark grey pile. What emerged was Phyliss' jewelry, some makeup, a vape pen, a few keys and a matching Gucci wallet.

"She obviously thought it necessary to leave all her personal item outside the house," Teri commented. "What do you have?"

Mason unzipped the bag and folded it open.

"I'm not sure."

Teri looked down at the odd collection and immediately recognized many of the items. Before her mother had fallen too far into the bottle, she'd woken up one morning when Teri was only a young child and decided that she had the psychic ability to cleanse unwanted spirits and planned to do so professionally. The fact that, up until that point, she had shown no spiritual interest or leaning had no bearing on her revelation. The venture had failed miserably, however, once her mother had recognized that she really didn't have any latent talents in the spectral department, she'd handed Teri her cleansing kit in lieu of a more traditional plaything.

The contents of her mother's kit was almost identical to what was laid out before them.

Recalling her girlhood memories, Teri recited what everything was and what it supposedly did as she pointed from one item to another.

"This is clear quartz and is used for soaking up negative vibes and clearing them. This is another white sage smudge stick which is used in every room of a house to clear energy for a renewal. This one is peppermint spray which is like an air freshener for positive energy. The rest are salt, juniper and rosemary all of which are to rid the home of bad vibrational odors and replace them with positive ones. This box here holds white tea candles which are burned slowly in each space in order to help guide the energy. And finally, we have white matches, which are to be used in the lighting of the smudge stick and the candles."

"You don't actually believe all this crap, do you?" Mason asked, concerned.

"Not now, but you should have heard my mother wax lyrical about their mystical power when used against dark forces."

"If I'd known her at the time, I would have had social services get you the hell out of that house," he stated.

"She was pretty harmless back then. The real horror started when she traded cleansing spirits to drinking them."

"Not wishing to change the subject, but if all this stuff was to help her clean this house, why the hell was it left in the car?"

"If I had to guess," Teri replied, "I'd say that Phyliss didn't want the entity to know what she had up her sleeve, and that by leaving the kit in the car she could lay the groundwork with the smudge stick, then pop back out as needed for some of the other tools of the trade."

"Only in Los Angeles," Mason said, shaking his head. "It's a shame she didn't bring a gun with her. Probably would have had a lot more stopping power than oregano or peppermint."

"Sage," Teri corrected him.

"Does it really matter?"

"You are a sceptic, aren't you?"

"My philosophy is that I'm only going to believe in things that have been proven."

Teri rolled her eyes. "Do you want me to try and get some background on exactly what services Phyliss was offering? I assume she must have a website."

"I was thinking of a more direct approach," Mason replied. "How about we drive to her house and see if anyone is at home?"

Teri looked unsure. "Shouldn't we stay here with the forensic teams?"

"Did you waste your time like that in Stockton?" Mason asked.

"No, but I don't know what the protocol is in Hollyweird. Don't forget. This is my first active homicide down here."

"There's nothing we can do while the CSIs are inside. If they do find something of note, they'll call, and we'll come back. Officers have already canvassed the other homes but nobody heard or saw anything. So, in the meantime, we need to find out what Phyliss Brimmer and Leticia Gold were up to."

Teri shrugged and advised Officer Applett that they were both leaving the scene and then signed themselves out.

After avoiding Sunset like the plague, they sped along Fountain Avenue till it dead-ended at Las Cienega, then dropped down to Santa Monica and stayed on it until they reached Camden Drive in Beverly Hills. Teri took a right then drove north to the foothills. She pulled up in front of what appeared to be a transplanted Mediterranean villa, complete with climbing bougainvillea and towering Cyprus trees.

"Phyliss appears to have had humble tastes," Mason said sarcastically.

Mason tried the elaborate, wrought iron framed doorbell and though both could hear its chime echo within the house, nobody came to the door. As there did not appear to be a garage or car port and theirs was the only vehicle on the property, it was clear that nobody else was home. The problem was, at that early stage, they didn't even know if Phyliss had a significant other or roamed around the mansion by herself.

Mason wrote the words 'please call me' on one of his business cards then left it wedged into the space between the front door and the frame.

Before they could make it back to the car, Mason's phone sounded. He answered it and listened intently for a full ten minutes.

"That was the crime scene manager," Mason said as he joined Teri in the car. "They've finished fingerprinting the main areas of interest and are about to start on the rest of the house. They expect that it will take the Latent Prints Unit a few days to match what they've found so far. I wasn't expecting much, considering that TV and movies have pretty much given any budding perp a road map of how not to leave trace behind. They did find one interesting thing. Apparently, the house has hidden security cameras for the front door and garage. They had a tech fast forward through the feeds, and apart from Phyliss and Leticia, nobody else has entered the place in two days."

"So, we potentially have another one," Teri commented.

"Yup. Another homicide that no one can explain."

"Unless Leticia has superhuman strength."

"I somehow doubt that," Mason responded. "Plus, she would have had to have been drenched in way more blood than she was if she was the attacker."

"What makes it really weird is that we know that there's absolutely no other way in or out."

"There is one thing," Mason mentioned. "This is the first time there hasn't been a party associated with the crime."

Teri didn't comment until they crossed over Sunset and were back in the foothills of Beverly Hills.

"I don't agree," she finally said. "I think there *was* a party associated with this one."

"How so?"

"I think that Harter's party in 2007 was the start of all of this."

"Any backup to that statement?" Mason asked.

"Absolutely none."

"Glad you're onboard," Mason said, shaking his head and smiling.

CHAPTER 27

Teri's grandmother called the next morning and advised that she and Mason were more than welcome to join her and Debbie Cohen at one o'clock for their regularly scheduled lunch at Spago.

While Teri looked perfectly acceptable in her dark pantsuit, Mason had forgotten about the potential lunch and had thrown on the same jacket and pants he'd worn to the morgue the previous day. They were both creased and fragrant with the enduring aroma of decomp. Teri read the look on his face.

"I've got some dry-cleaning spray in my locker. If you don't mind a slight hint of lavender, it should do the trick."

"Do I need it?" Mason asked. "Can you smell eau-de-morgue on me?"

"Like you bathed in it," Teri replied. "Try the spray. It works."

Before Mason could say anything, his phone sounded.

Seconds later, he disconnected the call and got to his feet.

"I'd better have a squirt of it now. We're going to UCLA."

"Leticia's back with us?" Teri asked.

"Apparently. The doc said we can have five minutes, though he doubted we'd get much out of her, considering what they've got her dosed up on."

"You head to the car, I'll swing by my locker."

*

"I smell like a fucking florist," Mason said as they tried to find their way through the maze of UCLA medical buildings.

"Maybe, but you don't smell like death which, considering where we're going, might just be a plus."

They eventually found their way to the neuropsychiatric clinic and were made wait almost half an hour before a prim little man with a goatee and rimless glasses walked up to them. His name tag read Dr Lafontaine.

"As I said on the phone, you've only got five minutes," the doctor said without preamble.

"You do know that your patient is the sole witness to a murder, right?" Mason asked.

"I don't care if she witnessed the birth of Christ. She's in shock and in need of long-term psychiatric care. My number one focus is on the patient, not the police."

"We thank you for your help and concern," Teri said putting a little silk into her voice. "I promise you, we won't overstay our welcome."

"I know you won't," the doctor replied haughtily. "I will be in the room with you."

"Actually, you won't. Unless you are her lawyer, you have zero right to hear what transpires between us and your patient." The silk was still in Teri's voice, but the material was definitely starting to fray.

"I'll have you know—"

"I do hope you're not using up our precious time with Ms. Gold," Mason said in a clipped voice. "That's called obstructing an investigation. I doubt it would serve any of your patients if you had to spend the rest of the day downtown with us."

The doctor looked from one to the other as if their very presence was offensive.

"She's in the Resnick Wing. Follow me."

Fontaine led them through a maze of corridors until he finally stopped at one particular room. He opened the door and stepped inside.

"Wait one second, while I let her know that you're here."

It was more like thirty seconds, but when Fontaine reappeared, he stood aside so that Mason and Teri could enter the room.

"Five minutes," he reminded them.

"Five minutes," Teri confirmed, before shutting the door in his face.

Mason was shocked at the figure that was lying on the hospital bed. She looked nothing like the realtor they'd encountered twice before. Leticia looked as if she'd lost weight and her normally tanned complexion had turned a pallid yellow. Her vibrant blue eyes were bloodshot and appeared unfocused.

"Leticia?" Mason said in little more than a whisper.

Her head lolled for a moment. Despite both of their attempts to get her talking, almost two minutes passed before Leticia even looked up at her visitors.

"We're sorry to have to bother you like this," Teri said. "But we need to know what you saw at the house."

"Phyliss?" she asked in a weak and croaky voice.

"What did you see?" Mason asked, moving closer to the bed."

"I don't know. I think I dreamed some of it."

"Some of what?" Teri urged her on.

"I don't know what was real and what wasn't," she managed to say.

"Tell us anyway," Mason said.

"Is Phyliss alive?" Leticia asked.

"Why do you ask that?" Mason questioned.

"In my dream, I saw her die."

"How did she die?" Mason nodded.

Leticia took a moment to gather her tranquilized thoughts.

"She was in the bedroom; the one with the red floor. She was chanting and had just placed her smudge stick on a saucer when the floor, that God awful red floor, rose up and tore at her."

"What do you mean, it tore at her?" Teri asked.

"I mean it seemed to have hands. Old, gnarled hands that pulled and—" Leticia lowered her head as a single sob wracked her body. She again raised her head and tears began running down her cheeks. With her hands restrained to the bed, she couldn't even attempt to dry them.

Teri stepped forward and grabbed a wad of tissues from a box by the bed. She gently dabbed Leticia's face dry.

Leticia gave her a brief nod of thanks.

"Oh, God!" she said, her voice drained. "I wasn't dreaming. She's dead, isn't she?"

"I'm afraid she is, which is why we need you to think very hard about what you saw in that room. You said the floor rose up and began to tear at her. Obviously, that didn't happen. What else could you have possibly seen that made you think it was the floor rising?"

Leticia closed her eyes and thought hard about what had happened. The problem was that she was full of a chemistry set's worth of tranquilizers and anti-depressants, that were designed specifically to stop such memories from surfacing. It was clear from her facial expressions that she was having to battle her own mind to gain access to what was locked within.

"It wasn't the floor," Leticia managed to say. "But it did rise out of the floor."

"What rose out of the floor, Leticia?" Teri asked.

Before she could answer, the door opened, and Lafontaine entered the room with two orderlies that looked to have been plucked from UCLA football's back line.

"You've had your five minutes," he stated as he nodded to the two giants.

"You'll have to leave now," one of them said in a low bass-filled voice.

"Just one more minute," Teri pleaded.

The two men pushed between them and the bed and began edging them towards the door, careful not to use their hands.

Mason was almost though the doorway when Leticia managed to say, "Wait."

"What is it?" Teri called back to her. "What rose out of the floor?"

Leticia sat as upright as her restraints allowed and stared wide-eyed at the two detectives.

"A monster."

*

Neither detective said a word until they were back in the car.

"That was a waste of time," Mason said as he tried to find a way out of the parking structure.

"Maybe," Teri replied.

"What does that mean? You're not suggesting that she actually saw some sort of monster rise out of the floor, are you?"

"No, but I think we have to accept that whatever she did see almost scared her to death. We have to start asking ourselves what exactly could do that to a person. What would scare you that much?"

"I don't know, but you're currently giving me the willies."

"All I'm saying is that all the vics appeared to have been terrified at their time of death."

"A guy attacking with a gun, or a knife would have that same effect on most people," Mason offered.

"Yes, but none of the vics were killed with a gun or knife, in fact we still don't know how the fatal injuries were caused."

"I don't get where you're heading."

"I guess I'm saying... what if Leticia was right? I don't mean about an actual monster rising up from the floor, but maybe we're looking at something that's not that easily explainable."

"Everything is explainable once you've got all the facts," Mason stated.

"We have all the facts; certainly all the ones relating to the three unsolved cases," Teri pointed out.

"No, we don't. If we had all the facts, we would have all the answers."

All Teri could do was to turn and stare at her partner.

"What?" Mason asked defensively.

"That is the dumbest thing I've ever heard. What we do is take a bunch of facts and weave them into precedential patterns that match our knowledge base of prior crimes. What I'm suggesting is, what if this time there is no precedent to what's happening here? These cases don't fit any mold, because nothing like this has ever happened before."

"You should have worn a mask while we were in the hospital," Mason said, without taking his eyes off the road.

"Why?"

"Cause I think you might have caught a small case of crazy back there."

"Nothing like what you contracted last time you visited a donkey ranch," Teri shot back as she glared out the window.

CHAPTER 28

Spago's in Beverly Hills was the jewel in Wolfgang Puck's culinary crown. The original had been perched on the side of a hill overlooking Sunset Boulevard and the long-defunct Tower Records in West Hollywood. It had been casual chic, noisy and you had to be on a first name basis with Bernard, the officious maître d', to get a table. Puck had closed the restaurant at the height of its popularity and reopened the revised version deep within the gilded bowels of Beverly Hills. The food was still spectacular, but it had somehow lost some of its fun and whimsical charm during the move.

Mason rarely dined in the city's finer eateries. However, nothing gave him more pleasure than to pull up in front of parking valets in an unmarked Ford Crown Victoria that had over two hundred thousand miles on it.

As usual, the valets looked at the car with an expression of distaste and disappointment, knowing that there was little chance of getting much of a tip considering the state of the vehicle and the fact that, with its black hubcaps, it was doubtless a cop car.

Once in the restaurant, they were led to a table in the central courtyard that looked more like something you'd expect to find in the south of France rather than in the midst of Los Angeles' sprawling mass.

Freeda and Debbie were already there and raised their wine glasses in toast the moment the pair were seated.

Freeda was dressed in a cream-colored Versace pantsuit that Debbie had given her earlier in the year. Because of her access to the serious A-listers in LA, Debbie was sent an astonishing array of clothing as a form of unpaid endorsement. As the 'arrangement' only required her to wear each outfit once, she was in a position to pass down some of the luxury items to less well-heeled friends. Freeda, being almost the exact same size as her, made out like a bandit.

Debbie, due to some very good scalpel work, could have been anywhere between fifty and seventy. The only giveaway to her being in the upper range were the liver spots on her bejeweled hands.

After some small talk, Debbie smiled at the two detectives and asked, "So, what can I possibly do to help Los Angeles' finest?"

Mason told her, with minimal detail, about the three unsolved cases. He intentionally omitted anything about the two more recent homicides.

"I can see how frustrating it must be to have so little to go on, but I'm not sure how exactly I can help. Most of my clients are more in the robber-baron category rather than

239

being involved in anything as dark as murder. Besides, I'm delighted to say that I had nothing to do with those three parties."

"We're not interested in any of your clients," Teri said. "We're actually more interested in the entertainment. The same performer was at each of the three events and has never been located. We simply want to speak with him."

"Do you have a name?" Debbie asked.

"We have three names but they're all bogus," Mason replied.

"That's a pity. I'm not sure how I can help without—"

"We do, however, have a picture of the man," Teri said as she pulled her iPad from her bag.

Once she had loaded the photo that had been clipped from the security video at the Bel Air party, she placed it in front of Debbie.

"Ah," she said, then sighed. "We may have a slight problem."

"Why is that?" Mason asked.

Debbie tried to find the right words.

"You signed an NDA, didn't you?" Teri suggested.

"I think I'm permitted to answer that. Yes, I did."

"What exactly is it that the agreement forbids you from discussing?" Mason asked.

"I am not allowed to disclose what he does, how he does it or give any details of his abilities."

"We understand that whatever he does seems to have some sort of fear factor involved with it. Can you confirm that?"

"I never actually saw his show."

"Then how—?" Teri started to ask.

"Would you give me two minutes to make a quick call. I need to get a little advice about this," Debbie said as she got to her feet, removed a bejeweled iPhone from her handbag and made her way to the interior of the restaurant.

"That was interesting," Freeda commented as she finished her glass of wine. "She's usually very outgoing and more than willing to share some of the more tantalizing bits of gossip."

"The problem we keep having," Teri explained, "is that the guy we're looking for has had just about everyone in town sign a nondisclosure agreement. Which means that no one can tell us much of anything."

"And you are both certain that he's the one responsible for the four deaths?"

"No," Mason answered. "He is, however, the only person who was present at the parties and who hasn't been interviewed."

"But you do believe that this man is responsible for the murders?" Freeda asked as a waiter topped up her glass.

"Actually," Teri said, "from what we know so far, we're relatively certain that he was at all the locations, but had left prior to the attacks."

"Then why the interest?"

"Because, whoever he is, he has gone to some serious lengths to not be found or even talked about. That, in and of itself, is highly suspicious."

"Sorry to have stepped away like that, but I wanted a quick word with my husband, who also just happens to be my lawyer," Debbie said as she sat back down and drained her glass of wine. "I never bothered to tell him about the agreement as it seemed inconsequential considering the numbers of NDA's I have to sign when dealing with my celebrity clients."

There was a pause while Debbie watched a waiter fill her wine glass.

"Alex, that's my hubby, advised me to stick to the letter of the agreement but that some, more general questioning might still be acceptable."

Such as?" Teri asked.

"Now, there's the rub. It seems that it can cloud the issue if I suggest the questions. That will be up to you."

"Okay," Mason said with a smile. "Do you know the person's name?"

"Actually I do. He has a number of stage aliases, but his real name, at least, the one that I was given is Carlos Quinn."

"We're making progress," Teri said, smiling.

"Thankfully, the agreement never mentioned anything about not giving out his name. Probably because he's always using those creepy ones which reference ghosts and ghouls."

"We've encountered some of those," Teri said.

"May I ask how you managed to obtain his real name?" Mason asked.

"I think that's probably permissible. Whenever I add a new vendor to my party roster, I insist on doing a full background check. You can't be too careful when placing workers in the homes of gazillionaires."

"And he was willing to let you do that?"

"He had no choice. If he wanted to do business with me, I had to know everything about the person I was about to bring onboard."

"Can you tell us what exactly he was going to do at your parties?" Teri asked.

Debbie took a long swig of her Montrachet, then shook her head. "That's one of the no-go areas."

"Can you at least tell us the type of entertainment that Mr. Quinn provided?" Mason asked.

"Still no. Sorry."

"I don't know if it will help us, but can you explain, not in relation to Quinn, but generally, the sort of entertainment that you provide at these A-list parties?" Teri tried a different tack.

"Of course. The answer is anything and everything. I've had Elton John play piano, and not sing, mind you, for a small dinner party in the Holmby Hills. I've also had Coldplay perform at an outdoor gala in Santa Barbara. You've got to understand that the super wealthy simply want what they want. Money is rarely the object."

"How much is an evening with Elton John?" Mason asked.

"A lot, especially as he was told not to sing. He almost didn't take the gig until the number got really big."

"Define really big?" Teri asked.

"Six million."

Mason had just sipped his water when he heard the figure and almost did a spit-take.

"That was an extraordinarily large fee, mainly because of the no-singing slight. I got Coldplay for two point five million. Then there's the more unusual acts. Having Cirque de Soleil perform in your garden was a big thing in the early 2000s. Then having magicians like David Blaine became the rage."

"Dare I ask?" Mason asked.

"He'll do a short show for around a hundred thousand. If you want his full Vegas act including all the props, it's well over a quarter million."

Can you tell me Mr. Quinn's rate?" Mason asked.

"That's getting a little close to the bone. May I just say that it was initially above a David Blain short show? I hear that it's risen considerably since I was interested."

"Got it," Mason said, nodding. "So, whatever he does, it's pretty special."

"That's what I hear," Debbie said as she flagged down a waiter. "I told them to give us a moment so we could talk, but I've decided I'm famished so, let's order."

Once they'd made their selections, Mason continued trying to get as much info from Debbie as was both legally and morally (for her) possible.

"Do you have a contact number for Quinn?"

"I did back when he was being considered, but he's gone entirely online now."

"Wait a minute. Are you saying that you never hired him for a party?"

"That's the funny thing. I couldn't, and ironically, it was his fault. Because of all the chicanery and legal nonsense, it was impossible for him to provide detailed references which my background search requires. Because of all his NDAs strewn across the city, even if he had given me some names, they wouldn't have been able to discuss his performance with the security firm I use."

"Yet, he still gets business," Teri commented.

"Does he ever," Debbie replied.

"I assume he doesn't have anything as pedantic as a website?" Teri asked.

"Yes and no. I've been told that he has something along the lines of a prospective client chat room on the dark web."

"Isn't that a little over the top?" Mason asked. "Why would any performer need to go to those extremes? In fact, if he's that secretive, how does he even get paid?"

"Bitcoin," Debbie replied with a shrug.

"Can you give us the URL of the dark web site?"

"I've never had it. Quinn used to use a phone with a number that would change every few weeks at which point I would get a text from a burner phone with the new one."

"Have you got any idea how we could get a hold of the web address?" Mason asked.

"You could try contacting Elite Acts," Debbie suggested. "They do a lot of the liaison between party planners and the agents for the talent."

"Won't they have signed an NDA as well?" Mason asked.

"Undoubtably."

"That brings up an interesting point," Teri stated. "Did Quinn have an agent?"

"Not that I know of."

"How did you first hear about him?" Mason asked.

"Initially, it was just rumored that there was this guy who could—" Debbie said, shaking her head. "I think I almost said too much."

"I know you can't say what he does now, but do you happen to know when his act became an A-list attraction?" Teri asked.

"I do, but I think the NDA covers all knowledge of Quinn's past as well as present, so I can't give you any specifics. However, suffice it to say, that at one particular party, the hostess and a waiter were later murdered, adding even more notoriety to his mystique."

"I assume that the event you are referring to was Cynthia Harter's bash. That's one of the cases we are investigating. How did you hear about it?" Mason asked.

"Obviously I heard about the deaths on the news. It was impossible to avoid it. As for the entertainment, I heard whispers that something extraordinary had happened earlier in the evening. It didn't take long before I was being asked to book the act for other parties. Somehow, Quinn heard about me and that's how the whole background check issue came to pass."

"People wanted the same thing as Harter, even though the evening had resulted in two murders?" Teri asked.

"As I understood it back then, the deaths had no connection to the show itself. In fact, from what I've heard, Quinn was nowhere near the Harter house when the murders took place."

Before either detective could ask another question, their food began to arrive.

"If I may be so bold," Freeda said to the others at the table," I think that's enough interrogation for today. How about we just leave that subject behind, enjoy our food and gossip about our friends and neighbors as we usually do?"

"Sorry, Gran," Teri said. "I have one more question, then we'll let it be. Debbie, was his act anything to do with magic?"

Debbie gave a long evaluating stare.

"Let's just say that what he apparently did was, from what I've heard, beyond anything anyone had ever seen before."

"So, it was some sort of trick?" Teri replied.

"No, my dear. What was so enthralling was that what he did was one hundred percent real!"

CHAPTER 29

After using every search engine at their disposal to run the name Carlos Quinn, Teri and Mason were disappointed by the results. The DMV showed two Carlos Quinns in the greater Los Angeles area, but one of those had seemingly vanished off the radar ten years earlier at the age of seventy-five. The other was for an eighteen-year-old boy who looked nothing like Quinn and lived in the bowels of South Central.

Having already done a search under Quinn's names and aliases nationwide, as well as checking with the talent coordinator that Debbie had suggested, they were none the wiser. Mason and Teri weren't sure where to focus their energies. Both were stunned that anyone could fly that far below the radar, considering the unavoidable number of modern-day biometric requirements. They even tried social media searches, but while that brought forth hundreds of Quinns, none were local or relevant.

As a Hail Mary, Mason put in a request for military records, just in case Quinn had ever served or even applied, then spent the rest of the morning with Teri focusing on the status of their primary case, the latest murder at the old Harter house.

The forensic teams were still finishing up gathering evidence within the property. Part of the problem was the size of the place, the other was the sheer volume of trace evidence that was found within the workings of the escalator.

There were so many particulates that just logging them all became a full-time assignment. Two loaner officers that had been assigned by Balisek had been given the daunting task of coordinating the trace evidence for DNA analysis.

When the DNA Unit saw the number of samples they were expected to process, they had gone crying to Balisek, who, in what was becoming less and less of a rarity, sided with them rather than her case officers.

"We know that just about every single one of those samples was randomly deposited after the escalator was installed which was a year prior to the Harter event," she barked at Mason. "We also already know who was in the house on the night of the 2007 party and on the day of the more recent murder. Even if the particulates contain any DNA residue, the timeline is off for the Harter crime and most likely irrelevant for the latest one. If you are so convinced that the perpetrator somehow managed to get into that house unseen by security, or the cameras, then I suggest that your next move is to find out if alternative access is even possible."

"We checked. It's not." Mason replied.

"Have you thought of using a forensic security consultant?" Balisek asked.

"Of course we haven't. I've never even heard of one."

"Well, you have now, and the good news is that the city has one on retainer. I'll get their details and send them to you."

"How is that going to help?"

"It will help because, if we can determine that exterior access was in fact possible other than from the garage and the front door, we might just be able to move the case forward for a change. Don't you think that would be a step in the right direction?"

By the time Mason got back to their office, he'd managed to get up a full head of steam.

"What's the matter?" Teri asked as he stomped to his half of the table.

"Ballsack's the matter! She's sided with the DNA Unit. They're not going to process the particulates from the Harter house escalator."

"I'm not surprised. We were clutching at straws anyway."

"I know that. I just wish that for once she'd back up her officers."

"What's really got you pissed off?" Teri asked. "You knew she was likely to say no."

"I'm pissed off because she wants us to use a forensic security consultant to verify any potential exterior access points that we might have missed."

"What's wrong with that? It's a good idea."

"That's why I'm so angry. It was her fucking idea!"

"Oh, poopsy-pie. Was momma bear smarter than you?" Teri said, trying to keep a straight face.

*

At their weekly briefing with Hardwick and Simpson, they learned that nothing much was progressing with the Tamacini case either. As with the three original unsolved cases, no trace of a murderer had been found.

"At least we know what killed our vic," Hardwick said, almost boasting.

"Then it should be easy for you two heroes to solve the case," Teri said in a faux, cheery voice, frustrated that she herself had found no trace of Phyliss Brimmer's house cleansing business and was starting to wonder if it was more of hobby rather than a paid profession. She even went so far as to search through the woman's Facebook, Instagram and X posts in case she'd made some mention of her purported calling.

Teri had found nothing.

Mason had made it a point to stop by Phyliss's house at least once a day and had so far had no success at finding anyone in residence. Even after canvassing the neighbors, nobody seemed to have had any contact with the occupants of the house, which made Mason wonder if Brimmer lived alone.

Leticia was still under heavy sedation, and when she did rise above the fog, made little sense, other than continually asking for forgiveness from both God and Satan.

"Want to spend Ballsack's money and have that dinner tonight?" Mason suggested after another frustrating day of making little to no headway.

"Can't, I'm going over to see Gregg," Teri advised. "You don't have to wait on me to go to that restaurant."

"I don't like eating alone."

"Then don't. You must have plenty of friends. I'm sure one of them will jump at the chance of a free meal."

"I *had* quite a few actually, but you'd be surprised how quickly even your closest buddies will abandon you when they think you're a cop killer."

"Some people, huh?" Teri said, trying to make light of his statement. "What about a date? You must have someone in your life."

"After all the approaches I got when I was a suspected killer, it's kind of put me off dating. I don't know that I'd ever trust whether someone is really into me or just trying to screw their way into some sick form of celebrity."

"That's sad."

"That's life in LA," Mason countered.

I'll tell you what. I've got nothing happening tomorrow night. If things stay this quiet, want to go then?"

"I can't."

"Why?"

"I've joined a fear of women group that meets once a week at Hooters."

For a moment, Teri thought he was being serious then saw the humor behind his eyes.

"We're on then," she declared. "But—"

"I know. No strings. It's a work dinner."

"I was going to say, let's try not to bankrupt the chief. So far, she's managed to keep the piranhas away from us. I'd like that to continue."

"Understood," Mason replied, deciding not to mention the encounter he'd had in the parking lot only a few days earlier.

CHAPTER 30

Mason saw the photo printout that had been pushed under his door the moment he stepped inside his new home. It took a second for his brain to register exactly what he was seeing. A dead coyote lay on a brick patio. Its head appeared to have taken the brunt of a direct shotgun blast. There was little left of it.

Mason turned the piece of paper over and saw the same handwriting that had been used in the threatening note he'd received earlier.

This time it said: 'I warned you. As you can see. I had to take matters into my own hands. I suggest you learn from this.'

Mason wanted to look at the photo again to confirm what he already knew but couldn't bring himself to do so. He knew it was Wolfy, just as he also knew that the neighbor had almost certainly lured the animal close with food. The coyote, having started to trust the routine with Mason, would have stepped into the open, making itself an easy target.

Mason was surprised that instead of the rage he would have expected himself to feel at the sight of the senselessly killed creature, he instead felt a deep, hollow sadness. That being said, he knew one thing for certain: the anger would soon follow.

*

The music was still blaring when Teri approached her grandparents' duplex. When Freeda opened the door, Teri immediately noticed the change in her grandmother. Only one day earlier, she'd looked happy, healthy and as she herself always said, full of beans.

The woman who greeted Teri looked to have aged ten years almost overnight. Her complexion was sallow, and there were dark circles under her eyes.

"Gregg's in the park with Bobby. He had the urge to play catch," Freeda said as soon as she closed the front door.

"Why did they go all the way to the park? They usually play in the backyard."

"We're letting Emanuel use the yard a little more. He's just had friends over."

Teri stepped past her and walked to the back of the house. She was puzzled at seeing the family room curtains drawn while it was still daylight. She opened them and looked out at Freeda's prized garden and patio.

The sight that greeted her felt like a punch to the gut. Their immaculate lawn was covered in empty beer cans and fast-food wrappers. The flower beds had been trampled and a lone soccer ball was floating in the vintage water fountain. Probably the saddest thing, at least to Teri, was when she saw the colorful clay pot that she had made for Freeda in school when she was only nine. Though a little misshapen, it had become one of Freeda's prized possessions.

It now rested next to a worn deckchair and was overflowing with cigarette butts. Even from Teri's vantage point inside the house, she could clearly see that its rim was chipped in a number of places.

Teri found Freeda sitting in the living room, her head in her hands, sobbing.

"Oh, Nan," Teri said as she knelt in front of her.

"It's all right," Freeda replied in a whisper. "He has a right to share the property."

"He has no rights at all. He's not even a legal tenant. You stay down here. I'm going to have a little talk with him."

"No," Freeda cried out. "That's what's caused all this."

"All what?" Teri asked as she reached out and gently held her grandmother's wrists.

Freeda grimaced and pulled her arms away. Teri knew the signs. She had dealt with more than her share of domestic abuse cases when she first joined the force in Stockton.

"Let me see." Teri reached out and gingerly rolled back one sleeve, revealing the black blue and yellow discoloration of a bad bruise across her wrist and forearm.

"Please don't do anything else. He said he'd kill us, and I believe him. I really do."

256

"He's a bully, Nan, and I have no intention of making things worse for you. I just need to clear up a few things while I'm here."

Once out of the house, Teri's face locked into a mask of pure rage as she ran up the outside stairs then pounded on the door.

Emanuel opened the door wide. In his hand was an aluminum baseball bat.

"What do you want? Gonna give me more shit about what I can and can't do on my own property. Well maybe it's time I give you a little lesson in respect."

Emanuel pointed the bat, fat end first, directly at Teri's face. His attempt at intimidation did not go as planned. Instead of the look of fear he'd expected, Teri laughed. Hard. So hard that she actually doubled over. Emanuel stepped closer with the intent of forcing her to look at him. Instead, Teri snapped back upright, catching his chin with her head.

"Oh, man, I'm so sorry," Teri said in an overly concerned voice. "I'm so clumsy sometimes. Here, let's get some ice on that." Wanting to ensure that any nosey neighbors only saw her trying to help, she managed to swing him around and almost frog march him back into the unit.

The moment she closed the door, all pretense of caring about Emanuel vanished.

"Yo, bitch. You can't just come into my home, ya?" he shouted as he raised the bat.

"First of all, this isn't your home. As far as the law goes, you are a trespasser. As far as I'm concerned, you're little more than a pathetic bully."

"Yet, you just got yourself shut inside here with me," Emanuel sneered. "Bad move."

Emanuel swung the bat towards Teri's head. Instead of trying to duck or avoid the swing, Teri stepped into it. She twisted herself so that her back was to the arm holding the bat then, in one fluid motion, reached out and grabbed Emanuel's wrist, yanking it down as she twisted it to the right.

Emanuel screamed as his wrist tendon snapped and the bat flew out of his hand and struck the wall.

"Now I'm gonna fucking kill you, you cunt," he said as he used his one good hand to draw a nickel-plated gun from his hoodie.

Teri stepped forward and brought her right knee up into his scrotum. As he folded over in pain she slammed the other knee up into his chin, immediately breaking his jaw and knocking him out cold. The entire exchange took less than fifteen seconds.

Teri picked up the gun, tucked it in her waistband then rolled Emanuel onto his back and sat on his chest. She patted his face until his eyes opened.

"You have two choices," she said, her voice cold and precise. "Option one: you leave right now and never come back to anywhere near this neighborhood again. Option two: I call this in, and you get booked for the attempted murder of a police officer. Personally, I'd prefer you take option one as that would save the cost of your trial and jail time. What do you say?"

Emanuel tried to move but was pinned under her weight.

"You're the one who's in trouble," he managed to say without moving his jaw. "You never told me you was a cop. That means you can't touch me."

"Thanks for reminding me," Teri said as she fished out her shield and tossed it to the far side of the room. "You attacked me the second I showed you my ID and knocked it out of my hand. Any other ideas?"

"I got friends," Emanuel replied, half-heartedly.

"No, you don't. I checked you out. You work in Culver City at a carpet warehouse. You have no gang affiliations, and your life of crime so far has been trying to steal a car when you were sixteen, but didn't know it was a manual and you couldn't use the gears. Your only other brush with the law was when you somehow got into a fight at a mall. From what I read, you grabbed some young woman's backside and her partner saw you. Just like today, you were knocked unconscious."

"The guy was huge."

"No," Teri continued calmly. "The partner was a woman and was smaller than me. Normally, I would have found a less violent way to make my point, but after threatening my grandparents, you're lucky to still be alive. I suggest you get your scrawny ass out of here within the next hour."

"Maybe I'll claim police brutality," he said.

"That's your right, sir. However, while you are in a gen pop holding cell, I can't guarantee that word about you being a gang informant won't somehow leak out."

"I'm not a gang informant," he squealed as his eyes opened extra wide.

"That's the thing with rumors," Teri said, smiling down at him. "By the time everyone works out what was true and what wasn't, it's usually too late to undo the damage."

For a moment, Teri thought he was going to cry.

"Want me to call you an Uber? I'll ask for a big enough one to hold all your stuff."

This time Emanuel did cry.

*

Teri stayed and watched as Emanuel packed up his possessions, including the retro boombox that had been responsible for all the noise. The going was slow, due to his injured wrist, and on a few occasions, he even gestured to a few heavier items hoping that Teri might help. She didn't.

By seven thirty p.m., he was gone, but not before pulling his hoodie up, giving Teri his best 'stink-eye' while offering a Latin Kings hand gesture with his only good hand. She simply laughed and shouted that he should stop by the ER on his way home to get his injuries checked out.

By the time she stepped back downstairs, Gregg and Bobby were back from the park and her son had had his evening bath. Freeda, with a renewed lightness to her step, cooked up some homemade fried chicken with sweet potato fries and a green salad.

The mood around the dinner table was light-hearted and comfortable. While she was eating, Teri couldn't help noticing that Freeda kept staring at her. She waited until the two of them were alone doing the washing up (Freeda didn't believe in dishwashers).

"What's up, Gran?" Teri asked.

"I don't know what went on up there, and I know you well enough to not expect an explanation, but I just want to say thank you."

"You've thanked me a hundred times already," Teri said with a warm smile.

"I watched Emanuel get into that SUV. It looked as if he'd been in a fight."

"Not unusual with his type," Teri replied.

"Latinas?" Freeda asked.

"No. Bullies. They need to dominate just to feel alive."

"I worry about you, sometimes. You have to mess with some very unpleasant people."

"That's my job."

"I know that. I just worry for you. It's a shame you couldn't live somewhere a little closer. Maybe a place where people could look out for you."

"What are you getting at Freeda?" Teri asked, as a fluttering sensation started in her stomach.

"You live all the way in the valley. It must take you forever to get to and from work, plus you're too far from your son."

"I used to be much farther when I was in San Francisco then Stockton," Teri pointed out.

"But you're not in those cities anymore. I understand the reasons why you don't feel it's a good idea for Gregg to be living with you, what with your hours and such, but what if you could be near him and us and have a much nicer place to call home?"

Teri, though battle-hardened by her years in the force, felt her eyes well up.

"As you well know, I no longer have a tenant living in the upstairs unit," Freeda continued. "It's twice the size of the shoebox you have now, and you could start seeing Gregg far more often."

"I thought we agreed that with my work, it was better if Gregg and I never really..."

"Never really what?" Freeda asked, with her hands on her hips. "Got close? Bonded? For God's sake, young lady, he's your son. The bond is already there, and the huge plus with you living upstairs is that it doesn't matter if you have to go out early or come home late. He's only a few feet away. You would no longer have to adhere to a rigid schedule. The two of you could just find your own timetable."

Teri was having trouble holding back the tears. Ever since she'd moved to LA, Freeda had had a tenant with a long lease. Now the place was vacant, and she was face to face with a fantasy that she'd never allowed herself to even consider.

"You know I can't afford to live in this neighborhood," Teri reminded her.

"What are you paying in studio city?"

"$1500 a month plus utilities."

"I'll charge you the same amount here, but include utilities. That means you are closer to work, closer to Bobby and me, closer in many ways to Gregg, and will at the same time be saving money. Also, I already know you have a cat and am more than happy to have Cheesecake be part of our little community. I can't wait to hear what feeble excuse you're going to come up with next."

With tears streaming down her face, Teri hugged her grandmother as hard as she could without doing any damage.

"Is that a yes?" Freeda asked.

"Unequivocally!"

"Good. Then go into the other room and play with your son. I know you'll find the right time and way to tell him the great news."

"Tell me what great news?" Gregg said from the kitchen doorway.

"Your mommy just notified me..."

Teri looked on in horror thinking her gran was about to drop the news herself.

"... that we get to have apple turnovers and ice cream tonight," Freeda finished.

Gregg's eyes widened to saucer size.

"Thanks, Mommy!" he said as he ran up to Teri and hugged her legs.

CHAPTER 31

Mason met up with the forensic security consultant at eight o'clock the following morning. He'd scheduled it that early so that he could still get to work before too much of the day had gone. Thankfully, he'd been wary enough of morning traffic to leave Beachwood Canyon at seven, just in case there was a problem.

It was LA, so of course there was a problem. There had been a building fire on the corner of Highland and Sunset that had snarled all of Hollywood, north of Santa Monica Boulevard.

Mason had needed the entire hour to reroute himself through the valley, then come over the hill on Laurel Canyon. Even then, traffic was moving at a crawl. During the trip, Mason had time to put together a mental image of what a forensic security consultant would look like.

He had a pretty good idea, having dealt with a myriad of technical experts throughout his time in the force. Whether it was an expert on rope strength or someone with microscopic knowledge of radiation burns, they all seemed to fall into the same visual grouping.

As he finally reached the turn off on Sunset, Mason imagined someone in his fifties or sixties, with greying hair and an academic look, right down to a corduroy jacket with leather patches at the elbow.

Elizabeth McDonald turned out to be in her early thirties and, judging by her tan, spent an inordinate amount of time outdoors. The only thing that looked even a little bit scholarly was that she had tied her blond hair into a ponytail, though even that could have just been how she liked to wear it.

"You look like the photo I saw of you on the news last year," Elizabeth said, as Mason emerged from his Jeep. "I always wondered if I'd run into you."

"Why?" Mason asked, his internal alarm having climbed to DEFCON 3.

"I always thought that you'd been royally screwed and yet had managed to always look like you were able to keep your shit together."

"That was an act," Mason replied.

There was an uncomfortable, at least for Mason, moment of silence.

"Want to see the inside first?" Mason asked as he entered the code for the concealed lockbox and removed the key.

"Sure. I hope this is one of those places that looks like crap from the outside then knocks your socks off."

"You like having your socks knocked off?" Mason asked, then instantly regretted saying something so completely inane. He could feel his face redden and couldn't do much to hide it. He turned away from her and opened the front door, hoping she hadn't noticed his blushing.

As Mason held the door open for her, Elizabeth spoke in a stage whisper.

"Blushing suits you."

Mason overrode the biometric lock on the second door by entering a ten-digit code in a concealed panel, then swung the door open, revealing the escalator with its 'in your face' view of the city.

"Consider my socks fully knocked off," she exclaimed.

Mason gave her the full interior tour. While impressed with everything except the master bedroom, she did admit to finding the whole place lacking in any warmth.

"I like a home to have at least some feel of coziness. This house is like a monument to minimalism. I know that's a thing for the super-rich, but give me a sunken living room and a roaring fire any day."

"Do people still have sunken living rooms?" Mason asked.

"I do," Elizabeth said as she made for the back deck. Once Mason had unlocked the security door, she stepped outside and walked alongside the pool until she was staring out at the city below.

"Whoever built, or at least modified, this house was very security conscious," she commented. "Usually, there would be access front and back, but they made sure there was no obvious ingress points."

"Apparently, the guy who made all these mods was paranoid about a home invasion."

"Not paranoid enough," Elizabeth commented.

"Do you see a way in?"

Elizabeth gave him a wink, then asked if she could see the area below the back of the house. Mason drove her to the street below and pulled up next to the steep incline that rose towards the Harter house.

"See what I mean?" Mason asked. "There's no way to get up to there from here."

Elizabeth parted some of the hillside vegetation and studied the slope and building far above it.

"Let's go back up top," she said as she climbed back into the car. Once back in the cul-de-sac, Elizabeth walked over to her vintage Ford Bronco and retrieved a large, black nylon bag from the cargo area.

"I want to try an experiment. You wait here. I'll just be a few minutes."

Mason exited his car and watched her head towards the house. He suddenly remembered that he was going to have to let her in the security door. Feeling smug, he leaned against the car and waited for her to reappear.

She didn't.

Elizabeth had no trouble remembering the code that Mason had entered upon their initial arrival at the property. Once inside, she made for the deck entering the seven-digit code for that door as well.

She opened the front zipper of her carrier and folded out two hanger hooks. She placed these over the wood railing facing the city, leaving the bag dangling over the drop. Her last chore was to unzip the front of the bag and retrieve a steel ball the size of a large marble. It had been drilled though and fishing line had been poked though the center, then tied in a knot, preventing it from slipping out of the ball. Also protruding from it was a length of bright red ribbon.

Elizabeth then retrieved a slingshot from a side pocket of the bag and placed the metal ball in the leather pocket. She studied the distance and drop to the street below, then calmly pulled the leather pouch as far as she could towards herself. She aimed up at a twenty-degree angle then launched the projectile. Without even waiting to see where it went, Elizabeth exited the house and climbed back inside the car as Mason looked on, perplexed.

"Let's go back to the lower street," Elizabeth suggested.

"How did you get into the house?" Mason asked.

"That's kind of what I do, isn't it. I'll explain when we get down there."

Once Mason was again staring up at the Harter house, Elizabeth studied the hillside until she saw the telltale red streamer just behind some dried vegetation. She parted the bramble-like branches and retrieved the ribbon and steel ball.

"What the hell is that?"

"If I'm right, it will show you one possible entry point to the house."

Mason looked at the fishing line that snaked up the hill and shook his head. "I doubt anyone's going to be able to use that to get up this hill."

Elizabeth smiled back at him, then retrieved a pair of leather work gloves from her jacket pocket. She began pulling the line, wrapping it between her left palm and upper arm. Mason was about to question what she thought she was doing when he saw a black nylon rope emerge from the bag she had attached to the deck railing.

"You'll notice that the rope is knotted every two feet to aid the climber."

Mason stood in silence until the end of the rope was in Elizabeth's hand.

"That's a great trick, but I doubt that anyone sane is going to try and actually climb this hill with nothing but a rope. They'd need some serious equipment."

"You'd be surprised," Elizabeth said as she handed him the fishing line and steel ball. "Race you up there."

Before Mason could say anything, Elizabeth started up the hill. He looked on in shock as she practically sprinted up the steep incline, her gloved hands pulling her up one knot at a time.

Though her climbing was impressive and she might well get up as far as the support girders upon which the deck was mounted, he couldn't see how she could ever scale a seventy foot dead drop just with a knotted rope. As Mason watched, Elizabeth began scaling one of the steel cross beams that rose up from the rocky hillside at a forty-five degree angle.

She began using the cross sections of the support beams as footholds and was already halfway up to the underside of the cantilevered deck.

"Shit," Mason said, as he realized that she could actually beat him to the top. He dropped the metal ball and fishing line then jumped into his car, did a half donut on the narrow road and drove like a maniac. For some reason, something deeply primal made beating Elizabeth a necessity.

He got back to the cul-de-sac in record time. For a brief moment Mason believed that he was in with a chance, then the front door opened and Elizabeth emerged looking none the worse for wear.

"That was impressive, however, I'm not sure that could be duplicated during a party that had extra security everywhere."

"It's not my job to solve your case for you. I'm just supposed to see if access to a property is, in fact, possible. That I've just done. Given time, I could probably find a few more ways to get in, but I think you get the point."

"Do you always find a way in?" Mason asked.

"If I want to get through the defenses badly enough, I will always find a way," she replied as she stared into Mason's eyes.

He wanted desperately to respond with some clever retort, but instead, felt his face begin to redden.

*

271

"I heard through the grapevine that that punk living above your grandparents ended up in ER at the LA Community Hospital last night," Mason said as he walked into their shared office.

"Really?" Teri responded. "What an amazing coincidence that you would end up hearing about something like that."

Mason couldn't fully hide his guilty expression.

"I didn't like the vibe when we were last there," he explained. "I may have put out a few feelers just in case the guy hit our radar."

"That include hospitals?"

"Of course."

Teri tried to look as disinterested as she could while at the same time, feeling a rising concern that he had found out about Emanuel. Though she felt she could trust her new partner with such information, if she was wrong, Mason could cause her some serious trouble. Not so much because of the altercation with Emanuel, but because she hadn't reported it.

"As it happens, once the cops finally arrived to interview him, he insisted he tripped on a curb, tried to stop his fall with his free hand then smashed his chin on the sidewalk."

"They buy that?" Teri asked.

"Why wouldn't they?" Mason replied coyly. "Unless you know something they don't."

Teri could see from his expression that Mason had a pretty good idea how Emanuel got hurt and it didn't involve a curb or a sidewalk.

"Why would I?" she replied, feigning disinterest. "How did things go with the security guy?"

"It was a woman, and she gave a very convincing demonstration that the house is not impregnable. I now have to work out if that means anything to our case."

"What do you mean?"

"She managed to climb that hill at the back and used the codes to get through the security door off the deck."

"That's good, isn't it?" Teri asked.

"It showed that it could be done, however, while a mountain goat might be able to do it, the question remains: why would anyone do that just to kill Phyliss Brimmer? Besides, the woman today had to use a shit load of climbing rope and hanging brackets. I think someone would have noticed such props after either murder."

"Did you just refer to her as a mountain goat?" Teri asked, smiling.

"Not in a physical sense. She was actually kind of attractive."

"Did you ask her out?"

"I'm not that interested."

"Then why the hell are you blushing, you big dork?"

"I'm a homicide detective," he replied in an extra deep voice. "We don't blush."

Teri rolled her eyes.

"What did I miss here?" Mason asked.

"Not much. Harddick and Simpleton are doing a second round of interviews with the guests from the Tamacini party, but so far nobody is willing to break the NDA."

"I was thinking, why don't I stop by the Tamacini house and talk to that butler again? After that, I thought maybe I would swing by the Brimmer place, just in case someone happens to be there."

"You do know that you could send a patrol car to check out if anyone's at home?"

"I know," Mason replied. "I'm just getting weird vibes about her and Leticia and what was really going on. If someone does show up at that house, it should be one of us who speaks to them first."

"Okay. I'm ready go as soon as you are."

"I need to make a stop," Mason replied.

"No problem. We can do that on the way."

"I kinda need to make the stop alone."

"Sounds intriguing. What's up?"

"I need to swing by my house before ten o'clock. There's a little matter I need to attend to."

"It's more than that," Teri stated already knowing when her partner was holding something back.

Mason wouldn't normally consider sharing any part of his private life with a fellow cop, but he was starting to think that Teri could be trusted not to throw any part of it back in his face. He briefly told her about Wolfy and the note he'd received the previous evening.

"I'm surprised you didn't kill the guy," she said, shaking her head in disgust.

"I probably would have, but I don't know which neighbor it came from. That's why I want to swing by the house. The mailman gets there between ten and ten fifteen and I want to check the mailboxes before he arrives, to see if they have any outgoing letters."

"Hoping to match the handwriting?" Teri asked.

Mason shrugged. "It's a start."

"What if the perp prints his envelopes?"

"I'm working on the assumption that if he's fool enough to send me a handwritten note, that's probably his jam. Most likely someone who likes to do things old school."

"What will you do if you find him?"

"I was thinking of tempting him out into the open with some food scraps, then shooting his head off," Mason said, straight-faced.

"That's great for a fantasy. What's going to be the reality?" Teri asked.

"I don't know, but I do believe in proportional responses."

"Isn't that the term for retaliatory acts of war?"

"It sure as hell is."

"I hate to point this out, but I have a feeling that taking a human life because someone else took a coyote off the map is not going to sit well with the DA's office."

"I know that," Mason replied. "It's going to take some creative thinking."

"Just don't fuck up the career you just got back."

"I plan not to."

"Good. You go off and do what you have to do, and I'll hold down the fort here," Teri offered. "Silly question, but why did you bother coming in, just to head right out again?"

"I only came up with the master plan a few minutes ago."

"Fair enough," Teri replied, smiling. "Good luck."

"Thanks. Try not to rough anybody up while I'm gone," Mason said with a wink, before exiting the office.

Once on the road and without Teri there to object, Mason turned on his favorite country music station and momentarily lost himself in Brad Paisley's impeccable guitar work.

As the morning rush hour was finished and the traffic jams had partially subsided, Mason jumped on the 101 freeway and then took the Gower exit. Once on Beachwood Canyon Drive, he slowed down and paid close attention to which mailboxes had their red flag in the up position, thereby letting the mailman know that there was something to be collected.

What with texts, email and the ability to buy and sell just about anything online, mail collection was used far more sparingly than a decade or so earlier. There were only seven flags in the up position and Mason ruled out four of those for being too far down the hill.

Once in his house, Mason grabbed an envelope and stuck a couple of food delivery menus into it then addressed it to Teri at work and slapped on a couple of stamps. With envelope in hand, Mason sauntered casually out of the cul-de-sac and walked to a brick fronted Tudor style house. He rang the doorbell and after getting no response, opened their mailbox flap and saw a single manilla envelope with a typed label. He quickly checked to see if there was a handwritten return address on the back, but there was none.

The second house with its flag up was across the street. It was a concrete square with oversized tinted windows and as much charm as a toothache. Mason was mildly concerned when he saw that the property had a Ring camera doorbell.

He pressed it and heard the distinctive electronically sampled tones and waited. Moments later a disembodied voice came out of an invisible speaker.

"Yes?" a woman asked in a clipped tone.

"I'm sorry to disturb you, but I don't have a mailbox yet as I just moved in and was wondering, as you've got your flag up, if I could put my letter in with yours?" Mason asked, holding up his envelope to the camera lens.

"Sure. Why not?"

"Thank you," he replied, without any idea if the woman was still even listening or was in fact anywhere near the house.

Mason opened her matt-black mailbox and saw a couple of white envelopes with handwritten addresses. He had memorized the writing from the threatening notes and could tell immediately that the lettering in front of him wasn't even close. Just in case the Ring camera was still capturing his actions, Mason added his prop letter to the others awaiting collection.

The last house was actually in the cul-de-sac. It was the one with the blue tarps covering the area where the roof should have been. Even before Mason reached the front of the house, he could hear the sound of hammering coming from somewhere out back. As the owner was doing all the work almost single-handedly, and the banging was happening at the rear of the property, it wasn't that big a leap of faith to assume that he was unlikely to see or hear Mason as he took a quick peek in his mailbox.

With the sound of banging still filling the air, Mason flipped down the lid and looked inside. He immediately felt his guts turn to ice. There was only one letter, and it was addressed to the *Los Angeles Times*. The handwriting was unmistakable. It was a perfect match to the writing on the back of the photo of Wolfy.

Mason closed the lid and smiled as he headed back to his home. There was something satisfying about identifying a perp. As a cop, it signaled the beginning of the end of an investigation.

As a hunter, it clearly revealed the prey.

Content with the knowledge that he now knew who had killed Wolfy, Mason drove to Franklin, then dropped down to Hollywood Boulevard as he made his way west. He wound his way down to Sunset, then up into the Trousdale Estates. Groves answered the door immediately and didn't seem the least bit surprised to see him.

"I still can't tell you anything more about the entertainment without risking a lawsuit," he said, once he'd

278

settled Mason in the kitchen with a mug of French roast in front of him. "Especially now since Tamacini is gone, as is my current employment."

"I was wondering about that," Mason commented.

"I got a call last night from London. One of his kids basically told me that my services would no longer be needed. I can stay here till Saturday at noon, at which point an extensive inventory will be carried out. Once that's done, I will have to immediately leave the property. I got the distinct impression that the heirs are worried that I might abscond with the family silver."

"Is there any family silver?" Mason asked, trying to make light of the situation.

"Not in this house. Ever since it became a trend to rob celebrity homes in the Hollywood Hills, the maestro had me ship most of his valuable possessions to the London home."

"How long were you with him?"

"Just gone twenty-five years," Groves replied.

"God. That's almost a marriage."

"I don't believe that one can receive what basically amounts to an eviction notice in a marriage."

"I got one," Mason corrected him.

Groves nodded. "I presume that was because of your little career hiccup?" Groves asked.

Mason laughed. "That would be correct. So, where will you go?"

"I'm not sure. Thankfully, the maestro paid me well and with my having been a live-in staff member, lodging and food was included and I managed to save up a decent nest egg. The problem is that I'm not sure where I want to live."

"Won't you look for another job?"

"I don't think so. After that long with the same employer, especially at my age, I don't think I could train another boss."

While Mason took a few sips of coffee, Groves studied him.

"I wish I could tell you more about the man and the performance."

"We've learned a few things since we last talked. His real name was Carlos Quinn."

Groves looked puzzled. "That's not the name that he used here."

"We know. He used a different pseudonym at every performance."

"I remember, but why would he do that?"

"When we find him, hopefully he'll tell us," Mason replied. "The reason I came back to speak with you is that another person has died."

"And you suspect this Quinn character?" Groves asked.

"Let's put it this way; wherever he seems to have performed, someone dies shortly afterwards."

"Where was this last event?"

"Actually, there wasn't a party, however, it did occur where one of the unsolved murders took place in 2007 after a party he did perform at."

"When we spoke before, you seemed pretty certain that the performer had left all the previous sites well before each death," Groves pointed out.

Mason scratched his head. "That still appears to be the case. You yourself saw him leave here when the maestro was still alive.

"I did. He had one of those oversized SUVs and a driver. Somehow, they got blocked in by the valets and Quinn raised quite a ruckus."

"So, he was in a hurry to leave?" Mason asked.

"I don't know. It's possible he just likes causing a fuss to get some attention."

"Let me ask you a question from a different angle. Was there anything about Carlos Quinn or his performance that could have played a part in the maestro's death?"

"At the time, I would have said, no, however, since being asked about the show and the performer, questions I wasn't permitted to answer, the idea of Quinn's involvement has kept me awake. I would now have to say that, though highly unlikely, he could have unknowingly been the cause of what occurred."

"It would make a huge difference if we knew exactly what the man did, or does, at these parties."

"I'll tell you what I can do," Groves replied. "Once you've located him and if he is formally charged, I believe the NDA ceases to be legally binding, and I will therefore answer all your questions."

"You do realize that by answering the questions now, it could greatly increase our chances of finding him and possibly even save a life?"

"I understand that, but again, I have to protect myself."

*

Once at the Junction of Foothill and Sunset, Mason debated whether to blow off the idea of stopping by Phyliss' house and head back to the office. He had little expectation of anyone being there, but that little voice that always seemed to keep him going in the right direction was telling him to keep trying.

Considering he was only ten minutes from North Camden Drive and probably an hour from work, he chose to have one last crack at checking the place out. After that, he'd request a daily drive by from the Beverly Hills police and leave it at that.

Mason parked a block from the house and walked the rest of the way. Despite his assigned car being considered unmarked, and therefore indistinguishable from the millions of others in LA, it wasn't. Anyone who still had enough brain cells to chew gum and walk at the same time knew full well that a black Ford Crown Victoria with black hubcaps and a light strip built into the rearview mirror was a cop car.

Once Mason reached the property, he was surprised to see a black Chevy Suburban parked in the forecourt. As he got closer, Mason could see a that there was someone on the far side of the vehicle, wiping down an area that had at some point been targeted by what must have been a sizeable bird. In Mason's mind, only a professional driver would go to that much trouble in the middle of the day. And from his casual clothing, Mason took a guess that he and his vehicle were on the clock for Uber.

The man didn't seem the least bit fazed at seeing Mason eyeing him from the sidewalk and even offered him a half-hearted salute.

Mason walked the long way around the property line so as not to be in direct line of sight from the street-facing windows. He made it to the front door unseen and noticed that it had been left ajar. Even before he could reach for the doorbell, he heard the sound of hard-soled shoes on a tiled floor.

The door opened wide, and a man appeared with a handful of assorted mail.

Mason was momentarily stunned. Though the man's hair was shorter and his face a little leaner, there was no doubt who he was.

Before the man could even react, Mason spoke.

"Carlos Quinn, I am placing you under arrest."

CHAPTER 32

Two hours later, Quinn was sitting across from Teri and Mason in an interview room only two doors down from their office.

"You sure you don't want something to drink. Coffee? Water?" Teri offered.

Quinn just stared back at her without speaking. In fact, during the arrest, the trip back to the station and the first thirty minutes in the interview room, he hadn't said a word.

"We can do this all day," Mason stated. "Why don't you just tell us why you happened to be at four different murder sites and changed your name for each event?"

It was Mason's turn to get the creepy stare.

"I don't understand why you don't want to talk to us. If you can satisfy our curiosity that you were not involved in the deaths, you can go," Teri explained. "At this point, we just want information. You having forced your hosts, their guests and their staff to sign nondisclosure agreements has greatly hampered our ability to investigate the unsolved cases, as well as the latest one in Trousdale."

284

Quinn blinked twice, then looked from Teri to Mason.

"When you arrested me, you said there were six murders?" Quinn asked, finally breaking his silence. "Just now you only mentioned the four parties you claim I attended."

"The fifth one didn't involve a party, however, it did take place at the same house where you performed in 2007 for Cynthia Harter. Victim number one," Mason replied.

Quinn looked well and truly shocked.

"Who was killed?"

"A woman by the name of Phyliss Brimmer."

Quinn's body sagged and his head fell forward. "Was... was Leticia there?" he managed to ask.

"She was," Teri replied, surprised at the man's reaction.

"Is she... alive?" Quinn asked in barely a whisper.

"She is," Mason answered.

Quinn looked up. His eyes were red-rimmed, and his face had gone pale.

"You obviously know both women," Teri said. "Maybe it's time to tell us how you knew them, and what exactly you did at the parties."

"If you wish me to divulge details like that, I will have to ask you to sign a—"

"Don't even think about asking us to sign one of your NDA's."

"Then that's that," Quinn said, as he crossed his arms and looked defiantly back at the two detectives.

"Are you refusing to answer our questions?" Teri asked.

Quinn looked down at the scarred surface of the metal table.

"Mr. Quinn?" Teri said, the frustration obvious in her voice.

"You said Leticia is alive. May I speak with her?"

"Not at this time," Mason replied.

"What does 'not at this time' mean?" Quinn asked.

Mason looked towards Teri to get her read on the situation.

"What is your relationship with Ms. Gold?" Teri asked.

"She's my wife... she *was* my wife. We're still close."

"We believe that she witnessed the death of Ms. Brimmer and subsequently had a mental breakdown as a result. She's at UCLA, in the neurology center."

Mason and Teri both expected to see a degree of concern or even sadness. Quinn however, started hyperventilating, while at the same time, his eyes darted around the small room as if looking for some means of escape.

"Mr. Quinn," Mason leaned forward across the table. "Please try and relax. She's in good care."

Quinn hung his head as he shook it from side to side.

"We need to know if you have recently been to the house on Cardwell Place. The same house where you gave a performance for Ms. Harter in 2007."

"I haven't been near that place in over sixteen years," Quinn replied.

"Do you have any idea what Ms. Gold and Ms. Brimmer were doing at the house?" Teri asked.

Quinn sat motionless for almost thirty seconds.

"I know exactly what they were doing there," he replied without raising his head.

"Can you tell us?" Mason asked, as he sat back in his chair, trying to appear relaxed even though adrenalin was surging through his system.

"Maybe I should talk to a lawyer," Quinn mused.

"Before you make that decision, after your lawyer gets involved, questioning becomes much more formal. Please, before you decide, have a look at these pictures."

Having discussed the idea ahead of time, Teri placed her iPad on the table and scrolled to a specific crime scene photo. It was a shot taken inside the master bedroom at the Harter house. Phyliss' body was in the foreground; her head lay on its side a few feet away.

The color drained from Quinn's face the instant he saw the screen.

"Is that—" was all he could say.

"That's how Ms. Brimmer was found. You can understand why her death had such a devastating effect on your ex-wife," Teri advised. "What concerns us most is that the scene isn't that different from this one."

Teri swiped the screen and a photo from the Harter murder scene almost sixteen years earlier appeared. Though coincidental, the CSI who took the photo had managed to use roughly the same angle with Ginetto's body and head separated from each other, yet have both in the same shot.

"Don't you think it's time to explain how you are connected to not just these two homicides but the other three as well?"

Quinn lowered his head again, but remained silent.

Mason again leaned forward.

"Carlos. Look at me."

Quinn lifted his head and met Mason's gaze.

"Did you kill these people?"

Even though he was clearly badly shaken, he managed to say, "No."

"Did you arrange to have these people killed?"

"No. Of course not."

"Were you involved in any way with the death of Phyliss Brimmer, Pamela Whitlough, Harry Groppel, Cynthia Harter, Pietro Ginetto or Gilberto Tamacini?" Mason asked.

Quinn used his unchained hand to rub his face almost as if he was trying to wear away his skin.

"Please answer the question," Mason prompted.

"I think I will need my lawyer now," Quinn said as he finally dropped his hand away from his face.

"Here," Mason said handing Quinn his cell phone.

"Can I ask you one last question before your lawyer gets involved?" Mason asked.

"What?"

"Whatever it is that's going on – will other people die as a result of something you've either done or instigated?"

Quinn looked across the table with an expression of defeat.

"Possibly."

As Teri and Mason rose to leave the room, Quinn spoke with his eyes shut.

"May I ask a favor?"

"You've not exactly done any for us," Teri pointed out. "We work on a quid pro quo system here. You help us, we help you."

"I'm not asking for help for me. I just want to make sure that Leticia is safe."

"She's in a psychiatric emergency center in UCLA. I don't see how much safer she can be," Mason observed.

Teri read something else in his face.

"What is it that she needs to be protected from? Is there someone still out there who plans to kill her?

"Not a someone," Quinn said, as he opened his eyes. "Something."

*

Quinn wouldn't say anything else until his lawyer arrived two hours later. Mason felt his heart sink the moment he saw her. Anita Bayliss was well known within the department. If you were guilty of any serious crime, she was the one you wanted in your corner. Your guilt or innocence was irrelevant, so long as you were capable of paying her exorbitant fees.

Bayliss was tall anyway, yet always wore red-soled, five-inch stiletto heels, enabling her to look down on just about anyone. That day, just like any other, she wore a dark grey suit that probably cost more that Mason and Teri's monthly salary combined.

After less than an hour conferring with her client, she asked to meet with Mason, Teri and Andrew Bernstein, one of the new breed of assistant district attorneys that preferred to negotiate deals rather than raise the department's visibility in open court. He and Bayliss had managed to reach more pre-trial deals than anyone from the DA's office could remember.

They met in the captain's small conference room, which was initially intended to be an office, but having no windows and a constant, yet inexplicable, smell of wet cat, it became a space for any meeting that required something a little grander than the bullpen or interview rooms.

"My client wants to trade information for leniency," Bayliss said without preamble.

"Define leniency?" Bernstein asked.

"No jail time," she answered.

"You do realize that we do not yet even know exactly what he has done," Bernstein pointed out.

"Then he should be released," she shot back with a smile.

"However, it does appear that he has been involved, in some way, with at least five murders," the DA continued intentionally leaving out murder number six; Phyliss Brimmer.

"Yet you can't prove that he was anywhere near any of the crime scenes at the time of those deaths. Come on,

Andrew. You know what I can do with this case. Let's find a compromise that works for both of us."

"I'm not sure if that's possible before we know exactly what part he played in all of this. He may not have been at the locations at the time of the murders, but he was certainly there prior to each one. Not only that, but was evading being questioned by changing his name."

"Lots of successful people change their names."

"Not right before a performance at which people died."

Bayliss studied Bernstein for a few moments.

"What if we could structure some sort of deal contingent on proving that my client had nothing directly to do with any of the murders?" she suggested. "That way, if you can actually tie him directly to any of the crimes, the deal becomes null and void."

Bernstein looked to be pondering the offer.

"You've got to be kidding!" Mason said, frustration oozing from every pore. "Six murders and Quinn is tied to every single one. I don't see how he wasn't involved."

"I said, directly involved," Bayliss pointed out. "Say a guy working for Hertz rented a car to someone who, later that day, intentionally runs over his wife. Is the Hertz employee guilty? No, of course not."

"This is about far more than a rental car," Teri said, shaking her head.

"Is it?" Bayliss replied. "The fact is that you have no idea what my client did or didn't do. That's my point. Once you know his involvement and that he was not culpable in any of the crimes, it really is the Hertz rental scenario."

"You know as well as I do," Bernstein jumped in. "that the DA isn't going to enter into any agreement without detailed specificity. So far, you are bargaining for leniency with nothing more than a theoretic promise of your client's innocence. Considering that, if his innocence is confirmed, charges would be dropped anyway, I'm not sure I even understand what it is that you're offering."

"Let me make it a little clearer," Bayliss said, feigning surprise that the DA wasn't able to grasp the simplicity of her deal. "My client will explain in great detail why he was at each of the crime scenes, what occurred and why he bears no direct responsibility for what happened next. In effect, he will enable you to close all five cases, in exchange for something along the lines of manslaughter two with three years' probation."

"And if we find that his actions directly led to the deaths?" Bernstein asked.

"Then the deal's off."

"Then what?" Mason asked.

"Then his fate is in the hands of a jury."

"I don't feel comfortable with this," Bernstein said. "So far, your client has not been formally charged with anything. He is here—"

"Unwillingly," Bayliss added.

"He is here for questioning. For your deal to make any sense at all, Quinn would have to be charged with the crimes, something that we have not yet done as we don't know what his involvement even was. Let me give you a counter suggestion. You have your client talk to these detectives and tell them what all the secrecy has been about and why he was at each location. We know he put on a show, but we need to have specifics about what he did, why everyone involved with the parties had to sign NDAs and why the last murder occurred in a property he hadn't even been to in over fifteen years. When he does that, we will be able to gauge whether he is, in fact, guilty of anything, and if so, whether it is to our benefit to plea bargain with you."

"Mr. Quinn was hoping for some sort of deal prior to saying anything else."

"But why? I don't see any benefit?"

"To be honest, Neither do I," Bayliss said with a shrug. "But my client wants the deal in place first."

"I bet he does," Mason said.

"Tell your client that we are receptive to making a deal, just not one based on smoke and mirrors. Give us the facts and we'll see what we can do," Bernstein said.

"He won't be happy about that," Bayliss said as she started to get to her feet.

"Then tell him option two is that we will have no choice but to formally charge him with all six murders."

"According to my client, it's five murders, and how exactly does that help if he's innocent?"

"We don't know that he's innocent. As far as we're concerned, we would be keeping a possible serial killer off the streets until we can sort all this out."

Even through her spray-on tan and carefully layered make-up, they all saw her cheeks redden.

"I will have to discuss this with my client."

"Good luck," Mason said, smiling.

CHAPTER 33

Russell McNeil drove from his office in Beverly Hills to St Cloud Road in Bel Air. Normally, he wouldn't have minded sharing commission on a listing of that size, but he'd only just found out that he was the designated hitter within Pure Gold Realty while Leticia was having a small 'procedure' at UCLA.

At thirty-eight, Russell was already considered one of the top earners at the brokerage. At just over six feet, a devoted marathon runner and with a passing resemblance to a younger Harrison Ford, he was well liked by all his clients, who in turn passed along their recommendation to friends who, in turn, brought in even more commission.

Neither he nor Michael Ellis, the co-owner and broker of record, knew that the small procedure was in fact Leticia recovering from a mental breakdown. They'd been contacted by Dr Lafontaine who advised that Leticia would not be able to return to work for a few weeks, and suggested that they make plans to service her clients until then. In addition, she advised that Leticia was not accepting visitors until further notice.

Once he'd disconnected the call, Ellis made up his mind that Russell McNeil was the obvious choice to take over Leticia's clients while she was otherwise engaged. He was almost as good a salesperson as Leticia and knew how to work with the ultra-rich. Though Ellis would never say so out loud, he believed that Russell deserved a share of Leticia's commissions as payback for her having stolen two, multi-million-dollar listings right out from under him in that fiscal year alone.

Russell profiting from her vanity surgery was, in Ellis' mind, just deserts.

Russell drove up to the vine-covered property and marveled, at just how stunningly beautiful the house looked. 'A slice of Old England' was how Leticia had promoted the listing. He agreed but had always felt that there should have been a second line. It could have read 'A slice of Old England, tucked away high above the chaos of Los Angeles'.

He parked his Lincoln Navigator away from the front entry so that the prospective buyer would have an uninterrupted view of the house and property. Russell checked his watch and confirmed that he had over an hour until the client would arrive. That gave him time to stage the house so that it looked as if the owner had just stepped away for a moment. Nothing killed a sale like an uncared-for home. Even though the current owner had vacated less than a month ago, it would still need some TLC to give it the feel of a lavish, yet inviting, property offered for sale at thirty-five million dollars.

It was the first time Russell had been to the house by himself, and it took a few minutes to formally orient himself to the layout. Once upstairs, he checked out all the secondary bedrooms first. Apart from a little dust and the need to let in some fresh air, they all looked as they should.

As Russell moved to the VIP guest suite, the first thing that hit him was the cold. The windows were all shut, yet an icy thread of air could be felt nipping at his ankles. The second thing was the smell. It had only been a week since Leticia had shown the property, but the room reeked not just of stale air, but of something far more invasive and dank.

Russell drew the heavy curtains and opened the room's two windows, hoping that the air would clear before the viewing. With sunlight flooding into the room like a couple of Klieg lights, he went into the bathroom to make sure all was show ready.

He checked the water pressure of the sinks, the shower and the bath. When he lifted the toilet seat to make sure there was no tide mark from sitting water, Russell stumbled backwards. The smell of decomposing flesh, coupled with the sight of what appeared to be a dead skunk, half submerged in a stew of water and bodily fluids, was a complete sensory overload.

Russell managed to get his gag reflex under control and stumbled down to the kitchen where, under the sink, he found a supply of Hefty garbage bags as well as an unopened pack of rubber, dish-washing gloves. Dreading the task ahead of him, he ran back up the stairs.

As he rounded the corner of the landing, he saw that the VIP bedroom door was closed, though he was positive he'd left it open so that the room could get some fresh air flowing.

Russell tried the handle, but it wouldn't turn. He tried using both hands, but with no success. After wasting a few more minutes trying to get it open, he ran back down to the kitchen where he'd seen a few basic tools under the sink.

With screwdriver and pliers in hand, Russell returned to the door and knelt down by the handle plate. He had just fitted the Phillips screwdriver into the screw head when the door opened on its own.

Russell was so surprised that he failed to immediately notice that the room was again in total darkness. The curtains were drawn, and the same icy whisper of air was slaloming between his legs.

Russell got to his feet and sensed, rather than saw, that someone else was in the room.

"Hello," Russell called out. "I'm the realtor for this house. I'm here for a showing."

His words were met with dead silence.

"I was told that the house was vacant," Russell added.

There was again, no response.

There was something about the low ceilings and small windows that gave the place a vintage creepiness that he normally quite liked, but that day Russell was feeling the full force of the property's character.

Knowing that the client was on his way, Russell knew that he had a limited amount of time to air the room again and clear out the small corpse from the toilet. He stepped towards the bedroom, then felt something heavy envelop him. It was as if he'd somehow fallen into a vat of moist earth which refused to allow him to move any part of his body except his head.

Even though he could clearly see that his body was not in any way surrounded by anything, he couldn't even seem to raise a finger.

Unable to move and alone in the house, Russell couldn't think of anything else to do but yell, hoping that someone would eventually hear him.

He had just opened his mouth when he felt whatever it was that was enclosing him tighten around his chest. Russell suddenly couldn't seem to catch his breath. The tightening continued until he felt something else within his bondage. It was moving from his waist up his stomach, eventually stopping at his sternum. Whatever it was hesitated for a moment, then, without warning, began to frantically claw at Russell's chest.

Unable to scream or even move, he began to feel pain. At first it was sharp, as if his flesh was being torn open, but then as the invader slowly encircled his heart, the pain turned to white hot agony.

The last thing Russell saw were two eyes staring back at him from the darkened bedroom. Even through the veil of pain-induced delirium, he knew that they didn't belong to anything human.

CHAPTER 34

Mason and Teri were killing time while waiting for word from Quinn's lawyer about whether her client was going to talk or not. As they reviewed the few witnesses who had provided minimal snippets of information about Quinn and his show, one of the loaner officers who'd been assigned to the task force stuck his head into their office.

"You mentioned wanting us to keep alert for any new deaths that could be related to these cases. Would an attack at one of the murder houses count?"

"Who was attacked?" Teri asked.

"A real estate agent by the name of Russell McNeil. He was found by a prospective client at the Groppel house in Bel Air."

"Is he alive?" Mason asked.

"Just. He's been taken to the UCLA emergency room. Apparently, he had a heart attack," the officer stated.

"How old is he?" Mason asked, as an icy chill ran down his back. Groppel had died of a suspected heart attack, even

301

though the autopsy revealed the organ as having exploded rather than there having been a blockage or rupture.

"Thirty-eight, and in what otherwise would have seemed perfect health. The guy runs marathons."

"Is he awake?" Teri asked.

"Yes, but sedated. The nurse said that he was probably going to make it and that she would give me a call when he's stabilized."

Once the officer was gone, Mason looked over the top of his computer monitor at Teri. "This is getting weirder by the minute."

"I just hope Quinn chooses to talk or else we'll still be swinging at nothing but air," Teri replied.

There was a gentle knock on the door.

"Come," Mason shouted back, loudly enough for his voice to go through the sound dampening padding that was glued to their side of it.

Bayliss stepped in and looked at the room with mild amusement. It was the first time she'd seen the converted space.

"Which one of you is being punished?" she asked, smiling.

"We thought having a private office was a reward," Teri shot back.

Bayliss eyed the wires hanging out of the glassless annex and only just managed to not laugh.

"What news from your client?" Mason asked.

"He still wants to make a deal, but it's the one that's already been rejected."

"He can't possibly believe that the district attorney would cut any sort of deal without hearing what he has to say first."

"He thinks his terms are fair."

"What do you think?" Teri asked.

"I think that as his lawyer, I have to follow his instructions."

"Understood," Mason said, reading between the widely spaced lines. "You know what comes next?"

Bayliss nodded.

Mason nodded at Teri, and both got to their feet. Bayliss stepped aside as the detectives walked down to the interview room where an officer had been stationed outside the door.

Mason walked in first and held the door open for Teri and Bayliss.

"This looks ominous," Quinn said, as he saw the hardened expressions on the two detectives.

"Please stand," Mason said.

As Quinn got to his feet, Mason spoke.

"Carlos Quinn, you are being formally charged for the murders of…"

As he recited the names of the old and more recent murders, Mason saw the other man's resolve melt away.

"Perhaps, if we talked a little more about—" Quinn suggested, before Mason interrupted.

"You have the right to remain—" Mason began the Miranda recitation.

"As council is already present and have explained his rights, Mr. Quinn will waive hearing them again," Bayliss stated for the record.

"Mr. Quinn," Mason continued, "you will now be formally booked and then held until further notice. Your lawyer will explain the process in more detail. Detective Grey will stay with you during the booking. I, however, have to meet with a witness to your last performance. At least, the last one we are aware of."

"Good luck with that," Quinn said, shaking his head. "If they were at one of my events, then they have signed a bulletproof nondisclosure agreement. They won't tell you a thing."

"That's the one problem with those contracts. Any contract, in fact. One of the few things that can nullify any such agreement is if either party is using the contract for an illegal purpose."

"I never committed any crime," Quinn insisted.

"That's the funny part," Mason said, grinning. "You've just been charged with murder, and by using your NDA to avoid detection and questioning by the police, it makes the NDA unenforceable. My guess is that once word gets out that your precious NDA isn't worth the paper it was printed on, we will have a long queue of party guests vying to tell us what went on at each event."

Quinn turned to Bayliss hoping she would interject something that would negate the detective's premise.

"He's right," she said. "I did tell you that earlier. Twice, in fact."

"Your best option at this point is to start talking to us," Mason advised. "If, as you've repeatedly told us, you had

304

nothing to do with these murders, the charges will be dropped."

Quinn simply stared up at him, his face a mask of fear and confusion, then lowered his gaze without saying a word. Mason shook his head and left the interview room. Bayliss stepped out with him.

"I don't see you jumping to the defense of your client," he said matter-of-factly. "Usually by now you would have accused us of fifty different legal infractions just by having brought him in for questioning."

"You noticed that, huh? The fact is, I was forced to take him on as a client. Judge Walker called me personally and told me that it was at the request of the court that I was to provide legal counsel. I told him that I felt I should recuse myself, but apparently no other lawyer wanted to touch the case."

"Why did you want to be recused?" Mason asked. "You've defended countless murder suspects."

"This one was different."

"How so?"

"Cynthia Harter was a friend of the family," Bayliss replied.

"Good reason," Mason agreed.

"Not good enough, apparently."

The two stood in the hall for a moment without speaking.

"I hear you're going to reinterview the party guests," Bayliss commented.

"That's our intention."

Before Bayliss could respond, a young officer came charging down the hallway.

"Detective Darby! Everybody's been trying to call you."

"We left our phones in the office. What's up?"

"Leticia Gold. She's dead."

Mason was momentarily stunned by the news, however, when he faced Bayliss, she had turned deathly white and was staring at Mason with a look of complete shock.

"That's another one to add to your client's list," he said in a lowered tone.

Mason then returned to the interview room and signaled for Teri to come with him. He then told the officer assigned to guard the door that he was to return the prisoner to the holding cell.

"What the hell is going on?" Teri asked.

"Leticia Gold is dead."

"How? Why?"

"I don't know. I just heard, but we need to find out."

"Was Gold killed or... what?" Teri asked, just as the officer opened the interview room door.

There was no doubt, judging from Quinn's expression, that he heard what Teri had just said.

He stared wide-eyed from one to the other, then dropped his head and began sobbing uncontrollably.

CHAPTER 35

The drive to UCLA took a third the time with the siren and strip lights on. Mason had stayed on Sunset until Beverly Glen, then headed south and wound his way through the residential streets so he could emerge close to the hospital complex.

As he sped past the plethora of mixed architecture, he couldn't help picking up the neighborhood vibe of comfortable affluence and perceived safety. Mason could never get his head around how these pockets of hoped-for seclusion and security were less than a few miles from raging gang wars. For some reason, having ADT install a deluxe alarm system gave the homeowners a feeling of relative invincibility.

What Mason knew from experience was that, if at some point, any one of these homes became specifically targeted, nothing was going to stop unlawful entry unless the occupant were better armed than the intruders, which was also a possibility in LA.

Even though he'd been to the same hospital only a few days earlier, Mason still managed to get turned around while surrounded by dozens of almost identical hospital buildings that made up the UCLA Medical Center.

Once he had finally parked and retraced his steps to the correct wing, Mason saw two uniformed officers standing on either side of what had been, until only a few hours earlier, Leticia Gold's private room. As he asked the nurses and doctor for their version of what had happened, they all relayed the same details.

Leticia had managed, through sheer determination, to wrap numerous tubes and wires that had been attached to monitors and drips around her neck then rolled herself out the bed. It was certainly not the most common method of hanging oneself, but it had done the trick.

After less than an hour of talking to the staff and responding officers, Mason knew that he was no longer needed. There was no crime scene, just a sterile hospital room where Leticia had decided to do a more permanent job of memory removal.

Mason hung on until the West Los Angeles coroner had deemed the death to have been self-inflicted before leaving. As he made his way through the labyrinth of neutral, beige-colored corridors, he saw Dr Lafontaine heading the other way, seemingly oblivious to the goings-on in his ex-patient's room. Mason knew he should just leave, but there was something about the presumptuous quack that had gotten under his skin the first time they'd met shortly after Leticia had been placed in his care.

As LaFontaine rushed past him, Mason whispered, just loudly enough for the man to hear, "I can see why you didn't want us around. You've done a bang-up job of looking after her."

LaFontaine stumbled and turned to confront Mason, but the detective had reached the end of the hallway and joined a throng of young trainee doctors as they tried to keep up with their medical instructor.

Feeling an unexpected sense of pleasure after goading the doctor, Mason decided that, while within UCLA's gargantuan medical facility, he might as well check in on the recently admitted real estate agent. It took a ludicrous amount of time to go from the psych hospital to the ER. At one point, a nurse he'd stopped between buildings had told him that she wasn't even sure that he could actually get to the ER from where they were.

Mason personally felt that any complex that gets to a size where you physically can't get to A from B has exceeded its practical envelope.

Finally, he caught sight of an ambulance turning behind a glass and steel tower. He followed its path and saw the emergency room entrance. He started to walk through the oversized sliding doors, when an officious security guard started to tell him that he couldn't come in that way.

After the battle to reach it, Mason had a strong urge to bark back at the guy, but instead, showed him his badge and was let in. Like all emergency rooms in Los Angeles, business was booming. Between the violence, the drugs and the city's adoration of overpowered cars and trucks, there was no shortage of mangled citizenry needing urgent attention.

Mason was kept waiting almost twenty minutes before a young looking doctor located him and led Mason away from the waiting hordes.

"You're timing is excellent," she said. "He's conscious and alert."

"Isn't that a little unusual after a heart attack?" Mason asked.

"His heart's fine. Whatever happened to him, it wasn't a heart attack. The symptoms were similar, but, in his case, the heart was actually bruised."

"How the hell does that happen?" Mason asked.

The doctor rubbed her glasses clean on the end of her white coat. "I've only ever seen something like it after a catastrophic chest injury, but in this patient's case there was no external trauma. It was as if something inside him was trying to crush his heart."

"But you have no idea what caused the bruising?" Mason asked, clearly confused by the doctor's last statement.

"Not a clue. There was no exterior trauma whatsoever. The good news is that there doesn't appear to have been any lasting damage to the organ itself, though, I should however warn you that Mr. McNeil's mental state is of some concern."

"How so?"

"I'll let you be the judge of that," the doctor said as she led Mason through the chaos of the ER area and into the relative calm of the intensive care unit.

With an aural background track of ventilators, monitors and gentle moaning, Mason was led to an area where the patients had private rooms while still in the ICU environment.

"Please try to make it as brief as possible. He may not be dying but he has most certainly just undergone a serious life event."

As Mason approached the bed, his first thought, even without knowing the guy, was how well McNeil looked, considering where he was. In fact, his skin was overly rubicund and his eyes, bright and focused.

"Don't be fooled by my rosy complexion. It's the oxygen. In reality, I feel like shit," Russell said in response to Mason's obvious interest in his appearance.

"I'm Detective Mason Darby with the Los Angeles Police Department. May I speak with you for a few minutes?"

"Grab a chair," Russell replied. "I wondered if anyone was going to show any interest in me."

"Did you know Leticia Gold?"

"Of course I did. In fact, I'm covering for her while she's having another of her 'secret' procedures."

"What procedures?"

"You know the ones. A little tuck here, a little tuck there," Russell said with an exaggerated wink. "Wait a minute. You said, 'did I know her'. Why the past tense?"

311

"She passed away earlier today. At this very hospital, in fact."

"My God," Russell uttered, clearly shocked. "I didn't think modern-day, western plastic surgery could kill you."

"That wasn't why she was here," Mason explained. "She was admitted to the psychiatric unit after witnessing a murder at one of her listings."

"Who was killed?"

"A woman by the name of Phyliss Brimmer."

Russell's head jerked, such was the impact of hearing the woman's name.

"I take it you knew her?" Mason asked.

"I wouldn't say that I knew her, but I was certainly aware of her. We all were. Leticia had her on some sort of retainer."

"Do you know what exactly Ms. Brimmer did?"

"As far as we could make out, she was some kind of psychic or mystic and did spiritual cleansing gigs for buyers before they moved in."

"Is that a normal part of the buying process in Beverly Hills?" Mason asked.

"Not even remotely, but Leticia brought her in a few months ago. The funny thing was that she only used the woman at a few of her listings, not all of them."

"Why is that funny?"

"Well, if Leticia was doing the cleansing as some sort of new-age gimmick, why not do it on all properties she'd listed?"

"When I told you that Ms. Brimmer had been murdered, you seemed more than simply shocked at the fact that she was someone you knew?"

Russell fiddled with a fingernail while deciding what to tell the detective. After all, the psych unit wasn't that far away and what he had to say would, if told to the wrong person, almost certainly guarantee him a seventy-two-hour staycation at the place.

"Does it have something to do with whatever happened to you in Bel Air?" Mason asked.

Russell tried not to look shocked at the almost uncanny way the detective had changed the subject back to the one he was reticent to discuss.

"I want to make it clear, before I say anything else that I honestly don't know what happened at the house," Russell said as a disclaimer.

He then told Mason how he'd gotten there early to give the place a once-over and make it show ready. He told about the state of the guest suite, the weird wind, the dead racoon in the toilet, and about going back downstairs to find some things so he could dispose of the body.

"And did you?" Mason asked.

Russell gave him a puzzled look.

"Did you dispose of the body?" Mason asked.

Even though he was talking about a dead animal, the way that the detective had asked him whether he had, in fact, disposed of the body made him suddenly feel oddly guilty.

"I don't think so," Russell stuttered. "No. I didn't. I never made it back into the room."

Mason slowly nodded, wondering if anyone had yet realized that Russell had had his cardiac issue in roughly the same place as where Harry Groppel had dropped dead of what the paramedics had initially thought was also a heart attack.

"Anyway, for some reason," Russell continued, "I couldn't seem to get the bedroom door open. I finally had to go back downstairs again and grab some tools. By the time I got back to the door and started to remove a screw, it opened by itself."

"Creepy," Mason commented.

"I didn't think anything of it at that moment. It wasn't until I felt something wrap itself around me that I started to freak out."

"Something wrapped itself around you? What sort of something? A scarf, a rope?"

"No. Nothing like that. It felt like one of those new weighted blankets that are supposed to make you sleep better, only I felt it cover every inch of me."

"Could you see what it was?" Mason asked.

"I couldn't see anything on me whatsoever, but something was there and whatever it was suddenly started to tighten, then it felt as if something was digging into me."

"Where?"

"My chest," Russell said, his breathing becoming faster and shallower. "Even though I could hardly breathe and

314

was about to shit myself, something made me look into the bedroom. That's when I saw it."

"What did you see?"

"At first, I only saw the eyes. They were slanted and way bigger than a human's eyes. I remember noticing that they were mainly yellow, but the pupils were red. Dark, dark, red."

"You said 'at first'. What else did you see?"

"I can't really describe it."

"Why? You must have been close enough to see it pretty clearly?"

"You don't get it," Russell said, shaking his head as if to ward off the images that were swirling within his mind. "I can't describe it because I've never seen anything like it in my life. Even in the movies they've never thought of a creature like that."

"Please try," Mason coaxed.

Russell lowered his head while he tried as hard as he could to offer a glimpse of what he had seen at the Bel Air house. The problem was the creature hadn't looked like any one thing. It was an amalgam of every childhood monster that had ever existed.

It was pure and unadulterated evil.

CHAPTER 36

As he started to make his way back through the maze of medical buildings, Mason turned his phone back on and was immediately assaulted by dozens of texts.

Quinn was, apparently, ready to talk. The death of his ex-wife had knocked any remaining fight out of him. Teri had advised that she would wait until Mason returned before restarting the questioning, however, she made it clear that Bayliss now wanted things to move in a more time-conscious manner. The hint being that Mason should get his ass back to headquarters as fast as possible.

As much as Mason hoped to turn up the fire under Quinn and maybe finally start getting some answers, there was one person he wanted to speak with before that happened. He needed some sort of overview of what Quinn actually did for his six figure shows, so that he had enough facts to know if the guy was telling the truth or weaving a new tapestry of bullshit.

Mason knew that he couldn't, or at least shouldn't, lie to his partner about why he wasn't going straight back, especially as she'd be doubly furious if she ever did learn that he felt interviewing the butler was more important than returning to headquarters as requested.

Groves was waiting outside the Trousedale house. Mason had expected to see a far more despondent man considering his imminent eviction and job loss. Instead, he was wearing shorts, a T-shirt and holding, if the celery stick was any indication, a Bloody Mary.

"You look happy for someone who's about to be homeless," Mason commented as he stepped out of the car.

"Things are never as bad as they seem," Groves replied, as he raised the drink in a toast then took a long sip.

"Your optimism is a shining example to us all. You ready to talk?"

"Come on in." Groves led the way to the living room then plopped himself down on an overstuffed white sofa and placed his feet on the carved Moroccan coffee table. "I would offer you a drink, but I know you'd refuse."

"Maybe once you're resettled," Mason said as he sat on the matching sofa directly across from Groves. "As I said on the phone, Quinn has been arrested and formally charged with six counts of murder. That means that, even though he has yet to be convicted, the NDA is no longer in force, as it relates to the ongoing investigations. Therefore, if you don't mind, will you please tell me what the hell this guy does at these parties?"

Groves laughed. "You've been busy."

"That and a few lucky breaks."

"I don't wish to appear ungrateful for how hard you are trying to solve the cases, especially the maestro's, but having been at the receiving end of some pretty nasty legal wrangling, do you mind showing me some proof of his having been charged?"

Mason smiled and produced his cell phone from his jacket. He signed into the LAPD site and entered Quinn's name. Though trying to appear confident, he was secretly praying that the booking process had been a timely one and that he wasn't about to look like an idiot, or worse, a lying idiot. After a few moments of watching a whirling circle in the middle of the screen, the file opened. Quinn's charge sheet was on page one and his booking photo was there for all to behold (well, all who had access).

Mason passed the phone across the table.

Groves looked at it, swiped the pages back then forward, then handed the phone back.

"I hope this helps," he said as he nodded his head.

"So do I," Mason replied.

"Quinn's act, or whatever you'd call it, was referred to as a spiritual awakening."

"That sounds awfully like new-age artsy crap," Mason commented.

"That's what I thought, but the maestro had heard whispers from friends and insisted that I would be blown away by what Quinn would do."

"Okay. What did Quinn do?"

"He pretty much did just exactly was it said on the can. He raised spirits."

"As in, made everybody feel happy?" Mason asked.

"As in awakened actual spirits. I don't know how the hell he did it, but he was able to make this... creature appear through a veil of black smoke. It took a while, but once the thing was in the room with us, it was fucking terrifying, if you'll pardon my French."

"If that was French, then I'm more fluent than I thought," Mason interjected. "Surely it was some sort of illusion? Maybe with all that smoke there was also a mirror or two?"

"All he brought into the house was a briefcase which held an old-looking book. That was it. He read from the book and after about ten or fifteen minutes, the room turned darker, despite all the lights still being on, and what looked like a black cloud started to appear just below the ceiling. Everyone thought at first that it was smoke, but as it grew, it looked more and more like a storm cloud. Eventually, an eerie light flickered from within it, and I swear I heard something that sounded exactly like thunder."

"And you are positive that Quinn couldn't have staged all this? That he couldn't have somehow snuck some props into the house before the party started?" Mason asked.

"It wasn't a trick or gimmick. The longer he read from the book, the stranger the atmosphere was in the room. You know that feeling and smell when a storm is close, and lightning is about to strike. Well, that's how it felt in here."

"That was his whole act?"

Groves laughed. "God no. That was just the beginning."

"Do you remember anything that Quinn read from that book?" Mason asked.

"No. Then again, I don't speak much Akkadian."

"But enough to recognize the language?"

"Hardly," Groves replied. "He told us up front that the book he was about to read was in Akkadian and that it had come from ancient Mesopotamia. He also said that it was one of the infamous black books of the early, dark arts. The one he had dated back to a time, thousands of years ago when demonic worship was widespread."

"You believed that?"

"Hey. It looked old and after what I saw him do... yeah, I believed it."

"So, what happened next?" Mason asked.

Groves finished his Bloody Mary as if he needed it to continue with the story.

"Quinn began raising his voice. It almost seemed like he was commanding the storm cloud. Then, without any warning, there was this godawful crack of thunder, right here in this room and the cloud started to swirl. Within seconds, it looked like a black tornado. Then the fun began."

Groves got to his feet and headed for the kitchen. He reappeared moments later with a bottle of Hennessy XO brandy and a highball glass.

"Sorry. I need a little help to get this out. I've been dreading having to ever talk about what I saw appear in the living room that night. I'll tell you one thing; I've never been so scared in all my life. Then again, I guess that's why the guy got the big bucks. He was offering a taste of raw and impossible horror that few humans could even imagine, let alone witness."

Groves poured himself four fingers of the amber liquid and downed the glass in one. He then shivered, grimaced and smiled.

"Better?" Mason asked.

"A little." Groves took a deep breath and resumed the tale. "The cloud thing was now a giant vortex than seemed to drop down from the ceiling. We could all see deep into it. It didn't stop at the ceiling. It felt like we were staring up hundreds, maybe thousands, of miles within the funnel. Lightning was coming from within its walls and the thunder was getting louder. That was when the wind started. It was a wind that had life and purpose."

"Here in this room?" Mason asked, getting more dubious by the second.

"None of us could move. We were completely transfixed waiting for whatever was about to happen. Something that only a few moments earlier we would have never believed possible."

Groves stopped to pour himself a slightly smaller brandy and downed it.

"The vortex suddenly began to contract, and instead of its tail trailing miles into the sky, it inverted and sunk right through the floor. The opening was right over there." Groves pointed to a spot to the left of where he was sitting.

Mason could only see an area of highly polished, white marble flooring.

"It just lay there spinning as Quinn's voice got louder and louder. Finally, he shouted one particular word and began repeating it again and again. Anyway, we were all watching the vortex thingy and personally, I expected it to give one last spin, or thunderclap then disappear. At that point it would have still been the weirdest and creepiest thing I'd ever seen. Turned out though, that was just the warmup."

Groves took a moment to pour himself another drink, this one smaller than the last jolt.

"Then the screaming started," Groves said after downing the brandy.

"Was everyone in the room screaming?"

"It wasn't coming from us. This wasn't your run of the mill screaming. This was deeper. Much deeper and seemed to be coming from somewhere within the vortex. As everyone watched and listened, a weak yellow light suddenly appeared within the spinning cloud of smoke then started strobing, and with each flash, the screaming started to sync with the light. It also got louder. It took a moment for me to realize that the increase in volume was because whatever was screaming was getting closer."

"What do mean, getting closer?" Mason asked.

"I mean that whatever the hell was at the other end of that vortex was moving towards us."

"Could you tell if the voice was a man or a woman?"

Groves laughed. "You're not understanding what I'm telling you. The sound coming from it was like nothing I've ever heard. You might think that Hollywood has managed to create some of the scariest monsters with spine chilling roars and stuff, but trust me, they've never even imagined a sound like the one that was coming out of that hole. It was almost as if it was made up of the screams from thousands of tortured souls."

Mason, finding what Groves was saying hard to believe, did his best to not let his reservations become visible.

"Was everyone as scared as you obviously were?" he asked.

"It would have been impossible not to have felt that way. Some appeared to be having a worse go of it than I was. One woman, directly across from me kept fainting and sagging back in her chair. I don't know if anyone else noticed and just didn't care, but nobody did a thing to help her."

"You included?"

"Me included, at least initially," Groves admitted. "To reach her I would have had to try to jump across the vortex in the floor. By that time, it was probably five feet wide and that just wasn't going to happen. Besides, the woman kept regaining consciousness and would then look over the rim into the void and pass out again. At one point, I was about to see if I could find a way through the crowd and circle through the dining room to try and reach her, but before I could make a move, a claw reached out of the hole and grabbed the rim."

That was as much as Groves could impart before taking a short break. Even though he clearly believed everything he was saying, Mason considered what they had seen to be a complete con. Somehow, Quinn had staged the whole thing. People seem to forget that special effects experts and some high-end magicians were able to produce impossible tricks designed to fool audiences around the world.

Mason turned on his phone for a few seconds, just long enough to see that not only had Teri tried to text him multiple times, but Ballsack had also joined the party. It appeared that Bayliss was starting to raise a stink back at headquarters, insisting either her client be questioned or released.

Mason sent two quick responses, one to Ballsack the other to Teri.

They simply said, 'On my way back'.

For a moment, he considered doing just that, but then, Groves returned looking both stronger and determined.

"You ready to keep going?" Mason asked.

"No, but I will."

CHAPTER 37

"The thing I remember the most was that when that claw latched onto the rim, a couple of people laughed. Despite all the tension and fear in the room, there was something about the claw's appearance that people found amusing. I suppose it was almost a 'jump the shark' moment; that Quinn had gone one step too far with his show. A swirling mass of black smoke spinning in the middle of the living room floor was one thing, but a hand (or claw) suddenly appearing like that was just too impossible."

"What did you think?" Mason asked.

"For a brief moment, I picked up on the vibe and thought that the visual was a tad over the top."

"Why only for a moment?"

"Because a few moments after the oversized purple and black claw appeared, the rest of the creature climbed out of the floor."

"Did any of the guests continue to see any humor after that?" Mason asked.

"Not remotely. Once the head and shoulders were visible, it became clear that what we were seeing was not an illusion. The thing was real," Groves insisted.

"Would you be able to describe this creature?" Mason asked, as he started to worry about the other man's grasp on reality. "Also, if the claw gave everyone the impression that the show was, in fact, staged, then why did seeing more of the creature reverse that sentiment?"

"It's hard to explain. First, there was the smell. It reminded me of when you light a match. There's that half second when all you can smell is sulfur. This was like that except the odor had depth. It wasn't just sulfur. There was also a mustiness and the distinct smell of something feral; something wild and unwashed. Have you ever been inside the monkey pavilion at the zoo? It was like that, but way stronger. Then there was the sound. Once the creature's head rose into the room, the screaming stopped and was replaced with this god-awful breathing. It sounded like a death rattle, but at five times the volume. Then there was the face. I don't know exactly how to describe it, other than it was constantly changing. The head itself was at least three times bigger than the biggest human head you've ever seen. It was huge. It looked a little like a rhinoceros, but instead of a horn, it had a gaping hole which, if I had to guess, might have been its nose. I only say that because a dark, yellowy-green ooze was flowing out of it. But as I said, it kept changing. Its flesh couldn't seem to lock into any one form. It moved in independent judders, forming and reforming around the one part that stayed the same."

"What part was that?" Mason asked.

"The mouth. Even while the face kept reconfiguring itself, even melding into more of a snout, the rows of blackened yellow teeth stayed the same. They were jagged and each one sloped inward at the end. Have you ever seen a great white shark tooth?"

Mason nodded.

"These looked a little like that, but way bigger, and there were so many of them it was impossible not to imagine what it would have been like for the creature to tear into human flesh."

"Did it leave the vortex?" Mason asked.

"Yes," Groves said, finally. "It ended up standing in the middle of the room with its head almost reaching the ceiling."

"Are you sure about that? This looks at least—"

"It's fifteen feet from floor to ceiling," Groves interrupted him. "And yes, I am sure. I could see its ears touching the beams."

"What did the rest of it look like?"

"I couldn't tell you. Its lower half seemed to drag part of the vortex up into the room with it. No matter how hard it tried to move away, it couldn't. It almost looked as if its bottom half hadn't yet been formed and was still within the smoke."

"How did this creature interact with the guests in the room? Was it scared... angry?" Mason asked.

"Angry doesn't quite cover it," Groves explained. "From the moment it emerged from the floor, it seemed hell-bent on attacking anything and anyone."

"Why didn't it?"

"Quinn seemed to have some sort of control over it. Whenever it tried to get any closer to the people that were surrounding it, Quinn barked commands at it, and it stopped moving any closer."

"Willingly?" Mason asked.

"I don't think so. I think it was fighting against Quinn's will, or power, or whatever, from the moment it first appeared."

"What else happened?" Mason asked.

"After about five minutes of the thing glaring and snapping at us, Quinn walked over to the maestro, and I heard him shout something about it not being too late. The maestro just shook his head. Quinn then stepped closer to the creature and started shouting some new command over and over."

"Can you remember what that was?"

"No. By that time my brain was mush. I've never been that scared in my life. Then again, I'd never before been in the presence of such evil."

"Why do you say evil?"

"I know this sound ridiculous, but looking at it, I felt I was staring at the devil."

"The actual devil?" Mason said, trying to keep a straight face.

"Well, not some horned red guy with a tail. I felt I was looking at the reason that devil worship ever existed. I fully believed that I was in the same room as the creature that spawned the myths and followers."

"How did the show end?" Mason asked.

"Quinn kept chanting at it. Whatever the hell it was that he was saying, the creature seemed to break from the vortex and for a moment, stood there. All of it was visible until it suddenly started to disappear right in front of us. The last thing I saw were its teeth gnashing together, then it faded into nothingness."

"That was it?" Mason asked.

"That was it," Groves replied. "Just so you know, that is the first and last time that I'm going to tell that story. I plan to do everything in my power to never think of that day again."

Mason studied the man for a good few moments.

"Do you think that the creature that you saw in this living room could have possibly been what attacked the maestro later that same night?"

"Of course I do. Something scared him so badly that closing the iron maiden on himself was the better option. Before that night, I would never have believed that something that terrifying could even exist. After seeing that creature, I think I might have done the same."

"And you have no doubt that what you and the others saw that night wasn't just an illusion?"

"I spoke to the maestro immediately after the guests had left the house and he said the same thing. Whatever it was, there was no doubt that it was real."

"Did the maestro feel he'd gotten his money's worth?"

"He did. He also said something odd about managing to get the package without coughing up any more money."

"What did he mean by that?"

"No idea. I never had any direct dealing with Quinn so it must have been something to do with the contract."

"But all in all, the maestro was happy with the outcome?"

"Oh yeah. He'd been told that Quinn's show would top any other performances that were doing the rounds of the A-list parties. All the guests, though in shock at what they'd seen, felt it was the most life-changing thing they'd ever witnessed."

Mason sighed.

"You're not believing any of this, are you?" Groves asked.

"I've seen more horrors than you could possibly imagine, but none of them went beyond the capacity of a depraved human mind. I do believe in monsters. Just not the kind that you believe you witnessed."

"You still think it was all some sort of trickery, don't you?"

"I have to, Edgar," Mason replied.

As Groves led him to the front door, Mason asked, "So when's moving day?"

"Actually, there won't be one. I found out last night that the maestro left the bulk of his estate to me. Apparently, he hated his offspring even more than he let on."

"They'll doubtless contest the will," Mason remarked.

"Won't matter. He made me executor as well as the main beneficiary. What's astounding to me is that he changed his will over ten years ago and I never knew a thing about it. He also started documenting the behavior of his heirs, specifically his son, and made note of the attempts that were made to get access to the estate long before the maestro even died. They are a nasty bunch, and our lawyers have volumes of documentation to show why they were excluded from the will."

"So, it really is all yours," Mason said, smiling. "That's got to feel pretty good."

"What would really make me feel good is if the maestro was still alive," Groves said as they reached Mason's car.

CHAPTER 38

Teri was furious. Mason had picked what was probably the most inopportune time to go off grid. While she trusted that he was fully immersed in police business, leaving her to battle an angry lawyer and the chief of police was, in her mind, unforgiveable.

She was about to try his cell again when a text arrived saying that he was on his way back. Teri decided that simply announcing his return wasn't sufficient information to pacify those at headquarters.

Just as she was about to redial his number, there was a gentle knock on the door.

"Come in," she called out.

"We've finished with Quinn. He's been processed and is back in holding," the duty sergeant advised.

Will Smith, no relation to the mega-star, was in his late sixties and contemplating full retirement in less than a year. Thirty years on the force had taken a toll. His thinning grey hair sat atop a face that had aged prematurely. His blue eyes had lost their sparkle years earlier and now looked cold enough to freeze water.

"Something came up when we uploaded his data," Will explained. "We got a match hit on his prints. It seems that Quinn didn't used to be Quinn. He had a record under the name Alex Fillerston."

Smith passed a data sheet over to Teri.

"I sent you an electronic version as well," he advised.

"Give me the abridged story," Teri requested.

"He was a quasi-magician who used to use some of his skills to con some low-level marks. It's basically nickel and dime crap, but he doesn't appear to have been that good at it. He seemed to get caught more times than not."

"Any outstanding warrants?" Teri asked.

"All expired years ago."

"And nothing under Carlos Quinn?"

"Nada, sorry."

Once Will was gone, Teri accessed the database and reviewed the charge list for one Alex Fillerston. The first thing she noticed was that his life of petty crime took place entirely on the East Coast, which explained how he'd managed to change his name and fall out of the system once he'd ventured west.

Fillerston specialized in sleight of hand and close-up magic. He did a lot of street work, using a folding card table and minimal props. Apparently, while dazzling the onlookers, he became somewhat adept at removing watches and jewelry from unwitting audience members.

Because he had practiced the necessary moves in a mirror, it was almost impossible to see what he was doing. His shortcoming was that he never bothered to practice using side-angled mirrors or cameras and therefore didn't realize that his illegal sleight of hand could, on occasion, be spotted by anyone standing at an oblique angle. Thus, he was caught red-handed on numerous occasions.

The only charge that had held any weight was from when he had somehow managed to get a gig at a birthday party in the Hamptons. Alex had cleverly ensured that his audience was seated directly in front of him and therefore assumed that no one could see if he stripped someone of their overpriced tennis bracelet.

What Alex hadn't counted on were the security cameras concealed within a number of elaborate chandeliers.

He was arrested before he could get off the property. After winning the courtroom lottery and somehow getting a half-decent public defender, he managed to get bail, which he immediately skipped out on and fled to the West Coast. What the data didn't give was how he'd somehow managed to go from being a two-bit crook to one of the most exclusive party performers in Beverly Hills.

Teri hoped that once her partner bothered to show up, they might just get that question answered.

She was about to check up on the CSI team's findings from the old Harter house when the office door opened a crack. Patty Gainer, the CSI investigator that had welcomed

Teri while working at that same scene, poked her head around the corner, grinning.

"So, you really are stuck in one of the interview rooms," she said, grinning. "I thought they were kidding."

Now unmasked, Teri was struck by just how attractive the CSI was. With the mask gone and the CSI unitard having been replaced by a form-fitting dark suit, Patty was stunning.

"At least it's private," Teri replied.

"I thought I'd bring down the updates," Patty said as she held out a flash drive.

"Thanks. I was literally just about to log in and see if there'd been anything new."

"Actually, there was one interesting hit. The guy, Quinn — that's not his real name."

"That'll muddy the waters," Teri said, feigning surprise at the news. "Next you'll be telling me that the guy was called something stupid like Alex Fillerston."

"I didn't take you for a smartass," Patty said, smiling.

"What did you take me for?"

"I don't know, but I was hoping to find out."

Teri felt a comfortable chill ripple down her spine. She was about to respond when the door flew open, and Mason walked in.

"Sorry for the disappearing act," he announced. "I wanted to hear Edgar Groves' version of Quinn's act before we continued the interview. At least now we have a baseline to see if he's giving us the whole truth."

"His real name is Alex Fillerston," Patty said as she squeezed by him. "We'll talk later," she said to Teri, before giving her a nod and leaving the office.

"I hope I didn't interrupt anything," Mason said, mildly curious about the 'we'll talk later' comment.

"Not a thing," she replied, even while trying to work out whether she and Patty had just had a moment.

Teri had never considered herself as gay, in fact, for the past two years, she hadn't had the time or interest to have sex at all. On a few occasions, she had felt a mild attraction for a few women but had never even considered acting upon it. Patty was the first one to stir something deeper. The problem for Teri was, that having never had a same sex relationship, she had no idea if Patty had been coming on to her or was just being friendly.

"You ready to restart the interview?" Mason asked.

Teri confirmed that she was and chose to forget about the brief exchange with Patty. If there was something there, it would just have to wait.

Mason called the duty desk and arranged for Quinn to be brought back to the interview room.

"I'll call Bayliss and tell her as well," Teri said as she reached for her cell.

Fifteen minutes later, Quinn stared nervously at the two detectives.

"I understand that you are now willing to talk to us again?" Mason asked.

Quinn looked at his lawyer, who gave him a subtle nod.

"What do you want to know?" he asked.

"Let's start by you telling us exactly what your act consists of?" Mason asked.

"I have a number of acts. You'll have to be more—"

"The one you get paid six figures to perform," Teri snapped at him. "The one that seems to result in people dying. Why don't we start with that one."

"There's been no proof that my client's show has resulted in any deaths," Bayliss said.

Quinn looked down at his lap and took a while to re-engage with the others in the room.

"May I answer your question with a little history?" Quinn asked.

"Your history or Alex Fillerston's?" Teri asked, hoping for some sort of reaction. She got one, but not from Quinn.

"Who the hell is Alex Fillerston?" Bayliss asked.

"Alex Fillerston is Quinn's real name and was the one he used until his mini crime spree forced him to move west and change his name," Teri explained.

"You could have told me," she stated, as she glared at Quinn.

"I would have expected you to know more about your client," Teri replied, smirking.

"Do you and your client need a minute alone?" Mason asked, enjoying Bayliss' discomfort.

"That was going to be my big reveal," Quinn said. "Yes, I was once Alex Fillerston and yes, I was a small-time crook. I'm not embarrassed by what I used to do, because if I hadn't lived that life, I would never have found the career I have now."

"I hope this career is something that can be continued in prison," Mason mumbled.

"Let's start with my journey out west," Quinn suggested. "When I left New York, I had no money, and thanks to a bench warrant, had no way to publicly perform my magic without attracting the attention of the police. I knew I wanted to get out of the city, but at that point I had no idea that I would end up way out here."

"This sounds like it's going to be a long story. I think we should jump to present day and talk about the parties in Los Angeles," Mason said.

"You need to know what happened to me in those few days otherwise, anything else I say is going to sound like complete bullshit."

Bayliss glared at both detectives before either had a chance to jump on that last comment.

"Go ahead, but please try and keep it short," Teri requested.

"Before I started doing magic shows, I used to play a lot of poker. In fact, poker was how I taught myself some of the basics of close-up magic."

"So you could entertain the other players?" Mason asked.

"No. So I could cheat," Quinn replied.

CHAPTER 39

"You've got to understand that the people I played with were not sophisticated gamblers," Quinn explained. "These were local guys who barely knew the rules. It was ridiculously easy to mess with the cards. A couple of times I even managed to get everyone so focused on my right hand that I was able to use my left one to skim some chips from the player next to me."

"While that was a wonderful glimpse inside your moral compass, I don't see how that has anything to do with the current situation," Mason voiced.

"It'll make sense in a minute. Anyway, while still not sure where I was going to end up, I headed west and was able to find a game in almost every town I stopped in."

"How were you travelling back then?" Teri asked.

"Good old Greyhound bus. I would go about a hundred or so miles each day, at which point I would get off and stay the night while playing a little poker with the locals. Each evening I'd earn a little more cash and the next morning catch the next Greyhound out of town. By the time I got as far as Nashville, I was starting to like the new lifestyle. Always moving and always earning."

"You weren't earning," Mason advised. "You were stealing."

"Hey. The guys turned up half expecting to lose their money. I just moved the needle a little in my favor. Anyway, one day, after the bus broke down, I ended up in some Podunk town in Mississippi. There was one crappy bar and a main street one block long. The place had been a Wells Fargo stage stop back in the day and for some reason the town decided to stick around, even after their only source of revenue dried up. Their only reason for still being in existence was a run-down service station with a motel attached. Considering that Littlebrook – that was the name of the place – considering that Littlebrook wasn't even on a main highway, pickings had to have been pretty thin."

"I bet that didn't stop you from taking their money?" Mason said.

"Of course not. There wasn't an existing game, so I had to start one myself. I managed to find three guys in the bar who were willing to play a few hands, but even then, they wanted to play for nickels and dimes. It wasn't until this big guy turned up and announced that he wanted the ante raised to a twenty dollar buy in."

"Sounds like the town had at least one high roller," Teri commented.

"That's the funny thing," Quinn replied. "The guy wasn't from the town. He'd been on the same bus as me

340

and was therefore stuck in the same hellhole for the night. Now usually, I wouldn't even consider trying to screw over someone else on the bus. I try to live by the credo to not shit where I eat, but I needed to top up the piggy bank and he appeared to be the only person willing to fork over some real coin."

"Wasn't that a bit of a risk?" Mason asked. "I mean, if things got hinky and he caught you doing your little parlor tricks, I'm not sure how you'd have been able to hide from him."

"I knew that was a possibility from the moment he joined the game. The guy seemed pretty mellow, but looked like a linebacker that had replaced weightlifting with cake eating. There was also something a little off about the guy. I won't go so far as to say that he was simple, but I got the distinct impression that his brain wasn't firing on all cylinders."

"Is this story leading anywhere?" Mason asked.

"We're almost there," Quinn reassured him. "I decided that between his size and missing brain cells, I'd better not mess with someone who looked like he could bear-hug me into a pretzel in nothing flat. So, I did something I never thought I'd do. I played it straight. No fancy dealing, nothing. As it turned out, I didn't need any help that night. After Hubert – that really was his name – after Hubert sat down and produced a decent-sized wad of twenties, the other players quit, leaving just Hubert, some guy whose name I forget and me.

"I cleaned the one guy of his entire fifteen-dollar stake, then it was just me and Huey. At least twice I thought of throwing in the towel and letting him keep some of his money, but he got really angry at the idea of giving up. The weird thing is that I don't think he'd ever really played cards before. He didn't seem to have a clue what he was doing."

"Did you at least find out why a guy like that had so much expendable cash?"

"I didn't have to ask. He must have told me fifty times that he was a courier, though he pronounced it 'career'. He'd been in Iraq and came back a little fucked up. This guy he knew, Jason Grant, had been in-country with him and the two had remained friends. It seemed that Grant always tried to help Huey whenever he could. He gave him odd jobs and stuff to do, just so Hubert could earn a little money. It seemed that Grant's main source of income was fencing low-end antiquities that troops smuggled back from Iraq and Afghanistan. This time round, Grant had paid Huey five hundred dollars in cash for him to carry a flat brown box all the way to Portland, Oregon, but the stipulation was that it could only travel by bus. It seemed that whatever was in it, Jason didn't want it to go through any scanners.

"Well, despite playing poker completely straight, I still won every cent the guy had. I've never seen anything like it. This huge guy just started blubbering and couldn't seem to stop. Finally, in an attempt to shut him up, I suggested that he try one more hand. Huey told me that he had nothing left to bet, and I suggested that maybe he did."

"You're a real charmer, aren't you?" Teri said, shaking her head.

Quinn looked over at Bayliss and was surprised to see that she too was viewing him in a new, and not very flattering, light.

"What? That's not me anymore. I'm a changed man."

"Of course you are," Mason replied with a smirk.

"Do you want to hear the rest or not?" Quinn asked.

"Just so long as the saga's almost over," Mason said.

"It is. Anyway, so I convince him that the odds were likely to be in his favor, so it was unlikely that he'd actually lose whatever was in the box. The poor guy took the bait and ended up with a pair of fours. I, on the other hand, managed to get three smiling kings. I swear I thought the guy was going to stroke out. He went all pale and jittery then stumbled out of the bar. I had my doubts about his ever giving me the box, but as I had already cleaned the guy out, I wasn't going to sweat it. Anyway, ten minutes later, Huey comes back into the bar and hands the package to me. He was still sniveling but didn't say a word. Once he'd given it to me, he walked right out again."

What about the next day on the bus?" Teri asked.

"That would have made for an interesting ride, but amazingly once they got it fixed and were ready to go, Huey never showed. We pulled out of Littlebrook at seven o'clock the next morning and there was no sign of him."

"Did you check if anyone in town had seen him?" Mason asked.

"No."

"And the bus left with one passenger not accounted for?"

"I may have suggested that Hubert found a ride and decided to leave the previous night."

"Did Hubert find a ride?" Teri asked.

"Beats me," Quinn replied with a shrug.

"I take it that whatever was in the box played some part in the creation of this new and improved you?" Mason asked.

"Oh yeah. As soon as I got back to my room in the motel, I tore the thing open, hoping it was going to be drugs or cash. You know – something easily exchangeable. Instead, there's this motheaten scarf or shawl thingy wrapped around some old book, and when I say old, I mean old. The cover was made of some sort of hide, but definitely not cow leather. And it was carved like a fancy saddle. The weird thing was that the back cover, and at least ten pages that were next to it, looked as if they'd been in a fire. I didn't know if that mattered or not.

"There were letters on the front, but I had no idea what it said. I opened it and when I checked the pages inside the book, there was the same sort of writing as on the cover, plus there were these weird-ass drawings – you know, the sort of sick shit you'd see in a really bad graphic novel."

"Do you mind defining 'sick shit'?" Mason asked.

"You know the stuff. Crazy-looking monsters ripping people apart. I was about to throw the thing away when it dawned on me that it had to have been kinda valuable for Huey's friend to pay for its transportation all the way across the country. I decided to keep it and do a little research at the next stop. This was before smartphones, so I had to do things old school and use a computer in the library in the next town. It took me freakin' hours before some geeky old, retired teacher helped me work out that the writing was from the Mesopotamian period, but he couldn't translate it. I had to wait until we reached Tulsa and found my way to the university there. I thought that maybe they taught that language, but some snooty kid at the main reception desk looked at the text and actually laughed at me and told me it was written in Akkadian and there were no classes that taught that language. When the jerk stopped giggling, I asked him what classes might actually deal with Mesopotamian history at the time when they spoke Akkadian. That shut him up. Apparently, their archaeology program specialized in Middle Eastern cultures, and part of the master's course required a basic ability to both read and write the relevant dead languages from the relevant Mesopotamian periods.

"I found this nerd who was working on his thesis on Mesopotamia; specifically on the period between 500 BC and 1500 AD. Guess what language was spoken back then?" Quinn asked.

"I'm going to hazard a guess at that Arkadian one," Mason replied.

"Akkadian, not Arkadian," Quinn corrected him, before he noticed the dark look on the other man's face.

"Anyway," Quinn continued. "Two hundred bucks bought me a rough translation of the cover and the unburned pages.

I paid him one hundred upfront and when I came to pick up what he'd done, the guy looked at me like I was some kind of monster. Instead of handing me back the book and his pages, he threw them at my feet and ran off. He didn't even want the second hundred."

"Was it worth all the fuss?" Teri asked.

"Yes and no. The book was called – though I must warn you that it might not have been the exact wording – *'The Rite of Bringing Forth the Demon God Pazuzu.'* In the book, it gave very precise instruction on how to carry out the ceremony. The problem was that he'd translated everything into English, including the actual incantation. That meant that though I could now understand the words, I had no idea of how to say them in Akkadian, which was the whole point if I wanted to see if the book was legit. It took me hours to track the guy down again and almost that long to convince him that I wasn't the spawn of Satan and needed him to create a phonetic version of the Akkadian words."

"This is what you've been leading up to?" Mason asked, clearly frustrated. "You're seriously going to tell me that your gimmick is to pretend to raise some long-dead demon? Really?"

Mason started to get to his feet. "We're finished here," Mason said, before turning to Quinn's lawyer. "There is no deal. Obviously, your client is unwilling to work with us."

"Wait," Quinn almost squealed. "Please. Hear the rest. You gotta let me finish."

"Finish what?" Mason asked. "Listening to you spouting a bunch of complete bullshit?"

"At least hear him out," Bayliss asked. "I kind of want to hear the rest of the story myself."

"You haven't heard this before?" Mason asked.

"My client refused to give me any details until there was a deal in place."

"He's got five minutes," Mason replied, reluctantly.

CHAPTER 40

"I managed to get a seat in the back of the next bus out," Quinn continued. "Which isn't that hard, considering it's right next to the toilet and the ventilation isn't always—"

"Perhaps if you stick to the point," Bayliss suggested.

"Sorry. Yeah. So, once we were out of the city, I start reading the guy's translation, as well as the phonetic version. It sounded pretty goofy, but with the spelling laid out in front of me, I started reciting the words."

"That must have been nice for the other passengers," Teri commented.

"I did it quietly. Anyway, after I was about two thirds of the way through the recitation, I noticed that the light above me had dimmed. I looked up and saw that there was black smoke swirling above everyone's head. The driver must have seen it at the same time I did, cause he pulled off the road and used an air horn to get everyone's attention. We all had to get off until he was able to clear the air and determine that it was nothing to do with the mechanics of the bus.

"I was the only one who knew that I was the cause of the smoke. I had no idea whether or not I could actually summon some monster from a couple of thousand years ago, but if the smoke was anything to go by, I was starting to think that maybe I could."

"You sound as gullible as some of your card-playing buddies," Mason commented.

"The next morning, once we reached Albuquerque," Quinn continued, ignoring Mason, "I rented a car and drove way out in the desert and tried it again. Sure enough, the black smoke appeared, but as I kept reciting the incantation, it turned into a weird tornado thing that suddenly sank into the ground, leaving just the open-end swirling like some sort of whirlpool. I gotta tell you, I was shitting myself, but for some reason I had to keep going. Finally, at the part where I had to keep saying the same word over and over, this fucking head started to rise out of the ground."

"What kind of head?" Mason asked.

"The kind that would keep you awake at night for the rest of your life."

"Did you keep going?"

"No way. Not then at least."

"What did you do about the thing that was coming out of the ground?" Teri asked.

"For some reason, as soon as I stopped the recitation, it stopped emerging from the whirlpool. All it seemed to be able to do was make this god-awful noise, like something out of Jurassic Park."

"So, it was more like a roar?" Mason asked.

"No. It was more like a scream. A deep, horrific scream."

"So, what did you do with it?" Teri asked.

"Nothing. I got back in the car and broke the speed limit all the way back to town. At some point, on the drive into Albuquerque, I started wondering if, instead of just selling the damn book, there was some way I could make some serious money just by making that creature appear."

Mason shook his head in wonder. "You really are a delightful human being. Before you finish your saga, we need to go back to my partner's question. You say you brought something up through the desert floor and then promptly ran away. What did you do about this supposed creature?"

"I left it there. It didn't seem to be able to get out of the hole and as we were miles from anything, I didn't see the harm in leaving whatever it was to its own devices."

"I get the distinct feeling that pretty much sums up the tenet for everything in your life," Teri said.

"What? Self-protection?"

"No. Leaving everyone else to clean up your mess."

Quinn shrugged.

"If any of this turns out to be true, could you still find that location?" Mason asked.

"Not in a million years. It was just some place out in the middle of nowhere. The whole point was to find somewhere far off the beaten track."

"We may go back to this point at a later time. I don't like the idea of there being some animal that was left trapped in the middle of the desert," Teri commented.

"It's almost certainly long dead by now," Quinn replied. "So you want me to continue, or do you have a few more potshots you want to take?"

"Not for the moment," Mason stated. "Please continue. I'm looking forward to hearing your next life-affirming action."

Quinn ignored Mason's comment and continued. "The first thing I realized was that whatever way I found to use the book for my benefit, it had to be somewhere with a lot of seriously rich people who weren't afraid to pay up big time for something completely unique. Then it dawned on me. Los Angeles. The place was riddled with celebrities and serious money. From what I'd seen on TV, they also seemed like the kind of people that would do just about anything to see something that nobody else had seen. That's when the idea came to me to use the book and turn it into some kinda act. By the time I reached the coast, I'd narrowed it down to it being more of an A-list party thing. After a little research, I found out just how much some people were willing to pay to wow their guests. The problem was, I had no way of breaking into that level of society.

"Then, just as I'm starting to doubt my own plan, I'm lying on this cheap bed in some dump of a motel in Barstow when this show comes on the TV about LA's top realtors. One of them was Leticia Gold. There was something about her that made me feel like she would be willing to back a guaranteed money-making scheme. Plus, she was already connected to some seriously rich buyers. According to the show, she routinely sold homes that were priced in the millions.

"As soon as I got to LA, I made an appointment to meet with her on the pretext that I wanted to buy an expensive house in Beverly Hills. The moment she saw me, she knew it was a scam. Maybe it was the JC Penny suit, or maybe I just gave off a certain vibe, but she called me out immediately. I had to practically beg for her to listen to what I was pitching. I don't know why, but she agreed to give me ten minutes. It only took five, but even after I showed her the book, she wouldn't believe any part of it. She suggested I leave immediately, and I suggested back that maybe a demonstration would change her mind. Amazingly, she agreed, so long as it was at a location of her choosing, where there were people around and if it was a bust, she could walk away and never see me again. I agreed and she suggested that we meet that afternoon in front of the entrance to the Hollywood Bowl. A celebrity she'd sold a house to was playing there and had asked if she wanted to come by for the sound check.

"When I got there, security had her name on a list and waved us through. She led me to the very back of the empty amphitheater while, much to my amazement, Ozzie Osbourne was belting out an old Black Sabbath song on stage. We sat down and I started reading from the book. Leticia started getting a little antsy after about ten minutes of nothing happening, but as soon as the black smoke started to form overhead, she got interested. At the point when it turned into that weird tornado-looking thing, two things happened at once. The band stopped playing and Ozzy's voice echoed from the stage."

"'What the fuck is that?' he asked. 'Whatever it is, I want it in my act.'"

"I was actually intrigued by that idea, but Leticia had other plans. She whisked me out of the amphitheater and drove me straight to Musso and Franks. You know it?"

"Of course we know it," Mason replied. "Keep going."

"Over martinis, a first for me, Leticia began planning everything. Even though she hadn't yet seen the creature, she felt that the vortex alone was worth the price of admission. She arranged for a private party at her own house with fifty carefully selected guests. In a stroke of complete genius, she also came up with the idea of the nondisclosure agreement, not just to protect the two of us, but also to add a certain panache, her word, not mine."

"Where was her house at that time?" Mason asked.

"It was off Coldwater Canyon drive, halfway up Cherokee Lane. Anyway, the night arrived, and all gussied up in a brand-new Versace suit, I made my appearance an hour into the party. Leticia cleared a large space in the middle of the living room and, after introducing me as Carlos Quinn, a name she made up on the spot, I started reciting from the book. The guests were initially curious about what I was doing, but after about five minutes they started to lose interest and began talking among themselves. I didn't care. I kept going. They pretty much ignored me until the smoke began to form up against the ceiling. Even then, their interest was minimal as they were used to high-end magic shows, and producing a little smoke just wasn't that impressive.

"It wasn't until the tornado of smoke settled into the ground, leaving the swirling hole twisting down into floor, that their interest was piqued. For the first time, I saw lightning within the smoke and started to worry that just maybe I was playing with something potentially dangerous."

"Yet you continued," Teri commented.

"I did. I tried not to let the audience see just how scared I was and acted like it was no big deal. At least, that's what I tried to do, however when this monstrous head started rising from the earth, I thought I was going shit myself. It was nothing like the one in the desert. This one was the manifestation of pure evil, and the guests went fucking bananas. At first, they were screaming their asses off, but soon, their morbid curiosity took over and they all moved a little closer. That was when the creature started struggling to release itself from the swirling cloud. As only the top two-thirds of its body had been formed it couldn't free itself, however, I didn't know that and as it began to howl and screech, I read the part in the book about forcing the demon back into its realm. Within a couple of minutes, the beast was drawn back into the earth and the smoke thinned, then it too disappeared."

Quinn took a deep breath then looked to the two detectives.

"That's how it started."

Mason didn't want to believe a word of Quinn's story, and in any other instance would have had him taken back to his holding cell, however, after having met with Edgar earlier that day and been given an almost identical story, he couldn't simply dismiss what he'd just heard.

"Let's say that I believe your story," Mason said. "What's the connection between your ritual and the subsequent deaths?"

"Let me first say that I never meant for anyone to get killed," Quinn stated. "We just got a little greedy, is all."

"Greedy, how?" Mason asked.

"After that party, Leticia paid for us to go to Vegas where I could get an expedited name change. She wanted to start 'marketing me', her words, not mine, while memories of my first show were still hot. She managed to get some high-paying bookings. The very first one was at this huge party in Montecito. The guy had been at Leticia's party and wanted to impress all his friends, which was fine with me. The only issue was that he wanted something extra."

"What more could someone possibly want?" Teri asked.

"He wanted me to not stop the ritual before the creature was fully formed. He wanted to see it become whole."

"Had you ever done that before?" Mason asked.

"Nope."

"But you did it anyway?" Mason asked.

355

"I did, but only after Leticia bumped the rate up to a quarter million."

Mason slumped back in his seat, completely stunned. "Two hundred and fifty thousand dollars for one show?" he asked.

"Yup. But you've got to understand that though it was only one show, it was the only one like it. It was unique. The host would have bragging rights for the rest of his life."

"Except he wouldn't because of the nondisclosure agreement," Teri pointed out.

"So, bragging rights within the circle of friends who'd also been there and signed the same agreement. It was still quite a coup."

"Did you do it?" Mason asked.

"I did."

"What happened?"

"It was pretty cool, actually. It was a different creature than the first two times. I realized at that point that I was never summoning the same demon twice. It totally depended on the location of the event as to which one came forth. Anyway, this time the thing was scaley and bright red, and I just kept repeating the chant until it finished forming and broke free of the smoke. I was terrified that it was going to tear the place apart, but after a couple of minutes, the host gave me the okay to get rid of it. I recited the reversal chant, and it got taken back into the ground."

"So, what went wrong at the Harter party?" Mason asked.

"Nothing. Nothing at all, at least initially. She was another host who wanted the extra program. This time the thing looked like some sort of distorted version of a deformed *Hell Boy,* like in the movie, but with the horns intact. I raised it out of the ground and let it fully manifest, then this stupid drunk who thought it would be cool to try and run off with the book grabs it right out of my hands. By the time we had the guy restrained and I had the book back, the demon had vanished. It had just faded away right in front of everyone."

"Did you never ask yourself where it went? I mean, you brought it into our world, then for a few extra dollars, let it go free. Didn't you consider that a risk?"

"Not initially," Quinn replied. "I assumed it went onto a different plane or something."

"What, like a connecting flight?" Mason asked.

"I don't think he means that kind of plane," Teri suggested.

"You know... alternate universe stuff," Quinn clarified. "I wasn't until Ms. Harter and that waiter were killed that I realized that these things might just stay behind."

"So, once you heard about what had happened, did you at least go back and try to use the reversing spell?" Teri asked.

"I know this will sound pretty stupid, but after hearing about the way they died, I decided that it was best if I stayed far away from the place."

"So, you never removed it?" Mason asked.

"No. I meant to get to it one day, but then I—"

"You what?" Teri asked.

"I guess I forgot."

CHAPTER 41

Bayliss and Mason decided it was time for a break and Quinn was locked back in his holding cell for the night. Balisek had decided that, to avoid any chance of Quinn telling anyone else about his demon raising, it was best to keep him isolated for the time being and approved a two-night stay at their internal holding facility.

The extra time was so that the DA's office could finalize the wording of the plea deal they'd agreed upon with Quinn. The big problem, at least for Mason, was that he still didn't believe that the prisoner was anything else but a con man who'd stumbled across some decent special effects. In an effort to confirm his suspicions, Mason arranged for Quinn to give a demonstration the following morning at one of the lesser-used training areas at the LA Police Academy.

Even though Mason fully expected the demo to be a complete and utter waste of time, he still needed to make sure that the environment was safe, secure and private. The last thing the LAPD needed was for the media to get wind of what they were doing. They had enough trouble with racial complaints and the growing 'defund the police' movement. If it got out that they were trying to verify whether a wealthy white man, who was already accused of murder, really could raise demons out of the Elysian Park grounds, the backlash would make the '92 riots look like a street fair.

Mason was exhausted by the time he got home. As he approached his driveway, he glanced over at the blue-tarped house. The lights were on, and he had a clear view of the front room and the owner sitting in his leather recliner. Mason now knew the man to be one Milton Gavish. Mason's reverse directory search gave him the name and using a $19.95 background search provided him with enough info to know that he was dealing with a perpetual troublemaker. Though Mason could have garnered the same information via the LAPD database, he didn't want there to be any obvious internal trail of his having been interested in the guy. He even paid for the information using a Venmo account with a fictitious name that he'd created years earlier for just such an occasion.

Gavish had a long history of bullying neighbors and making false accusations to the local police about anything that got stuck in his craw on any given day. While Mason's first choice may have been to take him out back and beat the bullying right out of him, he knew that such an action would doubtless do Mason more harm in the long run. No. He had to find a way to appease his need for suitable retribution while at the same time not appearing to be remotely involved.

Mason had considered waiting for the man's yappy little dog to be left alone in the backyard and either drugging it or simply relocating it up the hill far enough away so that the coyotes would find it long before Gavish ever did. The problem with that plan was that Mason, though he would never admit to it, was something of a softy when it came to animals. Besides, he wanted Gavish to be the one to suffer, not his little dog.

As soon as Mason stepped inside, he was struck at how uninviting his home was. Even though he'd only recently moved in, he knew he could have done more to make it feel a little more like home. Sure, he had the TV and sound system, but the walls and floor were still bare. After he was arrested and Chang left him, she took everything, not expecting Mason to ever see the light of day again. Once he'd been absolved of all charges, he had called her and suggested she return some of the paintings, rugs, ornaments and knick-knacks, but she had simply laughed then hung up the phone.

Mason knew he could fight to get at least some of his property returned, but decided that alienating the Los Angeles medical examiner would not be worth it just to get some stuff back that would neither suit nor fit his current home.

Mason promised himself that he would start spending some serious time fixing the place up once the Quinn case was closed. He certainly had the funds to give it a facelift. The problem was, he knew nothing about how to make a place look warm and comfy. He'd spent half of his life as a cop and lived a typical cop's life.

On the rare occasions when he wasn't knee deep investigating violent death, all he wanted to do was kick back, watch a few movies and catch up on sleep. Looking at rugs and fabric swatches was never going to make it onto his priority list.

In the kitchen, Mason looked to the back door and considered checking outside, but then asked himself, 'What for?' Wolfy was gone and though he was pretty sure that he could find another coyote who was willing to take his food, he'd felt some sort of kinship with the original one.

Mason grabbed a beer and his iPad, then searched the Uber Eats restaurant list, hoping to find something new and exciting. After becoming overwhelmed at the choices, he went with an old favorite and ordered the large chicken fajita platter from Justin Queso's in West Hollywood.

While he waited for his dinner to be delivered, he scrolled through Netflix's trending movie list and, not finding anything that had the chops to cleanse his mind of the day's events, went with one of his all-time favorites. Though it had hardly been a blockbuster at the time of its original release, there was something about *Vertigo* with James Stewart and Kim Novak that had grabbed Mason the first time he'd seen it and kept bringing him back for more.

*

On the other side of the Hollywood Hills, Teri, with distracting help from her cat, Cheesecake, had started to pack her belongings for her move to her grandparents' duplex in less than a week's time. Boxes were strewn around her rental townhouse, and she was starting to stress about her packing protocol. Being something of a planner, she'd wanted every box to hold items from one particular space. That system lasted about half an hour, at which point she realized that there was no way to ensure such packing purity. The first five boxes had been perfect. After that, she had to combine rooms when it came to the smaller stuff, which meant her process was already sullied. By box ten, she'd opened a bottle of wine and was cramming whatever fit into whatever box was closest at hand with zero regard for her initial system.

At one point, Teri became overwhelmed by just how much stuff she'd managed to accumulate. It wasn't as if most of it had any value, intrinsic or fiscal. Apart from some photos of Gregg and artwork he'd created at school, Teri felt she could easily throw everything else away and start over. It wasn't as if she hadn't done that a couple of times in her life already.

When she'd handed her son over to Bobby and Freeda and had run off to San Francisco, she'd taken nothing with her. Once the detectives who'd taken her under their wing were both killed in Los Angeles, all Teri had wanted to do was paint over the mistakes and tragedies of her life and start again. It took eighteen months of working at a couple of different restaurants to finally come to the conclusion that some things couldn't, or at least shouldn't, be swept under the proverbial rug. Some things, no matter how dark and depressing, become part of your DNA. What will make or break you is how you choose to live with them.

Within days, she had quit her job and enrolled at the Costa County Police Academy. She'd been terrified by the very concept of giving her life some sort of direction. That fear, however, was nothing compared to what she was about to do by taking a step closer to sharing her life with her son.

*

The following morning, Quinn (in handcuffs), Bayliss, Mason, Teri, two patrol officers, and, as a complete surprise to everyone, Chief Balisek, met up at the reception area of the Police Academy. The commanding officer of the training facility, an ex-marine and twenty-year LAPD veteran, met up with the group, then led them to the back of the academy property, before then returning to the admin building. As arranged, nobody at the academy was to witness or to know the intent of the small group.

"Unless anyone has anything they want to say, I think we should get this party started," Mason said. "Quinn? You ready?"

Quinn looked to the others, then up at the grey, June-gloom sky that was a regular weather factor any time from April through to August in LA. He looked down at the cracked concrete slab where it was deemed the demo should take place and studied it, while stalling for time. He had no doubts that he could prove to the onlookers that he was able to raise demons. His concern was what that could mean for him in the long run.

"I've gotta tell you," Quinn said. "I usually work in nicer surroundings."

If he'd hoped that his comment would add a bit of levity to the morning, he was wrong.

"Okay then," he mumbled. "I guess I'll get started. May I have the book?"

Quinn had already been advised that as the original hide-bound book was a vital piece of evidence, he would not be permitted to touch it. In fact, Teri herself had come in early, and with a uniformed officer videoing her the whole time, she had donned nitrile gloves and removed the ancient tome from its plastic evidence bag. She then used a special document scanner that could be held away from the actual pages, and copied everything within it, including the newer pages that Quinn had added after acquiring the book. What Quinn was handed was a plain black binder with copies of the original pages inside.

"As I said yesterday, I don't know if it will make a difference by not using the real book," Quinn mentioned.

"Why would it?" Mason replied. "You actually read the phonetically-altered version that's stapled to the first page, anyway. The book is nothing but a prop."

"It's a book that allows me to raise demons into our world. I don't know how it works. Maybe without it, nothing will happen."

"Let's try, shall we?" Balisek said.

Quinn shrugged and tried to hold the binder open but couldn't because of the handcuffs.

"I need these off," he stated.

"Yeah, right," Teri said as she took hold of the binder and held it open for him.

"This doesn't feel right," Quinn insisted.

"It didn't feel right for the victims either," Mason voiced.

Quinn didn't like the look in the detective's eyes and decided he'd better get on with it. He began reciting the phonetically spelled words. After years of practice, he was able to make his voice sound both mysterious and respectful. Even though he'd told the onlooker that little happened for the first ten minutes, their patience began to ebb after only three.

Finally, at the eleven-minute mark, the already gloomy day darkened even more. The observers all looked up and saw that beneath the grey marine layer, black clouds had formed and were swirling above them. Mason knew what he was seeing, but was still not believing Quinn's story. In fact, Mason was doing his best to catch sight of the gimmickry that was being used to create the illusion they were observing.

As the clouds grew and then began to form into the vortex, almost exactly as Quinn and Groves had described it, a cold chill ran down Mason's spine. By the time the funnel had sunk into the concrete slab only a few feet from where they were standing, he realized for the first time that he could be about to witness something truly supernatural.

Even though they were outdoors and able to clearly see the surrounding city and hills, they all felt the same sense of crippling claustrophobia. Mason took his eyes off the swirling chasm in front of him and looked to the other observers. They all had the same expression. The only one who didn't look as though she was about to lose it was Teri. She still had the expression, but at the same time, he saw that her jaw was set in sheer determination. For a brief moment, he felt a sense of pride that his new partner was not going to be put off by something as impossible as what was happening in front of them. He knew, at that moment, that nothing would ever stand in the way of Teri doing her job.

Mason was brought back to the moment when Bayliss screamed.

Mason looked back at the swirling chasm and immediately felt his knees go weak.

Something was rising out of the vortex.

CHAPTER 42

Balisek and Bayliss both took a few steps backwards as a head began to emerge from the pit. Mason stood firm and kept his gaze riveted on the thing. Teri, to everyone's surprise, including Quinn's, took a step forward, drew her gun and dropped to one knee as she aimed it at the emerging creature. Mason was about to tell her not to shoot, then realized that she had no intension of firing unless absolutely necessary and that she'd in fact just reacted exactly as trained, while he and the others stood there gawking.

The creature's head was now visible above the swirling smoke. The two versions he'd heard, one from Quinn, one from Groves, didn't do justice to the monster that was rising up in front of him. First of all, it was big. Impossibly big. Its head was at least four times the size of a human's. Its blackened features were grotesquely deformed and were covered in a glaze of slimy fluid that made Mason wonder if this demon resurrection was in fact, something of a rebirthing process and that the goo that was covering it was actually something akin to human afterbirth.

The worst part, if Mason had to pick just one, was the eyes. They were slanted and bulged outwards. They didn't blink as such, but rather turned blood red every few seconds in time with a strange, raspy, mewling sound that the beast was making between growls and hideous screams.

As the shoulders and torso started to appear, Balisek called out, "Enough. That's enough. We don't need to raise the thing any further."

Quinn looked to Mason for confirmation of the command. He nodded, thankful that Balisek had intervened to stop the freak show.

Quinn stopped the recitation and read the reversal incantation. The others looked on in rapt silence as the demon was drawn back into the vortex, screaming as it tried to break free from the black smoke. Within seconds, the head vanished, and the spinning cloud rose from the ground, and for a few moments swirled overhead, until it too faded then vanished from sight.

Quinn turned to Mason and grinning, asked, "Believe me now?"

"What I believe now is that you have an even bigger problem," Balisek stated.

"How so?"

"Remember how in the deal, there was a caveat that you had to help the police in any matter deemed necessary to both close and resolve the murders of Groppel, Harter, Whitlough, Ginetto, Brimmer and Tamacini?"

"We all agreed to the terms," Bayliss responded, her voice still shaky after what she'd just seen. "What's changed?"

"What's changed is that none of us, except Quinn, truly believed in his having the ability to raise whatever the fuck that was, from out of the ground. Now that we have been shown irrefutable proof that these monsters do exist, you Mr. Quinn, have one more task before the agreement can be ratified."

"I don't see what more my client can do that he hasn't already done," Bayliss responded.

"By my count, there are four of these creatures that were allowed to break free and remain loose among us. As part of resolving the cases, we now need your client to get rid of them."

"I don't know that I can. The reversal incantation has to happen when the creature is in solid form. Once it starts moving between realms, I don't think the spell will work."

"Realms?" Mason asked with raised eyebrows.

"That's what I call it," Quinn replied.

"When your ex-wife went back to the old Harter house with Ms. Brimmer, was it their intention to try and get rid of that particular one?" Mason asked.

"How would I know what they were up to?" Quinn insisted. "Leticia and I are divorced."

"May I jump in for a moment? Teri asked. "Last night I couldn't sleep, so I spent the night calling a party planner that you might remember. Does the name Debbie Cohen ring a bell?"

The color drained from Quinn's face.

"She very sweetly woke up a bunch friends who had attended some of the parties we're not investigating, as well as the ones we are, and informed them of your situation and found out something interesting. At a number of parties, you were seen to raise the creature completely out of the chasm. You even seemed able to restrain it somehow. What I found fascinating is that in each of those cases, after everyone had a good look at the thing, you had used a spell to return it back through the vortex."

"I don't remember—"

"It seems that you always offered two versions of the act. One where the creature is half exposed, another where it is fully out of the ground and freestanding. It seems that, right before the show, you informed the clients who chose the deluxe model that there would be a surcharge to return the monster back into the ground at the end of the act. Amazingly, most people paid the extra amount, but a few refused. Do you want me to remind you which ones those were?"

Teri hated the fact that she'd basically caught her partner completely off guard by not telling him what she'd unearthed, but she was pretty sure he'd understand. At least she hoped he would. She'd planned to tell him what she'd found before the demo, but Balisek dragged him off before Teri could get a chance to do so.

Quinn stared at Teri in shock. It was obvious that he had believed that his scamming of the clients was a piece of volatile information that would always remain locked behind the terms of the NDA.

"What that means," Teri continued, "is that you not only brought these creatures into our world, but forced your clients to pay extra to then remove them. As if that wasn't bad enough, when they refused to bow to your little extortion scheme, you intentionally left the creatures to their own devices."

"That's not entirely true," Quinn protested.

"I think you should shut up now," Bayliss snapped at him, furious that her client had turned out to be a monster in his own right.

"They can't leave the perimeter of where they appear," Quinn stated, completely ignoring his counsel's advice. "Plus, I've been wondering whether to say this or not, but—"

"Mr. Quinn, will you please shut the hell up!" Bayliss yelled.

"The event at the Sunset Tower Hotel. You keep accusing me of leaving a demon there, but they didn't even want the extended show. I don't know what killed that woman, but it wasn't one of my little monsters."

"Little monsters?" Mason growled and took a step closer to Quinn.

"I'm outta here," Bayliss said as she raised her hands in the air and headed towards the parking area.

"You're my lawyer," Quinn shouted after her.

"Not anymore!"

"You can't do this," Quinn shouted.

"Sue me!" she shouted back.

*

Once back at their office, Mason waved off Teri's apology for not letting him know what she'd found out about Quinn's extortion scheme.

"I would have done the same," he said. "It means that Quinn is not only eligible for murder one, but after adding three counts of extortion to the list of charges, we won't need a plea deal."

"You will if you want him to get rid of the entities," Teri said. "Plus, you said three counts, yet Quinn told us that he never brought a demon fully out of the vortex at the Sunset Tower Hotel. That means his little extortion trick only happened at the Brimmer and Tamacini."

"Then what killed Whitlough?" Mason asked.

"I think we need to go back over that murder book and look at it from a different angle. We lumped that case into the same category as the other deaths because of Quinn having performed at the party. If he's being straight with us, which at this point I feel he is, then we need to find out who really killed her."

"I assume you are dismissing the idea of her having drowned?"

"Unless she managed to do so in a large enough volume of Evian water to fill her lungs, and then somehow managed

373

to crawl, unseen, into the pool, then yes. Her death wasn't accidental."

"I'll tell you what. I don't want to slow the momentum on the Quinn cases or the Whitlough homicide. Why don't I stay on Quinn, and you take the Evian drowning?"

Before Teri could answer, Mason got a text.

"Fuck," Mason said as he read it. "Balisek wants to see both of us.

"Is that a bad thing?"

"She's your ex-stepmother. What do you think?"

"Maybe she wants to commend us for the fine work we've been doing."

"Is that what you really think?" Mason asked.

"Nope. Just trying to be positive." Teri replied.

"Let me know how that works out for you," Mason smiled as he opened the door for her.

CHAPTER 43

Mason had expected there to just be the three of them at the unscheduled meeting with Balisek. When he saw the district attorney, his lead ADA, Andrew Bernstein and Anita Bayliss all sitting waiting for them, he knew that something was off.

"I thought you quit?" Mason said, as he sat next to Quinn's ex-lawyer.

"So did I," she replied coldly.

"Detectives, I wanted you to be part of this meeting," Balisek began. "After witnessing the demonstration over at the academy and then conferring with the district attorney, we both feel that there is no way that the cases against Carlos Quinn can be brought to trial."

Mason felt his heart shudder and the blood rush from his head.

"What the hell do you mean?" he managed to ask. "He fucking confessed."

"Let's keep the profanity to a minimum, Detective. Yes, he did confess, but that will not be enough in this case."

Mason looked to Teri who was shaking her head in shock, wondering what political bullshit had been put in play.

Patrick Farrigan had been district attorney under three mayors, and if it weren't for his full head of grey hair, he could have passed for much younger than sixty-five. As he observed the look of shock and disappointment on the faces of the two detectives, he understood their reaction. In fact, he completely agreed with them. There was zero doubt that Quinn was complicit in multiple murders, yet he had no choice but to follow what he knew to be a foregone conclusion.

"You have both done an amazing job pulling together all of the facts that we now have before us," Farrigan said. "Quinn should be found guilty. There is no doubt about that. The problem is, we can't bring this to trial because of what Mr. Quinn did that ultimately resulted in the multiple deaths. The issue is not with the evidence or the man himself. It's because of what we would have to accuse him of doing. Quinn somehow has found a way to raise what have been described as demons or monsters. If we were talking about the human variation of those traits, say a Bundy or a Manson, that would be one thing. But we're not. From what I have read from your reports and from what Chief Balisek has relayed to me, these are actual, non-humanoid creatures, the likes of which have never been seen in modern times. There is no possible way that a jury in this day and age is going to accept the prosecution's case that these murders were carried out by demonic creatures, raised from the earth by Quinn."

"But we've seen them," Mason insisted. "Hell, I didn't believe in them until then."

"That's all well and good, but the jury will have not seen them and except for a very small percentage of the population, people believe that they only exist on TV, movie screens or game consoles. If we were to attempt to mount a case involving real life monsters, we would be crucified by the media and laughed out of every court in America."

"So, we just let him go?" Teri asked.

"Quinn has us over a barrel. He has nothing to lose by going to the media and showing his unusual talent, and also, conceivably, continuing to perform his act."

"Wouldn't that be a good thing?" Mason asked. "Then he'd, in effect, be showing everyone that the creatures do exist and that he's guilty."

"That may be, but if the public were to become aware of the existence of these creatures, it would almost certainly destroy that fragile veil that we all use to retain our sanity when faced with the impossible. Religions would be superseded with demon worship. Somehow, either the original book, or one like it would end up in the wrong hands and we could literally see these creatures on battlefields or in the Colombian jungles being used as guards for the cartel properties. If there is one thing of which I am completely certain, it is that Quinn's little monsters, as I believe he recently referred to them, must never become public knowledge."

"So, what happens to him?" Mason asked.

"That's where the irony steps in. He will have to sign our own nondisclosure agreement which will bar him from carrying out any more rituals and telling anyone about any of this."

"What if he ignores it?" Teri asked. "What if he does talk?"

"That's the beauty of the agreement. If he does disclose anything and it becomes public knowledge, the agreement is nullified and we get to have our day in court and by that time, the public would believe in the creatures and Mr. Quinn would have himself given up the tenuous hold he'd had on us."

"And you are going to resume being his lawyer?" Mason asked Bayliss.

"I'm not sure I have much choice," Bayliss replied, glaring at the DA.

"We still need him to get rid of the monsters that he left up here with us humans," Mason pointed out.

"We've already discussed that. Ms. Bayliss and I will structure an addendum to the NDA that makes his removing the creatures a leading caveat to the contract."

"We also plan on revisiting the Whitlough case," Teri added. "After Quinn's comment at the academy, we want to confirm that that creature didn't, as he professes, rise fully out of the vortex. If that is the truth, then we still have an unsolved case to deal with."

Balisek had clearly lost interest in the proceedings and simply nodded as she raised her phone to her ear.

*

While Teri returned to their office, Mason went to retrieve Quinn from lock-up so they could hit the first property. He had decided to start at the Trousdale house, as it was the only location still occupied. He also felt that he owed Groves for his having provided details of Quinn's show.

Mason stopped in the evidence storage area and signed out the infamous black book as well as the binder with the photocopy and phonetic translation. Just as he was about to walk down to the holding area, he had an idea. Mason stopped in at the duty sergeant's kiosk and got permission to make a photocopy down there, so he didn't have to go back up to RHD.

Once he was done, Mason folded the single sheet of copy paper and placed it in his inside jacket pocket.

On the drive to the Trousdale Estate, Quinn wouldn't shut up. Mason assumed that the man's verbal diarrhea was in reaction to his almost being a free man. He was angry enough that Quinn was no longer to be handcuffed, but he was really furious that the little shit was going to literally get away with murder. It took every ounce of Mason's willpower not to stop the car, put two in the guy's skull then leave him in the gutter where he belonged.

Instead of becoming too immersed in such dark fantasies, Mason took a couple of deep, cleansing breaths then turned on the radio loud enough to drown out anything that his passenger felt like sharing.

Groves must have heard them pull up, as the front door was already open by the time they exited the car.

Mason had called him right after the meeting with Balisek and had asked if they could come by and attempt to exorcise whatever was lurking within the property. He made it a point to not let on that Quinn was soon to be a free man in fear that Groves might finish the guy off there and then.

Once they were inside, Quinn asked whether Groves had noticed any unusual sensations within the house since the accident.

Mason and Groves both looked shocked at Quinn's choice of words. Clearly, neither felt that what had befallen the maestro could be classified as an accident.

"Not up here," Groves replied. "But on the few occasions that I've had to go down to the basement area, the temperature would suddenly drop and the last time, I could have sworn I saw smoke swirling on the floor."

"What did you do?" Quinn asked.

"I stopped going into the basement," Groves replied, matter-of-factly.

"Then that's where we should start," Quinn announced. "I'll need something to drink first. Perhaps a coffee. If you have any cookies, all the better. Detective? You want anything while the butler's getting my order?"

Mason had a momentary concern when Groves stepped up to with inches of Quinn.

"Would you perhaps like that coffee in enema form?" Groves asked in a surprisingly pleasant voice.

Quinn could only shake his head as his voice appeared to have temporarily left him.

"I hope you don't mind if I don't join you down there," Groves said to Mason. "As soon as you're done, I'm going to have the entire basement filled in."

"I don't blame you," Mason replied. "Why don't you go out for a while, and I'll give you a call when we're finished here."

"I'd appreciate that," Groves said as he gave Mason a friendly pat of the shoulder. "I'll be down on Sunset having a mooch in Book Soup," he said, referring to the iconic bookstore on the corner of Sunset and Holloway Drive.

Once Groves was gone, Mason followed Quinn into the basement and took in what had been the maestro's cherished torture chamber.

The iron maiden was gone. Mason knew it would never have fit in the evidence lock-up, so assumed it must have been hauled to the police storage garage instead. The concrete where it had stood was at least three shades lighter than the rest of the floor. The result of a lot of bleach and scouring to remove the blood.

As Mason looked around the collection of crude and yet terrifying devices, a freezing draft suddenly swirled at his feet, immediately chilling his ankles.

"What the fuck was that?" Mason blurted out.

"Good news," Quinn replied. "It's still here."

CHAPTER 44

Quinn positioned himself in the middle of the room and began the reversal incantation. To Mason, it sounded pretty much the same as the one he'd heard Quinn recite at the academy and hoped that the guy wasn't trying something cute. That was the one concern shared by everybody. If he attempted to bring another creature up through the vortex, Balisek had secretly advised Mason that he was to consider such an action as an attempt on his life and that lethal force against Quinn was acceptable to ensure the monster never fully manifested.

As seemed to always be the case, for the first ten minutes nothing happened, then without warning, a form seemed to emerge from the wall. Mason was shocked to see that unlike the one he'd seen at the academy, this thing was partially translucent. Its silhouette kept going in and out of phase as Quinn continued his recitation. At one point the monster seemed to solidify for a split second then began to diffuse even more.

The most unnerving thing was that the beast appeared to be howling and screaming, yet no sound could be heard except for Quinn's repeating of the last few phrases.

Everything seemed to be going better than Mason expected, when the demon suddenly solidified completely and started to reach out for Quinn. Mason looked on in horror as one of its massive claws looked about to grab him. At that instant Quinn read the last words within the text.

The creature froze in place then began clawing at the concrete as a hole opened in the floor and it began to be pulled towards it.

Within moments it was gone. Nothing remained of the creature or the chasm. The floor looked untouched and the temperature within the room began warming immediately.

"That wasn't so bad," Quinn said laughing as he closed the binder. "When's the next one?"

Mason wished that his tacit permission to kill the guy was still an option.

*

Teri contacted a couple of guests who had attended the Whitlough party, and after explaining that the NDA was no longer in effect, both confirmed Quinn's statement that he had never brought the demon fully out of the vortex.

Frustrated that so much investigative time had been wasted on the case by lumping it in with the other Quinn homicides, Teri re-read the Whitlough murder book twice through and realized that something was missed during the initial investigation, thirteen years earlier. The original detectives had interviewed the guests and wait staff. They had not, as she knew only too well, interviewed the performer as he was never, at that point, able to be located. What bothered her was that there was no record of them having spoken to the kitchen staff.

Both Teri and Mason had briefly spoken to one of the detectives who had been given the original case. Mario Gutierrez was now a lieutenant at the Hollywood Division and had been very helpful when they'd first talked. She only hoped he'd feel the same way now that she was going to have to question their methods.

Teri called Gutierrez on his cell phone. She fully expected to have to leave a message, but the call was answered almost immediately.

"Gutierrez," a slightly slurred voice said.

"This is Detective Grey at RHD. We spoke about the Whitlough murder."

"I remember." His voice sounded even more slurred.

"Are you drunk? Is this a bad time?"

"Damn right it's a bad time. I'm sittin' here on the terrace of the Roserita Beach Hotel doing my best to not think about that or any other case. If that wasn't clear enough, I'm on fucking vacation."

The call disconnected.

Teri immediately dialed the number again.

"I'll give you this," Gutierrez said. "You sure as hell got yourself a pair of cojónes."

"That's very kind," Teri tossed back, wondering how he'd take her sarcasm.

Gutierrez laughed. "You got two minutes while this lovely waitress brings me another Pina Colada."

"Thank you. Your case no longer fits our perp, so I thought I'd take another crack at it while the book was out of storage."

Teri waited for some sort of acknowledgement, but got nothing.

"I'm calling because I can't see any mention in the chrono or in the interview list of the kitchen staff having been questioned."

"That's because we didn't question them. They never came into contact with her and, as I'm sure you know, half of them were almost certainly illegal and the other half didn't even know that there was a special event in the ballroom. I had a quick word with the chef, and he confirmed that he wouldn't have allowed any of them to stray from their stations anyway."

"I don't see any mention of your conversation with the chef," Teri pointed out.

"The guy was a major celebrity back then. I don't suppose it's any big deal to mention him after all this time, especially now that he's in God's waiting room. Do you remember Patrick Maduré?"

"The Cajun chef? Oh my god. I used to watch him as a kid. I even have one of his cookbooks. What do mean, he's in God's waiting room?"

"Five years ago, drunk as skunk, he was speeding the wrong way on a freeway on-ramp. Luckily, he hit a big rig before hurting too many people. As far as I know, he ended up just like that Stephen Hawking guy, at least when he was still alive. You know, the one with the wheelchair and robotic voice, except from what I heard, Maduré could still talk, he just couldn't move.

"Hawking did not end up in that condition from a crash. He had ALS. Sound to me like Maduré was paraplegic."

"Whatever," the retired detective replied. "Anyway, I read the other day that he's circling the drain and probably won't need that wheelchair much longer."

Teri tried hard to disregard the man's blunt stupidity and couldn't help wondering how the LAPD had ever survived with his type existing within the detective ranks.

"I still don't see why there's no mention of you having interviewed him," Teri said.

"He was a celebrity. He didn't want his name on some report downtown where the press were bound to find it. After talking to him, I made the call that his statement didn't add anything worthwhile to the case, so I kept our conversation verbal."

"That was it? You just chose to not even document what may later have become a relevant discourse?"

"Do you remember the guy?" Gutierrez asked. "He was the size of a frigging house. He was sweating the whole time we talked and couldn't walk more than a few feet without getting winded. He couldn't have had anything to do with her death. He was just there to cook the food."

"Was he the regular chef? I thought Maduré worked out of New Orleans?"

"He did, but Whitlaugh's people paid him a ton of money to come out to LA and prepare the meal for her celebration."

"Did he and Whitlough know each other?" Teri asked.

"Not according to him."

"So, you did ask?" Teri pushed.

"I must have done. It's a pretty basic question."

Frustrated by the man's cavalier attitude, Teri didn't bother with any more questions and hung up the phone. The process of trying to pry information had been a depressing reminder of some of the bottom feeders that somehow find their way onto the force.

Teri opened the murder book and looked back at Whitlough's bio. She couldn't see anything relevant, so decided to try a different approach so as to check out the author's history. She went to a site that, though usually populated with half-truths, occasionally came up with important nuggets that a celebrity hadn't wanted made public, but the contributing fan-base uncovered anyway.

Teri created a username and password on realfanbase.com, then entered Whitlough's name. Seconds later, an unflattering picture of Whitlough, taken at a signing a few years before her death, popped up along with a list of search categories.

Teri selected *private life*, then *early years*. She was stunned at the sheer amount of info that populated the screen. The data appeared to have grown exponentially, as did the writer's fame. Needless to say, with interest in her not having burgeoned until her first mega novel became a global bestseller, her younger years were nowhere near as well documented.

In fact, there was little written about Whitlough's teens and early twenties. Instead, friends and family had uploaded an abundance of photos in order to give her a pictographic history for that period of her life.

Almost all were what you would expect from a young girl growing up in Chicago. Lots of pictures of her making snow angels, goofing off on ice and attending a multitude of parties. Teri's mind was starting to atrophy as she waded through hundreds of similarly-themed photos. With her brain doing everything it could to wander off to more stimulating mental pastures, she almost missed the needle in the proverbial haystack.

One strange anomaly that drew Teri's curiosity was that at one period in her life, the photos of Whitlough changed from the mundane to the intriguing.

It took a moment for her to even recognize what she was seeing. Once she did, however, Teri took her time focusing on her find. For what Teri judged was probably a twelve-to-fourteen-month period, a large proportion of the photos were missing one half of the image. Some appeared to have been carefully cut, some had been haphazardly ripped and a few even seemed to have had one half burned away.

The digitized pictures differed from everything else Teri had so far seen. For one thing, Whitlough herself looked happier. For another, the background of most of the pictures looked more like a travelogue than all the previous homespun moments. Teri recognized, Niagara Falls, Washington DC, the Santa Monica Pier and San Francisco's Fisherman's Warf. Whitlough looked both happy and in love in all the pictures.

What Teri couldn't make out was who exactly had been standing next to her, sometimes with their hands entwined, sometimes with arms around each other. Whoever he was, he had been an important part of her life at that moment in time.

Teri scrolled back to the earlier photos, focusing on the ones just prior to the first crude editing out of Whitlough's significant other. After another half hour of mind-numbingly uninteresting subject matter, she stopped her scroll and went back two pictures.

It was another shot of Whitlough and friends, many of whom were a constant part of her early photographic history. Teri wasn't immediately sure why it had caught her eye, then noticed that there was one new face among the familiar group. The picture had been taken in front of a fifties-style, red and chrome diner. Eight people were standing side by side next to the restaurant entrance. All were dressed for Chicago winter with the exception of one man who stood three from the left. He was beaming at the camera as Whitlough, her then brown hair fluttering in the wind, stood next to him, staring almost adoringly up at his grinning face.

Teri knew two things immediately. That she had found Whitlough's mysterious love interest, and more importantly, Teri recognized him immediately.

CHAPTER 45

At nine the following morning, Mason left Quinn in the car as he ran into Pure Gold Realty in Beverly Hills so he could pick up the keys to the St Cloud house. He had at first been surprised that they were allowing him to go into the property without one of their reps being present, but it seemed that after what happened to Leticia and then to their colleague, Russell McNeil, nobody wanted to go anywhere near any of Leticia's listings.

"Are you going to record whatever it is you plan to do there?" the office manager asked as she handed over the keys.

"Of course," Mason replied. "We record everything nowadays."

Mason felt little concern for having lied to the woman. The fact was, Balisek had made it very clear that there was to be no new evidence of the creatures. It was going to be hard enough keeping what they already had from the media. If a video emerged showing an LAPD detective supervising what, to all intents and purposes looked frighteningly like the exorcism of a demonic apparition, the department would never live it down.

As Mason approached the car, he could see Quinn fiddling with the dash-mounted computer.

"I told you not to touch anything," Mason barked as he climbed into the vehicle.

"I was just curious to see if I could access anything interesting."

"Did you?" Mason asked.

"No. You gotta have a login and password."

"Fancy that. You'd think we'd want to share all our little secrets with a douche bag like you."

"There's no need for names. May I remind you that I am in fact, helping you at the moment. By tomorrow, we'll be done, and I'll be a free man."

"If I'd had my way, you'd be locked away till there wasn't enough of you left to bury."

"Ah, but you don't get to have things your way, do you? That's the great thing about our society; people like you might have the power to catch people like me, but in the end, my kind always find a way out. It's called brains versus brawn. I mean, look at me. My monsters have killed at least six people directly or indirectly, yet here I am being chauffeured around by you. I have to imagine that's got under your skin."

Mason kept his face expressionless then started the car. He slipped it into gear and stomped on the gas for a split second before braking. Quinn had no time to brace himself before he was thrown forward, bashing his chest on the dashboard and his head on the windscreen.

"You might want to buckle up," Mason said as he pulled slowly into the morning traffic.

Despite Quinn whining that he had broken his nose and probably given him a concussion, Mason never even acknowledged his passenger until they'd passed through the Bel Air gates.

It had been sunny on both prior visits to the St Cloud house. That wasn't the case this time around. The marine layer hung low over the city and as they climbed the winding road, they found themselves in a dense, grey fog. During the few moments when a gust of wind moved enough of the cloud aside so that the house was visible from the drive, Mason was surprised at how its quaintness had vanished with the sun. Under the muted grey light, the place looked unfriendly and foreboding. The small windows which had previously given it a warm, almost inviting feel, now made it look claustrophobic and unwelcoming.

*

Teri started her day back at the Sunset Tower Hotel. She'd had a dentist appointment at nine, so was only able to get there well past the breakfast service. Inga Civalla met her at the reception desk then walked Teri to the hotel kitchen so she could give it a more thorough going over. It wasn't as if she had any concrete reason to do so, it was just that having seen the photo of Whitlough outside the diner, Teri felt that there was always the possibility of the kitchen being somehow tied to the case.

From the moment Teri had recognized super-chef, Patrick Maduré, she felt something click, even though she still had no idea how that sensation would play out. The only thing she knew for certain was that on each occasion when she'd had that feeling in the middle of an investigation, she'd been about to make some sort of breakthrough.

The kitchen was quiet. The breakfast service was all but finished and apart from one young kitchen porter working at the far end of the room, the place was empty.

"Where is everyone?" Teri asked.

"We don't offer lunch except on weekends. We found that our clientele preferred to walk down to Sunset Plaza if they want a sit-down midday meal. The chef and sous chefs usually arrive at around one or two."

"Who cooked the breakfast?"

"That's done by the late-night kitchen staff. They usually clock out at around nine am."

"So, the kitchen is left unmanned? What if somebody wants a late breakfast?"

"Filippo is here till the dinner crew arrive, though after ten o'clock we only offer a continental breakfast."

"Where is Filippo now?" Teri asked.

"If I had to hazard a guess, I would say he's outside having a coffee and a smoke," Inga replied.

"What about the wait staff and dishwashers. You must keep some around in case of room service orders?"

Inga shrugged and gave her a raised eyebrow look.

"Oh," Teri said, as Inga's expression hit home. "I'm not here to check immigration status."

"Doesn't matter to them. Police are police."

Teri nodded her understanding. "Do you mind showing me around the kitchen?"

"Sure. I'm not an expert on what every single thing does, but I can probably wing it."

Despite her disclaimer, Inga gave her an extensive tour explaining the function of each station as well as what each appliance and gadget was used for. The end of the tour consisted of a look at the walk-in fridge and a much briefer peek at the walk-in freezer.

Teri had never spent any meaningful time in a commercial kitchen and was fascinated by what she was seeing. She peppered Inga with questions the entire time. Even once inside the freezer, Teri's curiosity was stronger that her will to stay warm.

The racks were filled with unrecognizable shrink-wrapped objects that even stumped Inga.

"I'm sorry. I don't know what they all are when they're wrapped like that. I know we keep a lot of perishable luxury items in the freezer. New Zealand lamb, lobster, jumbo shrimp... stuff like that."

"I would have thought that customers would expect those things to be fresh," Teri commented.

"Trust me, most people can't tell the difference."

"What's all this stuff?" Teri asked pointing to large plastic wrapped blocks that took up an entire rack space on the right-hand side.

"That's ice for carving. You know, like for big parties."

"I always wondered where those came from," Teri said.

"We used to have to order each carving be done out of house, which was fine, except that on top of the carving fee, they used to charge us an arm and a leg just for the ice. The then manager decided to bring in an industrial water freezer. Now we just pay for the carver to come here and work on our ice."

"That must be fun to watch?" Teri commented.

"It is, but you can't get too close cause the chips fly everywhere."

"I can imagine."

"Do you want to see one that's already been carved. It's for a wedding tonight?"

"Only if it can be seen in less than five seconds. After that, I think I'm going to freeze solid."

"It's right here," Inga said as she removed a piece of insulated plastic sheeting that was covering one of the racks.

"Oh my god," Teri exclaimed. "That's amazing."

"I know. The guy used to carve marble then found out that he could earn ten times as much carving ice."

Teri studied the sculpture of cupid, his arrow at the ready.

"How do you get the ice to remain so clear? It almost looks like glass."

"Incredible, isn't it. The trick is to use very pure water. That way the impurities don't discolor the ice. We actually go one step farther."

"How so?" Teri asked as she felt another tiny click go off in her brain.

"We use mountain spring water. After some testing, we found that Evian, from France, was by far the best."

Teri stared dumbstruck at the other woman. Inside, her mind was weaving a tapestry of confluent data, that had, until that moment, been impossible to bring together.

"I don't suppose Barney Fisher is here today?" Teri asked once they were back in the relative warmth of the kitchen, referring to the older waiter she'd talked to on their previous visit to the hotel.

"Actually, he is," Inga replied. "He's on room-service duty. He's probably in the break room."

Inga used her phone to send a text. Moments later a response caused her phone to chime.

"He's on his way."

"Tell me more about the ghost you mentioned when we were last here," Teri asked. "You said the sightings started in '09?"

"I hope that wasn't a problem," Inga said, almost apologetically.

"What do mean?"

"When I first heard about the ghost, the manager told me that it only started appearing after they opened up some of the walls to add more power and air-conditioning. As I

398

hadn't been here that long, I assumed that work had been done in the '09 remodel. I checked after your last visit and found out that work had actually been done in 1967. That's apparently when the hauntings started, not in '09."

Teri smiled as another piece of the puzzle slotted into place.

Moments later, Barney appeared.

"Is there a problem?" he asked, always on guard for the other shoe to drop.

"Not with you," Teri replied and gave him her most endearing smile. "When we talked last time, you said you were here the night that Ms. Whitlough died."

"I was."

"This may seem a strange question but, was there any sort of issue in the kitchen that night? Anything out of the ordinary?"

"We had a celebrity chef that night which always causes an extra layer of chaos. That one was especially bad. He did nothing but scream and shout at the kitchen staff from the moment he arrived."

"Is that unusual?" Teri asked.

"Yes and no. We of course get our share of the Gordon Ramsay types, you know, the ones that like to lord it over everyone in the kitchen. That said, they all usually calm down once the service is well underway. Not this guy. He seemed to get madder as the night went on."

"Did he do anything unusual besides scream and rant?" Teri asked.

"I can't think of anything particular. No. Wait. There was one odd thing. He wouldn't let anyone go into the freezer except him. He said he was taking extra care so that no one damaged the ice sculpture."

"While a little OCD, is that really that unusual?"

"Maybe not, but what *was* unusual was we'd all seen the thing being carved earlier in the day and knew what it looked like, yet when we were finally allowed in so we could wheel the sculpture out to the ballroom, it was different."

"Different how?" Teri asked.

Barney visibly blushed.

"The woman who died, the one who's birthday was being celebrated, she was some sort of famous writer."

"We know that," Teri said, not sure where the man was heading.

"Apparently, her books were kind of..." he struggled to find the right word. "Salacious. Yeah. That's the right term."

"I'm not sure I'm following your—"

"Her publisher wanted to surprise her with something unusual. So, the carver guy, he was told to carve the ice to look like one of her best-known characters. I gather he's supposed to be something of a lady's man. We didn't see what all the fuss was about until the guy started working lower down on the ice block."

Barney raised his eyebrows as if that would clue in Teri. She just shrugged and looked questioningly back at him.

"The guy carved a penis," Barney said in a stage whisper. "A big one. One that was..." Barned raised his forearm and shook it.

"Erect?" Teri asked.

"Very."

"I see how that was a little unusual but, I'm not sure it helps me—"

"The thing is," Barney interrupted. "Once the show was over and we could come back up and do our jobs, a couple of guys went in the freezer to get the sculpture, and the... thing was gone."

"The sculpture was gone?" Teri questioned.

"No. Just the... you know."

He again waved his forearm.

"The penis was gone?"

"Yup. And not only that, but it didn't look like it was carved 'gone', if you know what I mean. It looked more like it got broken off."

"Did you see anyone go into the freezer before that?"

"Not during the service, but when the performance was happening, we were all told to go down to the staff lounge, which we did."

"All of you?" Teri asked.

"Yeah. All of us," Barney confirmed.

Teri sighed.

"All of us except that screaming chef. He stayed up here as far as I know."

"Was there any fallout to the broken sculpture?"

"Not that we heard. Then again, by the time we were allowed back upstairs after the show, the chef had gone and when we resumed drinks service in the ballroom, everyone seemed shellshocked as a result of the show."

"Was there anything else?" Teri asked.

"Not until they found the poor woman's body in the pool. After that, we were kept away from the guests once the police arrived on the scene."

"Were any of the wait staff or kitchen staff interviewed?" Teri asked, even though she already knew the answer.

"As the woman had gone missing while we were all in the staff lounge, they didn't seem at all interested in us."

"Or in the chef?" Teri asked.

"Not that any of us were aware of."

"Thank you for your time," Teri said, offering Barney her hand.

"No problem," he said then shook it. "Are you going to want to talk to me again?" he asked.

"Is there any reason we might need to?" Teri asked with an understanding smile.

"None whatsoever."

CHAPTER 46

Mason unlocked the front door and immediately felt the change inside the house. When he and Teri had first visited the place there had been an inviting smell of fireplaces, polished wood and cinnamon. Now all he could smell was dryness; something that before that morning, he didn't think even had an odor.

But as Mason stepped inside, he knew that what he was detecting must have been similar to what archaeologists encountered when first opening ancient Egyptian tombs. It was a mix of acrid desiccation and centuries of airless stagnation. The air smelled as if it had never been breathed by the living.

The odor itself was enough to raise the hairs on the back of his neck, but when he turned on the entry hall lights, the sight that greeted him sent a chill from one end of his spine to the other.

It had only been a few days since he'd been inside the house, yet the hallway looked as if it had been abandoned and left to rot decades earlier. Every flat surface was covered

403

in a thick layer of dust. Large cobwebs hug in cascading brocades that were wafting in a perpetual draft that seemed to be running freely throughout the house.

"This looks interesting," Quinn said, seeming unaffected by the house's new appearance. "You'd think these people could fork out for a maid occasionally."

Mason was about to explain that what they were seeing was not the result of poor domesticity, rather, from some force that Quinn himself had unleashed years earlier, but decided to ignore the comment and keep things on track.

"Let's get this over with," Mason said as he tried to swipe away an errant wisp of webbing that had drifted onto his face. "Where do you want to start?"

"Normally I'd say wherever the person was killed, but I'm sensing that the demon has spread throughout this dump. Want me to try it right here?"

"This is your show," Mason pointed out. "You decide."

Quinn nodded as he retrieved the binder from a Safeway shopping bag that Mason had been holding. He stepped to the center of the hallway and began reciting. Almost immediately, the draft strengthened into wind. The entry was soon filled with airborne dust and free-floating cobwebs. While Mason was racked with a coughing fit, Quinn kept his voice steady and strong as he continued reading the words.

Upstairs, on the landing that overlooked the entry hall, two enormous ceramic jars stood on carved wooden plinths. As Quinn reached the part where he began to repeat the one final phrase that would ultimately draw the entity back down into the chasm, both jars tipped forward and fell over the wooden banister, crashing only feet away from the two men.

Mason refused to show it, but inside he was feeling fear beyond anything he'd ever experienced. It wasn't that he hadn't had some terrifying encounters in his career, but as bad as some of those were, he'd always known that he was dealing with flesh and blood and that, if he did as he was trained and used his brain rather than reflex, he would walk away in one piece.

Standing in the Bel Air mansion as some ghostly manifestation focused all its attention on them, Mason felt no such assuredness that all would be well.

Quinn continued reciting, his voice seeming to grow in strength. Suddenly, the wind stopped, and the floor opened up as the vortex appeared between them. Almost instantly, every particle of webbing and dust that had been kicked up by the force of the wind returned to the hallway and began to form into a towering shape at the bottom of the staircase.

Nothing about the creature looked like anything Mason had ever heard or read about. The only part of it that appeared to have any recognizable form were its two yellow eyes that seemed to be looking down on them with pure hatred.

As Mason stood frozen in place and Quinn somehow managed to continue reciting, the creature began shrieking like a thousand tortured animals as it felt the force of the incantation drag it towards the gaping hole. At one point, it seemed to break from the spell and lunged towards Quinn, who somehow didn't even flinch and read the words even louder. The beast never made contact as its lower extremities began being pulled into the void. As it tried to stay above ground, its shapeless form solidified for a brief moment, allowing massive, blackened claws to latch onto the wood flooring surrounding the chasm. For a second, the beast looked like a cross between a giant raven and a thrashing alligator, then it was gone.

"I remember this one now," Quinn said as he dusted himself off. "It was pretty nasty back when I brought it out of the void."

"Yet that didn't stop you from leaving it here in our world?" Mason said, his voice low and menacing.

"Hey. It was nothing personal. These people had the chance to pay for the removal the same way they paid for me to bring forth the latency."

"Latency?" Mason asked.

"Yeah, latency. It's not like I created these things. They were formed way before mankind. Whatever they once were, their latent spirits are all that's left. I'm just able to bring them into our plane."

"And leave them here if you can't extort some more money."

"As I said, it was never personal."

"I think it was personal to all the people that were killed by them. What about your ex-wife? I know you took her death personally."

"She was never even touched by the creature in that house," Quinn insisted.

"Maybe her body wasn't touched, but her mind sure as hell was."

"That was unfortunate."

"Tell me something. What exactly was your ex doing with that spiritualist? Why did she care whether those houses were haunted or not?"

Quinn thought for a moment.

"From what my attorney tells me, the deal is cut and dry, right?"

"Right."

"So, whatever I tell you now won't change anything?"

"Not unless you have killed some other people we don't know about."

Quinn laughed. "Nope, just the ones on your list... except the Sunset Tower Hotel thing. I didn't leave one of my little monsters behind there."

"So you said," Mason replied with feigned calm.

"My wife and I had this arrangement. When I left one of the demons above ground, I'd let her know when and where. She'd then wait a while until she was certain that the demon had made its presence known to the current owners, then would get in touch with them and wrangle herself a listing on the property. She'd worked out that in the LA market nothing was going to devalue any of the homes I worked at. That said, she knew that what I'd left behind wasn't just some rumored spirit or wayward entity. It was the real deal, and no matter who ended up buying the property, they weren't going to stay long once the creatures had made the residents aware of their existence. Leticia managed to turn the Hollywood Hills house and this one four times since I started. With her commission being around a million a pop, she was raking it in."

"I assume you got a cut?"

"Of course. It was business."

"So, I get the part that the creatures would spook the owners, but why didn't the creatures ever get violent like now while people were living in the property? It's not like you were there to control them."

"That's the irony. Other that the immediate deaths after my performances as with that Harter woman, the demons remained more of a nuisance than a threat until Leticia had Phyliss perform those damn exorcisms, or at least, try to. All that did was rile them up. It was something about them being commanded to do something. Made 'em mad as hell!"

"So why did Leticia suddenly want to get rid of them?" Mason asked.

"Phyliss talked her into it. She felt that enough money had been made on the two homes. She thought that it was safer to end that side of the business."

"Why did Leticia listen to Phyliss? It wasn't really any of her business, was it?

"Not that it matters anymore, but she and Leticia were more than just friends, if you get my meaning," Quinn explained.

"They were lovers?" Mason asked.

"More than that. Leticia spent most of her free time at Phyliss's house. They were talking about making it permanent."

"That brings up an interesting point. What were you doing at Brimmer's place?"

"Collecting mail. I used it like a mini post office. All part of my low profile."

"Why would Phyliss let you do that?"

"As I mentioned, she and Leticia were somewhat of an item."

"So what? She was your ex."

"We may not have been married anymore, but we became more like friends with benefits." Quinn winked.

"And that was okay with Phyliss?" Mason asked.

"It was, when she got to take part. She used to call us the three muffateers."

"Jesus Christ," Mason said shaking his head as if trying to get the imagery out of his brain. "And yet both died because of you."

"Indirectly," Quinn emphasized.

"Do you have any remorse at all?"

"Of course I do. Do you have any idea how much money I've lost not being able to do my show in LA anymore?"

"You can't do it anywhere," Mason snapped back.

"As Carlos Quinn! But don't worry. I wouldn't think of staying on the West Coast again. I was thinking of starting up in Florida. There's some serious money to be earned down there. I was thinking I might become Christian Lafitte. That name strikes me as a real money maker."

"What if I keep the book and the copies of the phonetic translation?" Mason asked.

"Then I would have my lawyer sue you, the LAPD and the city of Los Angeles. Do you have any idea how much attention we'd all get from the media. I don't think your chief or the DA wants that to happen. Do you?"

*

Once Quinn was back in his holding cell for the last night of his incarceration, Mason headed home. He was both physically and mentally exhausted. As he drove towards the Hollywood Hills, he heard the radio weatherman remind his listeners that LA was about to get hit by a pineapple express. A storm system that originates around the Hawaiian Islands then, after drawing even more moisture from the Pacific, dumps massive quantities of rain down on the West Coast, especially Southern California. According to the man, it was due to hit in about two hours. Mason knew from experience that hillside homes always fared the worst in LA during mega downpours.

Mason stopped at Trader Joe's on Highland and grabbed a microwaveable shrimp stir fry and a six pack of Corona, which was still discounted after the pandemic virus of the same name halted almost all sales of the Mexican beer.

As Mason approached his driveway, he saw his neighbor from the blue tarped house getting into a chauffeured Lincoln Navigator with a woman half his age. Judging by their formal attire, Mason assumed they were either going to the opera down at the Disney Center or some A-list party somewhere swanky.

Mason downed the first beer before he even reached the kitchen. As he watched the microwave count down from four minutes, he polished off two more. Not usually a heavy drinker, Mason felt the need to exorcise all of the demons, real or otherwise, that had taken root in his psyche over the last few days.

The wind started just after seven. At first it was a gentle breeze that swayed the palm trees in the neighboring yards. Soon the breeze became a gale. The wind seemed to be howling from fifty different directions at once. Mason stood at the front window facing the street so he could see when the rain started. As he stood there, he could distinctly hear the sound of the massive tarps that were strapped down protecting his neighbor's roofless home. He could see the strapping straining as the wind pressure increased. For a brief moment, Mason wondered how much force those tie-downs could take.

*

Milton Gavish and his intoxicated date arrived back at his house at 1:24 in the morning. Though the full force of the pineapple express had passed, the rain was still tipping down. The SUV pulled up outside the house and at first Gavish didn't notice that anything was wrong with his home.

It wasn't until he opened his front door, only to be greeted by a torrent of water cascading down his stairway, that he realized that something catastrophic had happened. He was about to reach for the light switch, then thought better of adding electricity to the problem. As if the chaotic mess wasn't strange enough, Gavish, by the light of his sparking fuse box, saw his dog standing on the coffee table as it floated towards his kitchen atop turbulent waters.

His leggy date took one look at the interior of his house, laughed, then flagged down the SUV which was in the middle of doing a U-turn and got the driver to take her with him. Alone and confused, Gavish stepped back out onto the street and looked back at his house.

The problem was obvious. The storm had been too much for the tarps which appeared to have completely vanished, leaving his roofless home at the complete mercy of the storm.

Gavish thought of himself as a tough guy, yet staring at his waterlogged home, having only a few weeks earlier cancelled the flood insurance after they tried to raise his rate, he started screaming into the night.

CHAPTER 47

Teri got an early start the next morning, hoping to beat some of the 405 freeway's rush-hour gridlock. She was almost successful. She managed to get as far as the Redondo Beach exit in under forty-five minutes, then the traffic clogged and stayed like that all the way to Irvine. After finally clearing, she made the rest of the trip to La Costa in good time.

The elite spa and golfing community that was nestled less than a mile from the sea was dotted with expensive houses and condos, all with views onto manicured greens and fairways. The La Costa Rancheros, a luxury retirement facility, was at the far end of the course where real estate prices were lower and only a select few properties were close enough to actually see any green whatsoever.

Teri checked in at the main reception area and was saddened to see a row of wheelchair-bound geriatrics all staring out a long, grimy window at the facility's concrete driveway.

It was obvious that they had been left there in order to clean their rooms, but there was something depressing in the way that their vacant stares and slumped bodies were just parked there to ease the workload for the staff, almost as if they were both physically and socially in the way. Teri had heard the expression about that type of facility being nicknamed 'God's waiting room' but had never before realized just how depressingly accurate that was.

The facility promised luxurious retirement living in three separate areas. One housed residents who were still active and wanted to be near golf and the sea while living in stylish condo units. The second stage housed those that required some degree of care, but still wanted a level of privacy. The third and final stage – maybe too final – Teri pondered, was the main building where she'd seen the motionless, cadaver-like residents staring out at manicured oblivion. This was where Patrick Maduré currently resided. According to the facility manager who she'd spoken to the previous day, he'd recently been transferred from the second group after having had a stroke that had left him incapable of looking after himself.

Teri found dark irony in the fact that one of the world's greatest chefs could no longer even feed himself.

Teri was led to his room and was horrified when she saw her culinary idol. All his professional career, Maduré had been a large man, both in height and in girth. Now, Teri would have been surprised if he weighed over ninety pounds. If she had to guess, and that's all you can do at the latter stages of dying, she would have given him less than a week to live. The air in the room had a sweet pear-like aroma hanging in the background. That plus the blue tinges on the man's fingernails pretty much announced the fact that the La Costa Rancheros were going to be able to flip the room any day now.

Despite his frail condition, grey complexion and the blue tinge to his cuticles, his eyes still looked alert. As Teri walked alone into the room, they followed her the whole way to his bedside.

"Mr. Maduré, my name is Detective Grey. May I speak with you for a few minutes?"

"What about?" His voice was raspy and slurred.

"I'd like to talk to you about Pamela Whitlough."

Maduré laughed. At least, Teri thought it was a laugh.

"About fucking time. I've always wondered whether anyone would figure it out. You've left it a little late. I don't think I'll make it to trial, do you?"

"So, you remember that night in 2010?" Teri asked.

"Pretty hard to forget it."

"Did you kill Pamela Whitlough, Mr. Maduré?"

"Yes."

Just saying that one short word seemed to take it out of him.

"Would you mind telling me what exactly happened?"

It took a moment for Maduré to recompose himself.

"Do you want to record my confession?"

"I don't see the need. Not wanting to be too crass, but I don't see you hanging around much longer, which kind of negates the need for recording this conversation."

"I hope you're right. These fuckers forgot about my DNR instructions and revived me last month. Now look at me. If I was planning to live out the week, I'd sue their asses."

"All I need is an abridged version of that evening?" Teri asked.

"The evening, or just the part where I killed her?"

"That part would be very helpful."

"I don't know if you've worked it out or not, but we used to be an item way back in Chicago. We had a great time and at first Pam was a whole lot of fun. Then suddenly, she got all clingy and weird and started talking about the long term. I told her there was no long term and that, in fact, I was pretty much done with her."

Teri waited patiently while a weak coughing fit wracked his body.

"How did she react?"

"Not well, but I didn't really care. Even before I made a name for myself, just being a cook seemed to attract one hell of a lot of female interest."

"What happened after that?" Teri asked.

"Nothing. I never saw her again until that event at the Sunset Tower. When her people got in touch with me and said she wanted me to cook for her party, I thought she actually wanted to see me and maybe bury the hatchet."

"I take it that wasn't the case?" Teri asked.

"It was not," Maduré replied while trying to shake his head. "Turns out she only wanted me there so that could get back at me for the thing in Chicago. She was in that fucking kitchen every five minutes, bitching and moaning about something or other. Finally, she walks into the freezer while I'm checking on the stupid ice sculpture then closes the door and starts screaming at me. I don't know what happened, but something just snapped. I grabbed the schlong from the frozen carving, broke it off and rammed it right down her throat. It was weird, I didn't mean for it to go all the way in. It was just to scare her, but it did go all the way in. I should have remembered that she could do that with her throat, if you know what I mean," Madure said, with an exaggerated wink.

"Suddenly she starts choking. I was about to call for help, but then, looking at her face turning purple, I decided that maybe things were better left as they were. Once she stopped breathing, I waited till the kitchen was cleared and the show had started in the ballroom. Nobody saw me carry her to the pool."

"You carried her by yourself?" Teri asked.

"Okay. You got me. I wheeled her on a catering trolley. It only took a few seconds to get her to that stupid pool. All I had to do was hold her under water for a while, then she slowly sank. I had no idea that what with her black dress and the black bottom of the pool, she couldn't be seen. That was a surprise bonus."

Teri looked at him for a long time without saying a word.

"Thank you," she finally said as she headed for the door.

"What happens now?" Maduré asked.

"You die," Teri replied from the doorway before leaving.

By the time Mason arrived in Downtown LA to collect Quinn from the holding cells, the temperature had hit ninety and the city smelled of baked concrete. He retrieved the binder which held the text that Quinn had been using to reverse his earlier incantations, then stopped in his office to type up something that had occurred to him the previous night. He printed a copy and used a hole punch that he knew the day shift duty sergeant kept hidden under his desk. Before going to collect Quinn from the holding area, he added the page to the binder. Mason was none too pleased when he saw Quinn emerge from the lock up, freshly shaved and smirking as he said a final farewell to the officer that had retrieved him.

It took almost an hour to get to the old Harter house. The trip was made seem even longer by Quinn's incessant babbling about how, in just a few hours, he would be a free man again.

Mason wanted nothing more than to throttle the guy but realized that he needed him to be in one piece so he could get rid of the last remaining demon.

The only saving grace was that they didn't have to trek all the way to Beverly Hills to collect the key as Mason already knew about the lock box and inside security panel.

The moment they walked into the house, Mason felt a chill creep throughout his body. Unlike the Bel Air property,

418

this one looked just as it had the first time he'd seen it. In fact, he was relatively certain that it had been cleaned recently, as there was just a hint of bleach in the air.

Mason assumed that probably came from whichever biological cleaning company had been hired to scour away any trace of the poor spiritualist that Quinn's last demon had beheaded in the master bedroom.

"Getting any feel of where you want to do this?" Mason asked.

"I'm not sensing anything up here."

"Let's try the main bedroom," Mason suggested. "That seems to be its favorite spot."

When he had performed at the house in '07, Quinn had entered via the garage and had used the back stairs to get down to the living room. On this occasion, he was fascinated by the glassed-in escalator and the view of the city beyond. After descending a second level, Mason pointed towards the master bedroom. When Quinn saw the blood red floor, he initially thought that it was just that.

Blood.

"Why would anyone want a floor like this?" Quinn commented.

"Any sensations?" Mason asked, ignoring his question.

"I sense something, but it's a little different."

"Different, how?"

"It almost feels like the creature has become far more entrenched here. It's as if it's made this house its own."

"Well, you're the one to change its mind," Mason said as he handed him the binder with the incantations. "I'm ready if you are."

Quinn shrugged and took it from Mason. "I don't have to give this back to you once I've got rid of this one."

"I know. Once we're done, I'll drop you at headquarters where you can collect your belongings as well as the original book and the binder you created."

"Good. Let's get this over and done with."

Quinn stood in an open area surrounded by the sea of red lacquer. He smiled to himself and began reciting the text. After ten minutes, nothing had happened. Quinn didn't seem remotely phased. However, after ten more minutes, Quinn became concerned.

"It's not working."

"I can see that," Mason replied.

"I think I need to try it again from the beginning," Quinn advised as he flipped back the pages.

He repeated the recitation, but with far more force than the first time. It wasn't until fifteen minutes later that the room shook slightly. It felt like one of the smaller tremors that were relatively common in Los Angeles. After that, Quinn had to continue on for a further thirty minutes, during which time there were a few more shudders, but nothing else.

It became obvious to Mason that whatever Quinn had left there sixteen years earlier did not want to leave, and was doing everything it could to resist the incantation.

Finally, after starting again from the beginning for the third time, the creature began to manifest itself, and when it did, it chose, whether intentionally or not, to have picked the creepiest way possible of doing so.

The first indication that something was finally happening was when an area of the lacquered floor began to undulate as if it had turned to liquid. Initially, only one drop rose from the floor. It was a perfect blood-red tear drop and as it ascended higher, more of the droplets began to form and rise.

Soon, hundreds, if not thousands of red drops began to converge and, for a moment, formed into one large red mass that stood twice as tall as Mason. As the two men looked on, the mass began to gain detail as it transformed into a vaguely humanoid shape. For one instant, Mason thought it was actually turning into the iconic image of the devil as depicted in cartoons and one particular brand of canned ham.

Though it did have horns and it did have a tail, once it was almost fully formed, Mason could see that it was nothing at all like the storybook demon. For a start, its body was partially translucent. It seemed to have dozens of sharply angled rib bones which protected dark, almost charred looking organs that bore no relation to anything within the human body. The tail was rat-like and long, and whipped from side to side in an almost metronomic rhythm.

The horns were nothing short of grotesque. Instead of the fairy-tale, double twists of bone, these were made up of sinewy strands of decomposed flesh that never stopped moving as they intertwined again and again, each time in a different knotting dance.

None of those traits, however, was as horrific as its face. It was human and not human, all at the same time. It was as if there were two faces trying to fight their way to the surface. One, that of an impossibly old man, the other, a monstrous visage of a cross between a rabid wolf and the head of a deep-sea dragon fish.

Mason couldn't have moved if his life depended on it. Nothing had prepared him for the creature that stood in the center of that room. He knew that he would never again in his life be so truly terrified.

He was wrong.

When it said its first words, Mason would've bet a month's pay that his brain wouldn't be able to take any more and would snap like an overstretched rubber band.

At first, the words were unintelligible and sounded more like deep-throated barking. Then, with Quinn trying to read the reversal spell even faster, the thing managed one clear word.

"Stop."

Mason was already frozen in place, but the command momentarily halted Quinn as well. Something that neither of them wanted.

"For god's sake," Mason screamed. "Keep going."

Quinn resumed the recitation, though only after taking a few steps further away from the creature.

The incantation was definitely working, as the beast's legs were already being surrounded by the black vortex and its screeching had grown to an almost deafening level.

"Read the final part," Mason shouted. "Now."

Quinn had for some reason been holding off on the final words that when repeated, caused the funnel to lay claim to the beast and drag if back from where it came. Mason's command hit home, and Quinn turned to the next page and started reciting the final words, repeating the phrase over and over again.

The creature, instead of being filled with pain as it receded into the floor, seemed suddenly to be filled with a look of pure hatred. It started moving toward Quinn and in one sudden move, grabbed him with its clawed hand and dragged him to within inches of its snarling face.

Quinn, with blood oozing from his mouth, tried screaming the final words again. Just as the monster opened its fang-filled jaws and spread them only inches from Quinn's face, Mason retrieved a piece of paper from his jacket pocket and began to repeat the incantation, only this time using the correct words, not the one he had doctored back at the office and swapped with the one in the binder. The beast was immediately ensnared by the swirling cloud as it began to drag Quinn back into the vortex with it.

The last thing Mason saw before both it and Quinn vanished down the chasm was the creature's other claw take hold of Quinn's head. Thankfully, before it had the chance to separate it from the man's torso, they were gone.

Mason approached the hole to confirm that, other than the vortex, there was nothing there. He then kicked the binder that had fallen from Quinn's hands as the creature grabbed him and pushed it with the side of his foot until it too went over the edge.

Once he'd finished that one last piece of housekeeping, Mason continued to chant the correct words until the vortex rose from the ground, swirled overhead, then dissipated, until the very last wisp of smoke faded, then was gone.

CHAPTER 48

Lieutenant Montez stuck his head into their converted interview room and advised Teri and Mason that they had all been summoned to Balisek's office.

"How did she sound?" Mason asked in the elevator on the way up to the tenth floor.

"No idea. I just got word from one of her assistants."

"Can't be good if she didn't even make the call herself," Mason commented.

"Don't read anything into that. It's all about power with her. Remember when she first got the top job and tried to pretend she was still one of us?"

"Ah, happy days," Mason joked.

"Hope you don't mind us jabbering on about the chief, what with you being a relative and all," Montez said to Teri, watching closely to see what, if any, reaction there would be.

Teri's face grew crimson, but before she could respond the elevator stopped and the doors opened.

Balisek was alone in her office, which was a relief to Mason. He knew from experience that had anyone been there from internal affairs, legal or worse, the LAPPL, it most likely would have meant that one of their own was about to be served up as some sort of political sacrifice.

"Sit, please," Balisek gestured to the two chairs facing her.

There was a moment of confusion while the three tried to work out the etiquette for how three people were supposed to share two chairs.

"Sorry," Balisek said, as if noticing the issue for the first time. "Detectives Darby and Grey, why don't you sit down while Lieutenant Montez finds a third one."

Though recognizing the blatant slight, Montez left the room and could be heard asking her assistants whether he could use one of the ones in the waiting area.

Mason and Teri assumed that Balisek would at least wait for the lieutenant to return. She didn't.

"I want to thank you both formally in front of your supervising officer, then I am going to ask him to leave so that we may talk. Understood?"

They understood all too well. Montez might have been their supervisor, but like almost everyone else in the building, had not been fully read into the case results, at least, not the parts that involved Quinn's 'little monsters'. It was clear that Balisek didn't want to be accused of not involving their commanding officer, at least at that stage.

Once Montez returned and sat himself down, Balisek thanked all three of them for managing to close not just the three unsolved cases, but also the murders of Tamacini and Dorothy Brimmer.

Mason knew the moment he heard the term murder used in relation to Quinn's cases that the fix was well and truly in.

"Though we haven't yet located Mr. Quinn, now that we have indisputable proof that he was, in fact, a serial killer bent on murdering guests at some of this city's most elite parties, it won't take long before he is brought in and can be formally charged, and I have no doubt, convicted. I would also like to add my special thanks to you, Detective Grey, for managing to separate the Whitlough case from the others and to have found a link that led you to her actual killer. My only regret is that, with Mr. Maduré having died yesterday, his case will not be brought to trial, though I can't help feeling that in its own way, justice has been served."

Balisek turned to face Montez.

"I know that pairing Darby and Grey was more of a convenience-driven decision rather than anything strategic, but I feel that their partnership should continue."

"I was actually hoping, now that some of the initial bad feelings within the department have subsided, that I bring them both back up to the bullpen and rethink—" Montez started to say.

"I would prefer they remain in the converted interview room. In fact, I plan to make use of them for the next six months or so. I have a few special projects that I think might benefit from a fresh pair of eyes."

"I wasn't aware of any special projects," Montez said, clearly confused.

"Thank you for coming by," Balisek replied, ignoring his comment. "Would you mind taking the chair out with you?"

Montez obviously did mind, but nonetheless, grabbed the chair and waited for Mason and Teri to leave with him.

"They'll be staying up here for a little chat," Balisek advised.

There was no way the lieutenant could hide his anger and discomfort at not being included in a meeting with two of his own officers. What made things even worse was that Balisek, Darby and Grey remained completely silent until he had exited the room.

"That was mean," Mason said as soon as her office door was closed.

"The man's a sycophantic idiot. He's lucky I don't transfer him to the South-Central Parking Division."

"I didn't know we had a South-Central Parking Division," Mason commented.

Balisek smiled. "Exactly. Now that we can talk, I'd like to tell you about the aforementioned special projects."

"Just so long as it doesn't involve any more monsters," Teri said, joking.

Balisek stared right back at her without speaking. Teri was pretty sure she saw a slight twinkle reach the other woman's eyes and may even have seen the beginnings of a smile.

She knew back from when the chief had been her stepmother that neither were a good sign.

Balisek spent the next half hour detailing her plan to create an elite team to investigate cases that never have or will make it into the murder books. Cases that remain open and inexplicable. Cases that are known to very few people within the force.

As the two detectives listened, they became less and less able to accept what the chief was suggesting. Not only would the initial two-person team work autonomously, only ever reporting to Balisek, but they would be forbidden to discuss any aspect of the case with anyone except a very small cadre that Balisek had handpicked herself.

"So, what do you think?" the chief asked.

Mason shook his head as if trying to clear his addled brain.

"I think that this must be some sort of a joke."

"I was thinking the same thing," Teri added. "I was even wondering if we were being recorded for the Christmas gag reel."

"I can promise you that nothing in regard to this project will ever be recorded either aurally or visually."

"So, you are being serious?" Mason asked.

"Deadly. I have to go to a meeting with the district attorney, so let's leave it there. I would like to hear both of your answers by nine o'clock tonight."

"That won't be possible," Mason replied.

"Why not?" The frustration was plainly evident in the chief's voice.

"Detective Grey and I have a long overdue project that we plan to complete tonight."

"I'm not aware of either of you having any ongoing cases. I had Montez confirm that you were both clear and available."

"He doesn't know about this one," Teri replied, smiling.

"Why don't I?" Balisek snapped.

"You do," Mason responded as he got to his feet. "Tonight's the night that Detective Grey and I attempt to do as much harm as we can to your credit at the Palm restaurant. Remember the Harddick and Simpleton bet? Well, it's time we collected our winnings."

Mason turned to Teri, who'd also gotten to her feet. "I don't know about you, but I'm thinking the big surf and turf platter. You?"

"That sounds a little too gluttonous for me. I might just have a pair of their lobsters and a bottle of Bâtard Montrachet."

"I'm not a big wine guy. Is it expensive?" Mason asked.

"Very."

"Then I might have one of those as well."

The pair started for the door.

"I will be checking that bill," Balisek called after them. "And I want to hear your answer by noon tomorrow."

Once they had gone, Balisek had a strong urge to call the restaurant and tell them that she no longer intended to pick up the tab. She actually went so far as to grab her cell, when

430

it dawned on her that she needed both of them to manage her new department. Pissing them off right before they let her know their answer was probably not a great idea.

Balisek sighed and selected a different number on her contact list.

"Good morning, Mr. Mayor. Yeah, I pitched it."

There was a pause while he asked her a couple of related questions.

"Yes, I think they will, and I've given them until noon tomorrow."

After disconnecting the call, she stepped over to one of her office windows and stared out at downtown Los Angeles. She wondered what the population would think if they knew what she was up to.

Then again, she justified, something needed to be done before more people died.

EPILOGUE

Mason could hardly get his key in the door. Even the Uber driver had noticed his inebriation and had offered to help him inside. Mason didn't care how drunk he was. Between he and Teri, they'd managed to get the dinner total up to over seven hundred dollars and change. As if to make one final point, they'd added a gratuity of twenty percent. He knew that Ballsack would freak out, but also knew that for the first time that he could remember, she needed him. What she'd put him through came at a price. While eight hundred and fifty dollars was hardly going to break her, she would definitely know why she'd had to fork out this one time.

Mason stumbled to the kitchen and drank water right out of the tap. He considered going to bed, but needed to check on one thing. He'd been in a rush before and wasn't certain if he'd done a good enough job.

After grabbing a flashlight, he crossed the cracked patio and stopped at the far corner of his property. He parted some shrubbery and studied the area beneath it. The soil had obviously been recently disturbed, but that didn't matter, as that had been his doing. Even though Mason knew that it was very unlikely that anyone was going to search his yard, he just wanted to make sure that no one could see anything untoward over the side fence.

Mason used the light to check the area, and sure enough, at the far end of the disturbed earth, a small triangle of blue tarp was poking out. He prodded it back under the soil then added another handful before smoothing everything over and letting the sagebrush fall back into place.

Mason was about to head back into the house when he heard a rustling sound coming from within the overgrown vegetation.

Mason knew that the area had mountain lions as well as poisonous snakes and coyotes and wasn't in a fit state of mind to deal with any of those. He walked back to the rear door, glancing back every few feet to make certain he wasn't being followed.

Once in the house, he was about to lock the back door when a thought occurred to him. Mason removed the tinfoil-wrapped item from the Palm's branded carrier bag and opened it up. He cut off a decent size piece of filet steak, then chopped that into bite-sized pieces.

Mason opened the back door and placed the foil onto the concrete patio, then the steak chunks on top of that. He returned to the house and waited. He was about to give up and crash for the night when he heard a gentle scratching at his door.

Mason cut more steak from the leftovers and waited a few beats. He slowly opened the door and looked over at the patio.

A coyote was standing in the center of the slab, its eyes locked onto Mason's. The animal looked a lot like Wolfy, but it appeared more malnourished. Mason was about to toss the extra steak towards it when he noticed the animal's left back paw. It was black.

"Wolfy?" Mason called out.

The coyote turned its head questioningly.

"Is it you?"

In response, the canine slowly stepped towards Mason. The closer he got; the more certain Mason became that it was indeed the coyote he'd thought had been killed by his neighbor.

The animal walked right up to Mason and with astonishing gentleness took the piece of meat from his hand, before trotting back into the shadows.

The moment Mason got back inside, he grabbed the note that Gavish had left him showing the dead coyote. Mason studied the picture and realized that he'd been so upset when he'd first seen the image, he hadn't bothered to look for any confirming details.

The dead animal was posed in such a way that all four of its feet were visible.

None of them were black.

"Holy shit," Mason said to himself as he plopped down onto the couch.

Even inebriated, Mason understood that he had sought revenge from his neighbor over the death of a coyote that, it turned out, wasn't Wolfy at all. He tried to feel some sense of remorse, but the harder he tried, the more he felt justified in doing what he did.

Even if it hadn't been Wolfy, the neighbor had intentionally killed an animal that was just trying to find a way to feed itself. Just like the millions of Los Angelinos that were strewn across the city's seven thousand, five hundred square miles, all it really wanted was to find a way to survive.